The New Normal

By T.S. Dawson

Mrs. Gina,

Thanks you so
much for giving your
time to my books. I
hope you really enjoy
The New Normal.

B Dawson

1

<u>Other titles by T.S. Dawson</u>

Port Honor

In Search of Honor

The Price of Honor

When I was Green

A Horse of a Different Color

My Summer with the Senator

The Road to the White House

Available for purchase on Amazon.com for Kindle and in
paperback format.

Acknowledgements

Thank you to all of you have hung in there with me through the last two years. Thank you to those of you who waited patiently, those who have encouraged me to keep writing and those of you who have continued read and to spread the word about my books. I really appreciate all that you've done.

Thank you to the crew that makes the books of TS Dawson more than just my scribblings. Thank you to my beta readers and editors. To Donna Goss and Annette Saunders who have been with me since the beginning, thank you for all of your feedback on character and content development and preliminary editing. Thank you to Jenny Tysver who helped me get to the end and Lord knows she had to lead this horse to the water and make me drink. To Christie Demasi, thank you so much for letting me bounce ideas off of you on our drive to work in the mornings, for researching the little things and for making my words more polished. Thank you to the newest member of the TS Dawson team, Vicki Goodson who gave of her time to do the final edit on this book and for making me feel better about the finished product.

Thank you to the street team members, Christina Rhodes, Cyndi Stephens Lloyd, Shannon Bickle, Sandy Dunaway Norton, Laice Walden Dickerson, Judy Rowland, Gay Hattaway Morgan, Amanda Morgan Green, Jenny Tysver, Rena Allen Turner, Rea Davis, Saundra Phillips Gilbert, Vicki Goodson, Jennifer Ham, Kerri Rogers Smith, Kerensa Smith Tolbert, Sherri Brooks Weeks, Jill Rowland Marriott and everyone else who helps spread the word about my work.

Thank you to John Bryan who continues to give his time to make sure my books are formatted correctly. He has tried and tried to teach me, but I fear I may be a lost cause.

Thank you to my family for allowing me the time to keep creating and thank you to all of you who give your time to read my books.

Thank you all very much.

-Terri
Aka TS Dawson

"Normal is the Holy Grail and only those without it know its value."
— **Sarah Crossan, <u>One</u>**

PART ONE

Chapter 1

Alex...

It wasn't for the lack of trying on the part of no less than six women that I managed to make it back to the St. Regis alone. The filming was over and the wrap party was still going strong, but I was done. Save for the burn that lingered on my breath of half a dozen shots of whiskey I'd thrown back during the evening and the scent of cigarette smoke that hitched a ride back with me, I was indeed alone.

I propped my hand against the wall above the panel that held the up and down buttons. The lights shining off the gold plate surrounding the buttons was blinding and I closed my eyes as I leaned against my arm to steady myself. My head swam and the room seemed to spin and I regretted my decision to decline a couple of the offers I'd been given. A woman under my arm to steady me would have beaten my current situation.

The ding announcing the arrival of the elevator barely brought me to life and I didn't bother to straighten up until the last patron had left the car. I heard a voice behind me calling, "Sir! Excuse me, sir," but I didn't think anything of it. I crossed leg over leg and staggered into the elevator. I was past buzzed and a bit on the drunk side. The truth? I was damn near shit-faced and couldn't remember the last time I'd been this far gone.

The voice called again, "Sir, wait!" A bony arm jutted in between the closing doors of the elevator. The doors stopped and retracted, opening for a boy of about twelve years old to jump on. I thought to myself how it must have been nice to have that kind of energy.

"Hi!" the boy said as I squinted and blinked to focus. I could have easily been convinced there was two of him.

When my eyes focused, my head snapped and I was taken aback by the sight. Sandy brown hair, emerald green eyes, athletic, but tall and gangly too. He moved like a puppy who'd grown too fast to manage his limbs. I recognized everything about him and it definitely sharpened my senses. If I were his age, I would have sworn I was facing a full-length mirror.

"Mr. Allen," the boy cracked with a nervous voice that was on the cusp of puberty. "May I get your autograph?" He held out a pen and pad in my direction.

I rubbed the beard that had taken up residence on my face. I was a method actor and if the part called for a beard, I grew one. I liked to immerse myself in a character and preferred authentic as opposed to makeup and wigs. Since filming had only ended yesterday, I hadn't taken the time to shave away the four inches that lent believability to me being a Civil War general.

"Sir," the boy said again, politely, "Would you mind?"

He gave the pen and paper a little shake, trying to get me to take it.

"Oh, yes, of course." I reached for the items and the boy lit up.

I barely had the point of the pen to the pad, trying to concentrate on what to say and not just stare at him when he began to gush.

"Thank you so much! My mother is a huge fan of yours!" He paused and appeared to be working up the courage to ask something else.

From under my eye brows, I took my eyes off of the paper and stared at him. It was like looking at a walking, talking picture of myself from middle school. Committing to that idea gave me chills.

He had to be mine and the real giveaway was the mole on his right cheek. I had it. My father had it. My grandfather had it, too. I saw photos of my grandfather's father, an old black and white with a noticeable dot on his cheek. Yes, he had it as well. With each generation, it became a bit smaller so this boy had something barely above a freckle, but there it was, raised and dark brown and right in the same spot. Perhaps in my rational mind, the non-intoxicated version, I might have needed a DNA test, but in this state, the science was written all over the boy.

"Would you mind writing something to her?"

"Sure," I squeaked out and followed with the million-dollar question. "What's your mother's name?"

I'd been with more women that I could count on all of my digits. Some would have worn that as a badge and had no regrets, but that wasn't me at all. I had my fair share of regrets and I steeled myself for his answer. Unfortunately, here were better odds of his mother being in the nay category than the yay category.

"Anna Catherine Calloway. Folks call her Anna-Cat."

I might as well have been gut punched. That name knocked the wind right out of me. I dropped the pen and the boy scrambled to pick it up.

"Anna-Cat?" I gasped, looking at him for confirmation.

Unaffected by my start, the boy offered the pen back to me.

"Sorry," I shifted, taking it and apologizing.

The walls of the elevator were closing in and I was getting a bit nauseous. I wiped my forehead with the sleeve of my shirt to absorb the sweat that was starting to spring up.

"Yes, sir. She's seen all your movies." The boy was giddy, still oblivious to my reaction.

I was stunned again. "Really?" I asked, puzzled.

"Oh, yes, sir." His manners really were impeccable. "She will just die when she finds out that I met you tonight!"

The elevator car rose, but not because either one of us had pressed the button for my floor or anything. I'd all but forgotten about going to my room. I'd been caught so completely off guard by the sight of what was no doubt my son that I could have been on a mission to Mars inside that elevator for all I knew. He looked like me and sounded like me at that age, but I just couldn't believe it.

"I'm sure she will." I said under my breath, still unable to wrap my mind around what was happening or what *had* happened.

I went off topic. "How old are you?"

"Twelve." He pointed to the paper trying to get me back to writing. I was right about his age.

"And you live around here?" We were in the heart of Buckhead, a busy district of Atlanta, and he looked to be alone.

"No, sir. I'm just in town for a baseball tournament."

"But you're staying at this hotel?" I found that curious since the hotels I stayed in for travel ball when I was younger weren't anywhere near the caliber of the St. Regis.

Again, he answered, "No, sir. I'm staying at the Courtyard a couple blocks north of here."

"And you're wandering the streets of Atlanta alone and just ran into me?"

"No, sir, two of my teammates are waiting for me in the lobby. One of my friends has an uncle who is a pretty famous DJ on a station in L.A. My friend asked him to let us know if you were ever in the area so he let us know and he even found out where you were staying."

The kid had connections. I was impressed, but also still completely stumped by the entire situation.

"So, Anna-Cat?" I started to write her name on the pad and pondered what to say. After thinking it over, and with the boy looking on, I finally came up with something appropriate. I had to ask the boy's name to complete my thoughts.

"August Calloway. Everyone calls me 'Auggie.'"

I had trouble keeping my jaw off of the floor on that revelation, too. My whole name was Alex August Allen. She named him after me, but didn't bother to tell me I had a son. Who would do such a thing?

I tried to recover. "My friends call me 'Triple A.'"

"Why?" he furrowed his brow.

"Because my initials consist of three As."

"Ah," he sighed.

"Well, Auggie," I began as I wrote, "So you're in town for a baseball tournament, you said."

"Yes, sir," he confirmed.

I didn't have anything else to do and no place to be in the foreseeable future. "Where are you playing and what time are your games? If your mother is there, we can give her a real surprise. I mean, since she's such a huge fan and all."

The boy jumped up and down with excitement. "Oh my God! That would be so awesome! She will just die!" he exclaimed again before settling down to give me the location and time of his next game.

I finished writing the note and handed it back to him. He took a moment to read it. When finished, he looked up with a priceless grin. "She'll love it! Thank you so much!"

Overcome, the boy stepped forward and hugged me.

A wave of something I'd never felt before washed over me. I'd been in love before and I'd loved my parents, but this was something else entirely. At first, I'd stiffened, not expecting him to touch me, but without telling my arms to do it, I found myself wrapping them around him. I even leaned down and smelled his hair. I breathed him in and felt a peace that I'd never known before. Something I couldn't describe radiated from the child to me. It was euphoric.

The elevator stopped and a group of teenage girls got on and squeezed the boy and I together to allow room for them. I was used to the squeals from all ages of the female sex and I braced myself for it, but nothing came. The girls giggled to themselves and faced the doors. One of the girls pressed the down button and away we went. The beard camouflaged me again and I was relieved. I feared if anyone recognized me while standing next to Auggie, they would truly recognize the same thing about him as I did.

I didn't know what his mother's reasons might be for keeping him from me, but I was certain I wasn't the only one she kept it from. Auggie was just as in the dark as I had been. Surely had he known, this would have been an entirely different experience.

Reaching the lobby, the doors opened and the girls exited, followed by Auggie. I trailed behind him. I wasn't sure what move to make now. I'd given him the autograph and returned his pen. Our business, I'm sure as far as he was concerned, was concluded. For me, I wasn't done, not by a longshot. My curiosity was piqued and I had so many questions.

First of all, I wanted to know his birthday. Secondly, I was curious as to who he thought his father was. Surely his mother had given him some sort of explanation. The dreadful part was that I couldn't ask anything and I had no real way, well, no way to go about it without coming off as some weirdo, to try to get to know this preteen boy that I just met.

Auggie crossed the lobby, having thanked me and made his way toward two freckle faced boys of about the same size and age. They appeared to be twins and I paled at the sight of them, thinking what if there was a product to every fling I'd ever had and they started coming out of the woodwork? What if there was a pack of twins out there? My heart then reminded my head that what I'd had with his mother was no fling. What I'd had with Anna-Cat Calloway was the stuff of which romance writers made their millions.

"Is that really him?" one of Auggie's companions asked.

I'd stopped a few feet back and all six eyes turned on me. Auggie nodded, confirming that it was indeed me.

"He's taller than on TV," the other said, mouth dropping open. "I've never met anyone famous!"

With that statement, I stepped forward and introduced myself. I extended my hand and this gesture didn't help with the gaped, open mouth situation that the boys seemed to have.

Auggie nudged the other one of them and prompted him to introduce himself. "I'm Will," and shrugging in the direction of his brother, "This is Wyatt."

After the introductions, I asked, "What sort of chaperones do you boys have if you're out wandering the streets of Atlanta all hours of the night? Aren't you a bit young to be out this late by yourselves?"

The two lookalikes hung their heads, looking caught, but Auggie piped up with an explanation. He was about as full of shit as I was at that age and tried to convince me that the guy, third seat from the left at the end of the bar, was Will and Wyatt's father.

I might've bought it, had the boys not looked so surprisingly clamored, "Yep, yes, that's our dad."

"Well, I'll just go over and introduce myself. I'll buy him a drink for bringing you fellas over. I'll get you something, too." I glanced back at the three of them, walking hot on my heals towards the bar. "What-a-ya-have?"

They made all sorts of excuses as to why I couldn't speak to their father. One of the boys couldn't take the pressure and finally broke. I couldn't tell which one it was, and not because of the lingering effects of my voluminous alcohol consumption earlier, but because they looked exactly alike.

"He's not our dad!" He blurted out while tugging at my arm.

The other one quickly added, "No one knows we're here."

I looked at Auggie with a raised eyebrow, giving him the look my father had always given me when I was busted. I quickly lowered it, reminding myself just how absolutely insane all of this really was. This is not parental instinct kicking in. This was bad booze that made for a

14

bizarre dream. I would surely wake tomorrow morning with a hangover and, maybe, with some strange flashes of the dream and nothing more. For now, until I woke up, I would see the boys safely back to their hotel.

In no condition to drive, I had the concierge arrange the hotel car for me. As the four of us crawled in, one of the boys marveled again, "I've met a celebrity and rode in a limo all in one night!"

His brother gave him a high five and exclaimed, "Best night EVER!" He drew out the word "Ever" with emphasis.

All the while, Auggie looked unimpressed by the limo, but took the time to read what I'd written with my autograph again. He smiled at me and I could see a mix of my father and the young girl I'd known all those years ago. "She'll like this. Thank you."

"Auggie," I said, lowly as not to be heard by the other boys.

"Yes, sir?"

"While you're in town, please don't go out like this at night without an adult again. I've enjoyed meeting you, but going out like this isn't safe."

I staggered into my room at the St. Regis hardly an hour later than when I'd first pressed the "up" button for the elevator. Wobbly legged, but about as sober as I could be, I opened the door to a view of the city scape. The curtains were just as I'd left them earlier in the day, open, but the room did not appear as I'd left it. It was smaller or maybe the walls were just closing in on me. It seemed as if life itself had just closed in on me.

Lightening making bright spider webs across the night sky caught my attention. It drew me to the window where I stayed, watching and thinking of nothing until I noticed my reflection.

This was a departure from the way I usually kept my appearance and it was a far cry from the way I'd looked the last time I laid eyes on Anna-Cat Calloway. Watching the light show before me I let my mind wander back to the time I spent with her. The weather was much the same as it was tonight, humid, sticky hot and with a thunderstorm on the horizon. It was just another night in Georgia.

"I'm a father," I pondered out loud as I wrapped my hands around my skull. I slumped against the window that made up the wall behind me and slid down until I was seated on the floor, legs stretched out before me.

To this day, I didn't know what I'd done to lose her, but I had lost her and apparently, I'd lost my son as well. I let my mind drift back, searching for the answer as I had so many times in the past.

Chapter 2

Anna-Cat...

It was a rare occasion when I missed one of my son's baseball games. In fact, I could count on one hand the number of Auggie's games that I'd missed and he had been playing since he was big enough to hold a bat. Unlike the other boys, he had no father to pick up the slack so I felt compelled to make sure he always saw my face in the stands cheering him on. Unfortunately, today was one of the rare occasions that I couldn't make it.

I'd never been one to stay out all night or even up all night unless I was working so the drive home from the hospital this morning was done with the aid of a Grande Caffé Mocha in one hand and the steering wheel in the other. Fueled with caffeine and not much else, my car barely made it home to Wrens. Even through bloodshot eyes, the city limits sign was a sight to behold. I was exhausted and dreaming of my bed before I made it into my driveway.

My mother, myself and several of their church friends had been taking turns staying with my father at University Hospital. Last night had been my night and it was rough, but I really couldn't complain. So many people, including my father, had it way worse than just being tired.

I came close to napping in the car just to get up the energy to go inside. The only deterrent that kept me from doing just that was the fear of what my neighbors would say. They already talked about me enough since I was virtually the only woman around who had a child out of wedlock. It was bad enough that I was the town harlot. I didn't want to take the title of town drunk when it got around that I was found passed out at the wheel in my yard.

Dead on my feet, I made it inside and perked up once I felt the buzzing of my cell phone in my pocket. I had put my phone on vibrate while at the hospital. I kicked the

17

door shut behind me and slumped against it as I checked the phone, noticing the call was from a 404 area code. 404 was Atlanta and it had to be Auggie. That's where his baseball tournament was this weekend.

I answered the phone about as fast as anyone could answer a cell phone. "Auggie!" I said with the full enthusiasm of a mother who missed her son, not some run down, groggy thing that couldn't wait to get to sleep.

"Hey, Mom!"

"Hey, Baby." I toned it down a bit, but still referred to him by one of the pet names I had for him. He was twelve going on twenty and hated for me to call him "Baby" anymore, but I couldn't help it. He was my baby and probably the only one I'd ever have.

"Shouldn't you be getting ready to go to the game?" I asked.

"Yes, ma'am, but we've been rained out. Coach wanted me to call and tell you we're on our way home."

"Awe, Auggie, I'm sorry. So, this weekend's a bust, huh?" I was glad he was coming home, but I felt so sorry for him. He'd been looking forward to this tournament more than all the other tournaments this spring.

"Well, I wouldn't call it a complete bust. You won't believe who I met last night!"

"Who?" I was thinking he must have met one of the Atlanta Braves. He loved that team, especially Brian McCann, the catcher. I wasn't close with my parents, but they had a weekly call with Auggie, Sunday evenings at 7:00 p.m. without fail. Mostly Auggie talked baseball with my father.

"Alex Allen!" Auggie announced the name the same way he'd announced to my father that he'd hit his first grand slam.

I had no words. I dropped the coffee cup I'd carried in from the car. Luckily it was empty so it didn't make more of a mess than I was already in.

Auggie pepped up again, "Mom, did you hear me? I said I met Alex Allen! Can you believe it?"

I couldn't believe it, but I did hear him. I tried to match his enthusiasm, but I could hear the struggle in my voice. "I heard you."

I sounded fake and Auggie knew my fake voice as well as I did.

"What's wrong?" he asked. "He's your favorite actor. You watch his movies over and over again. I got his autograph for you!"

Oh, Jesus. I thought I was going to vomit.

Auggie had a point. I did watch all of Alex Allen's movies. I even bought copies of <u>People</u> magazine when he was in it. I read the covers of <u>The Enquirer</u> and <u>The Star</u> when he was in those as well, but I refused to buy them.

I cut the fake voice and responded as I would with any other kind gesture from Auggie. "Thanks, Baby. You're right. He is my favorite actor."

Honestly, I never thought the day would come when Alex and Auggie met. Alex Allen lived in L.A. We didn't even leave the state except for the one time we went to Charleston for a baseball tournament. Alex Allen went to Oscar parties. The highlight of mine and Auggie's social calendar was an end of season party at Chuck E. Cheese in Augusta. It's not like Alex moved in the same circles as those of us in little ol' Wrens, Georgia.

I'd always figured the odds of Auggie meeting Alex in person were about the same odds as there being snow on the hills of Hell. I guess someone could have put the same odds on me having met Alex Allen, but I had met him. Almost fourteen years ago, I met Alex Allen.

***

It was April 3, 1995, opening day of one of the biggest sporting events in golf, the opening day of the tournament of all tournaments. It was a big deal all over the world, but even bigger in Augusta, Georgia. It was the be, all end all for professional golfers and locals. I was a local.

I grew up in the hill section known as Summerville. Summerville was once a town in its own right, but was ultimately absorbed by the City of Augusta. It was where the prominent residents of Augusta moved after the fire of 1916 and the floods. My grandparents on my father's side were some of those who helped boost the population boom of Summerville back then. I grew up in, and my parents still lived in, the same house my great-grandparents first built.

The house was big, steeped with history and within walking distance to Augusta National. It was the quintessence of Antebellum Homes, white stately columns and Magnolias dotting the yard. It also had six bedrooms, a wraparound porch, a pool and a carriage house. Those were just the highlights of the house. It even had a name, High Water. The name was a nod to the reason my grandparents moved there.

For years, my father had talked about renting the house out for tournament week, but my mother always protested. Year after year, they had the same argument and my mother always won. There was no need for me to suspect this year's argument would have any different outcome. They hadn't told me a thing.

I opened the back door with my key and, as always, I had to put my shoulder into it and give it all the effort I could muster. The door was solid oak and original to the house. It had no less than fifty coats of paint on it and it tended to swell and stick in the warm weather.

As if the jarring sound the door made when it popped from the frame wasn't enough to announce my arrival, I called out, "Hello?"

I had no reason to suspect anyone would actually answer. My parents were the early to bed and early to rise type and it was after 9:00 p.m. on a week night. I was certain they were in bed, but I made the announcement again anyway as I went down the dark hallway toward the foyer. "Hello?"

No one answered and I gave up calling out. I made the turn at the bottom of the stairs, taking hold of the banister and starting up. I was met with an ear ringing "Pow!" followed by a fierce sting that ripped through my upper arm from front to back, at least that's what I thought and felt.

I screamed from fright and the pain and toppled backward down the few steps I'd taken. Tripping, I fell into the floor at the bottom of the stairs and crashed, knocking my head against one of the transom windows that outlined the front door. Stupefied by the shock of the questionable injury to my arm and the blow to my head, I couldn't make heads or tails of what had happened. Moonlight lit the area just around the door and a figure stepped from the shadows, coming down the stairs. It was a man and he had a gun in his hand and it was still pointed at me.

"What do you want?" he demanded.

It was then that I realized what the pop was and what the pain in my arm had been. I had been shot. I suppose I fainted, because I don't remember anything after that.

The next day, I woke up in my bed, not my bed at my dorm room, but my bed at home. Groggy and sore, I came to in a haze. For lack of a better way to describe it, I felt more hungover than I'd ever felt before. I'd only been hungover twice in my life and those two times paled in comparison to this. My head was pounding and the light that pepped around the edges of the curtains was searing to my eyes.

I lifted my hand to rub my forehead and caught a glimpse of the bandage on my arm. A flash of the night before came back, the pop, the pain, the...the shot. Even now my arm hurt as I moved it, picking at the bandage with my other hand to get a look. I peeled off the white gauze and found a rudimentary stitch job done to the entry wound on the front. I rolled my arm over and, ignoring the pain of movement, I got a look at the stitch work on the exit side. I was comforted by the fact that short sleeves would cover it.

All of the sudden I came to with a start. I'd glanced around the room for the clock as images from the night before started to come back to me. My brain reminded me again that I had been shot, there'd been an intruder in my house. It was then that I saw a man asleep in an arm chair that didn't typically belong in my room. It was a chair from my parents' room, the one my father sat in each morning when he put on his shoes and socks. I suddenly realized I had no idea where my parents were or what had happened to them. Their faces flashed through my mind. I sat straight up in bed.

"Mom! Dad!" I gasped. I had no idea how I had gotten to bed or where my parents were or if they were alright.

The man in the chair jumped up. "Are you alright? Can I get you anything?" For whatever his reasons were, he woke up in about the same shape I did.

"What?" I scrambled back pulling the covers up like some short of shield, as if they would protect me from him.

"Don't be afraid." He held up his hands, palms out. "I'm not going to hurt you."

"Where's my Mom and Dad?" I demanded in my deepest most threatening voice.

"I don't know," he answered directly, standing and still showing his hands.

I kept drawn up as close to my headboard as I could get and on the far side of my bed. My head still pounded and I couldn't decide which I needed more, Tylenol or hair of the dog. I also didn't know whether to rub my head or my arm, but I did neither as not to make any sudden moves or let go of the security that was my duvet.

"What do you mean, you don't know? What did you do with them?"

"I didn't do anything with them," he replied in a tone that shared with me that he did indeed have the nerve to be offended.

I was still skeptical and, inching out, one foot eased on to the floor at a time, but keeping the bed between us. Simultaneously, I eyed the door for my escape and I snapped off another question. "What are you doing in my house?"

"I rented it for the week." Again, he sounded affronted.

"You rented it?" This was news to me.

"Yeah, are you okay? Can I..." he ran his hands through his hair and looked me over. "Look, I'm sorry about," he let his eyes linger over my arm, "that." He nodded toward my wound. "Luckily, I'm not a good shot."

"Are you seriously trying to joke about having fired a gun at me in my own home?" The impulse to pick up the nearest object and hurl it at him came on strong. I probably would have thrown something except he hit me in my dominant arm so I wouldn't have been able to get the job done.

"Well, um," he stuttered, "I thought you were an intruder."

"Intruders don't have keys, asshole!"

His eyes flew wide at my name calling.

Then it occurred to me that he'd shot me and not bothered to call an ambulance or anything. "And why am I not at a hospital?"

"Because I don't need that kind of publicity?"

"Excuse me?" I translated what he said, giving the full impression of what an asshole he really sounded like, "*You* shot someone and *you* couldn't be bothered to get them help? *You* are some piece of work!"

"It's not like that and I did get you help."

I struggled to ignore the pain and threw my arms wide open for dramatic emphasis, "I don't see doctors and nurses running around here!"

"You didn't need a doctor!" He darted his eyes at my arm, indicating the patch job.

I gritted my teeth and twisted, giving him a full look at the subject of discussion. "I've seen better stitch work on a horse's ass! Seriously, did you have a vet do this or the farrier or something?"

He rolled his eyes. "You sure know a lot about horses."

Although having shot me the day before, this intruder, despite his insistence that he had rented our house, I still considered him in intruder, didn't look so menacing now. He didn't have a gun and he was in the light of day. He was taller than me and as my eyes were coming into focus, he looked vaguely familiar. I was enraged by his statement about publicity. I blinked back the headache, drew up my full height and screamed at him, "Get out of my house!"

"No." He said it plainly, but stern.

Still spirited, I quipped back, "What do you mean, 'No?' Get out!"

Realizing I was still wearing the clothes from the day before, I threw down the covers I'd taken with me from the bed and stomped my foot for further emphasis on my demand.

"No," he repeated even more calmly.

I cut him off and darted for the phone on the bedside table. "I'll call the police," I threatened. "And, remember the publicity." I flared my nostrils but smiled curtly.

"I have a signed contract and I paid to rent this place for a week," he turned and gave me a dismissive flip of his hand. "Call the cops. Screw the press at this point."

"I'll press charges because you shot me," I yelled after him.

He yelled back, "I'll show them the contract stating the house was to be unoccupied by the owner and tell them that I thought you were a home invader. I believe it's called self-defense."

"What?" I followed him, stunned and still steamed.

He was well on his way down the hall with no intention of getting out of the house as I intended. He proceeded down the hall toward the master bedroom at a fair clip, not stomping, but giving the heart of pine floors a beating with every step all the same.

"Where are you going?"

He stopped and motioned toward my parents' bedroom, "To get dressed," and he carried on.

"You can't go in there!"

"I already did!" He paused inside the doorway, rested a hand on the edge of the door and challenged, "Plus, remember what I said about the contract?"

I glared at him.

"It says I can go anywhere in the house that I want. It's as if it is *mine* for the week."

The effects of having been wounded were not lost on me. I was blurry eyed, weak more so due to shock, in pain and all of this was only slightly hampered by the fact that I was enraged. Were it not for those issues, the fact that I was only 5'6" tall and all of a hundred and 15 pounds, I would not have been kept from breaking down the door and violently assaulting the jerk. As it was, I was left alone in the hall with my temper and no idea where to reach my parents for help or confirmation of this alleged contract. These emotions prove more than I could bear and, unfortunately, unresolved anger led to frustrations which led to tears. I puddled into the floor a sobbing mess and I couldn't, despite my best efforts, be quiet about it.

The bedroom door opened slowly. A cautious set of footsteps came forward. I looked up, sniffled, and rolled my eyes at him. I all but grunted, "You again."

He squatted down and reached to put a hand on me and I slinked back. He didn't back off, instead he offered a kind tone. "Please don't cry."

"You shot me!" I sniffed and wipe my nose with my hand. It wasn't a very hygienic or ladylike. "And you didn't even bother to take me to the hospital."

"Yes. Yes," he patted my back and cuddled me to him and, strangely, I let him. "I'm sorry about that."

I was worn out, regardless of having only just got up. I didn't have the strength to fight anymore.

"Please don't cry," he repeated, begging and sounding sincere.

"My parents have never rented out our house before," I said, trying to hold back more sobs. "They didn't tell me."

I looked up at him as if he could provide some explanation, but that idea was far-fetched. What would he know?

"I see that," he replied sympathetically.

I twisted my neck and looked at him curiously. In all of this exchange I still had no idea who this man was, but had an odd feeling that I should.

"What is your name?" I asked as I took in the features of his face.

He had green eyes, dark lashes and freckles so small they'd likely be missed by anyone beyond this proximity to him. His lips were defined, thin on top and fuller on the bottom. My eyes lingered on his lips and I noticed how white his teeth were, too. They were like fresh from a dental cleaning white. These features made him easy on the eyes and the more I looked at him the more distracting he was.

Easing back to a seated position next to me, he made an attempt to lighten the mood and stifle my tears. "I'll tell you mine if you'll tell me yours."

"Anna-Catherine Calloway." I tried to smile, but I wasn't quite there yet. "Folks call me Anna-Cat."

He extended his hand. "Alex Allen." We shook. "Folks call me..." he paused and refrained from adding his nickname. "Folks call me Alex."

My mouth fell open. There was a good reason I felt I should recognize him. Volumes of explicatives rolled through my mind and I barely kept them from rolling off my tongue. It was as if one side of my brain was explaining to the other how stupid I really was. He must have thought I was some creature from under a rock not to have recognized him sooner, at first sight even.

"So, Anna-Cat, you're quite possibly the prettiest crier I've ever seen." He knew how to deliver a line. He raised a brow. "How old are you?"

My tears stopped abruptly as I took on a whole new shock. "Old enough," for what I didn't say and I wasn't flirting with him. It was just the first phrase that drowned out the string of curses over what a fool I was.

I circled back to confirm what he said, "Did you say you're Alex Allen?"

He gave a half-cocked grin and a nod, accompanied by a light glimmer in his eyes.

Now the comments about the press made perfect sense. Well, in one regard they did, but it was still selfish on his part. Apparently, Alex Allen wasn't just one of the most famous young actors of our time, but a mind reader as well.

"It wasn't a vet." He gave an indication toward my straggling bandage, barely clinging to my bicep. "I swear, if it hadn't been a flesh wound I would have called 911."

I scooted to the side, straightening my posture. I had a better idea of the answer, but feeling it impossible, I asked anyway. "Did you do this?" pointing to my arm.

No words at first, he just gave another tip of his head. After a substantial pause, Alex explained, "I'm no doctor..."

I stifled a laugh.

"... But I took an EMT course for a part once," he concluded. "I passed, got the certificate and all."

"Oh, Jesus," I sighed.

"You're not easily impressed, are you?" Alex's face was nothing if not completely serious, the slight freckles on his brow merging into a tiny constellation.

I shrugged. No one ever said anything like that to me before and no one had ever called me pretty when I cried before either. I looked at my arm. Alex was right. It really was just a flesh wound. In fact, my head hurt way worse than my arm.

Courtesy of the pages of Teen Beat, Bob, Tiger Beat and 17 Magazine, Alex Allen's face has been the wallpaper for my friend Sally Ann Watson's bedroom walls for the better part of our teen years. She was a devout follower of

"The Mysteries of Margaret", a TV show that came on every afternoon at 4 p.m. The show was based on a book series and Alex Allen got his start playing Margaret's little brother and sidekick. I preferred the books to the show so I rarely watched.

Alex's most notable part, the one that sent teen girls like Sally Ann into early puberty, was the movie "Steps to the Moon." He played a dance instructor and, as I reflected on the movie, I began to blush. Although it was on cable TV, Alex Allen was the first man I'd seen naked, at least from behind anyway.

He noticed my blushing, read my mind again and said, "It was a body double."

Forgetting my head, my arm and everything else, I laughed out loud. I laughed until my sides hurt. It was a good feeling.

Chapter 3

Alex...

I was used to staying in strange houses. I'd basically been a nomad for most of my teen years and now it had carried into my twenties. I wasn't used to guns, but my father insisted on giving me one. If I flew somewhere, he shipped the gun Fed-Ex to my hotel or rental house. If I drove to my location, he insisted that I carry it in a case in the front seat of my car. It didn't matter that I was an adult, he insisted and life was easier when I pacified him. Plus, just because I carried it around with me, didn't mean I ever had to use it, so I thought.

I heard a noise from downstairs, footsteps to be specific. Stepping from the shower, I threw on my shorts and remembered the handgun in the case by the nightstand. I crept down the hallway with the gun drawn. I reached the top of the stairs and then, quite literally, the perfect storm happened. There was a flash of lightening that lit up a figure on the bottom step. There was no time to count to one, let alone count one Mississippi, before I heard the thunder and felt the house tremble at the same time. Then, the unthinkable happened. I squeezed the trigger, not hard, just barely.

The figure stumbled back and dropped like a lead zeppelin. My hands shook and I dropped the weapon. In retrospect, the trigger had been so sensitive, I was surprised it didn't go off again.

On unsteady legs and, with my ears still ringing from the boisterous pop of the gun, I inched my way down the stairs. With each additional crack of thunder and lightning, shivers went up my spine. As scared as I had been when I saw the figure coming up the stairs, I was just as scared now. I was petrified that I'd killed someone.

Keeping an eye on the body on the floor, I searched for a light switch, gave it a couple of flips and found the cherry on top of this situation. The storm had knocked out the power. It was dark, but not pitch black. There was just enough light that I could see there was no movement from the figure. I worked up my nerve, while debating on calling 911.

Another round of lightening lit up the room and to my surprise the figure was a girl.

"Shit!" I gritted my teeth and felt my color drain.

I leaned down, reached for her wrist to check her pulse. She had on a tank top and picking up her arm, the wound became obvious. The bullet had gone straight through what fleshy part there was to her thin arm.

"Jesus Christ!" I wiped my profusely sweating brow.

It was a good-sized gash, but she wasn't dead or dying. She'd likely just fainted. She needed stitches. On one hand I was lucky I wasn't experienced with guns, I was a poor shot. I only winged her. On the other hand, had I been more proficient with the weapon it wouldn't have gone off at all.

I rolled her over and brushed her hair back from her face. Shadows fell across the room from the storm and the streetlight out front. The power was back and I could see her. She was sweet looking and peaceful. I wanted to get her help, but with help came questions and those questions would bring attention that I didn't want. I'd avoided attention like this all of my career.

"She's not dying," I said out loud, comforting myself and making the decision of what to do.

I could see a cordless phone lying on an end table in the living room. I shook off the temptation to get it and dial 911. "No, I've got this."

The storm raged on. All night I'd sat by her bed and watched her sleep. I would have given anything for her to have woken up. I was as panic stricken that I might have killed her with the Hydrocodone and Flexeril I'd crushed and put in the water I'd given her as I had been when the gun went off. I kept the drugs on hand for a back injury I suffered when messing around kite surfing last year. After giving them to her, I worried the dosage for my weight might be greater than what would have been given to someone of her size. I only gave her the drugs to keep her sedated while I stitched her arm. I told myself it wasn't like I was giving her a roofie or anything sinister.

In the amount of time it took for the drugs to fully take effect, I searched the house for items to use to fix her up. I found kitchen scissors, dental floss, a needle from the drawer of an antique sewing machine that served as a table in the downstairs hall and whiskey from a decanter in the formal living room. There was no trace of rubbing alcohol anywhere in any of the four bathrooms so the drinking kind had to do for sterilization. It had been like an Easter egg hunt for make shift surgical supplies.

Now, she was awake and feisty. I'd met my fair share of bitches in my line of work, but she was not like them. She might have been putting up a fight, and a damn good one, but it wasn't the same. She had spunk and fire and was fragile at the same time. When she broke, it got my attention. Just to think about it sounded crazy, but when she cried she was the most beautiful thing I'd ever seen. Best of all, she didn't recognize me. For a little while, I was just some guy and when she figured it out, she didn't go all weak in the knees and drooling. She was fascinating.

"Please don't cry," I'd begged her.

I had a sister, Ashley. She was older than me and, growing up, I never gave a shit when she cried. Ashley cried like most people blinked. It was like a gift and most of the time she used that gift to either get her out of trouble or me into trouble. My father fell for it every single time, but not me. My opinion of my sister's tears carried over to most other women I met, but not this girl. This girl I hardly knew had me by the heart with one tear. What was wrong with me?

I pulled her closer, pressed her to my chest and stroked her hair until the sobbing turned to whimpers. Eventually, those subsided, too.

31

She stiffened, straightened up, and pulled back from me. She set her jaw, wiped her eyes and insisted, "I'm fine. Sorry about all of this."

She didn't say the word directly, but she called a truce. She told me her name, Anna-Cat Calloway.

"So, why did you come home last night?" I assessed her and, although she didn't answer my question to her age, I guessed she was at least college aged. "I assume you don't live here full time."

Surely had she really lived here, she would have known exactly what her parents had done and where they had gone.

Anna-Cat began pleasantly, "No, I have a place at school."

With her use of the word "school" my mind leapt to the thought of her going to boarding school. Some kids I'd known growing up went to boarding school, but it gave me pause. She didn't look like she had any age on her, but I would have never guessed she was still in high school.

Shit, I'm crushing on a high school girl, I thought.

Before my face could shift and really reveal the return of the guilt for having shot her and be compounded by the thought that she was still a child, Anna-Cat continued. "I go to college about two hours away."

"Ah," I exhaled in relief. I'm not a pervert after all.

"One of my friends was supposed to work the tournament, but she's sick so I volunteered to fill in for her," she explained further.

"What time do you have to be there and do you feel up to going?" I asked her, knowing how hot outside it was on the course yesterday and that I wasn't sure she should be out in that kind of heat.

"Honestly, she rubbed her head again, "I feel hung over and I'm certain I look like Hell, but I have to go."

"Can't they get someone else?"

"There is no one else. All of our friends that normally stay in town for spring break are away at college or they are already working it."

"So, you're skipping class to help out a friend?"

"She'd do it for me."

This girl kept getting farther and farther away from being like the ones I was used to in my life. She was loyal, a bygone trait as far as I knew.

"Plus," Anna-Cat added, "I spoke with my professors and, since I haven't missed any other days, they were, reluctantly, okay with me missing classes."

She shifted the conversation and started to get up from the floor, "I really should get some ibuprofen."

I offered my hand to help her up and she accepted.

"Thank you. I think my head hurts worse than my arm." She gave a half smile and I was taken in by her eyes. It was probably due to her crying and the headache, but her eyes begged the question, were they silver or pale blue? I looked away, not daring to ask.

I did ask, "Are you sure you're going to be alright?" I kept hold of her until she was steady on her feet.

"You said it yourself," she again, acknowledging her arm, "This is just a flesh wound and," she paused, thinking and looking at me with a narrow eye, "you rented the place."

"Ah, right." I gave a pursed smile. "How many days were you expecting to have to fill in for your friend?"

Likely realizing she hadn't brushed her teeth yet, Anna-Cat covered her mouth as she replied, "Today, maybe tomorrow. I'm not sure. She said she had a summer cold. She went in yesterday, but after an hour of coughing and sneezing, they sent her home."

"And you don't think they'll notice that patch job on your arm and send you home?"

"Well," she thought, "my Polo shirt should cover it. Not to mention, I really don't have a home right now. So, they're stuck with me."

"Okay, about that..." Before I really thought about them, the words were coming out of my mouth. "I've got this place all to myself until the practice rounds are over. Why don't you just come back here?"

A look of complete astonishment crossed her face and I wondered if I had somehow offended her.

I quickly clarified, "I promise, I'm harmless..." I corrected, "Okay, I mean, virtually harmless. I'd say I've already done my worst."

Anna-Cat bit her lip to stifle a giggle, but it didn't work. It was the first time I'd heard her laugh. Her southern accent came through even then. She was pretty when she cried, but she was stunning when she laughed.

As funny as she found what was said, she still shook her head, disagreeing with my proposal. "I don't think my parents would approve."

"I won't tell them if you won't," I teased her further. "But, if you would feel more comfortable, why don't you take the carriage house? I hadn't planned on using it."

Anna-Cat grinned, but not too widely. She'd reigned in her laughter and held back any excitement. "Alright. Sounds like a plan."

"Should we high five or shake on it?"

Anna-Cat held up her hand. High five it was.

We went our separate ways. She went to the club to work and I went because I had tickets to that day's practice rounds. A ball cap and the course logo shirt I'd purchased the day before allowed me to move through the crowd just as any other golf enthusiast. It was a rare occasion when I passed through an entire day completely anonymous. I was doing a good job of it today.

The smell of blooming azaleas, beer, someone's failing deodorant and a lady that bathed in perfume made a mix that offended my nose. Shades and the brim of my ball cap came in handy, but barely took the sting out of the beating down sun. It was another blinding day on the course.

I caked on sun block before leaving the house, but I could feel my skin cooking. I tanned easily, but not until after the first burn of the season. There was no relief from the sun as every ounce of shade on the course was taken and, by the time the day was done, I would have that first burn.

I tried to focus on the game. I followed a few players I recognized. I even made it to the ropes along one of the fairways to see Tiger Woods put one on the green within inches of the cup. The crowd went wild and my ears rang well after the quiet sign went up for the next player.

All of my senses were under assault and I was at the most magical place on earth for adult males. This was the Disneyland for grownups and for as long as I could remember I dreamed of being here. But now that I was here, all I could think about was Anna-Cat Calloway.

No one had ever come between me and sports before and I'd even dumped a girl once for getting between me and the TV while watching a Cubs game. There was a bit more to it than that, but her failure to get out of the way was definitely the last straw. Nothing had been normal since I heard footsteps in the hallway last night. It'd been a whirlwind of odd events since I met her, and now, I could not shake the thought of her. I still hadn't made up my mind if her eyes were silver or blue and that in itself was a distraction.

I strode across the course determined to see Phil Mickelson tee off. He was my favorite golfer, but instead of catching a glimpse of him close-up at the next tee box, I noticed the concession stand. A girl with long chestnut colored hair caught my eye. Her back was to me as she worked the handle, filling cup after cup of draft beer and sitting them to the side. The next thing I knew I was in line ordering a beer. I didn't even like draft beer. At the counter, I asked the very polite young attendant to tap the girl on the shoulder. I was just going to say "Hi" and be on my way. To my surprise, I had to say "Hi" to a girl who looked nothing like Anna-Cat after all. She was not at all like Anna-Cat. When she recognized me, she let out the ever so familiar squeal that almost all teenage girls did in that moment.

The squeal was followed by the girl going into all out hysteria and announcing so that everyone around could hear, "Oh my God! It's you! It's Billy Ward!"

The girl panted and repeated the name of the character I played in "Steps to the Moon." I didn't hang around to see if she fell into some swoon. With beer in hand, I slipped back into the crowd and no one seemed too phased but her.

I continued to wander the course and I did catch up with Mickelson before he finished for the day. I broke with the thought of Anna-Cat to consider how much more fun I was going to have at the tournament when my father arrived. There've been points throughout the day when I felt alone among the throngs of people and ordinarily that wouldn't be a problem. Today, however, the loneliness was magnified because when I wasn't thinking about how fun it would be to have my father with me... I was thinking about a girl that I shouldn't.

I stalked around the course. I stalked looking for Anna-Cat with a glance at every concession area I came near until the final player rang the cup on eighteen. Then, frustrated with myself over my preoccupation, I returned to my home away from home.

Chapter 4

Anna-Cat...

"Nice of you to join us today."

I closed my eyes and braced myself, hearing the voice come from behind me as I put my apron on. It was Chris Bussey. One, two, three, I counted and there it was. Chris slapped my ass. I knew it was coming, but I jumped, somewhat startled anyway. For the last three years he'd been the supervisor of the concession stand to which I'd been assigned and that's the way he greeted me.

"Don't do that," I said sternly.

"Say please," he replied in challenge.

I turned and glared at him. "It wasn't a request."

"Kitty Cat has claws." He made a swatting gesture at me with his fingers curved into make-shift claws.

I ignored him and went straight to my usual station.

Chris wasn't a bad looking guy. He had dark hair, dark eyes and some of the girls around the stand actually fell for his brand of charm. I was not one of those girls. I hated him, but he had a mad crush on anything that had female parts, including me. Every year, he pursued me.

Chris followed me, nuzzled beside me and asked, "So, pool party at your place again this year?"

"No!" I replied as sternly as if he'd smacked me again.

Not only did I remember our renter at Casa de Calloway, which prohibited a re-creation of last year, I also regretted hosting the party last year. This year, I figured I was only in town long enough to fill in for Sally Ann and there wouldn't be time. I told myself I'd be back at college before any if this really even had time to register.

I jumped right in, taking over one of the draft beer levers and started filling the first logo cup. Chris wasn't done. He sidled up to me closer and I felt his hand on the small of my back. I cringed. A shiver, ran down my spine and his hand inched lower.

"You and me, tonight. We're overdue."

I sat the cup down with a jolt that caused a good portion of the liquid to fly up and plop back down, some landing in the cup and some landing all around it.

I whipped around, looking him directly in the eye. "Take your hand off of me! Touch me again and see what happens. Do I make myself clear?" I also positioned my knee between his legs. On lookers wouldn't have noticed anything, but Chris felt the nudge of my knee into his groin.

He took a step back and stormed away.

The rest of the day passed in a fuzz of cold stares from Chris, whispers from the other staff members, wonders of where my parents were and thoughts of Alex Allen. I had enough on my mind to make the rest of the day pass in a rush.

Exhausted, I pulled into the driveway and around back where I came to rest in front of the carriage house. I was bone tired which was normal according to my usual experience from standing on my feet slinging beer all day at the course. I smelled like the inside of a keg and that was normal, too. What was not normal was that I couldn't go inside my own house, take a soak in my bathtub and sink into my bed.

I'd heard from Sally Ann through a mutual friend at the course. She was feeling better, but felt it best if I took the shift tomorrow as well. So, it was 9:00 p.m. and I had to be up at 6:00 a.m. for the early shift the next day. When I worked the tournament in the past I'd typically worked full day shifts. Sally Ann was a bit more of a princess than I was. She only signed on for half day schedules. She didn't need the money nor was she accustomed to manual labor. Normally, I would have been put out by her being a light weight, but not now. Although my headache was gone and, the arm thing was going to leave a scar, it didn't really bother me, I was just so tired.

The carriage house only had a shower and I really needed to soak. I peeked between the blinds. There were a few lights on in the house, but no one was by the pool. A dip in the pool would be the next best thing to soaking in my tub. Unfortunately, I didn't have a suit.

Two ibuprofen, a change of clothes and thirty minutes later with no relief to my aching legs, I peeked out the window toward the house again. The lights were still on so I took a chance that Alex was still up.

I ventured across the yard, cutting by the edge of the pool and sticking my hand in to test the water. The temperature was cool, but not cold. I came close to just jumping in clothes and all, but I didn't. I continued to the back door. I hesitated before giving three solid knocks on the door. I wasn't used to having to knock at my own house, but I didn't dare go in as I had last night. No one needed a repeat of that.

I waited and there was no response. I knocked again, three times. Another thirty seconds or so passed before I heard footsteps coming toward the door. I steadied myself and rehearsed what I was going to say.

When I was sure he'd made it as far as the opposite side of the door, I called out, "Hey! It's Anna-Cat."

The sound of the latch in the door was audible on my side. The hinges squeaked as the door slid open to reveal Alex standing there in nothing but thin pajama pants. They were low slung on his hips and revealed that deep V that guys have who work out a lot. Catching myself staring at that area between his hips, I quickly looked away.

"Hi. Sorry to bother you…"

"It's no bother," Alex was quick to reply, while resting his extended arm against the thickness of the door.

I fumbled a little, losing my nerve for a moment before asking, "Do you mind if I get something from my room?" My few moments of rehearsal had been a waste.

"No, not at all." He shifted back, opening the door wider and allowed me to pass.

"Thanks." I eased by him and started toward the front of the house to head up stairs. Alex followed.

Halfway up the stairs, a strange feeling came over me. I had another concern that maybe I should ask his permission before I used the pool. The strange feeling was again having to ask to use the facilities at the home where I'd lived all of my life except for the last nine months that I'd spent at Georgia College.

I turned around to ask directly and found Alex about three steps below me. He bit his lip and I could swear he blushed when I asked if I could use the pool. Then he answered with a nod.

I cocked my head and gave a concerned smile when I came out of my room found Alex had waited outside for me. "Are you following me for a reason?"

"Oh... Uh... No." Alex stuttered. "I... Well, no. No reason."

"Alright." I still couldn't look at him without my eyes being drawn to his waist. I fidgeted with my swim suit strings that were dangling from my hand and tried to divert my eyes with them.

Despite knowing who he was now, I was determined not to go weak in the knees over him. I was doing a stellar job until seeing him like that. It wasn't because he was famous either. I was certain I would have drooled over most any boy with a body like that.

I headed back out the way I came and Alex continued to come along behind me. For whatever reason, I felt compelled to ask him if he wanted to come for a swim. I felt like a fool as soon as the words left my mouth and a bigger fool when he turned me down.

"No, thanks. I think I'm going to turn in. Maybe tomorrow night."

"Okay." I did my best to keep my voice contained and show no emotion. It wasn't like it was any sort of let down or anything. I told myself the only reason I'd offered was because I felt bad about him sitting in the house alone.

I started to walk away and Alex added, "Anna-Cat, I think the light on the answering machine in the house is blinking. I don't feel right about checking it. Do you..." I didn't make him finish the questions. "Sure."

Back in the house, I pressed play on the machine. The first message was Dr. Stall's office, calling to remind my father about his dental cleaning next week. The second message was my mother. My eyes lit up at her voice and I was relieved to hear her.

"Mr. Allen, we are trying to reach our daughter, Anna-Cat. We can't seem to reach her at her dorm room at college and," Mom paused. She seemed to have the same, polite hesitation for bothering him that I did. "My husband forgot to tell her we'd rented out the house for the week and, if she shows up there." She paused again, before adding, "Please ask her to call us." My mother then left a number.

I was so relieved to hear her voice that I hadn't really paid attention to what she said. I picked up bits and pieces, but the number she gave got right past me. I had to play the message again.

"Here," said Alex, handing me the phone. "Just hit the call back button. I haven't used the phone all day so it should call the last number that called here."

"Oh, thanks!" I laid my swim suit down on the table and pressed the number to call back.

Within moments my mother had apologized profusely for them not telling me where they were going and what they'd done. Relieved to know they were alright, even though I'd assumed they were and had taken it for granted, I'd eagerly told her all about my day, with the exception of Alex having shot me.

"Yes, I'm working in place of Sally Ann," I responded. "It's only through tomorrow, I think."

Mother also asked about Chris. I didn't think she would have remembered that I'd told her how he was after the pool party last year. She'd threatened to send my father down there to set him straight about putting his hands on me, but I didn't want us to end up on the evening news.

Plus, I didn't really think my father would say a word on my behalf, let alone threaten some teenager.

"Yes, Chris is still there," I replied with exaggerated disgust.

She asked how that was going, but likely knew from the tone of voice in which I'd replied.

"Well, I stand by my decision to not work this year thanks to him, but now I have to fill in for Sally Ann. He's still all handsy." I rolled my eyes before remembering Alex was still hovering. I smiled, embarrassed, that I'd just rambled on with my mother with him standing there. Not long after, I decided to sum things up and get off the phone.

"I should probably go." I yawned for good measure. "Thanks for letting me know where y'all are."

Again, my mother apologized. "We love you," she assured me. "Hang in there and if he gets to be too much, go to your supervisor."

"I love you, too and it's just for one more day. I can tough it out."

The phone was barely off when Alex asked, "What is it you can tough out and who's Chris?"

"You sure are nosey," I said, avoiding his question and starting for the back door. "Thanks for letting me use the phone."

Alex followed. "Seriously, is someone harassing you?"

"I'm going to the pool now. Good night, unless you are coming to the pool, too and in that case, you should throw on a suit." I kept the chipper tone in my voice. I saw no need to discuss Chris Bussey with Alex.

"Fine. If you'll tell me what's what with this Chris pervert, I'll grab my suit."

I stopped in the jam of the back door. "I didn't say I'd tell you anything."

"So, he's a pervert?"

I glared at him. "Don't you have some Hollywood starlet girlfriend to go and call?" "According to the Enquirer I do, but..."

I cut him off. "No offense, but I don't care." I didn't care, but I didn't want to hear the details either.

"Okay. Fine." Alex reached around me and opened the door to let me out. "So, he's a pervert, he's your supervisor at the club and he's harassing you."

"Stop." I don't know what possessed my hand, but I gave him a playful slap across the chest as I passed by him on my way out the back door. It was too familiar of an act, but I had done it. I just did it on impulse, like I would with any of my friends. I had to remind myself I wasn't friends with Alex Allen.

The corner of his mouth raised in a wry smile. "I'll get my suit on. Meet you by the pool in ten minutes."

I only planned on taking a dip in the pool, just being in long enough to take the edge off the ache in my muscles. Before I knew it, I was racing Alex from one end to the other. He was quick, but I put up a good fight.

"You're pretty good," he said, whipping his neck and slinging the water out of his hair. Even wet, I could still see the waves in it.

"I grew up with a pool in my back yard." I waved my arm around, gesturing to the yard.

Alex laughed. His voice was deep and husky. I was just starting to understand why Sally Ann had such a mad hot crush on him.

"So, Chris..."

"Still off limits." I dropped under the water and took off swimming.

When I came up at the deep end of the pool, Alex was standing there on the edge. "I tell you what," he said, leaning down and offering me his hand to help me out of the pool. "I'll answer any question you ask me if you'll do the same."

I pondered the offer, knowing there were a million reporters in the world who'd kill for such an opportunity. Regardless, it was getting late and I needed to get out before I pruned up any more than I already had. I took his hand and, in one tug, he plucked me from the water. I hadn't expected to pop up like a cork and, grabbing my bikini top with my free hand to make sure it stayed in place, I basically crashed right into him.

"Who says I want to know anything about you?" I responded, trying not to take in the fact that I was now standing chest to chest with him. I was so close to him I could smell the hint of cologne that the chlorine in the pool had missed.

Winning a small battle not to lose my composure, I took a step back. Alex's face morphed from a heated, challenging stare to a flash of something that looked like disappointment before moving on to complacency. I guess he wasn't used to girls who didn't fall all over him, ones who withdrew from his embrace.

Although I had not agreed to our game of Twenty Questions, Alex took for granted that I had. Offering me my towel from a near-by lounge chair, he suggested I go first.

"Come on," he said, drying off with his towel and taking a seat on the end of one of the chairs. "Ask me anything."

I sat down on the chair next to him and dabbing water from my legs and assessed whether he really was an open book or not. I definitely wasn't. Ultimately, I decided to play along.

"Have you ever had plastic surgery?"

"Excuse me?" His eyes widened, shocked. "Why would you ask that?"

I gave a flippant motion, nothing direct or accusatory, waving my index finger at his face. "Your nose is fairly..." I searched for the right word to put it gently, "pointed."

"You think I've had a nose job?" He covered the subject and acted offended.

I was quick to banter back, "That's three questions that you've asked me already."

"What?"

"Four."

"Oh, I see how this is." He ran his index finger down the bridge of his nose, slowly. Somehow he managed to make that seductive and, feeling the heat rise in my chest and my cheeks, I covered myself with the towel and looked away.

Alex added while stroking his nose, "Nope. This is all courtesy of the Allen family DNA. Now, my turn. Do you have any brothers or sisters?"

"No." My answer was short and to the point. I didn't elaborate. It wasn't exactly a lie, but it wasn't the truth. I'd had a brother and I still avoided talking about him.

"You grew up in this big old house alone?"

"It was my turn." I then asked a question he'd probably answered a million times.

Chapter 5

Alex...

"How did you get into acting?" Anna-Cat asked, ringing out her wet hair.

Her hair appeared to have a natural part from her left, hanging over to her right. She tucked the strands that fell toward her face behind her right ear with the bulk of her hair hanging over her right shoulder.

I still hadn't figured out her eye color. Right now, her eyes were tinged with red from the irritation of the chlorine. That would be my next question. I resolved to ask her.

It would have been the most mundane, over asked question imaginable, if she weren't the one asking it. I normally responded with a yawn, but this time it was different. This time not only did I refrain from yawning in response to how I got my start, I actually told her the real story, not the one I told reporters and the like.

"I was thirteen and I had just been sent to live with my father and my step-mother in Tampa. I stayed in trouble, hence the move. I was beyond what my mother could cope with at the time."

I sat the towel to the side and continued, trying to keep focused on my story and not the length and shape of her legs, which were long, lean and smooth. Anna-Cat was built for swimsuits and I could have easily put her in touch with any number of modeling agencies who would have killed to sign her.

"Rebellious was an understatement," I said. "Fighting and so forth. My step-mother quickly had enough of my antics, too. That's what she called them, 'antics.' So, one day, she said to me that I was such a good liar and since I lived in fantasy land, I should at least get paid for it. Forgetting the part about getting paid and only remembering her irritated tone, when she loaded me up in the car and started driving, I thought she was taking me to some YDC facility or one of those boot camp type places for troubled youth."

Anna-Cat secured her towel around her and to my disappointment, covered up the lavender colored bikini she had on. Although she momentarily caused me to lose my train of thought, again, she seemed genuinely interested in my story.

"Go on," she encouraged me.

"Well, instead of dumping me at some detention center, she drove me the hour and a half to Orlando to the Nickelodeon studios. She proceeded to push me into an audition for a show called 'Apples to Oranges.' It was about these two young brothers who win the lottery. My character was the wise ass friend of the boys."

She gave a little snicker at my use of the description, "wise ass" and then shook her head. "I've never heard of it," referring to the show.

"That's no surprise. It didn't make it past the pilot."

"So..."

"They liked me so much that a part was written specifically for me when they started The Mysteries of Margret."

"I was going to say," she started again, "so you now get paid for being a liar. I guess your step-mother really had your number?"

"Yeah, I don't think of myself as a big fat liar or anything, but she definitely saved me from myself."

Anna-Cat nodded in agreement.

Redirecting the conversation, I pointed out, "My turn."

We were now sitting on the sides of the lounge chairs, face to face. Anna-Cat was in a half-cross-legged position with one leg tucked under the thigh of her other. I sat with both feet flat on the ground. I leaned in to get a better look as I asked, "What color are your eyes?"

Anna-Cat visibly blushed. "It depends on what I'm wearing. They shift between light blue and gray."

"Ah," I gave a knowing sigh. That explained that. "I like them."

"Thanks." Her cheeks turned pinker and she tried to reign in a smile while vaulting her next question my way. "What's it like being famous?"

I ran my hand through my hair from front to back, wishing she would ask me something a little more original. It wasn't like I was starved for being asked that one.

"Why do you want to know?"

"You can't answer with a question."

"No, seriously, why do you want to know?" I'd always wanted to ask that question and I'd never asked anyone before.

"Because I'm not famous, probably won't ever be famous and I've never met anyone famous, unless you count the time that James Brown sped past us on the streets of Augusta while chasing his wife and exchanging gun fire."

I really couldn't believe my ears. "Excuse me? James Brown was in a car chase..."

"And shootout," she added. "It was 1988 and I was twelve. My dad was driving me to my orthodontist appointment and all of the sudden a car sped past and whipped in front of us. Then, there was this popping noise. My dad immediately knew what it was, slammed on the brakes and shoved me to the floorboard of our car, but not before I got a look at where the noise came from. Mr. Brown was leaned all out of his window with gun in hand. I still remember how surreal it was. I'd never seen my father so scared."

"Jesus Christ! That's crazy!"

"Yeah, it was. Now, tell me, what's it like?"

"Sometimes it's good and sometimes it's bad, but it's never car chases and shootouts for me."

Anna-Cat laughed and gave a couple of rolls of her hand, motioning me on.

"What? You want me to elaborate?"

With a glint and a shift of her eyes and the twitch upward of the left side of her mouth, she gave a slight nod. "Yes."

"When a movie comes out, I can't leave my house for weeks on end depending on how popular the movie is. If it's a box office hit, then I'm stuck. If it's a flop, well, I don't want to leave the house then either so I'm stuck."

"So, you don't like being famous?" This time there was skepticism and a twinge of sarcasm in her voice.

"I like what I do and I'll admit I really like the paychecks, but I could do without being...stalked..."

"You've been stalked?" She sounded surprised.

"Yes, more times than I care to count. And, women regularly try to make friends with my mother, my step-mother, my sister and some of my cousins in order to try to meet me."

"Rather full of yourself, aren't you?"

"Are you mocking me?"

"No." Anna-Cat tried not to laugh, but she didn't succeed. "So, all of the women in the world want you?"

"No. Not all of them."

"Not all of them?"

"Well, there's tribes in Africa and in the rainforests of South America who don't get copies of People Magazine, but I'm working on that."

Anna-Cat slapped at me playfully.

"My turn." I scooted my chair closer to hers.

"What's it like living in a place like this?" I looked over my shoulder, back toward the house.

The house was one of those Southern stereotypes. It had wide porches and tall white columns. It was draped in Magnolia trees and exactly what people picture when thoughts of a Georgia mansion come to mind. It called to me when I was looking for a place to rent for the week. One look and I had to have it.

"I really can't describe it..."

"That good, huh?"

"No. It's just that I don't have anything else to compare it to, other than my tiny apartment at college." Anna-Cat clarified, "It's the only place I've ever lived."

"Really?"

"Yes, and you ask that like living in the same place is such a foreign concept."

I laughed. "It is for me."

"What do you mean?"

"Nothing. Never mind."

"So, you're not an open book."

"Huh?"

"You said I could ask you anything," Anna-Cat reminded me.

"Oh, right." I pondered how to answer. There was no way I wanted to tell her I was homeless and make her feel sorry for me or worse, sound like the poor little rich boy with unwarranted complaints. Finally, I replied, "I'm a bit of a nomad. It's a job requirement."

Anna-Cat and I continued to exchange questions until finally she yawned one time too many and remembered her schedule for the next day.

"Shit." She yawned again. "I've got to get to bed."

I didn't want to stop talking to her, but I stood and extended my hand to help her up.

"Folks from Florida aren't usually as gentlemanly as you are, Mr. Allen," Anna teased as she gracefully put her hand in mine.

"I never said I was *from* Florida," I replied as she stood.

"Is there another Tampa?"

"I said we were living in Tampa..."

"Well, then where..."

I stopped her. "You need to get some sleep and we can do this again tomorrow night if you like.

Anna-Cat grinned. "Deal."

That night I sank into bed with thoughts of Anna-Cat. Her hair, her smile, those eyes of hers, she was beautiful. Anna-Cat was smart and forgiving. She could have easily hated me for what happened last night, but she didn't even bring it up.

With my fingers interlocked, I rested my head on them and stretched out over the pillows. Her voice with the heavy southern accent replayed in my head as I watched the blades on the ceiling fan go around. I hung on the way she said "y'all" and how she drew out the most basic words into multiple syllables. I'd worked hard to get rid of any accent I might have had yet Anna-Cat embraced hers.

I couldn't recall the last time I'd had a normal conversation with anyone outside of my family, let alone a girl I'd just met. She didn't show any of the usual signs girls showed around me. She didn't seem enamored with me at all. I always thought it would be a nice change, but not with her. I wanted her to want me.

Typically, I was asleep as soon as my head hit the pillow, but not that night. This was the second night in a row that I'd struggled to sleep and all because of the dark-haired wonder I'd shot. I'd gone from one extreme to another. One of the reasons I'd come to Augusta was to get away from a woman, only to find another one I couldn't stop thinking about.

Rolling around in the bed, the phone on the bedside table caught my eye along with the time on the alarm clock. I contemplated making the call, it was long overdue. It was 2:00 a.m. here in Augusta which meant it was 10:00 p.m. in Santa Monica. Cammie would still be up so I made the call.

"Hello?" she screamed, trying to hear over what sounded like a rave going on in the background.

"It's me," I replied.

"Shhh!" She demanded of whomever was there with her.

I waited, impatiently, having my decision affirmed.

"Triple A, Baby!" Cammie turned on the breathless, Marylynn Monroe voice that she used when speaking to men. The voice was as fake as her nails, her teeth, her boobs, the extensions in her hair and her personality.

"Cam," I sighed, giving a little fakeness back. The sound I was going for was forlorn.

"What is it, baby?" She oozed.

I'd been dating her on the downlow for about six months and, thanks to it, I was on borrowed time for ending up on the cover of The Enquirer. That was just one of the reasons I had to make the break. I always thought it was low class to break up with someone over the phone, but I'd always had a feeling Cammie was used to low class. The offer to give me head when she followed me into the men's room at the Hollywood Bowl on our first date was a clear sign. Considering I let her, didn't exactly bode well for my credibility when it came to classiness.

"There's something I have to tell you," I said cautiously.

Not seeing it coming as some women would, with my month-long absence and inability to commit to calling her on a daily basis, Cammie let out a breathless, "Yes?"

I couldn't think of a better way to put it than to make it all about what she might want. "I'm okay if you want to date other people," I told her.

"What?" she gasped in what might have been her real voice.

"It's just that I'm going to be on the road shooting for the next six months or more and I don't want to keep you..."

Cammie regained her composure and talked over me, "You know, that's what I love about you, Triple A, you're so thoughtful."

I thought enough to know I hated when she called me that. It was a nickname given to me by my childhood friends, one of which I'd made the mistake of introducing to Cammie. He called me that in front of her. She thought it was cute and now wouldn't stop. It was like nails on a chalk board when she said it. Streaking, grinding, ear piercing nails and she wouldn't stop even though I'd all but demanded it.

"Baby," I hated that nickname about as much, "I'll wait for you," she tried to assure me.

I became blunt at that point. "No! Please don't."

Cammie got the picture. Her real voice reappeared. "You're dumping me, aren't you?"

I allowed an extended period of silence on my end to answer the question.

"You are!" The noise that had been behind her was completely gone, even the thumping music was turned off.

"I'm sorry." I lied. I didn't want to hurt her, but I wasn't sorry.

"You'll be sorry!" Cammie Attaway, the former bubblegum pop princess, who'd got her start singing in a church choir, was a far cry from that sweet girl now. She sounded like a whisper rising out of the bowels of hell, downright scary in that moment.

Without another word, I laid the receiver down, rolled over and went to sleep. A weight had been lifted.

The next morning while brushing my teeth and looking myself over in the mirror, I realized when it came to me and Anna-Cat, I wasn't the one that was intimidating. With the exception of those in the industry, like me, my stardom, for lack of a better word, was intimidating to others. No matter how modest I was about it, and I usually was, it was intimidating. That wasn't the case with me and Anna-Cat. Cammie Attaway scared me and Anna-Cat intimidated me.

Rinsing my toothbrush and sitting it beside the sink, Anna-Cat's story about James Brown came back to mind. She said she was twelve in 1988. I did the math in my head and quickly figured out how old Anna-Cat was. I was twenty-four and she was nineteen. The suffix "teen" putrefied the remaining hint of the toothpaste in my mouth.

Chapter 6

Anna-Cat...

The next day I was slinging beers, smelling like a brewery, having doused myself with a full cup of Amstel Lite, and dodging roaming hands from Chris Bussey, when things at the course took a turn. My face was flushed from the heat and it wasn't even lunchtime yet. I was what my father would call, "busted and disgusted."

Memories of staying up too late picking the brain of my house guest were fresh in my mind. Despite our odd and painful introduction, the evidence of which was still shown by the new bandage on my arm, I enjoyed hanging out with him. And regardless of his status as an actor and a heartthrob who was wanted by women all over the world – I laughed recalling our banter about that – Alex Allen really was down to Earth. I seemed to be falling into a fast friendship with the kind of comfort that typically came from those I'd known for years. I couldn't bring myself to regret not going to bed at a decent hour, even though I was dog tired.

Letting my mind drift to what Sally Ann would do when she found out who was at my house and that I'd hung out by the pool with him until all hours of the night, I overflowed the cup I was holding under the beer tap.

"Jesus Christ!" I muttered, snatching the cup away and feeling a trail of a line drawn with a fingertip that went from exceptionally high on my inner thigh backward under the hem of my shorts. I jerked around and let fly my open palm as I screamed, "Keep your hands off of me!" as I slapped Chris across the face. I don't think he thought I had it in me to do anything more than to warn him not to touch me, let alone slap him.

I'd been concentrating on filling cups as fast as I could and passing them to the counter workers. My legs

54

were apart and I'd planted my feet firmly shoulder width apart. That's what allowed him to get that close to me.

"Kitty-Cat likes it rough." Chris gave a sneer, grabbing my wrist and twisting my arm.

I still had the half full cup of beer in my other hand and with my face flying hotter with rage, I slung the beer in an attempt to douse him in the face. I missed as he wrenched my other arm. I felt my knees buckling as he drove me down with his grip and my eyes watered from the pain. It was the same arm that had the graze from Alex Allen's misfire.

"Let go of me!" I screamed again.

Noise like this on the course was out of the ordinary, but despite the commotion, life went on for everyone else in the concession stand. None of my co-workers intervened. They kept at their work. Intervention came from the other side of the counter, from one of the patrons who noticed what was going on.

"Hey! Take your hands off of her!" The voice was familiar and threatening.

Everyone stopped then. Heads whipped around like all of a sudden my wellbeing mattered, but that wasn't it at all. Co-workers, beer drinkers and those that were in line all ready to order the famous chicken salad all recognized the voice.

Alex had a hand on the counter and was drawing up a leg to come across when I jerked free of Chris.

"You quit, right Anna?" He just called me Anna and held out his hand for me to come to him.

"I do," I beamed at him. I turned back to Chris, whose mouth was gaping wide open, probably in a state of shock and highly intimidated by Alex. Chris and I were about the same height whereas Alex was at least six or eight inches taller than us.

While Chris was distracted with Alex, I shoved my club issued apron into his groin with a fist and growled, "I quit!"

I didn't bother going around the counter. Those standing in line waiting to order and waiting on orders moved to the side as Alex helped me climb over. The staff members, still stunned in silence over the appearance of Alex and the fact that he seemed to know me, watched bug-eyed.

Chris staggered after me, holding himself. "I'll call security!"

"Do it!" I snipped in challenge as I starting to walk away with Alex.

"I will! I'm calling them! You're trespassing now!" He called after me.

Alex fished out a badge from his back pocket and, dangling it for a moment for all to see, he placed it in my hand and closed his hand around mine. With his other hand he tore off his ball cap and shades. "Call them if you want, but she's with me!"

I didn't even notice until we'd nearly walked halfway across the course that Alex was still holding my hand. When I did realize it, I looked down at my hand in his and slowly let my eyes glide back up to his face. I felt the smile creep across my face and I bit my bottom lip to try to control it.

Shifting a quick glance from the player taking practice swings in the tee box to me, Alex asked, "What?"

"Were you really about to come across the counter back there?" I asked sheepishly.

"Anna, I was about to whip his ass!" He called me just Anna again and I liked it. I also liked the testosterone coming off of him.

"So, not worried about the press anymore?" I laughed.

Remembering the fight we'd had the morning we officially met and what he said to me, Alex turned, looked me directly in the face and shook his head.

I curled my index finger back and forth to Alex, "Come here."

Skeptical, Alex leaned down.

I kissed him on the cheek. "Thanks!"

When he leaned back, Alex smiled at me and I saw what all of the fuss was about with him. He was so good looking he was almost hard to look at without that thought being conveyed on my face. *My God, he was really something.*

Straightening up after the peck on the cheek, Alex sized me up, letting his eyes glide over me from head to toe. "Let's get you out of those clothes."

"Excuse me?" My head snapped, clearly not hearing him right.

Alex clarified, "You can't very well walk around looking like you work here. Let's go get you something else to wear."

"Oh," I sighed, a bit disappointed. "Yeah, I guess I should give this back to you."

"Why?"

"Because I can't just walk around here looking like the help. I have to go home."

"Oh, please. I meant let's go get you something to wear from one of the shops."

I might have lived in a big house in the hill section, but I wasn't made of the kind of money it would take to reoutfit me from one of the souvenir shops at the course. It was as if Alex read my mind.

Again, Alex took my hand and led the way. "Don't worry. As long as you let me pick it out, I'll treat."

"I can't let you do that." I stopped and took my hand back.

"You can and you will." Alex paused and waved a hand at our surroundings. "I'm guessing you've never been a guest at the tournament and been able to go where ever you wanted on the course, right?"

I gave a nod of my head, acknowledging he was right.

"But you'd rather go home with your pride than stay and have fun with me and see the sights?"

I didn't cave right away, but I caved. "Fine."

57

Alex picked out a lavender sleeveless polo shirt and a straw hat with a matching deep purple, lavender and white paisley band around it. Perhaps he thought that was my color. I wondered if he remembered my bathing suit from last night.

"This should match your shorts. What do you think?"

I looked down at my shorts. They were khaki and that went with everything. "You don't have to. I could run home change and come back."

"And by the time you pay for parking again, I could just buy you the shirt."

Alex had a point. "Plus," he added, "I'm tired of walking around this place by myself."

I started walking toward the changing room. "So why are you here by yourself anyway?"

Alex followed. "It was a spur of the moment thing."

"You got these tickets spur of the moment?" I found that hard to believe. Tickets to this game were harder to get than tickets to the Superbowl.

"They were a gift from my management company."

Over the dressing room door, Alex went on to explain that since he released three movies this year and each made a significant profit, he was able to submit a wish list to his management company. All he put on his wish list was four tickets to the Masters and a black 1962 Corvette Stingray.

"I'm assuming that's your favorite car?"

Completely changed and with hat in hand, I opened the stall door in time for Alex's reply.

"It's my mother's. She had one." Alex looked at his feet and stiffened his posture with his hands in his pockets. His body language signaled there was a story there.

"What happened to it?" I looked up at him as I stooped to tie my tennis shoes.

"I wrecked it."

"You wrecked a '62 Stingray?"

"Yeah." Alex uttered with a complete lack of enthusiasm.

"You really are going to make me pull it out of you, aren't you?"

"The thing is, I really don't remember what happened."

"What do you mean, you don't remember?"

"I took the car without permission and three days later I woke up in Sacred Heart Hospital." Alex continued to explain as we got in line to pay for the clothes I was wearing.

"How old were you?" I asked.

"Thirteen."

Bells and whistles started going off in my head. "Is that when your mother sent you to live with your father?"

Alex dipped his head and I gathered, I'd hit the nail on the head with my suspicion.

"So, she sent you to live with your father because you wrecked her car?"

Alex corrected me, "No. She sent me to live with him because I 'nearly killed myself on her watch.' Those were her words. She loved the car, but..."

"She loved you more?"

"Yeah, and I was an ungrateful little asshole."

I leaned in so no one in line would hear my use of the word. "I don't think an asshole would wish for a car to give his mother."

"Maybe an asshole would ask for one to keep for himself."

Already knowing the answer, I questioned, "Is that what you were doing?"

"No."

"You never told me, why were you so rebellious?" I asked, looking him over long and hard.

"You never asked." Alex straightened my collar.

His fingertips brushing against my neck caused my mind to go blank. It took me a minute to focus on something other than his touch. "I'm asking now."

"My parents divorced. The marriage had been a sinking ship for years. Of course, now I realize that, but back then, as a child, I didn't understand. The divorce left me adrift while everyone else found a new life raft. My father remarried and had another child and my mother became a serial dater. I was basically left to my own devices and raising myself proved to be a bad thing."

We were next in line as I prodded the conversation further. "I'm guessing these tickets weren't for you either."

Alex grinned. "My father has watched every one of these tournaments on TV for as long as I can remember. We watched them together until I started traveling so much. I knew he'd kill to see it in person."

We were up next and I handed the girl at the counter, a girl who graduated high school with me last year, the tickets from my shirt and hat.

"Anna-Cat, is that you?" I wasn't sure why she had to ask. I looked exactly the same as I always had and we'd attended the same schools from kindergarten through senior year.

"Yep. How have you been?" I replied as she scanned the tickets and Alex made a last-minute addition to our purchase by tossing a pair of ladies Ray Bans on the counter.

"Good," I answered, wondering if she'd notice him.

The total sprang up on the register and before she could verbalize the amount Alex took out his wallet and extended his hand with the cash. It wasn't until then that Sarah Walton noticed him. She gave him a cock of her head, trying to decide if it really was him or not. His cap and glasses didn't do the full Clark Kent trick on Sarah.

It wasn't unusual to see celebrities at the course. Last year I served beer to Tom Hanks. It was surreal, but nothing heart stopping and Sarah Walton looked as if her heart had indeed stopped.

When she finally found her words, she said barely got my name out again, "Anna-Cat..."

Suspecting she was going to ask me who he was, Alex gave the money a little shake and introduced himself before she could finish her sentence. "August Allen."

Sarah's eyes widened.

"Brother of Alex," he added.

I cut my eyes at him. He'd mentioned a sister, but nothing about a brother.

Sarah was still star struck, but she took the money, gave him change and we scurried out of the little shop.

"August Allen?" I questioned just outside of the doorway.

"It's my middle name."

"Alex August Allen."

"Hence the nick name Triple A."

"Ahh."

Alex gave me the tour of the course based on what he'd learned in the two days he'd wandered around there by himself. He bought me lunch and I introduced him to the world-famous Augusta National chicken salad. We ate lunch sitting under a tree near the Butler Cabin.

"That's where they award the green jacket." I pointed to the little white house. I knew a few things about the course, too.

"Have you noticed there's not even a pine cone out of place around here?"

"And the rumor is that they use giant blow dryers on the azaleas to make sure they are in bloom in time for the tournament," I said off-handedly.

"Is that true?"

"I've heard it more than once growing up around here when we had a late freeze."

"Wow." Alex went about chewing his sandwich.

After lunch we meandered around the course some more. At the sixteenth hole we made it all the way to the ropes, the front row of the crowd. We were within five yards of him when we watched Tiger Woods tee off.

A gentleman pushing to get closer to get a photo of Tiger nudged me and I stumbled backward into Alex. When

I lost my balance, Alex steadied me. The crowd was thick and now I was pressed back to front with him. He slipped his arms around me and crossed them over my waist. Although I hadn't invited him to touch me like that, I didn't feel he was trespassing on me the way Chris Bussey did. It felt natural and I didn't push him away or slink out of his embrace.

In that moment of close proximity to Alex, he whispered, "Don't go back to school tonight."

My pulse quickened and my heart raced. I tried to keep in mind that this was all just some weird dream.

Chapter 7

Alex...

I don't know what possessed me to say that, "Don't go back to school tonight." The words fell out of my mouth that should have been safely locked in my head.

Nor do I know what possessed me to wrap my arms around her like that, clutching her to me and holding her. I could have steadied her after that asshole nearly knocked her down and let her go. I should have done that.

I don't know what possessed me to burn for her the way I was starting to do so. I knew Anna-Cat was basically forbidden fruit, but for whatever reason, I was possessed. And despite the constant reminder I gave myself, saying she was too young and clearly not the type of girl to have a fling with, I couldn't help myself. The more she seemed unaffected by me, the more I wanted her. The really funny thing was that I was typically unaffected by women. They turned my head and made my dick twitch, but Anna-Cat did more to me than that. I was possessed by a need to be closer to Anna-Cat.

I don't know how I expected her to respond considering I hadn't meant to have the verbal diarrhea that I had, but casually, as if she hadn't understood my meaning, Anna-Cat replied, "I was planning on driving back tomorrow morning."

I hadn't felt butterflies since my first onscreen kiss. It was the second season of Mysteries of Margret and I had to kiss Larissa McClure, a guest star from our sister show. Here I was now, standing in the middle of the most prestigious golf tournament in the world, the Mecca for the male species, and my thoughts weren't on golf at all. My typically sports consumed mind was fixated on a girl, a teenage girl, and my internal organs were behaving like those of a teenage boy. I was five years out of my teens, but

I was genuinely excited over the thought of spending more time with this girl.

The last player pinged their ball down the fairway and the crowd started to move. I released Anna-Cat and, keeping close to the ropes, we moved with the flow of the spectators. Down the hill, about halfway down the fairway, a voice called my name, "Alex!" There could have been a dozen men named Alex so Anna-Cat and I kept moving. When they yelled, "Triple A!" That got my attention.

I touched Anna-Cat on the shoulder. "Stay here a minute, okay?"

She nodded and I could see her eyes over the top of her sunglasses when she dipped her head. They were still blue, pale blue.

I walked the few paces back as Jacob Stein approached me. I knew I shouldn't talk to him as long as the litigation was pending, but I didn't want him continuing to yell after me.

As I neared Jacob, he stretched out his hand, "Hey, man, I thought that was you."

I lowered my shades with one hand, thinking the last thing I wanted to do was shake his hand, but I took it anyway. "Yep, in the flesh."

"I didn't know you liked golf. I would have hooked you up with tickets last year."

Hooked me up, the thought made me laugh with distain. It would have been me that hooked me up since it was my money he'd used to finance his lifestyle and everything else for the last three years.

"Ever been to Pebble Beach? I can get you in." He managed to say all of that before I could get my hand back from his grasp.

I wanted to take back my hand and slug him. We'd see if he could get in Pebble Beach with a caved in eye socket and a broken nose.

I remembered there were a hundred people within earshot, including Anna-Cat, so I chose not to make a scene. "Nah, that's okay. Really."

"So, who's the girl?" Jacob nodded behind me, indicating he'd seen me with Anna-Cat. "Latest model friend?"

I shook my head. "Negative. Friend of my little sister's." I preferred to keep my answers short. The less he knew about Anna-Cat, the better. I reflected on my decision to even bother speaking to him and regretted it. I didn't want him to know one thing about Anna-Cat.

"So, when are you coming home?" Home was how he referred to his agency.

I just stared at him, not believing my ears. "You've got some real brass ones, don't you?"

"We'll do lunch. I've got some new projects in the pipeline I think you'll love," he bragged, pretending not to hear my last remark.

Plus, even if we weren't in what my attorney called the "discovery phase" of my suit against The Stein Agency, his agency, the only work he could ever get me was more ab-showing, rom-com, same-old-same-old.

"Look," I said frankly, "I appreciate all you did for me, but I'm okay with Goldwyn mainly because they haven't stolen five million dollars from me."

"I was hoping we could put this behind us..."

"We can," I assured him, "if you have a cashier's check on you made payable to me for every penny you took."

Jacob immediately looked past me and pretended to spot someone else he knew. "My attorney will be in touch." He patted me on the shoulder like any old friend would before darting away.

As if Jacob Stein had rubbed germs on my sleeve, I brushed my hand over it feverishly, wiping away his touch while walking to catch up with Anna-Cat. She had waited patiently with nothing but a smile. I liked that she smiled fully every time she saw me. When she wasn't clad in sunglasses I could see that her smile was one that came from her eyes and oozed sincerity. In the steps it took for me to get to her I wondered if she smiled at everyone like that. I hoped not. What I wouldn't give to be the only one she looked at like that.

I reached for her hand when I neared her and she didn't resist. "Are you ready to get out of here?" I asked her.

"Sure. Who was that?"

Guiding her by the hand and with a touch to the small of her back, I began to lead her toward the exit. "Former manager."

"Not a fan of him, huh?"

"How smart are you?" I teased her.

"Not quite Mensa, but close."

I wasn't sure if she was being a smart ass or if she was telling the truth. I stopped and looked at her. Anna-Cat stopped and stared back at me.

"Are you serious?" I asked, curiously.

"Yes. I missed it by two points."

"You're fucking kidding, right?"

Almost offended, she demanded, "Don't I look smart?"

"Forgive me, but girls that look like you aren't usually the brightest bulbs..."

"So, I'm an anomaly."

I burst out in laughter and repeated the word back to her, "Anomaly. Yeah, you are definitely that."

I'd taken a cab to the course, but Anna-Cat had driven her little white Volkswagen Bug so she drove us home. She parked in the driveway and, halfway through the turn of her key in the lock of the back door of the main house, Anna-Cat remembered she wasn't supposed to be there.

"Oh, sorry." She backed off with her key still in the door.

"It's fine. Why don't you come in? We'll..."

"No," she walked backward toward the steps. "I've got to get..."

"Your suit so you can meet me by the pool?"

She blushed. "Is that the plan for tonight?"

66

"The plan is for me to make some dinner. We'll eat by the pool, we'll burn off the calories and then we'll just hang out again. Are you up for it?"

"I should get to bed." She gave me this look: Come hither, no, don't. "I should..."

Slowly, I closed the gap between us, "You should let me make dinner for you and..."

"I should go get a shower."

"And then meet me by the pool."

"You sure are pushy, Mr. Allen."

"I prefer the word, 'Persuasive.'"

Anna-Cat gave a playful roll of her eyes.

"By the pool in an hour," I insisted. "Don't make me come over there and get you."

"Fine."

An hour later I carried two plates to the umbrella covered table by the pool. The plates consisted of my specialty, ribeye steaks seared with garlic butter, grilled peaches and baked potatoes. I'd picked up the items at the grocery store the day I arrived. I'd planned on making them when my parents arrived, but figured now was as good a time as any.

Anna-Cat wasn't out yet so I left the plates and returned to the house for the salad and drinks I'd prepared. Looking at the bottle of wine sitting on the kitchen counter, I wondered if Anna-Cat had ever been wined and dined. Her age popped into my head again and I figured the answer was no. I looked the bottle over again, tempted, but left it in the kitchen. I grabbed two bottled waters and the salad plates and headed back to the table.

Ten minutes later, Anna-Cat emerged from the carriage house. Red bikini, matching flip flops and makeup free, she was stunning without even trying.

"Sorry I'm late," she said as I pulled out a chair for her. "I called my mother and she insisted on knowing how my day went,"

"Did you tell her about the guy from the course?"

"You mean you?" she asked playfully over her shoulder as I scooted her chair in.

"No. I meant that asshole that was man handling you."

"Yeah, I told her about him." Anna-Cat started to laugh. "She's going to make some calls. She swore by the time she's done with him he won't be able to get a job anywhere in Augusta."

After dinner, Anna-Cat and I had a repeat of last night. We raced each other from one end of the pool to the other a few times and finally I caught Anna-Cat and dunked her. Anna-Cat was lanky with slight curves where it counted and she was athletic. While under water, she managed to wrap her legs around my waist and using only her upper body she swam toward the bottom of the pool. She had a death grip on me with her legs and she managed to pull me under. As soon as I went under, she let go and popped up behind me catching me around the neck.

"You weren't expecting that, were you?" she giggled at her triumph.

I twisted in her arms and there was a brief moment, a locking of our eyes, when I felt compelled to kiss her. She was drawing me in and I could feel the earth move, but I resisted. I pulled away from her. I continued to remind myself, *I'm not right for her.*

"How's your arm?" I gave a glance to the white bandage swirling through the water as she paddled with her arms to stay afloat.

"I'll probably have a scar," Anna-Cat batted her eyes and laid on the guilt.

"Maybe you can get a tattoo to cover it," I suggested, floating on my back.

Anna-Cat splashed me and I jolted up, giving the water a swat and her a healthy dose of payback.

"Did you really do all of your own dancing in..." Anna-Cat paused, clearly trying to bring to mind the name of the movie.

I knew what she was talking about, but I couldn't decide whether to be offended that she couldn't remember "Steps to the Moon" or relief that I'd found one woman on the planet that hadn't watched it hundreds of time.

I finally helped her, "In 'Steps to the Moon'?"

"Right." She smoothed her hair from her face and finished her question. "Did you do all of the moves yourself?"

"Yes."

She looked surprised.

"It's not like doing stunts."

She was amused. "So, you don't do all of your own stunts?"

I glared at her, but only in jest and splashed her again.

Anna-Cat ducked and immediately volleyed water my way. We had a full-on water fight for about thirty seconds before I caught her and attempted to toss her over my shoulder and to dunk her again. Anna-Cat was slick from being wet and put up a fight. I didn't give up when I should have and, in the struggled to keep hold of her, somehow my fingers got caught in the string from her bikini that secured it across her back.

"Whoa there!" she said as it snapped and she hurried to make sure she was still covered.

"Turn around." Regretfully, I didn't see anything more than a bit of under boob.

Anna-Cat quickly complied, turning her back to me.

"Hold still. Let me see."

Anna-Cat tensed. "Excuse me."

"I meant, let me see the strings. Be still."

Again, Anna-Cat complied as best she could while floating in water that was over her head. Upon inspection, I noticed the knot that held them together had only been snatched loose.

I tied the strings as Anna-Cat said, "Tell me what it's like."

69

"What?"

"What on screen kisses are like." I couldn't tell if she was flirting with me or just being curious. Clarification came when she conveyed, "I hear they are awkward." She was teasing me.

Just talking about kissing with her was titillating so was sneaking a look over her shoulder and down her chest as I retied the strings to her top.

"I guess that depends on who's doing the kissing and..."

"So, you're saying that it's not awkward when you do it? Or, you're so good at kissing that there's no..."

"Hey now," I cautioned, "I'm no awkward kisser. To be clear, the awkwardness is from the fact that thirty people are getting paid to watch what you're trying to portray as an intimate moment. It's harder than you think."

"Really?" Anna-Cat sounded skeptical. "I suppose sex scenes are just the worst."

"They aren't fun."

She threw her head back and laughter bellowed out.

"What's so funny?"

She continued to giggle through her words. "I can't imagine any of my guy friends complaining about getting paid to dry hump gorgeous girls. It is dry humping, right?"

"Basically, but let me tell you, forty people standing around, the lighting guys, the cameras, the microphones..."

"The nakedness."

"No one's exactly naked." I then explained the concept of a modesty pouch to her. "So, you have a sock on your penis?"

"I can't believe we're having this conversation." With a couple of strokes, I had a hold of the wall of the pool. Somewhat embarrassed and wanting to avoid anything more on that topic, I pulled myself up the side and got out of the pool.

"Do you have a girlfriend?" she asked me, looking up from the water.

70

I reached down and offered Anna-Cat a hand to help her get out. "Does it matter?"

Anna-Cat lifted both hands and, with a snatch, I popped her up out of the pool. I bought her chest to chest with me, resting her hands on my pecks.

Anna-Cat looked up at me, biting her bottom lip until she released it only to state, "You didn't answer the question."

"No." I said low voiced.

Anna-Cat didn't budge other than to slide her arms around my neck. "Why?"

I should have stopped her. I should have backed away. I should have ended things right there, but I didn't. I answered honestly. "I just broke up with someone."

"Anyone I might know?"

"Yeah." I think everyone on Earth probably knew who Cammie Silver was. She had been a B-celebrity before signing on to an MTV reality show.

"Who?" Anna-Cat took two steps back.

"What do you care?" I snapped back a little harsher than I should have. Even though I had been trying to resist the pull toward Anna-Cat, I was disappointed the heat of the moment seemed vaporize.

Anna-Cat was rightfully taken aback. "I guess I don't."

She brushed past me and picked up her towel from the lounge chair behind us. "When did you say your parents are arriving?"

"Tomorrow."

"Good." Anna-Cat dried herself off and I couldn't help but watch. "I hope they like the house and have a good time."

She wrapped the towel around her herself, slipped on her flip flops and started toward the carriage house.

"Wait. What just happened? Where are you going?"

"I'm going to bed." She barely turned back to me. "Nope, I could be on the road in fifteen minutes..."

I cut her off, "You're leaving?"

She didn't say anything. She just kept walking.

I went after her. "Hold on. Are you mad at me?"

Anna-Cat cut her eyes back at me and gave them a roll. The last time she rolled her eyes at me she was playing. This time she was not playing. She was pissed.

I raised my voice when she didn't stop walking. "Anna!"

That got her attention. Her shoulders slumped and she paused. With a sigh, she asked, "What?"

I closed the gap between us and got around her, making her face me. "What did I do?"

She closed her eyes and let out under her breath, "Nothing."

It wasn't as warm out as it had been the previous night and there was a breeze. The scent of Magnolias from the trees in the yard floated in the air and chill bumps sprang up on Anna-Cat's arms. Hesitantly, I wrapped my towel around her.

She batted back tears in her eyes as she looked up at me. There was an air of helplessness in the way she looked at me. I never knew my heart could be broken with a look, but I knew now that it could.

"Tell me what I did," I begged her.

"You didn't do anything." A single tear slipped down her cheek and she was quick to wipe it away.

I pulled Anna-Cat into my arms and held her. Her face hit right at my shoulder and she buried it there. Her breath prickled goosebumps on my skin when she spoke. The feel of her left me fighting hard against utter arousal.

"I'm not one of those girls that's easily star struck and I'm not ever going to be any sort of celebrity so I know I'm not in the same league as you." She said it as if it was a fact and she wasn't seeking sympathy. "But despite that, I like you. I like you for you and I know..."

"Anna..."

She didn't finish her earlier statement. She simply

admitted, "I like it when you call me Anna. No one ever calls me just Anna."

"Anna," I said again, leaning back and lifting her chin so she would meet my eyes. "I can't tell you the last time someone liked me for me."

Anna-Cat's cheeks grew wide as a grin stretched across her face and tears escaped the corners of her eyes. Anna touched my face, cupping my cheek and lightly caressing me. A warmth flowed through me like I'd never known and I tilted my head into her touch.

"Your eyes..." I began to confess.

Her hair was the thing shampoo companies dreamed of in their models and her skin was the perfect combination of tanned, yet porcelain. Her ass was nothing short of amazing and the last two nights her legs left me dreaming of having them wrapped around me. Those attributes were great, but the highlight of Anna-Cat was her eyes. I tried to think of the right words to describe them, but I had nothing. Nothing I could say would do them justice. Nothing I could say would do her justice.

"...are an anomaly?" Anna-Cat interrupted me, slowly biting her bottom lip and letting her eyelids float up ever so gradually until her eyes settled on mine.

Our eyes lingered a moment before Anna-Cat reminded me, "I have to go."

As far as I knew this was our last night together. I didn't want our time to end, but again the sinking feeling stirred in me, *I'm not right for her*. That feeling fought against my strong desire for her and I let her walk away.

Only a few feet from me, Anna-Cat looked over her shoulder. "Good night, Alex."

The struggle was over and desire won. Quickly, I caught her by the hand, twirled her and dipped her. It was a move that women the world over would have died to do with me. It would be lost on Anna-Cat, but it was the finale to the last dance in "Steps to the Moon." Indeed, I did my own dances in that movie and I remembered them. This time I didn't just nuzzle my partner's nose before bringing her up for the kiss. I showed all of my prowess as a man and I took her mouth while holding her suspended. Every muscle in my arms, back and chest flexed as I kissed her for all I was worth. I'd been treated like a stallion since I was sixteen years old, but this was the first time I felt as though I really acted like one. *I'm not right for her* was stamped out by lust and some other something to which I dared not admit.

Anna-Cat gripped tight around my neck when I first took her down, but relaxed instantly and gave in to me. She trusted me and her reciprocation spurred me on. Her fingers tugged through the hair on the back of my head as she devoured me as much as I devoured her. It took all I had not to lay her down, right there on the walkway to the carriage house, and take her.

"Oh God," Anna-Cat panted when I let her up for air.

"Anna, stay inside with me tonight." I was as breathless as she was.

"No," she sighed. "I can't."

Chapter 8

Anna-Cat...

I was packed and aimed to be on the road before daybreak, well before Alex woke up. The Lord or some other force had different plans for me and I overslept.

It was well past daybreak when I reached for the handle of the car door and heard the newly familiar voice call my name. "Anna!"

I turned to see Alex clad in nothing but a pair of black shorts and sneakers running up the driveway toward me. I'd hoped to sneak away without having a drawn-out goodbye with him or any promises to see one another again or, worse, no mention of plans to see me again. Those hopes were dashed and my racing heart was glad of it as I took in the sight of Alex, shirtless, muscles flexing in all directions and skin glistening. I'd seen him shirtless by the pool the nights before, but this took it to a whole new level. I suddenly felt the urge to fan myself, but resisted.

"Hey!" He said, half out of breath, and stopping before me. "Leaving without saying goodbye?"

Again, I thought of the plan and shook the idea out of my head. "I didn't want to wake you."

"How considerate," he smiled, taking two steps closer.

I backed up, thinking this was not the time to go weak in the knees over him again. I needed to remain strong. I needed to get on the road and make it to class this morning.

"You're sweaty." It was only an observation.

Alex took another step toward me and I backed up a step or two until there was nowhere to go. My back came to rest against the car door.

Alex placed a hand on each side of me, resting them on the ridge where the door meets the roof of the car. I closed my eyes, having the mixed emotions of dread and excitement with the anticipation of what I thought was coming. I could smell the hint of his deodorant and a hint of pure Alex. I never thought I'd find BO intoxicating, but his? Oh, it was.

With eyes still closed, and not meaning to, I let my thoughts escape my mouth, "God, you smell good."

"Anna." Alex nuzzled his cheek to mine and nipped at my ear. "I could stand to get a bit sweatier if you're up for it."

Everything in me came alive, but I loved the way he said my name. I squeaked out barely above a whisper, "I've really got to get back to class," but I didn't fight him off. I did nothing to stop him.

Alex dipped his hips and pressed into me. I could feel his erection through his shorts and mine, especially when he grabbed my thighs and hoisted me up against the car door. My arms went instinctively around his neck and I held on, locking my legs around him.

"I'm not ready to say goodbye to you yet," Alex said, holding me up, he pinned me to the car.

Alex continued to plant soft kisses on my neck, digging a deeper hole with his tongue in that divot between my collar bones. Goosebumps sprang up over the entire left side of my body. He also worked his hips, giving me a hint of what he had in store for me.

Suddenly, my mind snapped to reality. A voice screamed in my head, "You're not that kind of girl!"

"Hold on," I said aloud and struggled to get my feet to the ground. "Wait!"

I hadn't even known him a week. I wasn't about to give up my virginity like this. I thought I might be falling in love with him, but who knew what he felt. This was way too fast. Perhaps it wasn't love at all. Perhaps I was enamored with him like everyone else in the world. Maybe that was it. Maybe I was just another conquest for him. It was just too soon, too quick to know anything and too quick for me to do anything.

It took a minute for Alex to reign himself in, but he did it. He didn't fully back off, but he stopped grinding into me and released me.

"What's wrong?" he questioned, softly with an air of confusion.

"I'm not that kind of girl."

Alex laughed. "Who says stuff like that?" He backed up a few steps and ran his hands through his hair. "What kind of girl are you?"

"Not the kind that gives it up to a guy she's only known three days."

That's when Alex had a full belly laugh at my expense.

I rolled my eyes and opened the car door.

He reached and caught hold of the top of the door with one hand and adjusted his shorts with the other. He wasn't very discrete about the adjustment, evidencing the rock-hard looking erection again.

"Where are you going?" Alex hardly even tried to cover his amusement.

"I've got to get back to school, back to my reality," I replied sharply.

"Seriously, wait a minute."

"Why, so you can laugh at me some more?"

"I'm not laughing at you..."

"You sure fooled me!" I took my seat in the car and started the engine.

Alex stopped laughing and squatted between the door and the cab. "Anna, I know exactly what kind of girl you are and I'm only laughing at the situation."

Still with a stern edge, I asked him, "What situation is that?"

"The one where I finally find a girl that is making me crazy for her and she turns me down. Normally, women throw themselves at me and then there's you."

"The anomaly." I pursed my lips and raised my eyebrow.

"Exactly." Alex paused, closing his eyes to contemplate his next words. When he opened them, their color caught in the morning light and my heart sank. I knew I wasn't the type to fall into bed with a virtual stranger, but we'd basically had a crash course in getting to know one another and it wasn't that I didn't want him. I wanted Alex something fierce.

Alex continued, "I don't want you to go. I told you that last night. Honestly, Anna, I've never had a girl meet my family, but for reasons I can't put into words, I want *you* to meet them."

"I would love to meet your family. I would love to be able to stay, but, Alex, how long can you stay?" I asked sincerely.

"I don't know."

"And don't you think that might be a problem?" Before Alex could answer, I went on. "I'm not one of herd that just wants a fling with the movie star. I want dates and kisses and build up with Alex the regular guy. I want to see where things could go with the guy I've been getting to know this week."

I left that morning with little more resolution than what I'd had the night before. At least the night before Alex had kissed me feverishly, stood me back on my feet and sent me on my way with an unexpected slap on my ass that made me skip a step. It stung and gave me something to remember him by even if it was swollen lips and a handprint on my behind. Today, my heart stung and my eyes watered. All the way to Milledgeville I reminded myself that I'd done the right thing. I definitely had something to remember Alex by... I had a broken heart, but I'd done it to myself. Doing the right thing sucked.

"Stupid, stupid, girl!" I banged my hands on the steering wheel as rolled to a stop in front of my dorm that morning.

I made it through classes. I made it through the drive to the video store on Highway 441 to pick up a copy of every Alex Allen movie they had in stock and back to my dorm. I even made it through eating a little something. Made it through, that's what I did. That's all I did.

I could still taste Alex on my lips. I could feel him through the fabric of my shorts if I let my thoughts wander that direction in the slightest. I couldn't get him out of my head.

Sally Ann, who was well enough to go back to work on the course called me as soon as she got off. I answered the phone, but didn't really feel like talking. I just wanted to keep watching Alex, keep hating the women playing roles opposite him and keep sulking about my regret.

"Who was the guy you left the concession stand with after kneeing Chris in the balls yesterday?" Sally Ann demanded.

I'm certain inquiring minds such as hers was twitching with the need to know all day, but I wasn't ready to discuss it with her. Well, I wanted to discuss what had happened with my best friend, but I didn't want to tell her with whom I'd had the epic fail.

"Oh, just a friend," I replied, knowing if I told her anything, she'd press me to tell her the whole story.

"The girls at the club didn't think he was just a friend. They said you were holding hands and you don't hold hands with friends."

Where I thought I was supposed to defend my first statement and opened my mouth for such, Sally Ann had only been taking a breath. She continued, "Plus, bravo on what you did to Chris. That perv had it coming. Some of the girls thought you were crazy..."

"I'm sure they comforted him just fine," I smirked.

"Yeah, but seriously, he threatened to fire me today because you quit..."

"But he didn't. Look, I hate to cut you off, but I've got some studying to do. Big test tomorrow." I lied. I just wasn't in the mood for talking and Sally Ann who'd known me longer than anyone could tell.

"What's wrong? Are you mad with me or something?"

"Or something, but I don't want to talk about it."

"Are you kidding me?" Sally Ann insisted on talking about everything. I knew every detail of her life. She was an open book and she expected that of me as well. Most of the time I cooperated, but not this time.

"I promise I'll tell you all about it soon."

"Soon?" She sighed heavily. "I'm dying here."

It took her a few more pressuring, begging questions, but I caved. I always did. It wasn't that I couldn't keep a secret, but I just struggled to keep one from Sally Ann.

"Okay, don't go nuts, but..." and I told Sally Ann the entire story, only leaving out Alex's identity.

She persisted with her demands to know Alex's name, but I stood my ground. I didn't budge.

"I really can't advise you that you're right to regret not giving it up, if I don't know who he is. I just don't know what we're working with here." Sally Ann was frustrated in her failed attempts to bring me to full disclosure.

"There's no redemption. It is what it is."

"I've half a mind to drive over to your house right now and find out for myself, you know."

"You wouldn't!"

"I would!"

"And I would *never*," I emphasized the word "never" and continued, "ever speak to you again!"

Sally Ann went to speak again and I cut her off.

"I mean it!" I affirmed.

Sally Ann stopped with the interrogation and reminded me why she was my best friend. "Okay, look, go back home, say you forgot something and get a do over if it's bothering you this much."

"I can't. I have class and I've got to work tomorrow night and his family is going to be there. It's just..." I trailed off knowing it just wasn't possible.

"I don't know what else to tell you," Sally Ann said sympathetically before giving me the line my mother would give me. "If it's meant to be, it will be."

"I'm sure you're right." I wasn't sure at all, but what else was there to say?

Before Sally Ann hung up she added, "Anna-Cat, I'm happy for you even if this isn't going exactly where you would like."

Sally Ann had a way of letting me know she was always on my side and I loved her for it.

"Thanks," I said, poking the corner of my right eye where I could feel tears starting to bubble up.

"Remember, it's better to have loved and lost than to never have loved at all."

"I didn't say I loved him. I couldn't be in love with him. I haven't even known him a week."

"Anna-Cat, this is me you're talking to. You're in love and it's not like your heart has a time table. And, if you didn't love him, you wouldn't be miserable like this."

"I've made a big mistake, haven't I?"

"No," Sally Ann reminded me again how well she knew me, "you just did what you normally do."

"What's that?" I asked.

"You guarded your heart."

"Excuse me?"

"It's instinct for you."

"Why would you say that?" I did not know what she was getting at.

"Anna-Cat, if my brother died and my parents acted like their sole reason for living died with him, I think I'd be a little guarded, too."

My brother was a topic I never discussed with anyone. Sally Ann had frequented our home enough over the years that she knew how it affected my family without me ever uttering a word. She knew I took a backseat to Chandler's memory and I guess I was lucky she only referred to me as "guarded" and not "messed up."

"Anna-Cat, it's not like they set the best example on how to love," Sally Ann explained.

"I didn't realize you noticed." Tears were forming in my eyes.

"We've been best friends since we were three years old, of course I noticed. Just because we never talked about it didn't mean I didn't see what was going on. Why do you think I always invited you to my house and rarely slept over at yours?"

I was in full bawl mode by the time she finished her sentence. My brother Chandler died when I was six and he was eight. He was my father's namesake. A flood of memories came back in that moment.

"You know, I can still picture my father flung over his little body. I could hear my father's voice as he screamed my brother's name. Being a dentist, my father had medical training, but none of it was worth a damn that day."

"My mother said your brother got hit by a car, but that's all she's ever told me." She didn't put it into a question, but I understood Sally Ann was asking what really happened.

"We had a dog, a golden retriever named Harry...He was so fluffy..."

"You had a pet?" Her voice went high at the shock. "I didn't think you were allowed to have pets."

"I haven't been able to have one since Harry." I cleared my nose, sniffling and continued. "Anyway, he was an indoor dog, but whenever the door to the outside opened, Harry bolted. It always infuriated my dad that the dog didn't mind and Chandler and I took our fair share of brow beatings over letting the dog out. One day, Chandler was coming in from school and he opened the door only to have Harry rush past him. I was headed in the door right behind him and Harry nearly took my legs out from under me as he darted for the yard. Dropping his book bag, Chandler sprinted after Harry. Harry ran right out in the street. Cars missed him, but Chandler wasn't so lucky. Chandler ran into the street and right into the path of an oncoming car. I had only been steps behind Chandler and my father was somewhere behind me. I saw the whole thing and so did my father. That was the day my father all but forgot I existed."

"Oh my God!" Sally Ann gasped.

"Not with all of the king's horses and all of the king's men..."

"I'm so sorry, Anna-Cat."

"The next day, after they came home from making the arrangements, my dad took Harry into the back yard and shot him. He didn't even bury him in the back yard. He just threw him in the big rolling trashcan. Mama tried to stop him..." I wiped my eyes and pictured everything all over again. "He said he'd do any damn thing he wanted. His boy was dead and he'd kill anything he wanted right then. I think she was afraid he was about to kill us all."

"That must have been when you went to live with your grandparents in Wrens for a little while."

"Yeah," I confirmed. "I lived with them for about three months. I wish I could have stayed with them forever."

"Again, no wonder you have the issues you do."

"I didn't realize I had issues."

"We all have issues," she tried to lighten the mood.

Sally Ann couldn't see it through the phone, but that made me smile. "Sally Ann, I love you."

"I love you too, Anna-Cat."

"They aren't bad people," I said, referring to my parents.

"I know," she concurred. "They've just been broken-hearted for fifteen years and they didn't seem to know how to cope with it or help you cope with it. Who knows how we'd be if we lost a child like that."

We were just about through with our goodbyes when Sally Ann gave me one last piece of advice. "If the guy really likes you, he'll come find you and you won't have to do all of this worrying and, if he doesn't come find you, forget him and know that he wasn't worth your time."

Sally -Ann succeeded in watering down my worry over Alex. Although I spent the rest of the night watching Alex Allen movies, memories of Chandler were pulled to the forefront of my mind. I tried not to think of my brother, but it was a losing battle. It had been a long time since I'd relived the day Chandler died. I'd never forgotten him and I missed him every day, but I hated thinking of that day or the months that followed. They might not have been the best parents, but they were mine. Thinking about it now, it wasn't that shocking that they didn't tell me they rented out our house or where they went.

Chapter 9

Alex...

"Alright, out with it!" My sister Ashley demanded as she took a seat in the lounge chair next to me, the same chair where Anna-Cat had sat the two nights before.

I didn't break the stare I had on the ripples in the pool when I replied, "Out with what?"

"Whatever is going on with you. We're all on Dad's and your dream vacation all day and you were a million miles away."

"I was not." I said, sounding affronted and turning to give her my full attention, I let my head fall over on the pillow of the lounge chair to face her.

Ashley persisted as she started to nurse her glass of wine. Ashley was three years younger than me and this was the first time I'd seen her drink. Even though Ashley was mostly right, I tried diverting the subject to her alcohol consumption.

"When did you start drinking?"

"When did you start keeping secrets? Don't change the subject. What's going on with you?"

I rolled my eyes. I knew I had been distant part of the day, but when we entered the gate that morning, my father and I practically danced arm in arm and kick for kick right on through like a pair of Rockettes. We drank beer together and smoked stogies like we were old money members of the club. We talked golf, the lay of the field, the speed of the greens, placement of trees and gushed together over Amen Corner. Unfortunately, things took a turn for me when we passed by the concession stand from which I'd rescued Anna-Cat yesterday.

Ashley leaned up in her chair, sat her glass down, folded her arms and gave me a good stare down. "Don't make me ask you again."

Ashley had a flare for channeling our mother. It was like a special talent or something.

"Yes, mother," I answered sternly.

I didn't want to tell my little sister I was stewing over a mad case of the blue balls from a girl that was for all I knew still in her teens, nineteen, but still, and a girl I'd shot not four days prior. Sadly, I needed to talk to someone. The upside was that Ashley was one of the few people in the world I knew would die before she breathed a word about me to anyone. That being the case, I started to give her the G-rated version of events.

"This is her house?" Ashley barely took a breath. "And, you shot her?"

If there was such a thing as a whisper scream that's how Ashley's last question came out.

I nodded, slowly, with pursed lips and answered her accusation.

"Jesus Christ! And she was okay?"

"Yeah, she was fine. I only pierced her arm, but it scared the shit out of me when it happened."

"I suspect it did."

I went on telling Ashley about the fight we had the next morning and how we got on afterward.

"You like her," Ashley announced well before I got to the good stuff.

"It's crazy, right?" By this point, I'd taken Ashley's wine glass and tossed back the last few swallows. The two of us sat almost knee to knee facing one another and I searched her face for the answer.

"I think it's all a hoot. You're falling for the one girl in the world who isn't starry eyed over you." Ashley didn't bother holding in the laughter. She let the chuckles roll and roll.

"It's not funny!"

"Oh, but it is!" She went on not bothering to tone down her amusement.

I sat wordless, waiting for her to stop.

"Come on now," Ashley finally quipped. "Surely you can see the irony."

"You think I only like her because she doesn't like me?"

"She's a challenge and you've never had a challenge a day in your life."

I glared at her and she corrected herself. "You've never had a challenge when it came to bedding woman."

"Ashley! Jesus! You're my little sister..."

"And I know you better than anyone else on Earth."

"But..."

"You think I don't know how you get ar..."

"No. Just stop. This was a mist..."

Ashley and I went back and forth cutting one another off and finishing each other's sentences. She did know me better than anyone, but I didn't like to think of her knowing about my sex life. I didn't even really like knowing that she knew what sex was.

"Alex, I'm just teasing you. If you like this girl, then go get her because quite honestly, I've never seen you like this."

I didn't have to ask, "Like what?" That went unspoken and Ashley described me.

"You are great at compartmentalizing, Alex. When you come home or meet up with us, you leave all of the Hollywood bullshit behind. You never bring home girls and you never talk about who you're dating. In fact, for a long time, Dad and Leslie thought you were gay."

"What gave them that idea?" I furrowed my brow.

"I just told you. You never brought anyone home. The only way we know about your escapades is by seeing glimpses of you on Entertainment Tonight and, let me just tell you, those girls aren't for you."

"What makes you so sure?" I asked.

"Because I know you. This whole acting thing is just a job for you. It's not a lifestyle."

Ashley had me pegged.

"I don't think she wants to see me again," I admitted regretfully.

"I'm sure you didn't do anything that can't be undone with an apology." Ashley reached over and patted my knee. "Just use that Allen charm and you'll be fine."

"I'm not so sure."

"Well what did you do that was so wrong?"

I didn't want to tell my sister that I propositioned Anna-Cat and then ground myself into her, all but dry humping her against the side of her car.

"I came on a bit too strong. I think I scared her off."

"Go apologize and see where it goes. Stop analyzing everything. Who's the girl, you? Or her?"

Ashley took another look at her empty wine glass. "I really should have brought the bottle out here."

"Yeah, you should have." I smiled.

Ashley stood and, taking her glass, she headed for the house, leaving me by the pool. I watched Ashley as she left. About ten steps away she turned back.

"I really envy this girl of yours," she said.

"Why?"

"This place is beautiful. Can you just imagine what it would have been like to grow up here?" Ashley waved a hand out, motioning expansively at the grounds and the house.

"You'd think she would be spoiled, but she's not. She's the most down to Earth person I've met in as long as I can remember."

I started to take a good look at my surroundings. Sitting by the pool at the Calloway house was some sort of enticement for great conversation. In the last few days I'd had some of the most meaningful conversations I'd have in a long time sitting next to it. Apart from Anna-Cat, I knew this pool was going to be the thing I missed the most when the tournament was over and it was time for me to leave.

"I'll be right back," Ashley told me before continuing inside the house.

I gave up the master bedroom to my parents. Ashley took one of the guest rooms and I took Anna-Cat's bedroom. That night, while lying in her bed, I drifted off to sleep while replaying my last few moments with her. She might have shot me down, but I knew without a doubt that she was as into me as I was to her. I resolved to enjoy the tournament with my family, but instead having my parents drop me off at the airport on Monday morning, I was going to find this girl. I wasn't ready to let her go yet.

The next morning, after my run, I made a call to my agent back home in California. More specifically, I called my agent's secretary. I tended to use Mrs. Margarite as my personal secretary from time to time. In the year I'd been at this firm, Mrs. Margarite and I had developed quite a friendship. Thanks to my many gifts like donating myself as a "win a date with" prize at her grandkid's private school, she was always willing to help me. Today's project, I had her track down exactly where Milledgeville, Georgia was, find out when Anna-Cat was scheduled to work again at the part-time job she mentioned she had at a coffee house downtown, wherever that was, and to rent me a house somewhere in the vicinity of Anna-Cat.

"Something with a pool," I instructed her.

"Yes, sir, Mr. Allen." No matter how many times I told Mrs. Margarite to call me Alex, she always called me Mr. Allen.

"And, I need a car. Something inconspicuous. Could you help me rent one and have it delivered to this address?" I then gave her the address to the Calloway's house.

"Of course."

After the call, I got dressed and headed to the course with my family. Today, I was back to my old self, equally determined to put my obsession with Anna-Cat to the side for the time and show my dad the time of his life. Although there was a constant reminder of Anna-Cat at every turn on the course, I succeeded admirably at the other. We managed to meet Arnold Palmer and Jack Nicklaus and we got within inches of Phil Mickelson.

By the time we returned from the course that afternoon, a black Ford F-150 King Cab was parked in the driveway. In the passenger's seat was a folder containing all the details of Mrs. Margarite's success. She'd found a house for me on Lake Sinclair and negotiated a three-month lease under the name of Triple A, Inc. She'd incorporated me a few months ago as a way of protecting my assets and shielding my identity. Mrs. Margarite was a true genius who always went above and beyond. The last thing I found in the folder, behind the directions to the rental house, was Anna-Cat's work schedule. Reading it, I wondered if this was the definition of stalking. Regardless, I was thrilled with Mrs. Margarite's work as always, not that she'd ever helped me stalk anyone previously.

That night my father joined me by the pool. I sat in what had become my spot and he took the chair next to me, the chair I'd always remember as Anna-Cat's chair. He handed me a Miller Lite before he sat down.

"Thanks!" I said, popping the top off of the bottle.

"So..." My father began the same way he always did when he wanted to talk to me.

I took a swallow of my beer and followed with, "Yes, sir?"

"When's the last time you saw your mother?"

My father always asked about my mother, but only as an ice breaker. They'd had a difficult divorce and I think he had given up on caring about her well before the papers were signed.

"It's been about six months"

"I trust she's doing alright."

"She's okay." The truth was she was the same as she always was, bitter about the divorce.

"She still lives in the same house?"

"Yep. I was filming in Memphis and she'd always wanted to see Graceland so I flew her up. She doesn't like to leave home much anymore, but I guess she decided to do it for Elvis."

My father snickered until it tapered off into silence again. My parents were the same age, but to look at them no one would guess. She easily appeared ten to twenty years beyond their fifty-one years. We continued to nurse our beers, both of us studying the ripples in the pool as we contemplated what to say next.

"You know, I've never really understood what you did with your life," my father stated. He didn't look at me when he spoke. He just put the statement out there.

I added nothing except, "I know."

"I was furious with Leslie when she got you mixed up in all of the TV stuff. I wanted you to go to college and get a good job and..." he trailed off. More silence passed until he spoke again. "The thing is," he paused, working to get what he wanted to say out. "The thing is I think you've done alright for yourself."

He seemed serious so I refrained from laughing about how he'd only seen the light regarding my vocation since I'd scored him the trip of a lifetime. Instead of laughing, I asked him something I'd always wanted to know and never had the courage to ask. "Have you seen any of my movies?"

I told myself his answer didn't matter, but in the end his answer was shocking. "Every single one of them and at the theater, too."

I looked directly at him when I'd asked so I could judge his sincerity. As best I could gather, he was telling the truth, not that my father was one to lie. My heart swelled and my cheeks widened with a smile that I couldn't stop.

More silence passed. Each of us stared at the pool, watched the ripples and became lost in our thoughts.

"I like this place," my father announced out of the blue. "It's peaceful."

"Yeah, I think I could sit right here forever," I sighed deeply.

"So, Ashley said you've had some girl trouble."

"I'm going to kill her."

He reached over and put a hand on my shoulder to keep me from getting up. "Oh please, she barely said a thing."

"Sounds like she said more than she should have."

"No, seriously, all she said was that you were having some girl trouble. Son, I promise, she didn't elaborate."

The quiet filled the air again as I pictured Anna-Cat's face. Sitting with my dad by the pool was fine, but what I wouldn't have given to have been sitting with her, I couldn't say. I would have wondered what she was doing then, but I didn't have to wonder about that. I remembered the schedule Mrs. Margarite put together and that it said Anna-Cat was scheduled to wait tables at a place called Brewers tonight.

"You wanna tell your old man about her?"

My first instinct was to say, "Not really," but I didn't. I filled my dad in much the way I'd done with my sister, softening the blow of the over eager way I'd propositioned Anna-Cat.

"I've been doing what I do since I was fourteen. Dad, the way women respond to me, well, you wouldn't believe it. They don't know me, not really, they think I'm one of my characters or another. Mainly they think I'm Billy Ward. He was a cool guy and I could stand to be more like him, but he's a figment of a writer's imagination. They throw themselves at me not even knowing me."

My dad didn't say anything. He just listened.

"The beauty of this girl is that she's not that into movies and TV and she hardly batted an eye over me. She'd never seen ""Steps to the Moon"" and the things that impress her are as simple as racing me from one end of the pool to the other, listening to her and talking with her. I could just talk to her for hours. I've never just talked to girl."

I scratched my head and tried to put all of what I was feeling into words without making my father wonder about my sexuality again.

"I was only with her for three days and that first day was rough, but once we got past that, it was like I'd found a best friend. I felt like I could tell her anything. Like Alex August Allen, the regular guy from Tampa could tell her anything."

Dad smiled. "Son, it sounds like you're in love."

"That's what Ashley said too."

"So, what's the problem?"

"According to her, she lives here. I mean, she lives at college, somewhere called Milledgeville, Georgia and, again according to her, I live in some other world."

"She's scared. Who can blame her?"

"She's only nineteen and she's so smart. She's way smarter than I am."

"Alex," my dad began to caution me, "you know my track record with women. It's not the best, so you can take what your old man's about to say for what you think it's worth. You need to be careful with this girl. She's got her whole life ahead of her and, after dating someone of your stature, there's nowhere to go but down."

I didn't want to hear this, but he thought I needed it and I showed him the respect of listening.

"You never went to college. You never had to. You're older and you've seen more of the world than most eighty-year-olds. She's right, Son, you live in another world than us mere mortals. She's got a right to be scared. If you think you love her, you need to be careful. A broken heart from one mortal to another is one thing, a broken heart from one of your type to another is one thing, but a regular Joe or Jane receiving a broken heart from the likes of Zeus is whole 'nother level of heartbreak."

I took in every word and I heeded his warning. I also heard my father compare me to Zeus and that was quite possibly the biggest complement he'd ever given me.

My father reiterated, "Just be careful with her heart. We were the same level, but I wasn't careful with your mother and we all know how that turned out."

The moon was high in the sky and peeping through the Magnolias when my father decided to call it a night. I stayed seated by the pool and pondered the advice he and Ashley had given me. I thought about the truck outside, the directions to Milledgeville, and the time it would take me to get there based on those directions. I had two more days of family time and, despite my father's sound advice, I knew I had to see Anna-Cat again. I vowed to be careful with her, but I couldn't just let her go.

Chapter 10

Anna-Cat...

By Tuesday, I'd reached a fever pitch of burn for Alex. I'd rented and watched all of his movies repeatedly. I hated all of the actresses who played opposite him, who got paid to kiss him, knowing I'd gladly kiss him from here to eternity for free. And mostly, I hated myself for not staying when he asked me.

The tournament was over, he was gone and I hadn't heard from him. I'd really hoped he would call, but he hadn't. Of course, he wouldn't call, normal boys called and Alex Allen wasn't normal.

To make myself feel better, I went to Macon that afternoon for retail therapy. I perused the racks of Macy's, Belk's and Victoria's Secret. I never bought lingerie before and had no reason to buy it then, but Victoria's Secret was having a sale. In one of the clearance bins I found a pair of black lace panties with roses stitched on them. In another bin, I found the matching bra, in my size. I didn't own a single matching set of bra and panties so I threw those over my arm and kept browsing. In yet another bin I found a pair of garters. I'd never even tried on a garter belt, but figured, what the hell. I purchased the whole set, plus a pair of black stockings and a new set of pajamas, something more feminine than the tank top and shorts to which I was accustomed.

That night I was scheduled to work as the hostess at Brewers so, when I got back to my dorm room, I paired the undergarments with the white button-up shirt and short black skirt I'd purchased at Macy's. I wore three-inch red pumps, which did nothing to amplify the length of the skirt. It was short, very short. I curled my hair and added more makeup to my face than I normally did. I told myself while standing in front of the full-length mirror that Alex

Allen didn't know what he was missing. I was damn sexy in this outfit.

The dinner shift was busy for a Tuesday night, but things were winding down by 8:30 p.m. By 9:00, I was all but clocked out, seated on a stool at the counter waiting on my to-go order. The servers were doing their side work, sweeping and stocking the condiments on the tables, and I was neglecting the door. I hardly heard it when it screeched across the floor and I certainly didn't turn my head for it. Whomever it was, was welcome to seat themselves and they did just that.

Watching the service window to see if it was my order that just came up, I didn't notice the stool next to me slide out. I didn't notice a thing until the new patron spoke.

"Good evening, Anna."

My heart stopped. I was almost afraid to turn my head to confirm it was him, but I worked up the courage. Slowly, I turned to confirm that I wasn't having episodes of delusional hearing. Complete with ball cap, shades and a slight stubble, I would recognize him anywhere now. He wasn't just anywhere though. He was here. Alex Allen was in Brewers, where I worked, and he was sitting right next to me.

A measurable shock ran over me and I couldn't speak. I twisted in my seat and reached out to touch him for further confirmation as he looked me up and down.

"Are you seriously wearing garters?" He lowered his sun glasses and peered over them, looking down at my thigh. My skirt had ridden up a bit when I squirmed in my seat.

I bit my lip, feeling my eyes blaze and remembering how I'd burned for him since I last saw him. I nodded in the affirmative.

"What were you thinking?"

I straightened my skirt and tried to tug it down enough to cover the tops of the stockings and the straps holding them up. That act also helped me to stall, figuring out how to respond. I wasn't about to tell him I was thinking about him. I blushed at the memory of talking to myself in front of the mirror before I left for work, but didn't say that.

"What were you thinking?" I shot back.

I wasn't the only one dressed to raise eyebrows. Alex was wearing a tight-fitting white, Levi's "Button Your Fly" t-shirt that flattered his abs, pecs, delts and biceps. My heart fluttered as I looked him over.

"What do you mean?"

"Never mind," I answered, diverting my eyes before my face flushed any more than it already did.

"What brings you to Brewers?" I asked him.

"You."

"Really?" My heart thumped hard enough that I was scared he was going to hear it.

"Yep." Alex reached over and plucked a menu from the stand on the far side of the counter. "And a good cup of coffee."

"Well, you've come to the right place." I tried not to smile so freakishly big, but I had a feeling I was failing.

Alex laid the menu down, crossing his arms on the counter in front of him and looking directly at me, he asked, "So, garters?"

Alex brought the conversation back around. He reached down and ran a finger under the elastic strip that went from the belt to the top of the stockings and which I had not successfully hid beneath my skirt. "Do you know what those do to men?" Alex quizzed me, keeping his voice low.

Goosebumps sprang up instantly from his touch and the pit of my stomach went flipping all over the place. "No," I whispered back.

"Anna, they are the recipe for an instant erection."

"Jesus!" I shook my head, embarrassed. "You…"

He leaned over my shoulder and peered down. I had two buttons open on my shirt and I'd intentionally let cleavage show that night. I felt it completed the outfit.

"Is that a black bra you're wearing with a white shirt? Christ, Anna, I'm going to need you to walk in front of me when we leave."

"When *we* leave?" I asked him to confirm.

"I didn't come all this way just for the coffee."

"You really have a way with just coming out with it, don't you?"

When I realized Alex was next to me, it was as if everyone else in the restaurant faded away until Molly put my to-go box in front of me. Before Alex could answer my question, Molly appeared.

"Here you go!" She plopped the box of chicken caesar salad down in front of me.

"Thanks!" Translation, "Beat it!" I'd already paid for my dinner so there was no further exchange needed between Molly and myself and I wasn't about to introduce her to Alex even though she stalled, waiting for the introduction.

"I'll see you tomorrow night," I told her and I started down from my stool.

"Let me help you." Alex offered his hand and I took it.

It was as if something came over me. Hardly thinking and leaving my box of food on the counter, I pulled Alex by the hand and told him to come with me. I led him down the hallway and out the back door of Brewers.

I kicked the door closed behind us and, brazenly confessed, "I really want to kiss you right now."

With the quickness of a lightning strike, Alex had me pinned to the door and, there in the dimly lit ally behind the restaurants and shops of downtown Milledgeville, he devoured my mouth with his.

"My God, I missed you," he said only moving back slightly to grab another breath before going for my neck.

Initially, Alex had taken my face in his hands, but he let go and roamed south, grazing over my breasts as he went. His hands didn't linger, but I could feel my breasts swelling beneath his touch.

Alex continued to roam until he found the hem of my skirt. He lifted it and spread my knees with one of his. Passion and complete abandon had taken hold of us when he grabbed me by the thighs and lifted me. Again, I was draped around him, feeling his erection between my legs. This time, he held me by my ass cheeks, his splayed hands finding their way into my panties, squeezing me and roaming further as he kissed me. He covered every inch from my mouth to my ears to the top of my cleavage. I arched my back and moaned as he slipped his tongue in the slit between my breast that the heavily padded push-up bra created.

"Alex," I breathed, straining and arching.

He didn't respond.

"Alex," I panted again with a little more volume.

This time he leaned up. "Anna," he said, locking eyes with me and, coming tantalizingly close to penetrating me with one of his fingers.

"Alex," I continued breathlessly, but not squirming to stop him, "I can't lose my virginity on the back of a door in an ally."

Alex stopped. He jerked back his hand and let my feet slide to the ground. He stepped away from me and looked me up and down. An air of self-consciousness came over me as he seemed to size me up, assessing the situation.

"Sorry," I started to apologize. "I didn't mean to teas..."

Instantly, he closed the gap between us and planted his lips over mine to stop me finishing my sentence. He was gentle, but the passion was still there. Easing only his mouth away from me, leaving his forehead pressed to mine and our fingers interlocked, Alex said, "It's okay. We don't have to do anything. I want to, there's no denying that." He kind of laughed, "But it's okay."

"What are you doing here?" I repeated my question from earlier.

"I told you. I missed you." He cupped my cheek and nuzzled his nose to mine.

Alex was making it difficult to concentrate on having a conversation, but I managed. "So, you just drove to Milledgeville on a whim?"

"No, not a whim at all."

"Really?"

"Yep. I..." Alex stuttered, having trouble finding his words. "I... I've got time before my next job so I rented a house out by the lake. It has a pool. I was thinking, if you weren't busy, maybe you could hang out with me at the pool some more."

I blushed uncontrollably. He rented a house to be near me. My knees went as weak as if he had kissed me again.

Alex followed up with an equally shocking statement, completely contradicting his previous actions. "About the virginity issue. Keep it. I know I don't deserve it."

"What?" I was not expecting him to say that at all.

"You heard me. Keep it."

How could I possibly keep it? All I thought about was what it would be like with him. I'd never been interested in anyone enough to give it away before and now he just told me to keep it.

Strangely, I found my inner courage and replied. "Maybe I will and maybe I won't. I just don't want to lose it out here like a common tramp."

Alex laughed. "There's nothing common about you and I think you are about as far from a tramp as one can get."

I blushed again and smiled, biting my lip. I couldn't seem to help myself. Still holding Alex's hand, I gave it a tug, pulling close to him. "Let's get out of here."

Having walked to work earlier in the evening, it was a no brainer to accept Alex's offer to give me a ride back to my dorm.

"In fact," Alex began his suggestion, "why don't you grab a few things and come hang out with me tonight?"

My mind swirled a little as he held open the back door of Brewers for me and I contemplated what to say. I'm not sure what I expected when I suggested we get out of there. I certainly wasn't going to take him back to my dorm, but I hadn't thought it through. Now, he'd made this offer.

Before I could answer, he added, "It's a three-bedroom house so you can have your own room and I promise I'll get you back in time for class tomorrow morning."

I assured myself I was a big girl and I could do this. I could stay over at his place and nothing would happen. I paced myself as not to seem too eager and replied after making several strides down the corridor that lead back into the restaurant, "Okay."

I picked up my to-go box, said "good night" to Molly as Alex waited for me by the front door. With dinner in hand, I headed for Alex. I couldn't take my eyes off of him. Despite what had transpired between us out back, I just could not believe he was here.

Alex held the door as we stepped out on the sidewalk in front of Brewers. It was hot and humid, typical of April in Milledgeville, but something I hadn't noticed during our time in the ally. Now, I noticed everything as I'd come alive with the excitement of just being in proximity to him. It had only been a few days since I'd last seen him, but it seemed like an eternity.

There was a hint of Magnolias coupled with the smells of a busy city at night; car exhaust, smoke from the open doors of the pool hall next to Brewers and a multitude of foods from the other restaurants on Hancock Street. It smelled like a mix of old and new south, but nothing compared to the smell of Alex. My hand in his and our arms intertwined, we waited at the corner for the light to change, for the figure to light up signaling it was alright for us to walk, and in that moment all I could smell was Alex. A splash of cologne, a hint of detergent and fabric softener and a hint of what I thought must be pure Alex. I leaned in closer so I could breathe him in and I failed at resisting the urge to kiss him again.

At the corner of Hancock and Wayne Streets, I stood on my toes and pressed my lips gently to Alex's neck. His hand tightened around mine and he drew me nearer, which I didn't realize was possible.

Alex whispered in my ear as I nuzzled his neck, "I guess you're okay with PDA?"I giggled and drew back. "Sorry."

"Oh, no, I'm completely okay with it if you are."

The light changed and Alex led the way for us to cross.

One week passed as I went to class, to work and when I wasn't at either of those places, I was out with Alex. I only went home to the dorm to sleep.

Alex and I went on dates. We went to dinner. We toured the Indian mounds in Macon and the Old Governor's Mansion in Milledgeville. We hung out by the pool and late at night, well after anyone would notice, Alex would deliver me back to my dorm. It was interesting that wherever we went, Alex took precautions not to call attention to himself. At home, he was Superman and out in public he was Clark Kent. Since his middle name was August, I took to calling him "Auggie" on the rare occasion that I need to address him by name.

By the end of the second week, I'd spent the night twice at Alex's. One night I slept in the guest room and another I'd fallen asleep on the couch wrapped in Alex's arms. I woke up the next morning with a comforter over me and Alex asleep on the floor next to me.

"You don't have to work, if you don't want to," he told me one night by the pool as he read one script and I read another he'd given me.

It was a nice offer, but I was not under any illusions about our time together. I knew he would leave sooner or later and, although I hated to think about it, it was inevitable. He would have to go off to shoot some movie in another state or country or God only knows where and my new normal would come to an end.

"No, thank you," I said, simply and not taking my eyes from my page.

"Really?"

I held my eyes steady, hearing him drop the bound pages with a thud and knowing he was looking at me. "Really."

"Okay."

I kept reading, but Alex didn't pick his stack back up. A few minutes of silence passed before Alex slung his legs around and sat facing me on the side of the lounge chair.

I lowered my binder and let my head fall to the side. "What?"

That conversation was the beginning of week three.

"I want you to stay here with me."

I didn't repeat the same question, but it must have been written on my face. My heart stopped. I thought I heard him ask me to move in, but I was scared to ask him to repeat himself for fear of looking like a fool. What if I'd misunderstood? We hadn't even known one another for a month.

"Of course, you can say no and things can stay the same, but I like having you here."

"Can I think about it?" I smiled, demurely, pleadingly, and freaking out inside at the same time.

"Well, it's getting late," Alex stood from his chair and offered his hand to help me up. "We should get you home."

Pulling me close to him when I stood, I came chest to chest with him. My heart was already swelling from his question, but the proximity to him always got me. The way that he looked down at me, that got me as well. It was as if he could see straight to my soul and like he could devour me, all of me. I loved it. I loved it every single time he did it.

I slid my hands up his arms and over his chest. It wasn't the first time I'd touched him like that, but every time I did, just to touch him was like a gift. He was smooth and tight. Even if he was just a regular guy, a nobody, I could imagine women swooning over him. I did. He took my breath away and I swooned over him.

It was close to midnight and Alex walked me to the front porch of Bell Hall, my dorm, as he had done almost every night for the past few weeks. On the steps of the porch, under the moonlight and the little street lamps that lined the sidewalks around the front of campus, Alex lifted my chin and kissed me. It was soft and sweet and left me dying for more as he always did. Not since the night out in back of Brewers had he tried to take things to another level, but I wanted him to try. I wanted him to try because he wanted me, not so I could turn him down again. I wanted him to try so I could give in to him.

"Well," he backed away, licking his lips after the kiss, "goodnight, Anna."

No one was out there but us, so I called him by his name. "Goodnight, Alex."

I watched him as he walked back toward the parking lot. Just as I turned to go inside, I heard running footsteps coming back and the calling of my name, "Anna!"

I slung my hair when I whipped around to see him running up the steps.

"Hey, that question I asked you..."

I looked at him wide-eyed. It hadn't been a question, it had been a statement.

"Are you really going to think about it or..."

I cut him off, "Yes..."

"Yes, you're going to think about it or, yes, you're going to come stay with me?"

"Yes, I'm going to think about it." I almost laughed. It was sweet seeing him sort of insecure, if that's what it was.

I hardly slept that night. It had been days since I spoke to Sally Ann, but this warranted a call. This was a big

104

decision and, I didn't need Sally Ann to make my decisions for me, but I tended to talk to her before I made the big ones.

Sally Ann rarely dropped the F-bomb, but she dropped it real good after I told her the whole story.

"You're fucking kidding me!" Sally Ann gasped right after I told her who stayed at my house the week of the tournament and again after I told her he was the mystery guy I'd regretted not giving it up to.

"Now, he's basically asked me to move in with him," I confessed, hardly believing the story myself.

"You're seriously having a fling with Alex Allen? He's in Milledgeville and you're not on the verge of a breakdown? Are you having a breakdown? Seriously, this is far-fetched."

"I know! Why do you think I didn't tell you who he was to begin with?" I all but shouted in the phone out of excitement.

"You know what I think?" I could see her shaking her head through the phone. She did that when she had trouble believing something and I figured she was having a pretty hard time wrapping her mind around this. I would have a hard time wrapping my mind around it if our roles were reversed and she'd just told me the same stuff.

"What?"

"I think you should do it!"

"Really?" I wanted to do it, but there were so many reasons why I shouldn't. Good girls didn't move in with guys after knowing them for only a few weeks.

"If I'm going to have to live vicariously, I really want you to go all in. I don't need any half-assed-ness."

"I'm not joking!"

"Honestly, neither am I. I think you should do it. You don't know how long you have with him and isn't it better to have loved and lost than never to..."

"I know the saying, Sally Ann."

"Then live by it, Anna-Cat!"

In all honesty, my decision had been made well before I picked up the phone to dial Sally Ann. I was going to say yes to Alex.

Chapter 11

Alex...

Anna-Cat called around lunch time. I was out and she left a message. She didn't want me to pick her up tonight.

"I'm going to drive myself out tonight. I have to work until 8:00 so I'll be out around 8:30 and I'll meet you by the pool," she said after the beep. "I'll bring dinner," she added before hanging up.

Worrying about a girl wasn't my style, but Anna Catherine Calloway made me worry. I worried that I'd scared her off last night so, for her to call, put me out of my misery.

Anna-Cat showed up closer to 9:30 and, again, I did that out of character thing. I worried. When she didn't show up by 9:00 I dialed the operator who put me over to Brewers.

"Hey, is Anna-Cat still there?" I asked the chipper girl that answered the phone.

The girl replied instantly. "Nope. Left about an hour ago."

"Okay. Thanks." That didn't help my nerves.

Then, I began to do an even more uncharacteristic thing. I paced. I paced in front of the living room window watching for the first sign of anyone starting down the driveway. When I finally spotted the headlights coming down the driveway, I immediately went out.

"Can I help you carry anything?" I asked to cover the neurotic tendencies I was showing and barely allowing her to open the car door.

"Sorry I'm late," Anna-Cat started, handing me the bag containing three to-go boxes. "You must be starving."

It wasn't what she said, but something about the way she said it. She was late and she sounded off.

"Yeah," I agreed, again covering my anxiety and wondering what was up with her.

"There was a horrible wreck on 441. I think someone got killed."

That statement didn't help my anxiety at all, but it was then that I really noticed Anna-Cat. She didn't seem herself. She was shaking.

"What the Hell, Anna?" I dropped the to-go bag and reached for her. "You're covered in blood. Are you okay?"

"Jesus, I don't know."

She fell into my arms, but I held her back, looking her over, searching for the source of the blood. It was on her hands, her knees, her shirt and just generally all over her, but she wasn't bleeding. Closer inspection revealed it was smears and dried patches.

"It's not mine," she assured me, her voice trembling and tears were building in her eyes. Further study of her and I could tell she'd already been crying.

"Oh, Babe, I've got you." I pulled her into me, wrapping my arms around her and cradling her head to my chest. "I've got you," I repeated soothingly over her head and held her as tight as I could without fear of breaking her.

"I stayed with him until the ambulance came," Anna's words came through in staccato like breaks between her sobs. "I haven't felt so helpless since..." She trailed off into gasping sobs.

"You can tell me all of it or as much as you want or I can just hold you. You tell me what you need."

"Just hold me." Then it was as if her mind changed directions completely. "No," she snapped and jerked back from me. She looked down at her clothes and gasped, "I've..." She sucked in one gulp of air after another. "I've... I've got to get out of these clothes."

I halfway feared she was about to strip there in the yard. She was going into shock.

"Anna, come inside." I grabbed her by one of her hands. She'd been ringing them and really losing it over the sight of the blood.

"Come on." I led her inside about as fast as our feet would carry us and right into the first bathroom we came to, the guest bath in the hall.

I cut the water to the shower on and instructed her to get in. "I'll get you some fresh towels. Do you have a bag in the car?"

She nodded as she started to unhook the buttons on her blouse. This wasn't the way I'd wanted to see her undress for the first time, but now wasn't the time for those thoughts.

"I'll get it," I said, referring to her suitcase in the car. I didn't let my mind dwell on it, but for a split second, I reveled in the fact that she'd thought to pack a bag. The other times she'd stayed over hadn't been planned. Tonight, she'd planned on staying and I liked that.

I left and went straight to the kitchen. I took out the bottle of scotch I'd put in the cabinet next to the glasses. I grabbed a juice glass and poured myself a shot. I downed it, stared at the bottle for a split second and poured myself another. Another glance at the bottle and I contemplated making a double for Anna.

I did it. I made a glass for Anna and returned with it and two towels, knocking before I entered. Over the running water, I heard her tell me to come in. The curtain was pulled over the tub shower combo.

"I'm going to take your clothes and put them in the washing machine." I told her, taking away her opportunity to worry about them and the opportunity for her to see them when she got out. "I'm also leaving a drink here for you. I think if ever anyone needed one, it might be you."

After putting Anna's clothes in the wash, I went to her car and came back with her bags, her purse, makeup bag and a suitcase big enough to indicate she had planned on staying more than one night.

I knocked again before entering. "It's just me. Not sure why I said that. Of course, it's me. Who else would it be?"

The curtain was still pulled and the shower was still running as I entered cautiously. The glass I'd left next to the sink was empty. She'd told me early on she wasn't a drinker, but no one could blame her for breaking that rule tonight.

"Alex, I'm so sorry," Anna said above the sound of the water.

"There's nothing to be sorry about."

"I should have gone to the hospital with him. He didn't have anyone..." She started to cry again and I could still hear her over the sound of the water. "I did all I could. I did everything."

I lowered the lid on the toilet and took a seat. I sat there listening to her. "Anna, do you want me to get in there with you?"

"No," I could hear her sniffling. "I don't want you to see me like this."

"Do you want me to get you another drink?"

"No. I still feel the burn of the first one."

Any other time and I probably would have laughed at that statement. As it was, I didn't even breathe a hint of a snicker.

"I just feel so terrible. I did everything my dad did for Chandler and it didn't help then either. I did everything, Alex!"

I had no idea who Chandler was or what she was talking about. "Anna, tell me what happened."

She didn't say anything, but I could hear her moving. It sounded like she slipped.

"Anna?"

"I'm okay." She reached her hand out from the curtain at the backside of the shower and nearest to where I was sitting.

I moved from the toilet lid to a spot on the floor and took her hand, locking her fingers in mine. She was sitting

110

in the tub with the water from the shower running over her. Only the curtain separated us.

Anna began again, "The accident happened right in front of me tonight. The road was wet and a car hydroplaned into the car in front of me. It was there in front of me one second and on its side in the ditch the next. I don't know how it missed me."

She gripped my hand tight enough that her knuckles went white. "It was there and then it wasn't," she repeated. "I managed to get stopped and I ran. I remember running and I think I pulled him from the car."

I listened as Anna searched for understanding. "It was like everything was in slow motion, but lightning fast at the same time. There was blood everywhere. Oh, God, it was everywhere. I don't think he was wearing a seat belt and I don't know how I did it, but I'm pretty sure I pulled him through the windshield. It must have been shattered. I don't know, but I had him on the ground and I started CPR. He wasn't breathing, I remember checking. I did CPR until the guy in the car that hit him pushed me away and took over. Then, I just held his hand until the ambulance took him away."

I didn't think it was possible, but she squeezed my hand harder.

"Alex, I don't think he was even as old as I am."

"We can go to the hospital if you want. I'll drive you. We can go check on him. We can go now."

"I..." Anna stuttered and relaxed her grasp on me, straightening her fingers and holding them stiff. It was as if she was holding out her hand to stop me. "I don't know if I want to know."

I couldn't see her, but I had a feeling she still hadn't stopped crying. The shaking in her hand and her arm, the catching in her voice, those things gave it away.

I felt horrible for the guy whomever he was, but I was so thankful it wasn't her. I just wanted to hold her and never let her go. I made do with holding her hand and listening to her.

"Shit!" came out barely audible. "I look like a prune." Anna withdrew her hand. "I should finish up and get out."

I got up and picked up one of the towels I'd brought in for her. "Here," I offered, slipping it around the back of the curtain. "I'll go and heat up dinner."

I left her things in the bathroom along with a t-shirt of mine. "I'm leaving you something you can put on if you want."

"Okay. Thanks!"

I started to leave and she stopped me with my name. "Alex?"

"Yeah?" I said, hand on the door knob already about to pull it shut behind me.

"Thanks for listening."

"You don't have to thank me for anything. I'm just so glad you're safe." The truth was, I wasn't sure what I would have done if it had been her in the accident. My stomach lurched each time I thought about the possibility.

It was late by the time we ate dinner, well, picked at dinner. We ate about as much as we could under the circumstances. After that we went to our comfort spot, the lounge chairs by the pool.

Tonight, we didn't bother with swim suits. I went with the pajama shorts I'd planned to wear to bed and a mate of the plain white undershirt I'd given Anna. She had on that shirt and it was barely long enough on her to cover the bottom of her panties. She was damn sexy in it.

Tonight, I also insisted Anna share my chair. She sat between my legs and leaned back on my chest. She intertwined her legs with mine and felt like ribbons of silk around me.

Anna was guilt ridden over the guy in the car and I did what I could to take her mind off of it.

"Tell me something about you that I don't know," I told her, playing with her fingers, twisting them in mine.

"I had an older brother. His name was Chandler," she began. By the time she finished, I understood why the guy in the wreck affected her the way it had. What she'd described about tonight's accident was horrific enough, but add her family history to it and it's no wonder she was a basket case.

"He died right in front of me and my father. He'd been hit by a car and my father, having medical training from being a dentist and all, he did everything he could to save Chandler, but it just wasn't enough."

My God, the picture she painted was devastating. I saw my own father over Ashley and I shivered at the thought.

"Chandler died and life as I knew it ended, too. I know I sound so selfish to say that." She covered her face with her hands, ashamed of what she'd said.

Anna went on to tell me how only her friend Sally Ann knew how it was for her growing up. She described her parents as having been zombies after her brother died.

"I don't blame them. They weren't mean to me. They were just emotionally unavailable. The older I get the more I understand what the death of a child can do to a person, but it's hard because I lost him but I lost them, too and they didn't notice that."

"God, Anna, I'm so sorry."

She twisted around. "I love it when you call me Anna." Her eyes were pure blue with red streaks, like veins of lightening crackling through the sky, and she was so pale in the moonlight. She had to be the most attractive crier I'd ever seen. Absolutely breathtaking.

"Anna," I said again.

That night Anna didn't give me an answer, but she didn't go home in the wee hours of the night either.

When she was finally so tired that she could hardly hold her head up anymore she asked, "Do you mind if I sleep next to you?"

"Of course not."

I had an internal body clock that woke me up at 6:00 a.m. every day of my life. Already being awake on the two occasions when Anna had stayed over in the past weeks, I'd watched her sleep, I'd made her breakfast and I'd woken her up in time to get her to class on time. This time, I'd been up half the night watching her sleep. It was unlike her usual peaceful, barely rolling over sleep. It was restless and fitful. I knew even in her unconscious state, she worried about the boy from the wreck and the wreck brought back haunting memories of her brother.

After praying to God to ease her mind, I decided to take the bull by the horns. Leaving her to sleep, I showered, shaved and dressed. I even trimmed my hair. When I was done, I looked like Billy Ward. Knowing the hospital staff would be reluctant to give out information to just anyone, I embraced the fact that I wasn't just anyone. Another look in the mirror and I was confident that this face would open the doors I wanted it to this morning. I didn't like to flaunt my celebrity, but this was for Anna. It was one surefire way to get the answers I needed to help put Anna's mind at rest and I knew in the pit of my stomach that I'd do anything for her.

Before leaving I left a note on my pillow. It said only, "Don't worry. I'll be right back."

In the short time I'd been in Milledgeville, I'd learned there were two McDonalds, two colleges, two Piggly Wiggly grocery stores, but only one of everything else. Not counting the state mental hospital, which Anna had told me all sorts of sordid tales about, there was only one hospital that would take in a car accident victim. I'd seen the signs for it on my way back and forth to pick up Anna so, this morning, I followed those same signs.

I found the hospital and got the information I needed. I even used my golden ticket, a little flirting with a nurse who nearly fainted upon recognizing me, and she let me into the room with the guy.

"It's time for your meds," she said and amped up the giddiness when she explained he had a visitor. "Look whose come to see you!"

They guy was indeed beat to Hell and back, casted on several limbs, and had tubes running to and from various monitors, but he was awake. His eyes fluttered upon the sight of me.

"I've died and gone to Heaven and this is who greets me?" With a dry mouth, he smacked and grumbled. "I want the angel from last night back and Heaven looks a lot like a hospital."

"He's a little groggy with the meds," the nurse explained with an embarrassed apology.

"Have you found his family?"

"Oh yeah, but they're flying in from Charleston," she answered, still all too thrilled to help me.

I asked as gently as I could, "Is he going to be alright?"

"Oh yeah. The worst part was last night and he's got a rough road ahead of him, but he's going to pull through."

"Okay. Good. Well, I'll check back on him..."

I was about finished talking to the doe eyed nurse when the poster boy for taking a licking, perked up. With slurred words he shouted, "I want the angel from last night back!"

"I should probably give him something else before he gets too worked up."

I agreed and made my excuses to leave. I could totally understand him getting worked up. If I thought I was dead and a guy that looked like me showed up as my prize in Heaven, I'd be pissed, too. I knew exactly the angel he was talking about and I wanted her right then, too.

I was just about out the door when the guy gave another shout. This time he sounded like he'd found reality, a bit of it anyway. "If I'm not dead when I blow this joint, I'm gonna find that girl and I'm gonna marry her!"

I thought, "The Hell you are!" But I only yelled back, "Get well soon," and kept walking.

Chapter 12

Anna-Cat...

I awoke the next morning expecting to find Alex next to me. I almost dreaded it. I'd dreamed about sleeping next to him and waking up with him ever since I'd met him and this was not what I'd imagined it to be.

Fluffy white covers with the hint of Alex's smell still on them, but no Alex. Where his head should have been on the pillow next to me was a note. I'd barely read it when he appeared in the doorway.

"Morning," Alex said, greeting me. He walked toward the bed and offered me what he had in his hands. "Here. A Bloody Mary might do you better, but we'll start with these."

Alex gave me two ibuprofen tablets and a glass of orange juice. He was a mind reader. My head was pounding.

"Thanks!" I smiled at him, tugging the covers up as I realized I was still wearing nothing but his t-shirt and panties.

Alex took a seat on the edge of the bed, the edge of the side where he had slept. He watched me as I swallowed the pills with a mouthful of juice.

"Where did you go?" I asked, giving a glance toward the note.

"Ah, right. I went to the hospital."

With those words, he had my full attention. I was scared to ask. I remembered everything that happened the night before and, on one hand I was desperate to know what happened to the guy in the wreck, but on the other hand, I was terrified to know.

Alex didn't wait for me to ask, he told me, "He's going to be okay."

I let out the biggest sigh of relief I think I'd ever let out. I felt as if a ton of bricks had been lifted from my chest and I immediately got to my knees and crawled across the bed, throwing myself around Alex.

Holding him tight, I exclaimed time and again, "Thank you!" Before coming out with the obvious, "I am so relieved!"

After a minute or two I unwrapped myself from around Alex. I stayed on my knees, straddling him and reached out, taking his face in one of my hands. I studied his eyes for a moment. "Have I told you how amazing I think you are?"

Alex blushed.

"I think you are," I paused, feeling the crushing relief wash through me again and my eyes starting to pool with tears, "...just about the best thing that's ever happened to me."

"Oh, Anna," Alex shook his head, "I couldn't stand seeing you like that last night." Alex put more emphasis in his next few words than he normally did. "If I could have done anything to stop it, I would have."

I leaned in and softly pressed my lips to his. Lightly, I kissed him, lingering in place as I felt my heart expand to fill my entire chest cavity. I loved him to the point that it ached.

"You know that thing you asked me?" I drew back so slightly that the air when I spoke rippled over both of our faces.

Alex nodded his forehead slightly into mine as his grip on my back tightened. He acknowledged he knew to what I was referring.

"There's no place I'd rather be than here with you."

"Thank you," he said between kisses he planted on my neck.

Finally, the moment was cooled by my bladder.

Accepting that it was too late for me to make it to class, I agreed to hang around the house with Alex for the day. All morning and half of the afternoon I fought against

117

a heated sensation in the pit of my stomach and between my legs. I stole looks at him when he wasn't looking. I snatched a glance here and a glance there. He was gorgeous. When I let my eyes linger on him for more than a few seconds, I found myself biting my lower lip and wondering what it would be like. What would it be like if I gave in to my desire for him? I wanted to more than ever. I knew it was in evitable. Slowly, I worked up the courage to make a big confession. It took me until the afternoon, but once I made up my mind, there was no stopping it.

I left Alex in the kitchen and searched through his closet. I found one of his button-down dress shirts and I slipped out of my tank top and shorts and put it on. I dabbed on a little perfume and let down my hair from the bun I'd had it in all day.

Alex was cutting cheese, putting together an afternoon snack for us and I made it all the way up behind him before he realized I was in the room. I wrapped my arms around him from behind and let my splayed hands roam down his chest and farther down to that deep "V" area leading to the top of his pelvis.

"You know that thing you told me to keep?" I asked him as my hands stopped their roaming journey and came to rest with my fingers pressed into the pit near his hips where his thighs met his torso.

I couldn't see his face, but I could tell as he sat down the utensils he had in his hands when I felt his whole body tighten. His chest heaved and I could feel him catch his breath.

I pressed closer to him, stood on the toes of my right foot and let my other foot slide up the outside of his left leg. I whispered against the bottom of his neck, "It's yours whenever you want it."

"Holy shit, Anna!" Alex gripped the edge of the counter top.

In one sweeping move, he turned around, picked me up, swiped the cutting board, cheese and knives to the side and sat me on the kitchen counter. He planted a kiss that was so deep I wondered if he was going to dig down and lap at my bursting heart. I'd never been kissed so thoroughly, so powerfully, so intensely before and I'd thought his kisses had been all of those things in the past. Those paled in comparison to this one.

Alex pulled back only to take one long look at me. My legs had been draped open with him between them. I didn't close them, but I tucked the front tail of the shirt between them, covering my crotch, but drawing up the sides so my thighs were bare, bare almost all the way to my hips.

Starting with my toes, he let his gaze work me up and down again. He ran his hands over his face, starting with his palms against his forehead and bringing them down, covering his mouth, which by the look of the way his eyebrows shot up, was open wide. He looked like he was caught somewhere between shock and awe.

Alex's voice came husky when he asked, "What are you wearing?"

I arched my back and looked down at my attire. With the change in my posture, the unbuttoned top three buttons of the shirt coupled with the fact that the shirt was entirely too big for me, allowed for the right shoulder to shift and fall, leaving the top even more gaped open. I almost flashed one entire boob and I felt the thrill of being exposed to him.

"Your shirt," I said, letting my eyes drift back to his.

"My God you wear it well." Not even bothering to hide the act, Alex tugged at the bulge in his shorts, obviously adjusting his erection.

Alex stepped forward and pulled me in to his arms and went for it all over again, feverishly kissing me to all abandon. A hand slid down my neck from where it had been gripped in the hair on the back of my head until it was cupped over my shoulder and under the shirt. Still sliding along, Alex kept going until my skin prickled everywhere he touched as he took away the material leaving both of my shoulders bare. The fourth button was still intact and held as the shirt slipped down, coming to rest just over my ever so erect nipples. Alex drew out a long line over my collarbone with his tongue, continuing over my left shoulder. Chill bumps sprang up down my arms and both legs.

"Tell me where," he seethed, husky voice persisting. "Here, the bedroom, where?"

"Anywhere you want."

"That's my girl!"

Gently, but swiftly, Alex scooped me up and carried me to the living room. He eased me down to the floor.

Alex hovered over me. "Are you sure?"

I sucked in my bottom lip and nodded before pulling him down to me and rolling him over and onto his back. I straddled him, squirming a little as I felt him bulge beneath me. I arched my back as I slung out my hair.

"You are the most beautiful thing I've ever seen."

The way he said it made my heart shatter. There was a twinge of ache to his tone. For just a split second my insecurities jumped to the forefront. I imagined all of those Hollywood actresses and models he's been around and wondered what was wrong with him that he thought I was the most beautiful.

Alex must have noticed the change on my face. "Whatever you are thinking, stop it. Come back to me." He hooked a finger around that spot where the button held and directed me down to him, easing it loose while I moved.

My hair fell around our faces as we kissed. His hands roamed from twisting my hair back to guiding my hips to palming my ass and back again. All the while, my hands propped on the living room rug and supported my weight.

Finally, breathless, I leaned up. I braced my hands against his chest and as I did the white dress shirt slid further down and pooled around my wrists and my waist. The only thing keeping me from being exposed as topless was my hair, which was long and thick enough to cover me on each side.

120

"I want to tell you something, but I fear you've heard it so much that it has no meaning for you."

"Tell me." Alex ran a finger from that pitted spot where my neck and chest meet all the way down between my breasts and farther down to the top of the shirt. "Tell me," he repeated as he went.

"I love you." I leaned down and kissed him once. "I love you for you." Twice. "Just the way you are." A third time. "Just you." Then, this time it was me that was devouring him.

I raised up and unhooked the last button, whipped my head, slinging my hair back and exposing myself to him. I'd always been self-conscious about my body, but, in this moment, I didn't give my insecurities any thought at all.

Alex sat up and my arms went around his neck. Now we really were chest to chest. He locked eyes with me, appearing to have still been completely taken off guard by what I'd said.

"You know you are going to break my heart?" He breathed heavily and inhaled the words with a sigh.

Alex moved my hair over my shoulder so the skin of my bare breasts laid against him. He didn't tell me he loved me right back, but I felt it. I swear I did. I loved him and he loved me. I knew he did.

Alex got to his knees, lifting me with my legs going around him, he carried me with him. He moved all one hundred and ten pounds of me as if I was nothing, maneuvering me, laying me down on my back.

A little pressure from Alex's touch, directed me to tilt my head. There was a slight quaking sensation in me each time Alex ran his tongue over my nipples. When his teeth grazed over them, the feeling down there was a bit more intense and a heated ache was building in that same spot. I ground my hips into him. I didn't know what it was to want a man inside me, but this had to be it.

Alex raised his head and a wave of disappointment came over me. "Don't stop," I pleaded.

"Oh, I'm not stopping," he replied as he assessed our surroundings. "I'm just rethinking our location."

After dragging his tongue over my ear lobe, he whispered. "I'm going to want to do this more than once so I can't have you getting rug burn on our first time."

Alex was bare chested and still clad in his swim trunks. He stood, adjusted his shorts and offered me his hand. I took it and before I knew it, I was over his shoulder. I let out a scream, one tinged with shock and glee.

Alex tossed me on the bed and I fell deep into the fluff of the comforter, featherbed and mattress. I giggled all the way down, but stopped abruptly as Alex tipped his nose to my navel and then his tongue. He left a damp trail with a wake of more goosebumps all the way up to my left breast. He drew a few circles and I squirmed and arched and tried not to burst into flames or full thrashing. I'd never let anyone see me naked, let alone touch me like this.

"Hey," he said in a breath as he reached my mouth.

My heart was beating in my throat, pounding in my chest and echoing in my groin. "Hey," I exhaled back.

"Are you su..."

Before he could finish his question, I took hold of the top of his swim shorts and asked, "May I?" as I began to inch them down.

"No."

I was stunned, but that immediately subsided when Alex stood from the bed and took them down himself.

I tried not to stare, but he was there, standing at the end of the bed, completely naked. He had the physique of those Greek statues I'd been studying in Art History class all semester: chiseled abs, that deep V, square jaw and yet, no leaf in sight. From the look of things, it would have taken more than one leaf anyway. His skin glistened with a thin layer of sweat, but that just made him all the more intoxicating. I could not tear my eyes off of him and it was as if he took his time standing there so I could look. I didn't know whether to thank him or blush.

I wasn't the only one looking, Alex ran a hand through his hair and took a long gaze over me, letting his eyes float from my foot to my face. Arriving at my face, he said, "You are one fine woman, Anna Catherine Calloway."

I don't think anyone had ever called me a woman before and that definitely made me blush.

Alex crawled up the bed, finding the back of my knee and swirling his tongue in circles over the back of the bend. I giggled and squirmed as it set off fireworks, nothing big, small fireworks like sparklers. Alex did the same swirls around my belly button and that's when I felt the real fireworks, the Roman Candle type.

He made his way up and up, setting off more and more fireworks as he went.

"Let's get rid of these," Alex said, hooking his fingers in the top of my panties.

I replied with a slight air of shyness. Considering I was topless, it might have been a little late for that, but it came out anyway. "Okay." I tried to cover the sound of my response by digging my heels into the mattress and raising my hips, cooperating as Alex started to slowly slide them down.

With panties slung to some far part of the room, Alex crawled up me again.

"I won't last long this time," Alex explained, gripping my hands in his and taking them over my head as he kissed me long and gently.

He failed to realize I needed more explanation as this was my first time, but the question, "What?" remained in my head. I couldn't say a word for kissing him back and having my breath taken when he pushed into me. I was expecting it, but I wasn't, not when it happened.

Almost out and back in time and again, Alex knew what he was doing. "Move with me," he panted into my neck, still clutching my fingers in his and driving our palms together and pinning my hands above my head.

I followed his instruction. I would have done anything he told me to do in that moment.

"Oh, Jesus Christ!" Alex bucked. "Anna! Jesus, Anna!" He bucked again and fell limp over me.

"Alex?" I questioned. I'd had health class and biology and an awkward conversation with my mother, but him passing out on top of me was not covered in any of those lessons.

"Anna?" My name came barely above a whisper.

"Are you alright?"

"My God," he rolled off of me, but pulled me over on to him. He started to laugh. "I'm better than alright." He planted kisses on my forehead, my cheeks and one luscious wanting kiss on my lips.

When Alex released me and fell back to breathe, I asked, "Not disappointed?"

"Are you kidding me," he swept the hair out of my face so my eyes could lock with his as he drove home the point. "I could never be disappointed. Plus, if anyone should be disappointed it's you my love."

"Why would I be disappointed?"

"Give me twenty minutes and I'll show you."

Chapter 13

Alex...

I'd had women that were more experienced. I'd had women in all sorts of places and positions. I'd had women that were nothing short of freaks. I'd had everything I could imagine until I had Anna and nothing prepared me for her.

I'd had sex with Anna just that once and knew I was just getting started. It usually took me about twenty minutes to get my second wind. Mentally, I was raring to go as soon as I'd orgasmed the first time, but my body needed time to rest and get it up again.

I fell onto my back and pulled Anna on top of me, resting her head on my chest. I could feel her breathing. My thoughts were jumping from one thing to the next.

"That thing you said earlier..."

I thought I was going to have to elaborate, but Anna acknowledged me with a simple, "Yeah."

"You said it probably didn't mean anything to me, but I want you to know, it means everything coming from you." I stroked her hair, softly, letting it flow through my fingers and she ran her fingertips up and down from my abs to the top of my hip bone and back. It tickled and I could tell it wouldn't take twenty minutes with her. "You being here with me means everything to me."

Anna twisted her neck and looked up at me wide eyed, placing a hand splayed across my chest for support.

"I mean it." I'd never told anyone other than my parents and sister that I loved them. I'd never even said it to my step-mother and, in all honesty, I couldn't remember the last time I told my mother. It wasn't a phrase that came easily to me so perhaps that's why I was reluctant to just reciprocate her sentiment. I did tell her, "I'm not going to say it to you under these circumstances."

125

Anna leaned up, snatching the sheet to cover herself. "Do you think I said it to you because I wanted to screw?"

I sat up immediately. "Of course not. I just... well, it's different for guys and I don't want you to think..." I struggled more to get my point out and immediately regretted not just telling her. It's not like I didn't feel that way about her. Lord knows I felt it to the depths of my soul, to the moon and back and all of those sayings at once.

As I continued to stammer over my words, Anna gathered the sheet and left the bed.

"Wait!" I went after her, not worrying with a stitch of anything to hide my nakedness. "Anna, seriously, did you not hear a word I said?"

"Yes, but Alex, I really have to pee."

I backed off, relieved. "Of course."

Anna nearly had the door shut when she cracked it and stuck her head back out. "And Alex, I don't care if you ever tell me. I know how I feel about you is how *I* feel and that really isn't affected by how you feel about me."

That really made my head spin. Ashley had cried on my shoulder enough for me to know that it meant more to my sister for her guys to say it back to her. How he felt and what he said had a direct effect on her self-worth. From what I'd seen on TV and in movies, Ashley's mindset was that of most women. Again, Anna reminded me that she was the anomaly.

Anna emerged from the bathroom and, with the sheet wrapped like a strapless toga, she strode over to where I was seated on the end of the bed. She was one Hell of a sexy sight in nothing but my bedsheet. In fact, it hadn't even been ten minutes, but the eye candy was definitely speeding things along.

As ladylike as she could, she hiked up the makeshift dress and took a seat, straddling my lap. She draped her arms over my shoulders as I positioned her over my thighs.

"Can I ask you something?" she asked, taking turns nibbling my earlobe and circling the top of my ear with her tongue.

"You can ask me anything," I replied, feeling the rising between my legs and wondering how I would answer anything when I was quickly forgetting my own name.

"Am I doing okay?" She hesitated. "Did you like..."

"My Lord, Anna, yes, you're great and couldn't you tell that I liked it?"

Anna gripped me tighter and held me to the point of near suffocation and then her body relaxed. Then the reality of the situation really dawned on me. Anna wasn't just a virgin, she was completely unaware of how things actually worked. I began to doubt that she even knew what an orgasm was. That realization was titillating and amazing at the same time. I'd never been a teacher and lover to anyone before.

"Anna..."

She leaned back, smiled slightly, almost dreamily and so seductively, then she started back. "There's something about the way you say my name..." Bringing her face closer and closer to mine, she left off her words and kissed me. She had a talent for kissing, a real God given talent that made my dick stand at attention and my toes curl each time.

When Anna came up for air, she made one more declaration. "I've never been in love before and I've never told anyone else I loved them."

Unwrapping her from the sheet, my voice came out in a husky, lusty rasp that I hardly recognized as my own. "You are some Christmas present." I licked my lips before sinking my face between her breasts.

I circled one nipple with my tongue and the other with the pad of my thumb. Her tits were the size of ripe oranges, perfect, round and erect. The one time my father had a candid explanation about sex with me he'd said more than a mouthful was a waste, but he was wrong. Anna's were a handful and there was nothing wasteful about them.

Anna's head was thrown back when she moaned, "Where did you learn how to do that?"

She immediately added, "No, don't tell me! I wouldn't know whether to send them a thank you card or a mail bomb."

I laughed.

Coming down from the amusement, I couldn't stand the wait any longer. Anna didn't gasp this time when I entered her like the first. This time she knew better what to expect and this time she was just as tight, just as wet and wanting. I sank into her finding warmth and wonder for the second time.

"You feel so good," the husky voice came from me again, but broken with the pauses of me moving in and out of her.

This time she urged me on and she moved with me from the beginning as I'd asked her to do earlier.

"I didn't think I would like it," Anna admitted as I thrust back and forth, "But I do. I love doing this with you."

There was no more thinking on my part. As much as I understood the things Anna had never done before and never felt before, there were aspects of what went on between us that I'd never felt or done before either. For the first time in my life, I took my time. Instinct took over between us and there was no more instruction. For the first time in my life, I made love to a woman. I didn't just fuck some girl.

Slowly, rhythmically, I slid in and out and drug out the friction from our pelvic bones all the way up our bodies.

"Oh God, Alex." She gave the verbal indicator, but she didn't have to, I could feel her pulsing around me, tightening, quaking, and gripping me deep inside her and taking all of me.

It was too much for me to take... there was no choice about it and I came with her. Limp over her and too weak to pull out, I had to catch my breath.

Struggling to catch her breath as well, Anna whispered, "Thank you. That was amazing."

128

We laid there together, still one, each of us spent until I found the strength to ease away.

Anna secured her legs around my back. "Alex," she paused, having caught me, "I love having you..."

She loosened her legs as she stopped herself, still timid.

"Tell me," I urged her.

Anna looked away, somewhat embarrassed.

I repeated, "Tell me what you like. Tell me what you love. Tell me everything."

She said it like ripping off a Band-Aid, "I love it when you're inside me."

What a confession.

Regardless of climax or orgasms, from every kiss to the clutch of our intertwined hands to the feel of her legs locking around me, the passion I felt with Anna was beyond anything I could have ever imagined. I could have lived and died with my face buried in her hair. The scent of her was intoxicating to say nothing of how she tasted. My version of Heaven wasn't streets of gold, it was right here with her in my arms.

Long after our encounters, I still couldn't take my eyes off of Anna.

After dinner, we sat by the pool in our usual spots. Watching Anna with her studies, I remembered going to my grandparents' house and witnessing the love between them. My grandmother had her chair and my grandfather had his in the living room where they watched TV. I remember going there as a child and even some as a teenager and noticing that he liked looking at her as much as he liked watching any television show. Every now and then, she would catch him looking and just smile. Well into their seventies, he kissed her goodnight, kissed her good morning and kissed her countless times in between. Nothing, lusty or inappropriate, he just appreciated the fine woman he had and he never failed to let her know it. To my grandmother's credit, she never failed to smile for him, a slow rise of her lashes and blushing smile. I never saw her back away from his advances. I only saw warm exchanges between them. I remembered wanting what they had when I grew up.

"Stop looking at me," Anna lifted her eyes from her text book and cut them at me from under her lashes. She didn't have on one smudge of makeup and her freckles were on full display.

"I can't."

Her cheeks filled and she looked away. "Stop."

"I told you. I can't."

Anna pulled up her book to shield her face from my view.

"Anna?"

She held the book firm. "Yes, Alex?"

"Let me see your face."

"No."

"Please."

Anna lowered the book just enough so that I could see her eyes.

"I love you," I told her. "I mean it."

She dropped The Advances in Chemistry and curled her index finger at me while biting her bottom lip. "I'm going to flunk out of college over you," she laughed, still motioning me over.

I complied, allowing her to kiss me once. "You're not flunking out because of me. One of us needs a good education."

"You could always go to college."

"I probably should. If I did, I might notice sooner when my manager is skimming millions off of me."

"What?" It took her a moment, but she pieced it together, remembering something from our day on at the tournament together. "That guy at the course. You said..."

I didn't remember saying anything to her, but I guess I did. To be honest, I really only remember being with her that day and our time at her house. "I really don't remember what I said, but, yeah, the sleaze from the course is my former manager. It took me a while before I figured it out, but as best I can figure, he stole about five million from me."

Anna sat bolt upright in her lounge chair. "FIVE MILLION...Dollars?" She was quite loud with her verification of the figure, but quieted, speaking the denomination, having noticed the light flick on at a nearby neighbor's house.

"Yes, five million dollars."

"If I miss five dollars, I'm out of sorts. What did you do?"

"I threatened to kill him," I ran my hand through my hair and hung my head. "Admittedly, not my finest moment, but after getting past that I fired him and filed suit against him."

Anna sat, shaking her head. "There's nothing I hate more than a thief." She thought about it and quickly corrected herself. "Well, I hate child molesters and rapists more, but thief is definitely in my top five. I don't blame you for threatening him. I probably would have, too."

I'd seen her fighting mad before so I took her at her word. I'm sure she would have threatened him. She might have even landed a few blows on him which would have served him right. I tried not to fall over laughing at the mental picture of Jacob Stein's office staff pulling Anna kicking and screaming off of him.

"While we're on the subject of the suit, I might as well go ahead and tell you that I have to fly out to California next week for a hearing." I paused, assessing the shift on her face. She looked exactly as I'd hoped she would, disappointed over me leaving. "Would you like to come with me?"

"I can't. I have finals."

"Damn finals," I sighed in jest.

"How long will you be gone?" She shoved her textbook even farther away and snuggled up to me on my chair.

"Just two days."

The conversation subsided and Anna laid her head on my chest. Crickets chirped and the pontoon with a group of night fisherman fired up its engine and puttered out of our cove. The sounds of the country were all around me and I reveled in every minute of it.

"What are you doing this summer?" I asked her, breaking what silence there was.

"Taking molecular Biology, English Lit, racquetball and probably one other class."

"Seriously, you're staying in school?"

"It's called being focused."

"I get that but..."

"I have to work extra hard if I want to get into the Medical College of Georgia, especially since I didn't go to somewhere like Georgia, Georgia Tech or Clemson."

"You want to go to medical school."

"That's how folks usually become doctors."

"You want to be a doctor?" I heard myself, but didn't believe the abnormally high pitch that it gave off when asking that question.

"Yep, ever since..."

With all sorts of curse words exploded in my head, I cut her off. I didn't want her reliving any of that again tonight.

"Right. So, you have like eight more years of school?"

"Plus, residency," she clarified.

"You've really thought all of this through?"

Of course she had thought this through. And of course she would want to be a doctor, having witnessed her brother's death at such a young age and having felt completely helpless. Her statement was also a reminder of just how smart she was.

The conversation had progressed until that point with Anna's head still on my chest, but as she continued to hold up her end, she ran a finger downward from between my pecks, between my abs and down to my happy trail.

"I haven't accounted for everything," she said, reaching the top of my shorts.

The light touch of that one finger tickled and I squirmed and that all but caused my dick to rise to the occasion. We'd already done it three times today and I didn't want her to think I was some sort of sex addict so I did my best to curb my enthusiasm. It was a chore, but I managed, barely.

The next morning Anna woke early and resumed her routine of going to class, but this time she came home to me. She wanted to go to the hospital to check on the guy from the wreck, but to my relief she called and found out he had been transferred to a hospital near his home in Charleston, South Carolina. I couldn't have some helpless guy proposing to my girl. I never told her about his declaration the morning I met him. I'd never been one to be insecure, but I knew if I were him, I couldn't be trusted not to follow through with that statement.

Days passed with Anna going to class, coming home to me and going to work three nights per week. I hated it when she was gone, but feared she would get bored sitting around the house with me if she didn't go. While she was gone, I used my time to call my sister and let her know how things were going, read scripts, talk to my agent about putting off new projects, and I performed all sorts of other domestic tasks. I even ran errands like grocery shopping. We were establishing our own routine and it was the closest thing to normal I'd ever had.

"I tell you what," I said to Anna two nights before I was scheduled to fly out to California, "I'll get myself to the airport, if you will come pick me up."

"I can take you. I don't mind," she insisted, pulling back the covers on the bed.

Anna slept in my arms every night since the first night she stayed over. After making love each night until I was utterly spent, my chest was her pillow and her hair was my Nytol. I never slept better than I did with my chin resting on the top of her head. In fact, I didn't know how I was going to sleep without her in the coming days.

"No, picking me up will due," I crawled across the bed and took her face in my hands. "But I definitely want this face to be the first one I see when I get off of the plane."

She rested her forehead against mine. "I wish you didn't have to go."

"If I could get out of it, I would."

Anna stroked my nose softly with hers before allowing her upper lip to touch mine in that same soft, wanting manner. Her lips moved against mine and I could feel her more than I could hear her. "I love you." The words drifted out and her lips closed against mine.

It was the little things like that that got me the most with Anna and I would miss her to the ends of the earth while I was away.

Calculating the time difference, I managed to wait until 9:00 p.m. Tuesday night, her time, before I called her. My heart dropped when no one answered the house phone. I looked up the number and dialed Brewers. It wasn't her night to work, but I didn't know where else she might be.

"Brewers, this is Molly. May I help you?" The chipper girl I'd met that first night I went to find Anna.

"Hi. Is Anna," I fumbled over her name, correcting myself, "I mean, Anna-Cat working tonight?"

"Nope." I could hear the sound of popping gum through the line. "Sorry." She popped the gum again. "Can someone else help you?"

"No. Thank you anyway."

I'd looked forward to hearing her voice all day and now I couldn't find her. I waited another thirty minutes and tried the house again. Still, there was no answer. This rattled me.

10:00 p.m. the phone in my room at The Beverly Wilshire rang.

There was no greeting. Anna just went right into what she had to say. "I can't believe you are staying at the same hotel as the characters in Pretty Woman!"

134

"You could be staying here, too. You should have come with me," I teased.

"You didn't ask me to come," she replied promptly.

"Didn't I?"

"No." I could hear her breathing through the phone as clearly as I'd heard the girl chewing gum and blowing bubbles earlier. "Hurt my feelings, too."

"You're lying. You had class and you can't miss any more class Dr. Calloway."

"That's future Dr. Calloway."

"I love your laugh." I loved a million things about her, but I started there as it was coming in loud and clear.

Anna giggled the way she did when she was embarrassed. "How did the hearing go today? Any closer to getting your money back and kicking that asshole in his financial balls?"

"Whoa, Dr. Calloway. My virgin ears," I joked. I truly had never heard her talk quite like that before. "And, seriously, guys don't tend to kick other guys in the balls, even the financial balls, but that was a funny analogy."

Most of the time I would consider Anna the picture of a southern girl, genteel and tenderhearted, but I'd seen her punch one guy in the family jewels already and now with her comments about smarmy Stein's financial balls, I wondered if she might have a stash of venom in her character. Not the volume of venom that I'd seen with the models and actresses I'd mix myself up with in the past but a watered-down version. She was nothing near straight poison like Cammie Attaway, who should have some sort of diamond type pattern tattooed on her back to warn others. The more I thought about it, comparing Anna to a snake, admittedly a ridiculous notion, I decided she would likely be one of the nonpoisonous ones, the kind that only makes you sick to your stomach the same way a swift kick in the balls would.

Distracted with my thoughts of snakes and venom, I almost missed when Anna asked, pointedly, "So, how did it go?"

135

"He's fighting it," I rolled my eyes, "but it's pointless. We've hired a forensic accountant and it looks like we've got him dead to rights."

"What's there for him to fight?"

"I don't know. I guess we'll find out."

"You're not scared? I mean that's a lot of money for someone to just steal from you. Seriously, fly me out, I'll kick him in his real balls for you. The guy code doesn't apply to me so I'll do it and you can watch. I swear, it will make you feel better."

I made a hissing sound and laughed.

"What was that?" Anna asked, having missed my private joke.

"Nothing." Silence. "Thank you for the offer, but you're scaring me a little. I hope I'm never on the business end of your knee."

Anna laughed again. "When are you coming home?"

"Ah, home," I sighed. "I like the sound of that. You know, this is the first home I've really had. I mean, one that I rented myself."

"You're kidding right?" Confusion clouded her voice. "Don't you have some apartment in LA or somewhere?"

"I've stayed in hotels and camped out with friends mostly. I've been on the road working, going from set to set, place to place, since I was a teenager so there was never any point in buying a place."

"That's kind of sad."

"I never really thought much about it. Honestly, I never had the time to give it much thought. It's just the way it was."

"And now you have a house in Milledgeville, Georgia. That's a far cry from The Beverly Wilshire."

"True, but you understand it's not about the house or the hotel, it's about who is there that makes it home for me."

There was a long silence on Anna's end. It was so long that I asked if she was still there.

"Yes. I'm still here. I just don't know what to say. You continue to surprise me."

"I wish you were here."

More silence.

"Talk to me, Anna."

"Sorry. My mother just knocked on the door. I didn't want her to hear me on the phone."

"What?"

"She showed up at my dorm this afternoon. Luckily, I stopped by here after class."

That explained why I hadn't been able to reach Anna at the lake house. She was at her dorm.

"So, your mom just showed up?"

"She decided to drive up and see me. Apparently, she'd called a couple of times and hadn't been able to reach me. Now she's spending the night." Heaviness in her breath gave away her anxiety over her mother being there.

"You can take her out to the house if you like."

"And how would I explain that?" Anna was direct.

"Point taken, but that doesn't mean I wouldn't like to meet your parents." I'd never met a girl's parents before, never even wanted to meet them.

"Meeting my parents is one thing, but taking my mother to the house where I..."

"Live with..."

Anna cut me off, "My mother would call it 'shacking up'."

"Well, we'll just put a pin in that conversation for now."

"Yeah, it's only been a week and I've had camping trips that lasted longer so I don't know that I would admit to living with you just yet. Anyway, I've got to go before she comes in the bathroom to check on me. That's all I need." Anna ended her statement with a long, "Ugh."

"Anna, I love you and I'll see you at the airport tomorrow. I can't wait to get back to shacking up with you."

"I love you too, Alex and I can't hardly wait to get back to camping with you."

"Anna, is 'camping' a euphemism for something?"

Anna squealed, but quickly followed with a hushed, "Shut up!   Goodnight, Alex," and giggling, which it appeared she had no control over.

"Night Anna.   I'm going to go dream about 'camping' with you now."

Chapter 14

Anna-Cat...

"Anna, are you alright in there? It's been thirty minutes and I haven't heard the water cut on yet." My mother hammered on the door again. "Are you talking to someone?"

"I'm fine. I'll be out in a minute," I answered through my shirt which I was pulling over my head. "Perfect time for her to take an interest in my life," I said under my breath.

"What was that? I didn't get that last part." I could picture her with her head tilted and ear pressed against the other side of the bathroom door.

"Nothing," I shouted back to be sure she heard me through the door and over the sound of the shower which I'd just cut on.

I have lived in the dorm since the moment I arrived at college towards the end of August last year. I wasn't one of those who went home every weekend. In fact, I could count on one hand the number of times I've been home since I moved to college, and that included Christmas break and the recent stint when I met Alex. Even though she was only staying one night, having my mother underfoot all afternoon called attention to just how small my dorm room was and just how small the whole campus was for that matter.

My mother had been sitting on the steps of Bell Hall when I returned from Chemistry that afternoon. I'd had every intention of packing a few more things and heading out to the lake house, but that plan was shot. Thankfully she'd caught me on the way in and not on the way out or I would have had more explaining to do about where I was going than the explaining she required about where I had been in the last week that she had not been able to reach me.

"Out with friends, out studying and working, that's about it," is how I covered my inability to be reached.

Although I did not go home all the time, I did check in quite frequently. Before Alex I had nothing better to do with my time than study, go to work and make the obligatory call home two to three times a week. I hadn't realized it, but I hadn't called in a week and when she couldn't reach me, she hopped in the car and headed right over.

In a way, it was refreshing to know that she cared and she wasn't that put out by driving up here to visit me, but I would have rather spent the next few hours lying in bed talking about everything under the sun with Alex instead of having to rush to bed because my mother had to drive back early for her bridge club.

"Anna, is there something you want to tell me?" Mother asked as she unmade my bed and prepared to get in.

I stood up, frozen, from my own chore of unmaking my roommate's bed. I'd been lucky that my roommate mostly lived with her boyfriend so she would never even know that I slept in her bed let alone care that I did.

"About what?" I asked, afraid to face her.

"Anna," she drew out my name, "You can tell me you have a boyfriend, you know."

Just when I thought it wasn't possible, the dorm room got smaller and the dinner she'd treated me to at Choby's bubbled up in my esophagus. Knowing it was what had to be done, I turned around and faced her with caution. I'd never had a boyfriend before so I wasn't sure how she was going to take the news.

"Oh, don't be embarrassed. We've all had boyfriends and this makes so much more sense now," she said and with a giant smile on her face.

Embarrassed and confused, it must have been plastered on my face. "What makes you think I have a boyfriend?"

"You haven't been calling so you must have something else to fill your time. Plus, you snuck the cordless into the bathroom." She pointed to the open bathroom door to where the cordless phone could be seen lying on the back of the toilet.

"Oh, right." I did any number of things that further gave away my embarrassment including biting my lip while smiling broadly.

"So, tell me about him," she insisted as she got into bed.

"His name is Alex and he's really nice."

"Nice?" She shook her head. "Well, I'm your mother so nice will do."

My qualms about my mother showing up were starting to dissipate as I went on to tell her a stilted, PG version of my time with Alex. "I met him while I was in Augusta working for Sally Ann a few weeks ago at the tournament."

I further skewered the truth by saying his family had a house on Lake Sinclair. I hated lying, but I wasn't about to tell her my actor boyfriend rented a shack pad on Lake Sinclair and I had moved out there within weeks of meeting him. She seemed open minded to me having a boyfriend, but Gretchen Calloway, the longstanding President of the First United Methodist Church of August's Women's Club, would not be amused by the details of one's love life especially not those of her nineteen-year-old, unmarried daughter.

I went on to describe his looks and I described him exactly as he really was. I told the truth on that account.

Mother sounded satisfied with the details I gave her. "He sounds lovely. I'm assuming he's older than you are?"

I couldn't see her face and she sounded unphased by any age gap so again I answered honestly.

"He's twenty-four."

"Well, be careful. Don't give away your prize just because he'd older and expects it."

141

Thank Heavens I'd cut the light off moments before because the wattage coming off of my face combined with any light blinded her. I knew what it felt like when I went all red from mortification and this was definitely it. I could not keep out the thought of "little did she know," I'd already given away the prize.

"Anna?"

"Yes, ma'am?"

"I'm happy for you."

"Thank you."

I laid there with the covers drawn up looking at the glow in the dark stickers of stars and constellations on the ceiling just thinking. I found it funny how I was now glad my mother was here. Even though I didn't tell her the whole truth about Alex it felt good to talk to her about him. This seemed like a moment normal mothers and daughters would have and, if there was one thing I'd always wanted from my parents, it was normal.

"Mom," I said out of the silence.

"Yes, Anna?"

"I love you and I'm glad you came to check on me."

The next morning Mom was up at the crack of dawn. She was in a hurry to get on the road and I couldn't convince her to go to breakfast with me. We barely had time for conversation as she put on her makeup.

"No, no," she dismissed the notion. It's almost two hours back to Augusta and I have to stop by the house and make lunch for your father. Plus, I have to supervise the setup at the club, so I've really got to get going."

"He still can't make his own lunch?" I frowned, scooting next to her to get a look in the mirror.

"He'd rather starve than crack open the mayonnaise himself."

I couldn't remember ever commiserating with my mother about my father like this. It was kind of nice. I never knew she thought this way about him. I thought she hung on his every whim.

"He amazes me." I poked through her makeup bag, looking for her favorite shade of lipstick.

"How so?" She missed her lashes and applied mascara to her eyebrow as she shot another question my way.

I finished applying her lipstick to my bottom lip and replied, "The man can perform root canals, but can't toast bread or slice a tomato. Heaven forbid anything ever happen to you."

"Stop making me laugh before I look like the lead singer of a heavy metal band!" That was by far the funniest thing my mother had ever said.

Not fifteen minutes later, she hugged me goodbye in the parking lot of my dorm and was on her way. I watched her drive away until she turned the corner onto Hancock Street. While I watched her go, I wished I had more moments like this with her and I wished I could tell Alex all about my visit with her right then.

I arrived home from class to another surprise. This time it wasn't in the form of a parent sitting on my front porch. It was a message from Alex.

"Hey, my girl!" The message started.

My heart almost burst over him referring to me as his girl. That was better than when he called me just "Anna".

The message continued, "I was thinking, maybe you can pick me up at the Indian Creek Marta Station. That way you don't have to come so far and I hear rush hour in Atlanta can be a bear and I don't want you to get caught in traffic. Anyway, be at the station around 7:00 p.m. I'll be the one with the raging...Never mind. Use your imagination."

I squealed at what he was suggesting.

Alex closed with, "I'm about to board the plane so I'll see you soon. I love you."

I squealed louder when he said he loved me. It was probably loud enough that the girls on the far end of the hall probably heard me.

Alex had only been gone for two days and my mother had been a great distraction, but I missed him to the point that my heart ached for him. All through the day, I itched to get on the road to Atlanta to pick him up and now hearing his voice on my answering machine only made me want to jump in the car and drive like I was on my way to a fire just to get to him.

When I turned into the parking lot for the MARTA station, Alex was a vision. I didn't realize he had one, but there he was wearing a Georgia College t-shirt, ball cap and jeans. The t-shirt accentuated the muscles in his chest. It was pulled so tight and made me wonder if he shrank the shirt or bought it a size too small. His jeans were a boot cut that hung on his hips and the legs pooled just a little at the tops of the Timberland boots he was wearing. The pooling of the hem didn't make him look short like some guys. Alex looked as tall as ever. He could have been the model for Leonardo da Vinci's the Vitruvian Man, that drawing showing the man with perfect proportions.

Alex was waiting on the curb with flowers in hand, a dozen lavender roses to be exact. He knew how to do a homecoming. As I pulled up next to him, I tried to reign in the huge smile I had. I knew it was from ear to ear and I tried to keep my libido in check as I felt the heat rising between my legs.

Alex open the car door, handed me the flowers and threw his bags in the backseat.

"You are a sight for sore eyes," he said, sliding into the passenger's seat. "Come here."

I lowered the roses from my nose and eyed him. I could still feel his kiss on my lips from when he left on Monday afternoon, but now he was back and a fresh kiss promptly replaced the old one. My toes curled in my sandals as I stood on the brake, keeping the car stopped and getting leverage to reach Alex. Everything about me wanted to lean his seat back and climb on top of Alex right there. It hadn't been that long, but the loss of it didn't even warrant

144

an afterthought. I just wanted Alex, the intimacy with him, the rapture.

When he pulled back, I asked him, "Would you like to drive?"

"I can if you want me to," he offered.

"If you aren't too tired."

Alex kissed me again, a peck compared to the initial greeting, but the way he answered was just as hot as that first kiss. "I'm not tired at all."

I nodded and put the car in park and laid the wrapped bundle of roses in the backseat before we changed sides. As soon as Alex had the seat adjusted to his comfort we got on the way.

"Thank you for the roses. I love them," I said to him as we left the parking lot. "Now, tell me all about California.

"Tell me all about the visit with your mother." Alex cut his eyes at me, making the turn onto the ramp to head toward I-285.

Between 285 to I-20 and out toward Covington where the median wall ended and the grass began, we talked about all that had happened while we were apart. With the sunset behind us, I bided my time and waited for traffic around us to die down and for full darkness before I made the move I'd been wanting to make since I suggested Alex drive.

Noticing me unbuckling my seat belt, Alex asked casually, "What are you doing?"

"Making up for lost time." I replied, my voice sounding breathy.

With a hand on his high thigh for balance and my knees in my seat, I leaned over and planted a series of kisses from his ear down to his shirt collar.

"I like your shirt."

Alex held the steering wheel with his left hand and reached his right hand into my hair, holding me near him. "I like everything about you including that little dress you're wearing."

Headlights whizzed around us, but I didn't care. I ran a hand under the bottom of his shirt, feeling his chest as I nibbled at his collarbone through the material. "I'm so glad you're back," I said in between bites.

Alex slid his hand down from my hair to my neck, over my back and farther down over my ass, which in this position was barely covered my dress. "You're going to make me wreck."

"Do you want me to stop?"

"God, no!" Alex gripped my ass tighter and pulled me closer. "I want to pull this car over."

Alex lightened his touch as a set of lights whipped around us. When the car was safely up ahead, he continued to describe what he wanted to do. "And lean your seat back and…"

"And I'd let you."

I let my hand travel south and was just about to unbutton Alex's jeans when he applied the brakes, both figuratively and literally. As the car suddenly lunged forward with the quick efforts to slow down, I lost my balance and rolled toward the dash. Alex caught me and slung me toward my seat.

"There's a wreck or a road block or something up ahead. Get your seatbelt on," he said, sternly.

I giggled. "You've got to be kidding me." It was only a figure of speech as I'd looked ahead and, sure enough, there were blue lights across both east bound lanes of I-20. I took a hard look, "It's not a wreck. There'd likely be red ambulance lights if it was a wreck."

Alex paid close attention to the road and the cars stopping in front of us. "Do they typically have road blocks on the interstate?"

I'd traveled this stretch of the interstate between Augusta and Atlanta, not often, but enough times to safely say, "I've never seen one before."

"Something's up." A level of concern shown in his voice that I wasn't used to seeing and it definitely put the kibosh on any notions I'd been having about starting our reunion in the car on the ride back home.

Although I added, "I'm sure it's nothing," his stiffening and worry did not help me convince even myself.

"Lay your seat back," Alex instructed.

"What?"

Alex repeated himself, adding, "I had a couple of drinks on the plane. They've probably worn off, but I don't want to chance it. We are far enough back no one will notice if we swap places."

I looked ahead of us, assessing whether we could even attempt this and get away with it.

"Trust me. Lay the seat back," Alex gave the command again. "When we come to a stop, I'm going to lay mine back too. I'll go under and you go over, but we have to be quick."

Alex maneuvered us behind an eighteen-wheeler in the outer lane and, when it came to a stop, we followed suit. No sooner had he put the car in park than Alex commence our maneuver. Secured in the passenger's seat, he didn't raise the seat back up.

"Is this one of those protect your identity moments?" I asked him, taking the car out of park and inching up behind the black Club Car transfer truck in front of us.

"Yeah."

"In that case, put the ball cap over your face, turn toward the door and go to sleep." I cut my eyes at him and kept inching up in line.

The troopers were efficient in their processing of vehicles. It wasn't five minutes before I had my window down, a trooper leaning in with a flashlight in my eyes.

I smiled with all of the cheer and wattage I had. "Good evening, officer," I said causally, but kept my voice low as I handed him my driver's license and insurance card.

"Evenin' Miss," the Georgia State Patrol officer greeted me while looking over my license and insurance.

Handing back my cards, he shined his flashlight over Alex, but didn't linger. He continued scanning through the backseat while asking me, "Has anyone in the vehicle been drinking tonight?"

I nodded in Alex's direction. "I haven't, but I can't say about him. I just picked him up from the airport. He's asleep. Do you want me to wake him up and ask him?"

"No. That's not necessary." He hit me in the eyes with the flashlight again, but not on purpose. He was standing up from my window and motioned me on. "Go on. Have a good night and be careful out there."

The truck in front of me was a quarter mile ahead at that point so I gave it the gas, still cautiously. Once the color had come back to my cheeks and my knuckles from gripping the steering wheel as the officer had done a visual search of my car, I reached over and smacked Alex with an open palm across his chest. "You can get up now!" I meant for my words and my hand to give him a sting.

"What was that for?" He flinched.

I'd succeeded admirably with the slap.

"That was not fun. Jesus, what if they had seen us switch places?" I huffed. "You should have said something about having a couple of drinks before you got behind the wheel if you were concerned about it!"

"I wasn't concerned until I saw the entire State of Georgia out in force!" Alex tried defending himself.

"And another thing, if you are so worried about being recognized out here, then maybe you shouldn't be out here!"

"Whoa there!" Alex demanded. "The only reason I'm worried about being recognized out here is because it would bring an end to the peace and quiet I have out here with you. Do you know what it's like to be chased and stalked..."

"No, but..."

"Let me tell you, it's not that fun..."

"But it's the price you pay?"

"Right."

148

I snarled at him, "I liked you better when you were pretending to be asleep!"

"I liked you better when I had my hand on your ass and your lips on my neck! So, look here, I don't expect anyone to sympathize with me or pity over it, but of all people who might want to keep things quiet, it might be you, Anna."

I glared at him.

"Anna," he said more calmly, "our time wouldn't be our own anymore. Home wouldn't be the same. Sitting by the pool and just being us, it would come to a stop. You would go from being just Anna to being tabloid fodder. You'd be the latest in a string of conquests for Alex Allen. I don't want that."

"A string of conquests?" I snapped, taken aback and not quite ready to play nice again.

"You know what I mean. I told you the first time we met about the paparazzi and I'm not one to make conquests. You are not a conquest. You know that."

Alex reached a hand over to me and caressed my cheek. I was weak and immediately started to melt by his touch, but I refused to say anything.

"If anyone's been conquered, it's me."

I took my eyes off the road for a split second, just long enough to look his way. Alex was staring at me as he twirled my hair between his fingers.

"I couldn't stop thinking about you the whole time I was away. I just wanted to come home to you."

The rest of the way down I-20 there was nothing but road noise in the car. It wasn't until I turned off the interstate onto Highway 441 toward Eatonton that Alex spoke again.

"What kind of doctor do you want to be?"

"General practitioner."

"How long will you be in school?"

"Forever."

149

Alex seemed to ponder over my answer before he followed up with another question. "Where do you plan on going to medical school?"

"I would like to get into The Medical College of Georgia, but it's really competitive for instate students, or so I've heard."

"Are your parents paying for your school?"

"They are paying for my undergraduate degree, but we haven't discussed it further."

"I'll cover the rest. You just study and I'll take care..."

"Alex, that's sweet, but how long is the lease on the house?"

I see from the corner of my eye Alex was perplexed. He'd been playing with my hair, but he took his hand back.

"Three months. What does that have to do with anything?"

"We've only been together for what, a month? And, I'm already 'camping' at your house? Don't you think we ought to..."

"I see. Slow things down, right?"

"More like see where things go."

Alex was quiet.

"Alex," I said, taking the time to look at him as another set of oncoming lights lit up the cab of the car, "I love you. I've never been in love before and it's pretty strange for me to feel like I actually need someone and that's how I feel about you. I feel like I need to be with you and it's a pull more than wanting to be with you."

Alex nodded like he understood and I kept explaining.

"The thing is, I like that you seem to want to take care of me. It's sweet, but I'm very used to taking care of myself and I don't want your money. I just want you to be here. So, for now, I'm okay taking things one day at a time. There's going to be work for you that takes you away and school for me and let's just see how that goes."

"I can do that," he admitted, but he wasn't overly excited about the compromise.

Chapter 15

Alex...

"Shit, Anna, I'm sorry!" I said immediately after I came. In our haste, I'd forgotten to use a condom.

Anna was still breathless and pulled me down on top of her, kissing my neck and coming down off of her own orgasm. "It's okay. I'm on the pill and I've been remembering to take it."

"Oh, thank God!" I was relieved, but that did nothing to sooth the ache I had from drawing up so quickly.

"Alex," Anna said my name, wrapping her legs around my back and pulling me down, my cock rubbing against her. "I liked it like that."

Running my hand from her thigh all the way up her side, feeling the curve of her breasts, and continuing upward until I found her hand. I locked my fingers in hers. I hovered over her, propped on my other elbow. "We can do it like that all the time if you want. I'll do it again. Just like that, but better."

"Better? I don't think there's any such thing." She arched her back and rubbed her tits against me. I think that sensation alone cut the time it would take me to catch another erection in half.

I couldn't count the number of women I'd been with on two or three pairs of hands and I wouldn't go so far as to presume that I pleased all of them, but with Anna, she left no doubt that she was pleased. I'd never been praised or felt wanted in the way she did. No one was even in the ballpark of making me feel the way she did. She wanted to see how things would go and I wanted things to stay just like this, wrapped up in her.

Things did progress. It was my first Georgia summer and it was hot. The humidity was all that I'd been warned that it was, but the heat came mostly from me and Anna. She went to class, studied, kept up her job at Brewers, I bought a truck and we had adventures. We took weekend trips to the Blue Ridge Mountains hiking and tubing down rivers and to Tybee Island beach. I took another quick trip to California and Anna used that time to visit her parents. Mostly, we couldn't get enough of each other and being away from her was torture for me. She was my new normal.

Summer ended and fall classes began for Anna. I read scripts that didn't remotely interest me and she began sophomore year of college. By October I was forced to honor a contract for a movie I'd signed on for well before I met Anna.

"It should only be for six weeks and you can come out on the weekends. I'll fly you out," I insisted.

"You can't fly me to Canada and back every weekend." Anna shook her head as we discussed how we would survive the distance.

The movie, a romantic comedy, was scheduled to shoot in Toronto. It would be my second film that had been shot outside of the US. The first one I'd enjoyed. I liked seeing the world, but that was before I had her and a home. Now, I didn't want to see anything without her.

"I don't want to leave you." I followed her through the kitchen, catching her and wrapping my arms around her as she scraped our dishes for loading into the dishwasher.

"You're not leaving me," she said, squirming free to rinse the plates. "You're going to work and it's only for six weeks. It's not like you aren't coming back. Plus, I'm going to be right here and it's not like we won't talk on the phone two and three times a day."

I took the plate from her and sat it on the counter. "Anna," husky voiced, I wrapped an arm around her waist and pulled her back to me. "I want so much more than talking on the phone with you."

"I want that to, but we have commitments."

It wasn't something I thought about before I said it, but what I said was true. We'd been together six months and that's longer than I'd ever been with anyone so being committed to her was a forgone conclusion. It really went without saying, but I said it anyway. "The only commitment I care about is the one I have to you."

Anna's face lit up and she blushed. She never failed to be amazed when I made any declaration of my feelings toward her.

Barefooted, Anna stood on her toes and stretched up to kiss me. "I love you," she said, "and I'd follow you anywhere."

"Promise me you'll come up at least once."

"I promise." She kissed me again.

"And I'll do my best to come home as much as I can."

"Alex," Anna sighed, between kissing me again, "stop talking. You're wasting what time we have left."

Anna was right. I was scheduled to fly out in two days and I didn't want to spend our time doing anything that would fuel my fears about leaving her.

That night, in our usual spot by the pool, Anna tucked between my legs with her head laid back on my chest and shoulder as she read the latest in biology text books, I asked her, "Are you going back to the dorm while I'm away?"

Although she didn't need it because she lived with me, Anna had kept her dorm room for the sake of appearances with her parents. Her friend Sally Ann had started Georgia College this year and since she was the one person on Earth Anna trusted, she made the ideal dorm roommate for Anna. It was a win for Sally Ann as well since she got the cubby hole of a room all to herself.

153

She leaned her head farther back on my shoulder and stretched her neck to look my way. "I don't like being here without you."

I began massaging her shoulders. "Why don't you have Sally Ann come stay out here with you?"

Sally Ann had also been a regular at the lake house. She'd even slept over a time or two. I liked her and admired the friendship Anna had with her.

"I don't know..." Anna relaxed and let the book drop to her lap. "I just feel like I'll miss you more here."

"I want you to miss me," I said frankly.

Anna moved the book from her lap to the ground beside lounge chair. She twisted, crawling around until she straddled me. "Don't you get it yet?" Anna asked, taking my face in her hands.

Every time she touched me, I felt electricity surge through me and this time was no different. It clouded my mind and left me craving more.

"Get what?"

She rested her forehead against mine as she explained, "That I miss you when you leave the room, when I go to class, when I'm at work, so you can stop wanting me to miss you. It seems to come naturally to me and I don't know that I could stop it if I tried. It's torture."

My arms were already around her, but I squeezed tighter. "What are we going to do?"

"Get through it the best we can." She fought them, but tears streamed down her face. "I don't want you to go, but I can't ask you to stay."

Before I left, Anna relented and agreed to stay at the lake house.

Three weeks passed as Anna and I spoke on the phone at every possible moment. She'd stayed at the lake house as things with Sally Ann hadn't worked out. One of our first conversations involved details of how Anna had arrived at the dorm room to move in only to find Sally Ann and, what Anna called "The Flavor of the Month" in the midst of oral sex.

154

"What did you do?" I asked her.

"I slammed the door and haven't been back!"

"Have you spoken with Sally Ann since?"

"Yes, but..."

"It's been a little awkward?"

"Well, it's one thing to hear her describe her adventures, but it's another to witness them. I'm sorry. I must sound like a prude."

I laughed. "What would you do if someone had caught us?"

"Be embarrassed probably." I could just see Anna blushing through the phone. "What about you?"

"I might just be damn proud."

"What?!" I completely caught her off guard with my answer.

"Yeah, I wouldn't mind the world knowing I can get a girl like you."

"A girl like me?"

"Smokin' hot, sexy as Hell, into exhibitionism..." I teased her until she cut me off.

"You are awful, Alex Allen! Just awful!"

We talked two and three times per day like she said we would. I gave her a wakeup call in the mornings and tucked her in with a call each night. We talked for hours at a time. At the end of October, I flew Anna up for the weekend.

"My God, I have missed you," Anna explained as she threw herself into my arms in the middle of the airport.

I held her tight and nuzzled my cheek against her face. "I'm never going to let you go."

Not caring who was around us, I kissed her with complete abandon. The taste of her lips, apple Jolly Ranchers, the feel of her in my arms, firm and soft at the same time, the scent of her hair, apricots, and losing my mind over the sight of her; all of my senses came alive.

People from all walks of life buzzed around us and I never gave two thoughts to them. I had one thing on my mind, getting Anna back to what had become my temporary

155

abode. It was modern, stainless steel countertops, cement floors and exposed beams and ductwork in the ceiling. Now that she was here, the loft apartment with a rooftop deck I'd rented in downtown Toronto might stand a chance of feeling like home. It was a far cry from the cozy lake house, but it was Anna that made that place warm. I figured with just her being here, and what I planned to do to her this entire weekend, surely we'd warm the place up. From the way she placed her hand high on my thigh and snuggled into my shoulder for the ride to the apartment, I figured we might do more than warm it up. We might start a fire.

The elevator doors had barely closed before Anna stood facing me and ran her hands under my shirt and up my chest. "I've missed everything about you." She closed her eyes and exhaled slowly, allowing the words to slip away.

"Jesus Christ, you're all I think about." I pulled her closer to me, any closer and we would have melded together.

The door of the elevator opened and we stumbled out blindly, kissing and groping. I assume the elevator door closed, but I had no way of knowing.

I barely broke my lips away from hers. "Let me get the key." I fished for it in my pocket with one hand while keeping the other clutched to Anna's ass.

"Alex, I love you. I love you. I love you."

Hearing those words, I gave up on the key. I caught Anna by the thighs and lifted her against the door of the apartment. I was swift and we hit the door with a thud.

Anna giggled, "You have a thing for up against doors, don't you?"

"I only have a thing for you." I pinned her, balanced on my hips and used my arms and hands to relieve her of her shirt.

I ducked my head and ran my tongue between her breasts. They heaved and swelled in her bra. With my face buried in her cleavage and with the flick of my thumb and forefinger, I unhitched her bra and took it away.

I inched back over and marveled at the wonder that was before me. I marveled that she was mine. I studied her face, her full lips, puffy and rosy from our kisses. Her eyes were that nearly translucent blue that gave the illusion that I could see all the way to her soul if I just looked hard enough and even hooded, they blazed. Her hair was a tousled mass of brown silk curls, from my hands having gone all through it.

For only a second my eyes caught that pink line across her left bicep. She didn't have a tattoo of my name on her. The branding that she was mine was subtler than that. It was the scar that remained from what started all of this. I was thankful my stupidity that fateful night had not done more damage, but seeing the scar gave me pause to smile. As long as it was there, it would never let her forget me.

Downward my eyes fell, pulled as if they were magnets to her chest. Her tits were more full, firm and perkier than I'd recalled and I thought I recalled them quite well. I took one in my hand and another in my mouth. Anna arched her back against the door, offering me all I wanted of her, moaning and guiding me with her hands in my hair.

"I love you," she moaned again and, again, her words were as effective as any aphrodisiac to me.

Between the steel door to my apartment and the threshold of the elevator was a space of about five by five feet and in that space, up against the apartment door and then on the floor, I made Anna fully aware of just how much I missed her. By morning, I'd made her aware no less than four times.

"Do you really want to see Toronto?" I asked her, caressing her fingers, entwining them with mine, releasing them and doing it again. Her fingers were long, fine boned and thin. I noticed her leg as it was on display out from under the covers and hooked over mine. Bared from high hip to toe, her leg could be described the same as her fingers. I couldn't look at it without remembering how I ran

157

my tongue from her instep to inner thigh and beyond making her scream and writhe.

"No." Anna shook her head and her hair tickled as it moved back and forth across my chest. "I'm content to stay right here all weekend if you are."

We stayed in, ordered take out and didn't go anywhere beyond the roof deck until it was time to go back to the airport.

"I hate it here," I told her as we made the drive to the airport. I feared I sounded like a child being left on the first day of kindergarten as soon as I said it.

"And I hate you being here, but you'll be home in a few weeks and I'll come back here if you like. All of this will be over before we know it."

I kissed Anna goodbye at the gate and had that nagging feeling again. I watched her all the way down the passageway to the plane, suffering from a gut churning warning to prepare myself that I might not ever see her again.

We continued to talk on the phone day in and day out, multiple times. I carried on with the wakeup calls and tucking her in at night from afar. We played phone tag through our answering machines. If a thought popped in our heads, one dialed the other and shared.

I went home in November and my family, all but my mother, met me at the lake house. Anna spent Thanksgiving Day with her parents in Augusta, but told her mother a watered-down version of the truth in order to make it back to be with us on Thanksgiving night.

"I've been invited to have dinner with my boyfriend and his family at their house on Lake Sinclair," she reportedly told her mother.

Anna and I cooked a turkey and all the trimmings. Again, I was warm and content with being at home. I was surrounded by family and I loved life. I never wanted to leave.

It was a warm night, typical of November in Georgia from what I'd learned and Ashley and I took a stroll to the dock leaving Anna with my father and step-mother cleaning up the kitchen.

"I love her. She's like the sibling I never had," Ashley teased me.

"You have a sibling," I nudged her playfully as if I was going to throw her off the dock.

"I know, but you've never been much of a sister," again Ashley ribbed me.

"Be serious," I said. "What do you think of her?"

"Does it matter what I think?"

I shrugged.

Ashley's demeanor changed and all joking was laid aside. "She's perfect for you."

"How do you know?"

"It's the way you look at her when she's not looking and the way she looks at you when you're not looking. I wish I had what you have."

I stayed through Sunday in order to make it back to the set and report for work on Monday morning. I shared a ride back to the airport in Atlanta with my parents and before I drove away, I looked back at Anna. She was waving from the front stoop of our house and I felt the churn that was becoming familiar and heard the whisper in my mind. It told me this might be the last time I saw her. I shook it off because there was one certain thing I knew to my core and that was that I would never let her go.

After one particularly grueling day on set, having endured the most graphic sex scene I'd ever had to perform, I sank into the bed in the apartment and I dialed the number to the lake house. The answering machine picked up and, without thinking, I told her, "I don't want to do this anymore."

It was my job, but I felt as if I'd betrayed Anna somehow. The actress I was working with lacked all inhibitions. I wondered what normal man would have these complaints, but her methods seemed more suited for porn. She offered to "do anything for the craft". She didn't even bother to wink when she said "anything". Of course, the crew egged her on and the director was disappointed over my lack of enthusiasm.

By the time I arrived back at the apartment, I was chafed from being dry humped for five hours. I knew from reading the script that I'd finished the worst of it so I would tough it out and finish. Part of finishing meant I had to return to the set that night. What got me through it was the promise of hearing Anna's voice when I got back.

She was usually more forthcoming, but "Call me," was all she said and there was an unfamiliar tinge to her voice. Something was wrong.

"I can't come this weekend," she explained.

"Why?" I was quick to question.

"Can you come here?"

"Why can't you come here?"

"I just can't. I need you to come home. I have to tell you something and I won't tell you over the phone."

The whole world stopped and the color drained from me. In my mind, there was only one thing I could think of that she would not tell me over the phone.

Chapter 16

Anna-Cat...

I'd always known the sex talk my mother gave me hardly covered the bare minimum, but she'd failed completely to tell me anything about pregnancy. She hadn't breathed a hint of what the signs might be. I knew that a missed period was a surefire sign, but beyond that things were a mystery.

At first, I thought my breasts were just sore because I'd overexerted myself in my tennis class. I'd gained a little weight lately so I'd been giving it my all in class and running up and down the driveway at home to burn some extra calories. I thought maybe the freshman fifteen was finally going to hit me and I was not about to turn the other cheek for it.

A few weeks later, exercising became a moot point. The smell of any sort of food nauseated me, but the smell of fried foods finished the job. The only parking spot on campus one afternoon was outside of the dining hall. They were frying chicken for the evening meal. I stood up out of the car, got a nose full of the stuff and dropped to all fours by the car door. I puked up my toenails.

It was an all day long battle of smells and perseverance on my part. I didn't know what it was, but I knew it wasn't the stomach flu. With the flu, I wouldn't be able to choke it down as I had in some of these instances.

My emotions were out of whack, too. It wasn't my first biology lab or my first dissection of a fetal pig, but it was the first time I'd thought of it as more than a grade. Thoughts and what ifs over its poor, sad life over took me and before I knew it, I was cutting into it with a shaky hand and tears streaming down my face. All I could really think was that it was someone's or something's baby.

I never kept up with my period. It always came and went as it wanted. I wouldn't have described myself as

161

regular and my inability to remember to take the pill didn't help that situation. Plus, I'd never been too concerned about taking the pill since at my first OB/GYN visit the doctor explained that I had a tilted cervix and I'd likely never get pregnant without assistance, medical assistance and, not the doctor's exact words, but a heaping helping of it.

Finally, worry took over, worry of what was wrong with me, and I went to the campus clinic. As it turned out, the OB/GYN I saw when I was thirteen might have been a moron. I hadn't needed any help at all getting pregnant. I'd done a fine job of it almost all by myself.

I staggered down the steps of Ennis Hall from the student health clinic in complete shock. Anyone looking at me might have thought I was reading the paperwork in my hands when I missed the last two steps and stumbled to the bottom, barely catching myself. I wasn't really reading it. I just couldn't focus my mind to look at anything else.

I didn't know what I was going to do. I didn't want to tell Alex, but there wouldn't be any hiding it. The same went for my parents. The doctor said I was three months along and any idiot would figure it out soon.

I managed to make it to my car before I completely broke down. I cried over the death of my dreams of being a doctor. I cried over what I considered the humiliation of being two weeks away from my twentieth birthday and already being pregnant. I was quickly becoming a statistic. I cried mostly over what Alex and my parents would think of me. He might think I'd trapped him and God only knows what my parents would think. I could only hope that my father would continue to treat me as if I didn't really exist and, if that was the case, he wouldn't have an opinion at all so it wouldn't matter. I wondered what my mother would think. Surely this would be an embarrassment to her among her church friends.

It was the start of December, but the sun beat through the windshield of the car and it was as warm in there as any summer day. I wasn't sure how long I'd sat there, but I'd sat there long enough to break a sweat and to cry myself into dry heaves. For once in the last however many days, there was nothing in my stomach to come back up and that was a relief.

I drove home to the lake house and wondered if I was living there on borrowed time. Entering the front door, I saw the light on the answering machine blinking. I longed to hear his voice all the time, but now more than ever. I longed to tell him and hear him say everything was going to be alright. Of course, I wanted to marry Alex. I wanted to keep this life of ours going, but I hadn't planned on it going like this. I didn't want it like this.

I pressed play on the machine and listened as Alex sounded tortured. "I don't want to do this anymore."

My heart sank. What did he mean by that? I picked up the phone and dialed him back. I got his answering machine and left a message of my own. "Call me."

I looked down at my belly and gave it a rub. "Oh, Baby, it might just be me and you," and I started to cry again.

I would have loved to talk to Sally Ann, but I didn't want a soul to know about this until I'd told Alex. In all of the years I'd lived in the shadow of my brother's death, not even then did I feel as alone as I did right then.

A slight relief came that night when Alex returned my call. As it turned out, he wasn't breaking up with me. He just didn't want to be an actor anymore. His situation was not improved with my backing out of flying up there to visit him the coming weekend and insisting he come home.

"I have to work this weekend," he told me. "I don't know when I can make it back. We're running behind schedule and..."

"Just come home soon. I have to tell you something and I don't want to tell you over the phone." I wanted to see his face when I told him I was pregnant. If he was going to leave me over it, he would have to do it to my face.

Before hanging up, Alex told me he loved me and I reciprocated, but I wondered how long he would still love me when he found out.

"No matter what," I told the flutter in my stomach, "I'll take care of you. I don't know how yet, but I'll get it done somehow."

Another week passed and Alex and I continued to talk on the phone as we'd been doing.

"I won't be home this weekend, but I'll try to call you from my parents' house," I explained.

"Why are you going there?" Alex asked.

"It's my birthday and I don't want to celebrate it by myself."

"Holy shit, Anna, I had no idea! I'm so sorry."

"Don't worry about it," I quickly replied. "We never talked about it so it's okay."

"How've we never talked about that? You're turning twenty, right?"

"Yep, twenty."

"I'll try to come home next weekend and we'll celebrate then, okay?"

I wasn't sure if I wanted him to come home. I was starting to show and he'd figure it out. There was no way of hiding it, but as long as he was in Canada, I could pretend that everything was the same. No, I wanted him to come home and I wanted to get on with it. Come Hell or high water, Alex deserved to know and I deserved to know where I really stood with him.

Two days later I was home between classes when the doorbell rang. It was the UPS delivery man and he had a package for me.

He chattered away while I signed. "All the way from Canada, ma'am. I don't get many deliveries out this way from our neighbors to the North."

"I guess it's like a snowflake," I replied.

He looked puzzled.

I clarified, "We don't get many of those in these parts either, but every now and then we get a snowflake or two."

"Ah, right," he laughed heartily, taking back his clipboard and pen. "Well, have a good afternoon, ma'am."

The UPS man made off like a bandit, sprinting to his truck and with a wave as he put it in gear to reverse down the driveway.

I paused from my struggle with ripping open the large envelope to wave back to him, but immediately returned to my task. I was perplexed as to what it contained as I could feel what appeared to be a small box. The package was getting the better of me, but I was not to be defeated. I found a knife in the kitchen and slit the well taped envelope from top to bottom. Turning it upside down, out popped a little pale blue box, the size of which usually contained a ring. My heart dropped and I gasped at seeing the word "Tiffany & Co." written across the top of the box. In my shock, I almost missed the envelope, the type that usually contained a letter, that also fell out.

On the outside of the letter, where an address would typically be, it said "Anna, read me first."

I tore open the top of the smaller envelope with little to no effort at all. On a folded piece of stationary with his initials embossed across the top, Alex wrote, "I've probably gone about this backward, but I saw it and thought of you. I'm told it's called an eternity band and I am certain I will love you for an eternity. Wear it with any sentiment you like, on which ever finger you like, but know that I plan on adding to this one day. Happy Birthday and I look forward to coming home and seeing you wearing this and nothing else. – Yours Always, Alex."

I opened the little box and found a circle of diamonds. There were twenty emerald cut stones encased in what appeared to be platinum. The ring was thicker than my mother's wedding band, which was the only comparison I could think to make to this ring. I was scared to imagine how much Alex might have paid for it, because whatever it was, it was way too much.

I slipped it on and watched as it sparkled in every direction under the florescent lights of the kitchen. I put it on my left ring finger and I studied my hand and how it looked. This ring wasn't just beautiful, it was amazing.

I continued to study the ring as I dialed Alex's number. There was no answer other than the machine.

"Hi. Please come home soon. I'm wearing something of yours and I want to tell you 'thank you' in person." Tears started to fill my eyes as I turned the ring on my finger. It was exactly the same all the way around. "I miss you and feel like it's been an eternity since I've seen you. Please come home."

I was due at my parent's house that evening so I finished packing, slowly, hoping Alex could call me back before I left. I was only supposed to be there for two nights so there was only so slow I could go in packing for that little time. I assessed what I'd put in my overnight bag.

"Luckily, Empire waist tops were in and I'd stocked up on them," I thought to myself. I held one up against my torso and gave myself a good looking over in the mirror. I wasn't far enough along that this wouldn't do for keeping my secret.

For a moment, I thought about leaving the ring at home. Not wanting to have another secret, I kept it on. I waited until almost 4:00 p.m. before getting on the road and still Alex hadn't called. I wasn't concerned. I'd just find a way to call him from my parents' house that evening. That had been the plan from the beginning anyway.

Keeping my left hand on the steering wheel, as I usually did when I drove, I had the opportunity to stare at the ring all the way from Milledgeville to Augusta. The way the kitchen lights made it shine and twinkle was nothing compared to what the sunlight did. It was blinding and obviously expensive. I really didn't know how I was going to explain it to my parents, but I wasn't taking it off.

166

I was barely in the back door of the house when my father came barreling in waving what appeared to be a folded letter in his hand. Startled, I dropped my duffle bag and purse and threw up my hands.

"What is the meaning of this?" He demanded to know in a heavily raised voice while still flinging the letter all about.

My mother chased after him, yelling at an equal pitch. "Chan," that was my father's nickname, "Enough already! I'm sure it's some sort of mistake."

I wasn't used to them being heated in this way and was taken aback, but still responded sweetly. "What are y'all talking about?"

"The results of your pregnancy test from the clinic at your college! That's what we're talking about!" My father had not bothered to lower his voice one bit. In fact, he seemed to be growing more enraged by the word. He balled up the letter and threw it at me.

My blood drained and I felt faint and nauseous all at once. This was not how they were supposed to find out. The letter had not had the weight to carry far enough to hit me and fell at my feet.

"Goddammit! I thought they said you were smart!" He glared at me. "Smart my ass!"

My mother tried to get between us, but he threw out a hand blocked her. "Get out of my way, Gretchen!"

He circled me and I whirled as he went around, keeping my face to him. "I let you go away to school and this is what you get yourself into. Who's the father?!!"

Tears were coming and I tried to hold them back, but there was no stopping them. My father had never gone on the attack at me like this, ever. In fact, no one had ever spoken to me like this in my entire life.

"Excuse me? You *let* me go away to school? I got into Oxford and Columbia, but you only *let* me go to Milledgeville!" I cried through my defense. "And it's a fine time for you to suddenly take an interest in my life!"

"An interest? I pay for your life!" As we crossed the threshold from the back of the house into the foyer, he took a swipe at the table that lined the wall with his arm and knocked everything including the lamp and framed family photographs to the floor, shattering it all.

I screamed and jumped back to get out of the way of flying shards of glass and ceramic.

"Who is the father?!" He screamed at the top of his lungs.

I was trembling at that point and couldn't speak.

He quickly added. "It doesn't matter." His voice settled to a stern bite, kind of a growl. "You'll get an abortion."

At that I found my voice again, perhaps it was motherly instinct coming out already. "I will not!" I clutched both arms to my stomach as I screamed back at him.

"She will do no such thing!" My mother added with all seriousness. "That is against God."

"Gretchen, what the fuck?"

Her mouth fell open, equally shocked at the way he'd just spoken to her.

"Where was God when she was on her back? Out of wedlock!" Again, he screamed loud enough for the neighbors three doors down to hear.

I went into full blown hysterics. "I won't do it! I won't do it! I won't!"

He gestured at my attire with a flippant hand. "Look at you, trying to hide it! If you're so damn determined to have it, why are you hiding it?"

My mother grabbed at him. "Stop it, Chandler!"

He slung her off and stalked after me farther toward the front door. It was as if he was the lion and I was the prey. I'd never seen him so mad and I'd never been so terrified.

I continued to back up, the wooden front door was open, but the glass one was closed. I didn't exactly back into it as much as I backed through the glass door.

I remember bits and pieces of glass and blood and being able to see the very spot where it had all begun with the gunshot all those months before, but I was on the front porch this time.

My mother was screaming and my father yelled at her, but it wasn't the same as before. "Call 911!"

"Oh, Anna-Cat, I'm so sorry." He was on his knees tugging at my leg.

I had a very faraway feeling and remember looking at my arm, but it was like looking at someone else's. I had enough wherewithal to realize I was crying and there was blood all over my hands, so much blood I could not see my ring anymore.

"Jesus, Gretchen, bring me a belt or give me your panty hose. Hold on Anna-Cat."

There was a squeezing sensation all through my abdomen. I bolted upright and clutched my stomach. "Oh my God, no!"

"Just breathe, Anna."

My father never called me Anna, but he channeled Alex. I bit my lip, shut my eyes as tight as I could and pictured Alex. I prayed through the pain and didn't stop praying, begging God not to take our baby. I prayed and begged God repeatedly until I passed out.

PART TWO

Chapter 17

Alex...

I fell asleep sometime in the wee hours of Sunday morning. I'd had the good sense to crawl onto the bed at some point as I recounted my time with Anna and those memories faded into dreams. When I awoke shortly after noon I did so with a jolt. I sprang bolt upright in the hotel bed with a fever to find her right that moment. I was owed an explanation and, after all these years, I was going to have one.

With single minded determination, I called the front desk and had them help me arrange a rental car. I hurriedly showered, shaved the beard and trimmed my hair. I did away with all that made me look like I'd stepped out of a history book. It might have been twelve years later and I might have had the beginning of some crow's feet around the corners of my eyes and more than one or two gray hairs at my temples, but I saw a guy in the mirror that Anna Catherine Calloway would recognize.

By the time I'd packed and straightened the room for housekeeping, the front desk called. They had a car waiting on me.

Last night I'd planned on going to find the Georgia Tech baseball stadium and taking in Auggie's game, but the storm had raged all night and it was still raining this morning. I was confident the games had been cancelled, but that only fueled my determination. I would see my son again and I would get to the bottom of the question that had plagued me. I would find out once and for all why things ended with Anna. I knew the reason her father gave when he threatened to call the cops on me for trespassing on his property, but the biggest regret of my life had been that I believed him.

I didn't know where to find Anna-Cat and Auggie, but I figured I'd start by going back to where it had all begun. Pulling out of the driveway in front of the St. Regis, I pointed the Corvette the hotel concierge had so graciously picked out for me in the direction of Augusta, Georgia. I'd had the good sense to have the hotel give me a map with directions to Augusta and I figured once I got closer, things might start to look familiar. I remembered the name of the street her parents lived on and I could see that house in my mind as well as I could see my own parents' homes.

Almost three hours later, and to my amazement, I found the Calloway home. It was just as I'd remembered it. White, tall columns across a broad porch that spanned the façade of the house, it was a picture right out of some magazine like <u>Southern Living</u> and every inch of that picture held another memory of Anna. I took it all in as I pressed the bell.

Cars passed on the street and wind blew through the magnolia trees in the yard, those noises were a distraction as I waited, praying for the sound of footsteps coming to the door. I pressed the bell twice more before my ears were rewarded by the sound of someone approaching. The steps were in tune with the beating of my heart and I barely heard them above it pounding in my chest. I actually felt my knees shake as I allowed myself to imagine the possibility of laying eyes on Anna-Cat, my Anna, when the door opened.

To my dismay, the door opened and I found myself looking in the eyes that undoubtedly belonged to her mother. They were the same color and shape and, in that moment, they were as full of Southern hospitality.

"May I help you?" The look of hospitality faded to sheer wonder. It was the look when people see me and try to figure out from where they know me.

I stopped her with a word before she rang her mind completely trying to place me. "Hi. I'm sorry to bother you, but I'm looking for Anna-Cat Calloway."

"Shit fire and save the matches!" The woman's mouth fell open. Her eyes grew as big as saucers and she fanned herself profusely.

"Ma'am?" I questioned. "Excuse me?"

"You're him." It wasn't so much as a question as it was a flabbergasted statement. "The resemblance is..." She looked me up and down and quickly sought to straighten her face and reign in the words that were seeping from her brain straight out of her mouth. She threw both hands over her mouth, but the word, "uncanny," slipped out despite her efforts.

"You know, I thought so, too." I smiled widely with a cheeky edge.

Her face fell and she answered my initial request. "She's not here," the woman said abruptly. With no further explanation, she tried to get back through the door.

"Wait!" I reached to catch the door before she could get through it. "Hold on. Please. I need to find her."

Shocked at my forwardness, she demanded, "Let go!"

"Please," I begged again.

Then she gave me an ear-full of built up grievances, "How dare you show your face here! Honestly, after all these years, now you want to see her? Where were you when she found out she was pregnant? Where were you when she was bed ridden for six months and when she had to have him cut out of her?"

My mouth fell open as Mrs. Calloway berated me. She could have just said C-section and I would have gotten the idea.

"Where were you when she nearly lost him time and again? When she fought to keep him? When she gave up everything she'd ever dreamed of being for him? Were you off getting someone else's young daughter knocked up?"

172

She finished with a scream that rang my ears and sent me stumbling back a step, "WHERE WERE YOU THEN?!!!"

Anna's mother snatched the door away as she'd finished, but despite the tears that were building in my eyes and the wrenching in my gut over the picture she was painting of what Anna had gone through to have Auggie, I snapped to and jumped to shove my foot between the door and the jam.

"Please wait," I pleaded, grabbing the door knob on my side.

She gritted her teeth and I saw another glimpse of Anna. Their eyes blazed the same way when they were mad. "I'll scream for my husband!" she threatened.

"You do that, but this time I'll not be run off so easily!"

"What?" Again, she was taken aback, but glared at me all the same and pulled at the door.

I held firm to the knob with one hand and swiped the other across my eyes. "That's right," I added, "I didn't just leave her. I was here every day for three weeks in December 1995. Every day," I emphasized. "I came even after your husband threatened to call the cops."

She loosened her grip a little and her eyes softened, but she hadn't let go of the door yet.

With the hand I'd used to wipe my eyes, I fished in my pocket for my wallet. I couldn't open it with one hand so I had to let go of the knob.

"You got her pregnant and..."

"Apparently, I did, but..." I managed to flip my wallet open with one hand, but there was no way I could open the little pocket without both hands. I glanced at the button and back to the door. I risked it and loosened my grip, testing her. "I didn't give up until he gave back," I paused to let go of the door, trusting her to give me a chance and she did.

173

"Until he gave back this," I opened the little pocket on the wallet where I'd carried the ring since the day her father gave it back.

"I'd parked in the street, expecting her to show up on Christmas Day. That's when he walked out to my car, tapped on the window and gave this back to me. It's not a traditional engagement ring, but it was a promise and it bound me to her." I held the circular, diamond encrusted band in my open palm for her mother to see. "I didn't leave her. She left me."

Mrs. Calloway nudged the door and it opened wider. Her eyes filled and she quickly wiped each eye, trying desperately to keep me from seeing that I'd gotten to her.

"He said she didn't ever want to see me again. He wouldn't tell me where she was. On Christmas Day of 1995, your husband forced me to take back the ring I'd given her. When I resisted, he told me I'd take it from his hand or I could pick it up off of the street. That wasn't my first encounter with him, but it was the first time he'd had what I considered to be definitive proof that Anna didn't want to see me again."

There was no stopping her tears. They fell down her face and she shook her head, muttering, "Christ, Chan, what did you do?" She took a few ragged breaths and stepped from behind the few inches of the door that had remained covering her. "Anna came home for a visit. We found out she was pregnant. That hadn't been a part of our plan for her and it was a big blow for us. Anna and her father fought. Of course, it wasn't physical. He'd never lay a hand on her, but there was an accident and Anna got hurt."

Mrs. Calloway sniffled. "It was really bad. She almost lost the baby. She was in the hospital for a while and, when they let her come home, she was placed on bedrest for the remainder of her pregnancy."

Mrs. Calloway reached for the ring and I didn't object. She picked it up and studied it as she continued,

"She had me search the hospital high and low for it before we left there. She was convinced someone stole it and I guess they did." She continued to shake her head, appearing completely disgusted.

I assured Anna's mother, "I didn't know she was pregnant."

She handed the ring back to me. "I think she tried to call you when she got home, but I know her father made that impossible for her as well. He took the phone out of her room so she wouldn't be disturbed and by the time she'd had the baby and was on her feet again, she couldn't get in touch with you."

Mrs. Calloway, hung her head. "He even told her that you would have come for her if you wanted her."

I was outraged. "I did come for her!" All this time I'd thought she broke it off with me and what must she have thought of me?

"A thousand times I wished I could take away her heartbreak..." Mrs. Calloway seemed again to be speaking her thoughts, but they weren't really directed at me or in response to my statement. She took another swipe at her eyes. Her mascara was starting to run, but her attempts to straighten her face were fruitless. She only dragged the black smears outward toward her temples. Although I noticed this about Mrs. Calloway's appearance, it was little distraction to the tailspin my head was in.

"Mrs. Calloway," I said, but she was still lost in her own thoughts.

"I just can't believe it..." she trailed off again as I said her name for the second time.

"Mrs. Calloway, I would really like it if you would tell me where Anna, I mean, where I could find Anna-Cat," I paused and cleared my throat, having verbally started to stumble over the thought that kept running around in my mind and I started to explain further. "I met my son for the first-time last night."

Mrs. Calloway bit her bottom lip, her top left two teeth over the same side of her lower lip. I never thought an expression like that would be hereditary, but I remember Anna making the exact same face on a number of occasions. Mrs. Calloway loosened her bite and stepped to the side. "I guess you ought to come in off the porch."

My mind jumped to conclusions that I couldn't believe. Could she really have been right where I first met her all along? The answer was revealed as soon as I crossed the threshold of the front door.

"Anna-Cat lives in Wrens now," her mother began to explain as she moved around me to escort me toward the living room. "It's a little town just South of here."

My eyes hit the staircase, flicked to the top and right back down to the place on the floor at my feet. For a moment, I envisioned that first night. The crack of the thunder, the feel of the gun in my hand and the blood on the floor, I was there again. I rung out my hands and snapped back to reality.

Although some things in the foyer were exactly as I remembered them, there were new additions. I stopped for one of the additions, a large framed photo of Anna and Auggie. It was a black and white and he appeared to be about two years old. They were on the dock of a lake and she was throwing him in the air and catching him. The photograph was taken from a distance, but the look of joy on his face was unmistakable.

I ran my hand over their figures and blinked back tears of my own. Looking at the picture both broke my heart and warmed it at the same time. I should have been there with them, but they were happy. I wasn't in their lives, but they looked happy and I was glad for them.

There were more photos along the wall leading through the foyer and down the hall. There were more up the wall of the staircase. I followed Mrs. Calloway into the living room and she offered me a seat on the couch. Next to the couch, on an end table, there was another set of photos. Everywhere I looked there were picture of Anna and Auggie. Each one caught my eye and then there was one in particular that stirred another emotion in me.

Mrs. Calloway had started to say something, but I didn't really hear her. "He taught Auggie to throw." I said it again, slower, through my gritted teeth, emphasizing the first word, "*He* taught *my* son to throw a ball."

Seeing the photo of Mr. Calloway in a matching baseball uniform with Auggie, parallel to one another with him clearly demonstrating how to throw, made my blood boil. I picked up the frame from the table and held it out to Mrs. Calloway.

"With his lies and trickery, that man stole my son and stole all of our lives." I wasn't sure if I came off accusatory or confused because I was both.

She started to speak, but I stood. "I don't want to hear it!" I took a couple of quick breaths, trying to calm myself as she got back to her feet. A rage was building in me like I'd never felt before, not even during the ordeal of the lawsuit and the theft or when my parents divorced. I'd never been so angry before in my entire life.

"I just want to find...I want to find my family!"

"I know, but..."

"But nothing. Can you even begin to imagine what losing her did to me? I've never been the same and, now, to find out I have a twelve-year-old son? Do you know what it's like to miss out on your child's life?" I caught myself as their family history, the story of Anna's brother, rushed through my mind.

Mrs. Calloway stood there, mouth gaped open as I took a moment.

"I'm sorry. Of course, you can. Anna told me about your son." I ran my hands through my hair, trying to calm down. It hardly helped. "Please. Just tell me where I can find them."

She didn't give me the answer I wanted straight away, but she began again with what she'd started telling me before I exploded. "My husband is dying."

She gestured toward the couch again, but I held my spot, keeping my feet planted and my arms folded across my chest.

177

"He's in the final stages of prostate cancer. It's been difficult." She forced a smile, the kind that begs sympathy, but I had none.

Mrs. Calloway continued and I gave her the respect of listening. "Anna spends the night with him on the weekends. For a long time, they didn't get along."

"I can imagine," I sighed, thinking about zombie parents.

"Anyway, Anna always made sure Auggie had us as grandparents, but things were tense with her. She's only just made up with her father..."

"Because he's dying..." I said curtly.

She cocked a daring eye at me. "Like I was saying, they've just made up and he's only got days left so..."

"Are you asking me to wait to see them?" I was astonished.

"You said yourself you didn't even know Auggie existed until last night so what's a few more days?"

"And after that there's the funeral and then the period of grieving and well sometime after the tenth of never might be a good time for you?" If I sounded like a complete smart ass, it was because I meant to.

"That's not fair."

"Fair?" I plopped down on the couch. "Fair? There's nothing fair about this. My parents always told me life ain't fair and, let me assure you, they were right. There is nothing about this situation that's fair at all and we have no one but your husband to thank for that."

"In all fairness, you got our nineteen-year-old daughter pregnant."

"In all fairness," I laughed, "you didn't even know she existed after her brother died. She told me that, you know. She said she practically raised herself so her one shot at happiness, and let me assure you, we were happy together, was stolen from her. It was stolen by her father. What kind of parent does something like that?"

I could tell by the look on her face that I'd dealt her a blow with the comment about her son and how Anna felt

178

about them. She tried to regain footing. "I can't do anything to change that..."

"You're right, but by God, with or without your help, I will do my best to fix this."

Mrs. Calloway then dealt a blow of her own. "You assume she would want this fixed. She's not a girl anymore and I doubt she will be starstruck over you this time."

I wasn't one to come off superior because of my status and I made a rule never to brag about the clout that came with star power. This time, I made an exception to the rule. I raised my chin and looked down my nose and challenged Anna's mother. "Then you, Mrs. Calloway, you underestimate my charms."

I gave a delivery that was cold, deliberate and detached, but fearing her mother was right. I hadn't thought any of this through, but before she could smell my insecurities, I popped off another declaration. "Auggie is my son and that's what this is about!"

"Is it? If it's all about your son, then you need to take a moment and think about what your sudden appearance and any revelation you plan on making will do to him. Often, being a parent means thinking beyond yourself."

I left there with little more information than what town she lived in and I could only assume it was in Georgia.

"Fuck!" I beat my head on the steering wheel and dropped two more F-bombs.

Chapter 18

Anna-Cat...

I peeled myself out of the arm chair in my living room where I'd first sat down while on the phone with Auggie. I'd been certain I was going to pass out from exhaustion, but I hadn't. I'd sat there, riding down memory lane, until the bird in my grandmother's old coocoo clock busted through his door and alerted me to the hour.

"Shhhhhhitttt!" I huffed, getting to my feet.

It wasn't the first time the bird had done its job, but it was the first time I'd taken notice. It had been three hours since my legs had first given way. Between the lack of energy and the shock, it hadn't taken much for me to drop and stay there. Now I had to get moving. I had to get up, get a shower and be at Chalker Field to pick up Auggie in about thirty minutes. I had to put all thoughts of Alex Allen out of my head and get myself looking like I wasn't functioning on two hours of sleep in the last twenty-four hours. I also had to prepare myself for further details of Auggie's encounter with Alex.

Lathering up my hair for a quick wash, it occurred to me that the secret of Auggie's parentage was safe with him. Auggie is nothing if not an open book. He would have said something had he had the slightest suspicion. Had I not been dead on my feet, it would have occurred to me sooner that Auggie wasn't the only one I should worry about. I'd given up years ago on Alex ever finding out about Auggie. All of my attempts to contact him back when I was pregnant and for a year after I had Auggie had been fruitless. The cherry on top was the pictures of Alex in all the tabloids basically having sex with the actress from the movie he'd been filming in Canada. While I was back home with my father in my ear, he was screwing around.

I stopped scrubbing the shampoo into my hair and listened to my father's voice in my head. To this day, I could still hear him. "If he wanted to find you, he knows where to look." My father told me that every time I brought up the subject of Alex until I finally gave up.

I shook off the voice in my head and rinsed the soap out of my hair. I wondered if Alex ever thought of me. I had a daily reminder of him, but what did he have. What we had was still real to me, but I always wondered if it was ever real for him.

No sooner had I pulled back the shower curtain did I hear the phone ring. Slipping and sliding with wet feet all over the tile and hardwoods, I sprinted back to the living room where I'd left the phone. Ever since my father's last diagnosis, I'd jumped and ran at every ring, but whenever Auggie was away on tournaments, at sleepovers or just out of my sight in general I tended to jump and run over any ring of the phone.

"Anna-Cat, it's Mom." Of course, I recognized my own mother's voice, but she never failed to identify herself as if I would never guess.

"Is Dad okay?" I blurted out. "Did the hospital call?"

"Yes, he's fine. I didn't mean to scare you."

I let out a breath of relief.

My mother then got to the purpose of her call. "I just had a visitor that might be headed your way."

"Really?" I couldn't imagine who would warrant what came off as a warning call from my mother. "Who?"

"Auggie's father."

She didn't say his name. My mother had never said his name to me. The few times we'd ever broached the subject, she referred to him as "That man." Not in ten years had we mentioned that Auggie even had a father. They kind of treated Auggie like the second coming in more ways than one.

"Alex was at your house?" I rubbed my weary eyes. "He knows??"

"He knows," my mother confirmed.

One meeting with Auggie and he figured it out. "Figures."

I didn't know what else to say. I didn't know what to think or feel in that moment. I certainly didn't know what to do.

"I didn't tell him where you live. I mean, I told him you were in Wrens, but…"

A calm came over me. "It's okay," I assured my mother. "If he shows up, I'll figure it out."

"Anna-Cat, there's something I need to tell you, but I don't want to tell you over the phone."

"What is it?"

"Can you come here?"

"Mom, Auggie's due back any minute and I have to pick him up. And, I'm so tired there's no way I could drive back to Augusta right now. Just tell me."

"Not over the phone. I'll come to you." I think she was on her way to hanging up, but added, "Promise me you won't open the door for anyone until I've had a chance to speak with you."

Very perplexed, I replied, "I guess."

I hung up the phone and returned to the bathroom. I dried my hair, studying myself in the mirror and contemplating the thought of seeing Alex Allen in person. I'd gained about fifteen pounds over the years. Having Auggie gave me curves that I'd never shed. My hair was a little darker now. With my dad being sick, I hadn't been able to get out in the sun as I normally did so my hair had no natural highlights and I was pale. I didn't really look like the girl I'd been back then. It had been so long and so much had changed, but one thing hadn't. That one thing didn't matter so much. What mattered was how I was going to explain to Auggie.

Auggie wasn't stupid. By ten years old the kids at school had already started cluing one another in on the birds and the bees. He knew he wasn't delivered by the stork and he knew I didn't get him at the baby store, which is what I told him when he was small. He also knew he wasn't the second coming.

Auggie had asked about his father a few times over the years. He wanted to know why his father didn't come out to play baseball with him like the other dads. After that question, my father filled in. I didn't like my father being so involved, but I allowed it for Auggie's sake.

He asked about his father once in front of my mother and she replied with the most endearing thing she'd ever said about me. She told him, "You have a mother that is so amazing that God decided you didn't need a father."

It was sweet, but it was a lie. Everybody needs a father, especially a boy.

"Hey, Baby," I leaned over and moved my purse out of the passenger seat as I greeted Auggie.

He lifted the seat up and threw his equipment and duffle bag in the backseat. "Hey, Mom!"

I missed the days when he called me "Mommy." It was rare when I let him go anywhere without me beyond one night so this trip to Atlanta had been unusual in more ways than one. I knew he wasn't a baby, but he would always be my baby and I'd missed him to the point of tears at times last night while I couldn't get comfortable and sleep in the guest chair in Dad's room.

As soon as he was settled, I started to pull out of the parking lot around the baseball field.

"Wait!" Auggie said abruptly. He quickly turned and started digging in his stuff in the back. "Gimme a minute. I have something for you."

Finding what he was in search of, Auggie got back in his seat and put his seatbelt back on before handing me a folded piece of paper. "I hope you like it."

With the car still in park, I took the note and braced myself before opening it.

I wasn't going fast enough for Auggie. "Come on!" he demanded. "Your favorite actor wrote you a personal note. Don't you want to know what it says?"

I looked at my baby, sitting in the front seat and every bit as tall as I was. That kid never failed to amaze me. "It doesn't matter what it says. What matters to me is that you went to the trouble of getting it for me. How did you do that anyway?"

Auggie blushed and unintentionally deflected my question. "Read the note!"

I unfolded the piece of paper. It was definitely Alex's handwriting. I remembered his tiny little block style lettering. "You sure have a good-looking son. I'm a fan of any woman who can raise a boy that's this well-mannered. He is a real credit to you and I couldn't be prouder to have met him. – Alex Allen."

Holy shit! Alex definitely knew. The first line of the note gave it away. Auggie looked just like him and that one sentence was his way of letting me know he knew. My mother warned me, but I didn't know what to do with that information then. I didn't know what to do with it now, but I put the car in drive and Auggie and I headed home.

"Mom, he was really nice," Auggie gushed as I kept my crisis internal. "You would really like him."

It was a struggle, but I kept my response demure. "I'm sure I would."

I white knuckled the steering wheel, wondering how I was going to explain to Auggie that once upon a time I'd done more than like Alex Allen. I'd loved him to the point that Auggie was a product of it.

Any notion I had that I would catch some shut-eye before the summit with my mother was dashed as I pulled onto our street. We lived five minutes from Chalker Field and it had been only thirty minutes before that when I spoke with my mother, but it appeared she'd made it from the hill section to what she called "the middle of nowhere" in record time. There were two other black Cadillac's in Wrens that looked just like the one pulling in at my house, but one belonged to the locally known drug dealer and the other belonged to the funeral home and neither of them tended to darken my door. There was never any doubt, it

184

was none other than my mother. Every time I thought about her having the same taste in vehicles as a part-time pimp and full-time pusher, I got a laugh.

"What's Grandma doing here?" Auggie was quick to ask as he noticed her car not long after I did.

I made light of the question and replied dismissively. "She said she wanted to talk to me."

"Must really be something. I can't remember the last time she drove all the way out here for something other than one of my ball games and, even then, Papa drove her."

We came to a rolling stop in the driveway behind my mother. I turned off the engine and casually moved my elbow to the arm rest on the inside of my car door. I laid my face in my palm and took a moment to try to steady my wits. Auggie didn't need a moment. He bounced out of the car, forgetting to grab his luggage and baseball gear. This time I didn't bother calling him back and issuing a reminder. I let him go as I became lost in a memory that flashed quickly before my mind's eye.

This time the memory was little more than the feel of my cheek against the curve of Alex's neck. I breathed in deeply, inhaling the memory of his cologne, sandalwood and leather. I leaned in and easily felt his stubble on my face. For the first time in a long time, I wanted to cry over him.

In all of these years, a day had not passed that I didn't think of Alex. It never took much to send the thought of him to the forefront of my mind. A smell, a commercial for golf, the trailer of a new movie of his or just one glance at Auggie who bore a striking resemblance to him, it really took no effort at all to think of him. Today he was everywhere and not here at all. I missed him every day and from what my mother had told me on the phone seeing him in person again was not just a possibility, it was imminent.

I lifted my eyes from my daydream and noticed my mother. She was standing beside me, hands on her hips, staring me down with impatience. Her unspoken words were louder than any screams. She shot daggers demanding I get out of the car as Auggie passed her. He gave her a peck on the cheek and a "Hello, Gramma," but she didn't flinch.

I'd barely cracked the door of my car when she said the obvious, "We have to talk."

Luckily, Auggie was about as tired as I was. He took my mother's cues of wanting to speak to me alone and he happily went to his room to take a nap, but not before telling her who he met last night.

"Well, that explains that," she said, unamused.

Auggie rolled his eyes and left the room. He had a special bond with my father, but his relationship with my mother had always been a bit strained. I always figured she just didn't know what to do with little boys. I remembered her being pretty much the same, standoffish, with my brother.

With Auggie safely out of ear shot, my mother began.

I'd only thought my world was turning upside down, but now I insisted that my mother confirm it. "You mean to tell me, Alex didn't leave me? He came back for me and y'all told him I didn't want him?"

"No, Anna-Cat, no. Your father..."

"Dad did this? He put me in the hospital and almost caused me to lose my child and then he...he..." I gasped for air, unable to repeat the horror that had been done to me, to Auggie.

"Anna-Catherine," she said my name in that way that she did when she was issuing me a warning.

I was no child for her to warn about anything. What punishment could she dole out at this point?

"How dare you warn me? You've already done your worst, you or Dad, you stole my life." I drew in a sharp breath, but kept my words low as not to bring Auggie out running to see what was the matter. "You stole Auggie's life!"

My mother fell apart at that point. "I didn't know. I swear." Then she did the most unexpected thing. My mother grabbed me and threw her arms around me. "I've loved you all of your life, more than anything or anyone I've ever loved and it killed me to see your heartbroken. I promise, my darling." She hadn't called me that since I was small. "I would have taken the hurt for you a million times over."

She repeated herself as I started to cry with her. "I had no idea that your father had sent him away. No idea, I swear."

My mother stroked my hair as I cried. I cried for Auggie more than myself.

I'd always known what I had with Alex was as real for him as much as it had been for me so I never understood why he never came to find me. Now that I knew, I wasn't just hurt for me and Auggie, I was furious. I was furious with my father and it didn't take me long to communicate that to my mother.

"How dare he!" I said through gritted teeth as I pulled away from my mother, tears fresh on my face.

"There's nothing you can do about it now, Anna-Cat. You have to forgive him." She eluded to my father's health. I knew as well as she did, he only had days left.

"Isn't there?" I sniffled and wiped my eyes. "You all but said yourself, the main reason you told me now and didn't wait until he was gone because you were afraid Alex would get to me first." I paused only to think for a second before continuing, "I need you to take us to the hospital. We need to go now."

"Why?" She twisted her head, cocking it with confusion.

"So that my father can apologize to Auggie and tell him what he did."

"You can't be serious."

"I am and it's the least he can do for Auggie." I went on to explain, "I don't know if I will ever forgive him for what he's done to my child, but he's going to give back what he's taken. He's going to be the one to tell Auggie what he did even if it's the last thing he ever does. He's going to tell

187

Auggie who his father is and that it wasn't Alex's fault. He's going to make sure Auggie knows Alex never abandoned us."

It wasn't without further coaxing and insistence, but my mother finally agreed to my demands. She drove us to the hospital to see him. Once there, I asked Mama to wait with Auggie while I went in to see Dad.

"Hi," I greeted him softly. He was groggy and the lights in his room were dim, but he knew it was me.

"Hey." He held out his hand to me and I went to him.

"We've already talked about how things are for you," I reminded him.

He nodded. He was fading. In the last few days the cancer had spread from his prostate to his lungs. It was the cancer in his lungs that had sped up his progress and would ultimately finish him. He'd been placed on oxygen and had tubes in his nose to help him breathe, but last night was rough. The slow suffocation had begun. He looked so pitiful that it took effort on my part to remember that I was angry with him.

"Is there something you want to tell me and Auggie before you go?" I asked him.

All the way to Augusta I'd rehearsed this conversation in my head. I'd imagined him as his old self, not the skeleton in this hospital bed.

"I love you," he replied.

"I know," I gently patted his hand in mine, his hand that didn't have the IV in it, "but that's not it. Is there something you did to Auggie and to me, that you want to get off your chest? Something about Auggie's father?"

His eyes didn't normally look too big for his face, but now the thin skin of his face and his drastic weight loss, made them seem as big as saucers as they rolled around while he contemplated what I wanted him to admit. It finally came to him and his breathing became more labored. He knew I knew and he looked away.

188

"I think you need to tell Auggie what you did. I think it would be best for both of you if it came from you."

Dad fumbled with his breathing tube, distracting himself from having to look me in the eye. "I don't want him to remember me like this."

"But you don't want me to tell him what you did and him to remember you as the villain that stole his father from him, do you?"

If he could have hung his head while lying in the hospital bed, he would have.

I'd entered the room expecting a fight, expecting to find my father as I'd left him that morning, on a downhill slide, but not at the bottom of the hill. I expected to relieve all the frustrations that had built as the day went on, the frustrations that had been building for years. My expectations weren't met and the opportunity to take my frustrations out on my father vanished and they did so without a gripe in my head.

Fighting was something my father had done well with me, but there was no fight to be had. All fight was gone from him and to my joy, and distress, he agreed to tell Auggie everything. It took little coaxing at all on my part.

"Thank you, Daddy," I said as softly as the light that barely shown in the room.

I hadn't called him Daddy in as many years as it had been since my mother called me her darling. A long, long time ago my father had been a great man in my eyes. He was once a lion and I was just a little lamb. Now I was the lamb again.

"Of course," and then my father said something he'd never said to me before, something I didn't think he was capable of saying, let alone being. He said, "I'm sorry."

My mother stayed behind at the hospital to be with my father and Auggie and I borrowed her car to go home. Knowing that time was near for my father, I didn't drive us back to Wrens. I drove us to my parents' house. The drive between University Hospital in downtown Augusta and their house in the hill section was only about ten minutes.

Auggie hadn't said anything since he'd left the room with my father, but that wasn't especially unusual. Auggie was no Chatty-Cathy even on a good day. He was for the most part a quiet kid, unless he wanted something and then, like most kids, he turned on the charm. He tended to tell me everything, but in his own time. I trusted him to be that way now. Although I was dying to know what my father said to him and what he thought, I didn't press him. I let him mull things over and process.

I had my back turned, locking the back door behind us when Auggie started to come around.

"Granddaddy said that sometimes parents make decisions for their children based on what they think is best for the children." Auggie's speech pattern broke a few times between words as he struggled to get his thoughts out. "He said he made a decision for you that he thought was right at the time, but he realized now that it wasn't his decision to make."

He paused before going on and I waited patiently, guarding myself to keep him from seeing that my heart was aching for him.

"Granddaddy said that God had taken his son from him a long time ago and he'd hated God for a very long time. He said he understood now that he'd taken me from my father and..." Auggie's voice cracked as he started to cry.

"Auggie," I pulled the boy who was as big as I was, the boy who would always be my baby into my arms as he started to sob.

"He said it wasn't your fault that I didn't have a dad." Auggie cried harder. "I never missed not having a dad because I had him, because I had Granddaddy and now..."

I tried to tell Auggie that it was going to be alright, but I knew I wasn't convincing. I started to cry, too. We hadn't completely shielded Auggie from my father's declining health, but none of us understood that the disease would progress as fast as it had, so today Auggie got two shocks.

190

It took a while, but Auggie told me how my father told him the whole story. My father told him how he'd made Alex believe that I didn't love him anymore and he even told Auggie how awful my pregnancy was and how I struggled to keep him. He told Auggie what a wonderful mother I was. He heaped on praises of how amazing I was that I was able to balance finishing college and going to medical school despite having a baby at such a young age and doing it all by myself.

"Auggie, I didn't do it by myself," I corrected him. "I had you and my grandmother."

"Mama, it looked like it hurt him to talk and I told him he didn't have to tell me all of this, but he said he owed it to me to be honest. He said telling the truth was the most important thing in life and I should always remember that."

I took his face in my hands, gently forcing him to look in my eyes. "Auggie, you inspired all of us to be the best we could be and you inspired me to not let anything stop me. I had to take care of you because for the most part, it was just me and you. I've always been so lucky to have you."

"Mama, is Alex Allen really my Dad?" He immediately followed with a second question, the one I dreaded most. "And why didn't you tell me?"

"Yes, Alex is your father and I didn't tell you because the whole story seems so far-fetched. I'm just me, a girl from Augusta, and he's..." I shrugged off the ending of the sentence.

"He's really nice and..." Auggie searched for a word and ultimately added, "famous, but I'd rather have Granddaddy. I don't want Granddaddy to die."

Again, Auggie started to cry and I couldn't help myself either. I dug deep to keep from full on sobbing with him and managed to scrape by with just a few tears.

"Aww, Auggie, I don't want Granddaddy to die either, but the issue of Alex is a separate subject. It's not one or the other."

Auggie smiled sweetly through his tears. He seemed to understand.

"You know, I named you after both of them and my brother too."

Auggie's eyes lit up.

"His full name is Alex August Allen and you are August Chandler Calloway."

"I thought you just named me that because you liked that month best."

"Nope, baby." I said, pulling him close and stroking his hair. "You look just like him."

"You still love him, don't you?" He was a perceptive child, a perceptive child with a square jaw line, green eyes and sandy blond hair like his father.

"I've always loved him. He gave me you and you are the best thing that ever happened to me."

Chapter 19

Alex…

"Ashley, hey. Are you busy?" It seemed like a stupid question considering I could hear the wail of my niece through the phone.

"Trying to survive teething," my sister answered with an air of desperation. "Kids," she sighed heavily, "you should try having one."

"That's actually why I'm calling." I bit the inside of my lip and took a seat on the side of the bed.

When I left the Calloway house, I found myself aimlessly cruising down Walton Way in Augusta until I came to the Partridge Hotel. I figured I needed a place to stay, a base camp, as I searched for Anna and Auggie. I pulled in and rented the penthouse suite. Then, I started tapping my resources. I called my sister first. Ashley was always the first person I called when I needed a confidant or advice. Now, I needed both.

Addie, my sister's seven-month-old daughter let out another ear-piercing scream and completely derailed her mother's train of thought. "What?"

"You are not going to believe this," I prefaced and then laid it on her. "I have a kid."

"You what?" There was movement on Ashley's end, swift steps, swishing through the line and Addie's screams were still going strong, but more distant. "Shhh…Mommy will be right back."

"Excuse me? What are you doing?"

"I put her down and now I'm hiding in the pantry," Ashley explained in a whisper before redirecting the subject. "Did you just tell me you had a kid? Did I hear that right?"

"Yes."

"What have you done?" I heard what sounded like a slap.

"It's not what I've done. It's what I did. And did you just slap your forehead or something?"

"Shut up! Don't try to change the subject."

"I'm not. I called to..."

Ashley spoke over me, "I didn't realize you were seeing anyone in particular."

"That's the thing. I haven't seen anyone in particular in over almost thirteen years."

"What's that supposed to mean?"

In a matter of about fifteen minutes, I'd told Ashley the whole story. I started with my encounter with my little doppelganger last night to my hunt for him and his mother and my trip to his grandmother's house earlier. Ashley already knew my history with Anna and it was Ashley's couch I lived on for almost a year while I tried to get over Anna, so I didn't have to give her the back story on that. She also knew as much as I did about how things ended.

Between her questions, Ashley kept saying, "Oh my God."

"Yeah, it's pretty unbelievable, huh?"

"Oh my God," Ashley gasped again. "I liked her. How could she keep this from you?"

"I don't think..."

"You had a right to know..."

"Ashley, she would never..."

We continued to interrupt and cut one another off. That was pretty typical of us and the way we bantered back and forth.

"Apparently, she did," Ashley was quick to point out and she was pissed. "You didn't know about him until last night and she wasn't the one that told you."

I didn't say anything.

"Dear, Lord, you still love her!"

Ashley's accusation had been spot-on so there was nothing for me to say, not that she gave me time to reply.

"She broke your heart and didn't even do it to your face. She sent her father to do it and..."

I then reiterated to my sister what Anna's mother had told me about the fight she had with her father when she told them and the accident.

"She couldn't get in touch with you and tell you after she got better?"

"It's not like I have a home phone number listed in the book and do you know how many calls my agents get per day from women demanding to reach me because I'm the father of their child? Did you know I've even been sued for paternity three times by women I've never even met? I pay a lot of people to protect me from being bothered with such things and I don't tell you everything."

"So, you're saying she couldn't reach you even if she tried."

"It took you four days to get in touch with me when Dad had his heart attack and you've got all of my numbers and your names are on the list, but they still didn't let you through."

"It doesn't help that you are always having to change your cell phone number," Ashley added.

"And now you know why."

"Well, look, Fussy Pants out there isn't interested in crying herself to sleep," Ashley let loose of an over exaggerated sigh. "I'm going to have to pull up my big girl panties and go back out there in a minute so sum it up. I'm telling you, if I would have had her first there wouldn't have been a second."

I grappled for her attention, knowing she had to go and this wasn't her problem. "Ashley, I need you to help me. Tell me how to find Anna."

"Call that girl whose name rolls in the credits as Mr. Allen's personal assistant and have her do her job," Ashley suggested.

"No!" I replied abruptly. "I don't want anyone to know about this until I figure it all out."

Ashley didn't keep up the banter. It took her a moment to reply. "Try calling the hospitals. Find out where her father is. You'll either find her or you'll go there and have an opportunity to have a conversation..."

"And what should I say to him? 'You ruined my life and now I hear you are dying?'" I hadn't finished, but Ashley stopped me.

"I wouldn't start with that, but depending on what shape he's in, and if you can get in to see him, you might find out why he did what he did."

"Thanks, sis. I love you."

I thought the conversation was over, but Ashley wasn't quite done. She must have cracked the door to the pantry because I heard Addie scream bloody murder again.

"Alex..."

"Yeah?"

"This isn't just about you and some girl. Before you do anything, you really need to think about this boy. Do you want to be a parent? It's not easy."

"I know."

"Alex, you don't know. You've never really had anyone to take care of but yourself and there's been times when you weren't great at that so I really want you to think about this. Do you want to be a father? If there's any doubt, even the slightest amount, walk away now. I'm serious, Alex."

"I'm not walking away, Ashley. I never wanted to leave her to begin with..."

"Alex, you're not listening. This isn't about her and it isn't about you. It's about your son. Do the right thing, Alex."

I was taken aback. "And just what do you think that is?"

"That's for you to decide, but I'm telling you to put the best interest of this boy first. What's best for him?"

"Having a father."

"Maybe."

"What's that supposed to mean?"

Addie continued to fling her fit and the noise of her tantrum was coming in clearer. Ashley split her attention again shushing Addie and cautioning me.

"You and I both know there's more to being a father than having *made a deposit*. It's about commitment and putting the needs of someone else first. It's about more than a phone call here and there and a Christmas card with some cash in it."

She hit home with her last line since that's all we got from our father for a couple of years right after our parents' divorce. It took him getting remarried for him to get his priorities straight.

"I swear I hear you and I am in it for the long haul. I promise."

"It's not me you have to promise anything to."

I can't say I thought long and hard about Ashley's advice regarding walking away. That wasn't an option for me. I knew it wasn't just about Anna, but it wasn't just about Auggie either. I also knew it wasn't just about what I wanted either.

I did take Ashley's advice on how to find Anna. I called the lobby of the hotel. I asked for room service, a burger and fries since I hadn't eaten since sometime the night before and I asked for a list of all of the hospitals in the area. Fifteen minutes later I had dinner and a list complete with phone numbers to each hospital and the room service attendant had a $100 tip. We were both happy.

The list was in alphabetical order and I went down the list calling as I ate. I'd nearly given up when I dialed the last number to University Hospital.

"Hi," I replied after the hospital operator's greeting, "Do you happen to have a patient there by Chandler Calloway?"

"Could you spell that for me, please?"

I spelled and the operator clicked away on a keyboard that I could hear through the phone.

197

"Please hold and I'll put you through," the operator instructed politely with a sweet twang in her voice that reminded me of Anna's.

I verbally jumped to catch her before she put me on hold, "Thank you, but would you mind just telling me which room he is in?"

"Room 314. Could I help you with anything else, sir?"

"No, ma'am. Thank you so much!" My inside's quaked with nerves.

I wasn't half finished with my plate, but I was done. I was itching to get to the hospital, but I was torn as to what I would say. I knew the confrontation I'd dreamed of having with that man was pointless. I didn't have it in me to kick someone when they were down and, from what Mrs. Calloway had told me, her husband was down and he wasn't getting back up.

I'd checked into the hotel using my Florida driver's license, the one I had issued in the name of A. August Allen. No one's ever questioned me on it as long as I had on my disguise, a ball cap, shades, clean shaven, jeans and a Florida State t-shirt. Regardless of showing the I.D., the rest of the disguise got me into the hospital without anyone recognizing me. I passed by people in the hallway as if I was just another visitor, someone visiting a sick relative.

I found the room by following directions on signs and didn't have to ask for help. I peered in the door to find Mrs. Calloway seated at her husband's bedside, holding his hand. I could also see what appeared to be a doctor who was checking Mr. Calloway's vitals and adjusting a hanging IV bag.

"You may want to call your daughter and any other family, it won't be long now," the doctor advised.

Mrs. Calloway nodded, agreeing.

"I've upped the morphine dosage to keep him comfortable. He won't suffer," the doctor explained.

"Thank you," Mrs. Calloway sniffed as she reached over and stroked her husband's hair.

I couldn't get a good look at him from where I was standing, but from what I could see, a frail hand draped across the slender form under the white bedsheets, and from what the doctor said, the time to discuss anything with Mr. Calloway had passed. I knew this wasn't the time or place to demand answers and the decision to leave them in peace came easily. Despite what I thought of Mr. Calloway, I couldn't help, but feel sorry for both him and Mrs. Calloway in that moment. I also wondered how Anna and Auggie would take it.

I was winding down my spying when the doctor told Mrs. Calloway how sorry he was, she thanked him again and then mentioned, "I need to call my daughter."

My stomach dropped. Anxiety, nervousness, and anticipation gripped me as the opportunity to see Anna and Auggie materialized. Those feelings were immediately followed by an overwhelming sense of guilt. I wanted desperately to see them, to talk to each of them again, but not like this.

I went back to the hotel and waited. I checked the local paper the next day. There was no obituary for Chandler Calloway. I waited, using my time to put my agent on notice that I was taking some time off. I was reminded of my commitments to press junkets for the two movies I had coming down the pike and my obligation to attend the premiers.

"Don't worry," I shook my head, not pleased with the reminder, but agreeing to keep up to my contracts. "Just let me know when and where I need to be and I'll be there, but don't send me any more scripts."

Kip Chrispen, my agent for the last ten years, wasn't amused.

"You're not retiring on me, are you?" he asked jokingly, but not joking at all.

"Not yet, but I need a break."

His concern was not put to rest. "So, are we talking a couple of weeks or months?"

I could almost smell him sweating through the phone. He had other clients, but I was his top earner. If I wasn't booking jobs, he wasn't getting his percentage. I'd taken breaks before, but consistently made movies and money.

The next day I checked the paper again. It was there, his name listed in the little block near the bottom of the front page.

I flipped to the page that contained the full obituary.

Dr. Chandler Mason Calloway, beloved husband, father and grandfather entered into his eternal rest on May 13, 2008, at University Hospital, the same hospital in which he was born in 1947.

Dr. Calloway, a native of Augusta, was the only child of the late Chandler James Calloway and Anna Mason Calloway. He was born and raised in the Hill section of Augusta. After high school, Dr. Calloway enlisted in the United States Navy, serving his country proudly. After his service, Dr. Calloway attended the University of Georgia where he obtained a degree in Pre-Med.

Dr. Calloway met Gretchen Lawson of Wrens, Georgia while they attended UGA and after college they married and returned to the Hill, to his ancestral home. Dr. Calloway then attended The Medical College of Georgia. After his graduation from dental school, Dr. Calloway remained in the area to start his dental practice and raise his children, Chandler Lawson and Anna Catherine.

Dr. Calloway was a beloved dentist, preserving the smiles of countless Augustans throughout his thirty-five-year career. He served on the Board of Directors for the dental college at The Medical College of Georgia and founded the Smile Bus, a mobile dental office that provided dental care free of charge to needy school children in the CSRA. Founding Smile Bus was one of Dr. Calloway's most prized accomplishments. He enjoyed helping children more than anything else he ever did aside of spending time with his family.

Dr. Calloway is preceded in death by his parents and his son, Chandler Lawson Calloway. He is survived by his wife of thirty-six years, Gretchen, daughter Dr. Anna Catherine Calloway and grandson, August Chandler Calloway "Auggie." His family was the joy of his life.

Services for Dr. Calloway will be held at The First United Methodist Church of Augusta at 3:00 p.m., Friday, May 16, 2008. The family will receive friends at Poteet Funeral Home on Thursday evening, May 15, at 7:00 p.m.

I reflected on the obituary and remembered something Anna's mother said to me. She said while laying out her blame on me that Anna had given up all of her dreams because of me, because she became pregnant and because I left her. I wondered what she meant by that. Anna and I weren't together a full year, but I knew her and the only dream I knew she had was that of becoming a doctor. According to Mr. Calloway's obituary and despite the things her mother accused me, Anna fulfilled her dream. She became a doctor. As far as I knew, she became a doctor and she was raising our son all by herself.

I bummed around the hotel that day, not knowing what to do with myself. I wanted to be there for them. In a long-lost way, they were my family. Reveled in pride over what it appeared Anna had accomplished, but a question crept in. Was she raising Auggie alone?

Surely her mother would have thrown it in my face if Anna had someone else. Surely a husband would have been listed in the article if she had one and her last name would have been different. I convinced myself Anna wasn't married, but paranoia rooted itself in my head. She might not have a husband, but what if she was seeing someone?

"It doesn't matter," I said to my reflection in the mirror as I got dressed the next morning.

I'd dreamed of Anna and Auggie. In the dream we were at the house by the lake in Milledgeville. I was reliving the time of my life with her, but Auggie was there too. We

201

were a family. The dream was a glimpse of what I could have, a vision of what I wanted. I wanted my family.

I'd bided my time all week. Time for the funeral approached and I came close to throwing on a suit and going, but I didn't. Time for the funeral to start and end came and went. I paced around my room until I couldn't stand it anymore. I had to know how they were, where they were and, if ever I'd felt the need to be useful, it was now.

Chapter 20

Anna-Cat...

It was standing room only at the church. The who's who of Augusta turned out in droves. It was a beautiful service with military honors for his time in the Navy, dozens of white floral arrangements from patients, colleagues and friends and gospel music, lots of gospel music. He loved the stuff and Mama pulled out all of the stops.

The best part of my father's sendoff was Mrs. Patsy Revere belting out the lyrics to "Softly and Tenderly" a cappella. She gave it all she had and it sent goosebumps down my arms and tears to my eyes. The song was heart wrenching, but it was the tears of my child that caused me to ruin my makeup.

It was hard, harder than I thought it would be, to say goodbye to my father. It wasn't seeing the casket or the flag draped across it or the soldiers from the base fold and present the flag to my mother that broke me. It was knowing that today was the day Auggie's childhood ended. I feared my sweet boy's innocence went to the grave with my father.

Most of Auggie's friends were from Wrens, where I'd taken Auggie after he was born when we went to live with my grandmother. He had a couple of friends he'd made through going to church every fourth Sunday with my parents. One of his friends from church insisted Auggie come home with him after the funeral, but I was reluctant to let him go.

"Let him get his mind off of things," the boy's grandmother, a dear friend of my mother, persuaded me. "I'll take them for ice cream and have him home around 7:00 p.m."

Auggie begged to go and I caved.

Other friends insisted on taking my mother out to dinner after the funeral. I was invited too, but I really just wanted to go home and get out of my heels. I wanted to go home to my house, but had to settle with going back to my parents' house where I had to wait on Auggie and where I promised my mother we'd spend another night. I wanted to be alone, but she didn't. She hadn't wanted to be alone since my father died. In fact, my mother had never been alone. She moved straight from her parents' house after high school to a dorm room with a roommate at college and from college she moved in with my father when they got married.

I put my keys on the kitchen island after letting myself in through the back door. I paused for a moment kicking off my shoes and noticing the stove. I could picture my father cooking pancakes for me and Chan on Christmas morning when we were little. I wondered if Chan was there to meet him at the gates of Heaven. I pictured that for a moment, Chan behind these great big golden gates, wearing the plaid Christmas pajamas that matched the ones I had the year he died and my father running to him and scooping him up in his arms. I could just see my father giving him a hug that would go on for years. It was the saddest, happiest thought I'd ever had. I knew they were together now.

I shook off those thoughts before my tears returned. I continued down the hall past all of the family photos on the wall, candid shots of our lives, moments in time that made one think that we were one big happy, normal family. It was all an illusion. Nothing about us was normal.

I ran a hand along the photos, touching the face of my father in a photo of him making snow angles with Auggie, the one time in Auggie's life that we'd seen real snow in Augusta. A hint of a smile, a forced, sorrow filled smile, came over me. My father was as much of a kid in that photo as Auggie was. I might as well have been looking at a pair of seven-year-olds.

I moved on to Auggie, taking in the light in his eyes, the slight dimples in his cheeks. What little upturn there was to the corners of my mouth faded as I looked at him.

He was three in the particular photo on which I'd settled. He was happy. I lingered a moment then passed to the next. He was nine in the next one, eating Superman ice cream outside a shop at the beach. He was in Heaven in that one. There were other photos and I moved from one to another.

I'd worked so hard to make things normal for him, but everything he knew as normal was shot to Hell in the last few days. I wanted to drop into a heap of crying and build of puddle of tears right there in the hallway, but I couldn't. I had to start rebuilding normal.

I tore myself away from memory lane and continued on my course to change clothes. I gave a chuckle as I stepped over the spot that still had a little reminder on the floor, a dark spot where my blood had stained the wood. It was the very spot at the bottom of the stairs, the spot where I first met Alex and I always made a point of stepping over it.

"I guess we'll come full circle soon," I said over my shoulder to the spot as I took the first step headed upstairs. Little did I know then how close I was to full circle.

I went to my bedroom, the one that had remained mine since childhood. No matter how old I was, that would always be my room, just like the first room on the left at the top of the stairs would always be Chandler's room.

My mother redecorated every room in the house like a woman on a mission every other year, but she never touched our rooms. Chan's room was decorated just as it was the day he died. It had the same plaid wallpaper, same books on the shelves, Hardy Boys that once belonged to my father, and the same little Bible verse in cross stitch hanging in a frame on the back of the door.

Mine was decorated just as I'd left it when Auggie and I moved out and went to live with my grandmother. The white wicker bassinet where Auggie slept when he first came home from the hospital was still standing in the corner. Looking at it now, it was hard to believe Auggie was ever small enough to fit in that thing.

I'd been camping out in my room in the days since Daddy died and Auggie had been camping out in Chandler's old room. I imagined for Auggie it might have been like sleeping in an antique store, but he never complained. Every morning I woke up in my room, I felt as if I was waking up in a bad dream. The last time I'd lived there was probably the lowest point in my life. The only saving grace was that I left there with Auggie.

I unzipped my dress and slinked out of it as I crossed the room. I went to the closet and redressed in jeans and a t-shirt. I straightened what was left of my makeup and used the bathroom. I emerged and sat down on the bed to put on socks and tennis shoes. The curtains and blinds over the window were open and something moved in the yard, catching my eye. Someone was out there.

"Well, that's great!" I muttered, thinking about the warning the church ladies had given us about people trolling the obituaries and then robbing the house while the family was at the funeral. I thought it was preposterous at the time, but now not so much. Now I was actually a little scared.

I hurried along with my shoes and then went to my brother's room. From the windows in his room I could look down on the driveway. I made it to the window as I started to question whether I had locked the back door when I came in. I pulled the cord to open the blinds slightly and I peeked between the slats. To my relief, I saw a red Corvette parked in the driveway. I was fairly confident robbers didn't drive vehicles with no room for loot. Despite my relief, the question remained as to who the car belonged to and who was creeping around the backyard.

I made my way downstairs all the while expecting a knock at the door, but one never came. I went to the back door and found I had locked it. Another wave of relief came over me, but that soon dissipated. I looked through the door to the backyard and that's when things came full circle.

My breath caught in my throat. My heart started to race and my hands and arms got all tingly. I was caught between excitement and panic as I watched Alex Allen standing next to our pool.

I knew this was coming. My mother had warned me. At times I'd focused on the possibility of seeing him again; imagining how it would be, how it would go. Those thoughts got me through the past few days. Other times I had to focus on my family and thoughts of Alex were as far away as they'd ever been. Today, I'd all but forgotten him entirely.

Alex's hands were in his pockets and he looked like his knees were locked. From the back, he looked exactly the same, broad shouldered, slender waist and long legs. If he wasn't an actor, he should definitely be a Levi's jeans model. I'd never seen a man wear a pair of jeans better. The way they hung off of his hips and clung to his ass had me licking my lips. The panic attack was over, but the nervousness remained.

I worked up my courage and opened the door. I kept my eyes on him and he didn't even flinch as the door hinge screamed for a good oiling. I didn't tiptoe out. I walked normal, a bit of jittery hesitation, but certainly not light footed. Alex should have heard me coming, but he still didn't turn around.

I wasn't sure what to say so I simply said, "I don't remember you being so tall."

Alex turned around and his eyes went over me from top to bottom and back again. "I don't remember you being this beautiful."

I hung my head, blushing. In an instant the years fell away and I was that same young girl that was enamored with him. I didn't know what to say or how to respond.

"I'm sorry about your Dad," he said. His voice was exactly the same, a little husky, sweet, sincere.

"Thanks." I flashed a look to his face and then diverted my eyes again and then back. I couldn't look at him, but I couldn't look away either. I really just wanted to stare at him. He was everything I remembered.

Awkward silence set in. Alex stiffened his posture again and he ran a hand through his hair. My knees went weak and I fidgeted with my hair, pulling it over one shoulder as I worked up the courage to say something.

"Everything looks exactly the same as I remember it," Alex said, locking eyes with me. I didn't know whether he meant the house or me specifically.

A little more small talk and stolen glances at one another passed between us before I got to the real question. I thought I knew the answer, but I asked anyway. "Alex, what brings you here after all this time?"

He'd taken his hands out of his pockets a few minutes earlier and relaxed a little, but as he answered, a hand went back in to the pocket of his jeans and he pulled something out. "I have something of yours and you have something of mine."

Alex took a few steps toward me and held out his open palm to me. Laying in his hand was my ring. The sun caught it and it sparkled in all directions. It had more bling than I remembered.

My mouth fell open. "How did you... I mean, I thought someone stole it..."

"Your father gave it back to me when..."

Here came the tears again and there was nothing I could do about it. I remembered what my mother had told me that my father had done, but she didn't tell me that part.

"Here. It's yours." He held his hand open for me to take the ring.

My fidgeting continued and consisted of twisting my hands, one inside the other and rotating. I was skeptical if I should take the ring or not. I wanted to touch it, but I just wasn't sure. I could hardly believe what I was seeing on all accounts. "I can't believe you kept this all this time."

"Of course, I kept it. It's been in my wallet ever since..." He trailed off, not rehashing the event. "It wasn't mine to get rid of." He took another step closer to me.

"Seriously," he said, insisting I take the ring. "It's always been yours."

I reached and picked it up from his palm with my thumb and index finger, but then there was the question of what to do with it. I slipped it on my index finger just for lack of a better idea.

"Now, I believe you have something of mine."

My mind went blank. I was overthinking it, searching for what object I would have had of his until it occurred to me that he was talking about Auggie. The color drained out of me as I realized what he meant.

"Is he home?"

I was guarded, but I corrected him. "We don't live here and, no, he's not here."

"Why didn't you tell me..."

"I tried...but... and then there were those photos of you and I thought you had moved on... and my father... and..." Tears fell down my cheeks, but I didn't sob.

"I know," he said softly, reaching and taking my hands and stopping me. "I wouldn't have left you. Not ever. And what photos are you talking about?"

I snapped, jerking away from him, "The ones of you tied to a bed being ridden by..."

"Ah, right, those. They weren't real."

"Looked pretty real to me!"

He glared at me. "Well, they weren't. Those were part of the movie."

"Funny, I didn't see them in the movie."

"I made sure they ended up on the cutting room floor." He then added, defensively, "I don't do porn."

"It doesn't matter now anyway," I went back at him.

"It matters to me!"

I crossed my arms over my chest and turned my head. I didn't want to hear any more of it.

"Look, Anna, I didn't know you were pregnant and I never did anything with..."

"Don't worry about it."

"No!" Alex said defiantly. "I waited out front for you and I had no idea you were…"

"Stuck inside on bedrest," I smiled through my tears. "I thought you'd left me and you thought I'd left you. What's done is done."

I took a few more steps back from him. I wiped at my face, probably smearing what little mascara I might have had left. "It's been a long day."

"Wait. Hold on," he reached for me.

"No." I jerked back, struggling for self-preservation. It would have been so easy to fall into his arms and bury my face in his chest, but there was more than me to think about.

"Does he know?"

"He didn't before, but he does now."

"And now what?"

"I don't know, but today has been a lot for him. It's been a lot for all of us."

"I get that, but…"

"But what? Alex, we have a life here and he's twelve and…"

"And he's great and he's mine…and…" Alex furrowed his brow and appeared to search for more words. He seemed to struggle audibly to come to terms with everything. "And his childhood was stolen from me."

When he came out with it, he really came out with it.

"Now wait just a damn minute!" I snapped.

"Not by you," he whipped back, ringing his hands through his hair and rubbing at his temples. "My whole life was stolen, you, Auggie, everything that was supposed to be…" He took a breath and threw down the honest accusation. "What right did your father have to do this to us? If he wasn't dead, Anna, I swear I'd kill him!"

I backed up more as Alex gained momentum.

Alex popped off a bit more and then stopped abruptly, realizing he was in full rage and knew he'd spoken out of turn. "I'm sorry. I'm sorry. No, that's a lie. I'm not sorry."

I shrugged it off. "I know exactly how you feel. I only just found out what he did right before he died and it was really hard to come to terms with, not that I really have come to terms with what he did, but..."

"But he's your father so you forgave him."

"For the most part, but it wasn't for him. It was for me and for Auggie."

Alex changed the subject. "You named him after me."

"After you and my brother. August Chandler Calloway."

The wheels turned in his head as he mulled it over. "It's fitting." Alex grinned and, without consciously doing it, I found myself mirroring his look. I was smiling back.

"He's a great kid and he looks just like you."

This time, it was Alex's eyes that filled with tears. "Tell me what to do. Tell me how to get to know him. Tell me everything about him. Tell me I'm not too late to be a part of his life."

"It's never too late, but as much as it pains me to say, you'll have to get over the animosity towards my father or you'll never stand a chance with Auggie. If you asked him, my father hung the moon."

Alex didn't like the idea, but he nodded. "He really got me good, didn't he?" He asked the question and it almost sounded as if he was joking, and then answered. He wasn't joking. "He not only kept me from being a father to Auggie, but let me guess? He filled in and was basically the only father Auggie ever knew."

I couldn't dispute it. "If I had known, I would not have let that happen, but I didn't know. I'm so sorry."

"No, this is on me. I should have fought harder for you."

Chapter 21

Alex...

Heat rose in me at the sound of her voice. I hesitated. The thought of laying eyes on her had me melting in the very spot where I stood. I'd imagined the moment for so long that I could hardly believe it was really happening. I pushed past my hesitation and turned.

From head to toe I looked her over and back again. Anna-Cat Calloway hadn't aged a day. She looked exactly the same as the portrait I kept in my mind of her. She was absolutely remarkable, the very definition of the word as I was already playing out the commentary I would have with my sister over the phone later that night. I would be giving an account of every detail of her and how she set me on fire for her with a glance even after all this time. She was still the same Anna, my Anna.

Anna was dressed simply in a tank-top, jeans and sneakers. She was a little puffy around the eyes and the makeup around them was a little smudged, signs of her having cried at the funeral. She was gorgeous and I wanted her. I'd never wanted a woman as badly as I wanted her.

I kept my hands snug in the pockets of my jeans to stretch the front and allow room for the arousal I couldn't seem to contain. It was as if I was a pubescent teen all over again. I could hardly get a hold of the physical effect she was having on me, but I could try to cover it as not to embarrass myself.

There was small talk, an exchange of explanations of what went wrong with us and the part her father played in it, shared regrets and talk of my son. She really had named him after me and that really brought the thought home. I was looking at the mother of my child.

"August Chandler Calloway, I like it," I told her.

I did like it. I'd driven away that Christmas all those years ago with her father having given her ring back

212

to me, thinking she hated me. From what she was telling me now, and the fact that she'd bothered to name our son after me, making him a daily reminder of me, I knew that that couldn't have been farther from the truth.

There was also a heated exchange between us which came to a head with my calm admission, "I miss this."

"What?!" she griped without missing a beat.

"Fighting with you."

Anna was complete thrown off kilter with that statement and begged clarification. "Fighting with me?" she asked in a pitch high enough to hurt dog's ears.

"I'd rather fight with you than make love to anyone else." I quickly added when she blushed crimson, "It's a quote from a movie, but it's true."

"Well I don't want to fight with you!" Her face was beat red and she was still pissed.

I would have died if she would have said she would have rather made love. I would have obliged her first and then died. I would have taken her right there on the grass in the backyard of her family home.

"Do you ever miss it?" I asked, turning the conversation again.

"What?" She went from mad to confused and never lost one ounce of beauty along the way.

"Me and you. The house by the lake. I miss it all the time. I bought the place, but I couldn't ever bring myself to go there. It stays rented."

"You bought it?" Any trace of anger in her voice was gone. It was replaced with straight wonder.

"Yeah. I thought I wanted it. The house, I mean. I thought if I was there I could..." I trailed off, feeling like a fool trying to explain that I wanted to live in the past with her ghost. "So, I rented it out. I've had the same tenants for the last five years according to the leasing agent. They've tried to get me to sell it, but, well, I can't live there, but I can't sell it either." I gave a half chuckle, laughing off my ridiculous predicament and then changing the subject before Anna could comment. She just looked on in what appeared to me mild shock or amazement. I wasn't really sure which.

There was a pause, I really didn't know what to add to that, so I took the opportunity to walk over to the chairs by the pool. They were exactly where they were the nights we'd raced in the pool and talked for hours, first getting to know each other and where I stopped fighting the fact that I was in love with her.

"Where are you going?" she called after me. "You aren't leaving, are you?"

My insides did flips at the notion that me leaving seemed to affect her, that she seemed to care.

"God no!" I looked over my shoulder at her. "I'm just going to my chair." I motioned toward the one that had always been mine. "Join me?"

Anna followed and we didn't fight anymore and that didn't bother me at all.

I waited for her to sit down before taking my spot. I sat facing her, placing my elbows on my knees, casually. Anna mirrored me, with the exception of her posture. She fidgeted with the ring, toying with it, but not putting it on her finger.

"So, you became a doctor after all?" I urged her to tell me more.

She nodded, affirming her status.

"Your mother said something about you giving up all of your dreams." The only dream I knew Anna had was becoming a doctor so I asked her what her mother meant.

"Oh...nothing. So other than movies, what have you been up to?"

"I don't think it was nothing." I redirected her and pushed for the truth through more of her avoidance until she answered.

"I was engaged."

I felt as if I'd been gut punched. "Oh."

"It's not such a foreign concept you know!" she insisted with an edge.

214

"You were engaged, but you're not now?" I sought assurance.

"No. It ended some time ago."

"What happened?"

Anna tried to avoid answering, but I pressed on until she confessed.

Her eyes misted and she fidgeted more, looking from the ring to the grass at her feet as she explained. "He wasn't you, but he reminded me of you constantly." She blinked back tears as she met my eyes.

I scooted my chair closer to her and took her hands in mine. It was the first time I'd touched her and the electricity was still palpable between us. It sent voltage through me that made my knees tingle and would have dropped me had I not already been sitting. I was basically a giddy girl on the inside, realizing she hadn't snatched her hands back and she hadn't eased them away either. She let me hold them.

"You met him once," Anna continued as I tried to think of anything, but kissing her. "Remember the guy from the wreck that night? The night I was so late getting home and you were worried? The guy you went to see in the hospital to make sure he was okay so I would feel better?"

I did remember him. I remembered what he said about Anna the morning after the accident too. I kind of laughed at the thought. "He was delirious on pain meds. I wasn't sure if he was going to make it." I could see him all casted and hooked up to tubes and wires, the heart beat monitor and IVs. "Despite all of that, he called you his angel and told me he was going to marry you."

Anna shot me a quick glance as her cheeks filled with a smile. "He tried."

Images of them together, mainly a vague one of the guy from the hospital filling my spot irritated me, but I held it in. I didn't ask for any further details. In fact, I changed the subject altogether. I wanted to know all about her, but I didn't want to know about that.

"So, you're a doctor. That's awesome!" I said with enthusiasm. I was so proud of her.

"It wasn't easy. Jesus, the student loans..." She stopped immediately, took her hands back and tucked her hair behind her ears.

Anna parted her hair down the middle now, which was the only change in her that I'd noticed. The other thing I noticed was in that moment and it was how my heart shattered at the removal of her hands from mine.

"It was harder than I thought it would be," she went on, "but Auggie and I survived. I was fortunate to have my grandmother to help me with him."

I urged Anna on to tell me every detail of what it took for her to complete medical school while raising Auggie. She allowed her parents to see Auggie as much as they wanted, but drew the line at their insistence on taking him to raise.

"I never even considered it. And, I never asked them for a dime either, not that they offered." She was adamant.

There was a period of silence between us.

"I'm sorry I wasn't there." I didn't know what else to say.

This time, Anna changed the subject. "Tell me what you've been up to. Tell me the things I couldn't read in People magazine or see at the movies."

"Well," I bought time trying to figure out how to explain I had also gotten a doctorate degree. "I went to college."

"Really? That's great! Tell me what you majored in and when you had the time."

"Ha! Making time was more challenging than the classes. I'm sure you know how that is."

Anna nodded in agreement and looked on with complete interest as I explained.

"At first. I threw myself into my work. Three and four movies in a year, but then I decided I didn't want to do

216

it anymore. I was burned out and bored, but I didn't want to quit altogether. I mean, what else was I going to do?"

"I'm sure there's a million things you could do." I always loved the confidence she had in me.

"Maybe, but..." I shrugged. "I decided to go to school. I found a school that was discrete and I applied. I liked history so I decided to get a degree in that. I did one movie a year in the summer just to keep up appearances and the rest of the time I went to school. I got a Bachelor's of Science in History, then I got a Master's degree and then I..."

She cocked her head, drew in her eyes and questioned, "You got a doctorate degree?"

"Yep."

Still skeptical, "So you're doctor?"

"Not the same as you, but you're looking at Dr. Alexander August Allen."

She busted out laughing. "I like the sound of it."

"What so funny?"

"You were bored so you got a doctorate degree," she carried on laughing, "Who does that?"

I focused on her first question. "Well, that's not the only reason."

"Why else, because you needed the money?" she teased me, holding her sides and doubling over as she cackled.

I laid the real reason on her then. "No. I got the degree because I wanted you to be proud of me the way I am of you. If I ever saw you again, I wanted you to..."

Anna stopped giggling with the effect of a car throwing on the brakes. She reached out and touched me. It stopped the words in my mouth. I couldn't speak. I just stared at her hand on my knee and felt the warmth of her touch coming through my jeans.

"I may not have shouted it from the rooftops that you were the father of my child, but I never regretted a moment we spent together. I have always been proud of you."

217

Silence hung in the air between us as I blinked back emotions that were inching toward my eyes.

"What was his first word?" I wondered out loud, thinking of her reference to my child and making an attempt to keep myself in check.

"Shoes." She quickly corrected herself. "Not to make you feel bad, but he said Dada a lot. It's easier for babies to say than Mama. He said, 'No!', but his first real word was shoes and the way he said it was all drawn out," Anna then mimicked him, "Shoooos."

"Tell me everything about him. How much did he weigh when he was born?"

"He was huge. 8 pounds, 12 ounces and twenty-two inches long. He was so big and snuggled in that he wouldn't budge. I had to have an emergency C-section."

"Oh," I twisted my face at the thought.

"Yep, bedrest for weeks on end culminating in seventeen hours of full-blown labor to end in having to have him cut out."

I drew up at the mental image she painted, shuddering at the pain she must have gone through and all without me. I should have been there to hold her hand, to be the first person to hold my son. I should have been there.

Guilt was the next feeling that washed over me. It went straight to my core where I knew it would stay forever.

I tried to push it down and drew on every acting technique I'd ever learned to hold back the next emotion that came over me. Anger wrenched in my gut and I strained to keep the veins in my head from bulging as I was reminded just what her father had stolen from me, from us, but most of all, from her. I couldn't begin to fathom how scared she might have been.

"Don't feel bad, it was only one day out of my life. I'd do it again. I mean, I wasn't a fan of being pregnant, but I could definitely do child birth again, one day."

"Do you want to have more children?"

"I hadn't given it any thought. I just meant, I'd rather take one day of agony over nearly ten months of inconvenience anytime."

Anna went on to tell me all about Auggie's first steps, his first day of kindergarten, the first time he hit a ball out of the infield, all of his firsts. She gave details to the point that I realized again how I'd been left out and it hurt.

"How do I make up for not being there?" I asked her.

"I don't know."

I wish she would have said, "Be here now," but she didn't. The conversation moved on and on and we talked for so long that we lost track of time.

"Look," I said, "I'm dying to see him again," probably not my best choice of words, "but, I know today isn't the best time."

Anna tipped her head, giving a slight nod of understanding.

"What do you want me to do? I'll do whatever you want, but I'm..." I stammered over my words. "I'm not going anywhere. I'm staying down the street at the Partridge Inn. You can call me there or..."

"I'll call you," she stopped my rambling.

I stood and offered her my hand to help her up. Anna took it and our eyes locked and I did more than help her up. I snatched her, bringing her chest to chest with me. Anna's breath hitched in her throat and she let out a little squeak of surprise followed by a generous smile with her top teeth gripped over her bottom lip as I slipped my arms around her.

I wanted to kiss her something fierce, but I didn't. Without breaking eye contact with her, I tilted my forehead to hers. Her eyelids slowly lowered as did mine. The anticipation heightened the pull between us, but I refused to give in to the urge to devour her. I simply stroked the bridge of her nose with the tip of mine. I could feel her pulse quicken as her chest beat against mine and I simply said, "Thank you," barely above a whisper.

"For what?" she panted, breathlessly and I reveled in the effect I seemed to have on her.

"For giving me a son."

I caught a tear with the pad of my thumb as it slipped down her cheek. "Call me. I promise I'll come running."

Chapter 22

Anna-Cat...

I laid awake that night, staring at the ceiling and thinking of my father, of Auggie, and of Alex. Mostly, I thought of Alex. I wondered the same thing I always wondered. What would life have been like if he'd never gone away? Scratch that, if my father had never sent him away.

Minutes ticked by as I marveled at the timing of all of this. My father's health had deteriorated to the point that his death was eminent, but Auggie finding Alex, well, I couldn't decide if that was God's reward for Auggie or some sort of rotten cherry on top of the relationship I'd had with my father. Even in his final days, I couldn't fully make up with him and find it in my heart to feel that unconditional love that's supposed to exist between parents and children. I knew that kind of love existed. I had it with Auggie, but thanks to my father's selfishness, it would forever elude me with him.

I'd been on the brink of forgiveness, but then Auggie found Alex. I recounted his version of events, the same version my mother sprang on me days before, but not the version I'd known all of Auggie's life. The image of Alex's face shown through the darkness as he recounted his side. The glistening in his eyes lit up my ceiling like a movie screen. I could see his emotions written in his eyes as he recounted how Dad gave my ring back to him and on Christmas Day no less. I could see his face pale when I described giving birth to Auggie and how scared I was and how I'd wished he was there with me. His color immediately returned with a vengeance as he learned my father was the first man to hold Auggie when he was born. I could hear every emotion in his voice coming with the image on the ceiling. The hurt rang clear when he asked me about Auggie. It broke my heart to see him like this.

Beyond all of that, my heart had stopped at the sight of him and I recalled that moment, too. TV and movies never did Alex justice. His physique was like superglue for my eyes. As hard as I tried, I couldn't stop looking at him. His eyes, especially when they got misty, were as clear as the waters of the Gulf and they pulled at every part of me, heart, soul and in places that made me blush.

There was more to Alex than his eyes. His hands were soft, but they contained some sort of magical electricity. When he touched me, just held my hand, I experienced almost instant orgasm. My attraction to him was as powerful as ever.

I laid there in my bed thinking how ridiculous I was. I was growing more uncomfortable with a need for him.

I rolled over and looked at the clock. It wasn't the first glance I'd taken at the time, but it was the first time the card from the hotel with Alex's number on it got my attention.

"It's after 2:00 a.m.," I mumbled to myself, looking from the numbers on the clock to the numbers on the card. "No, you shouldn't call him."

Of course, I stretched for the phone and pecked out the numbers on the keypad.

A groggy Alex answered on the first ring, "Hello?"

"Dr. Allen?"

Alex chuckled, a raspy, coming to chuckle.

"You said you'd come running."

I could hear his breath catch as he yawned. I'd clearly woken him up. "I'll be there in five."

"No, don't." I covered my smile, concealing it as if he could see me through the phone.

"I don't mind." I could hear him moving around.

"I don't know why I called. Go back to sleep."

"Let me throw on some clothes and I'll meet you by the pool."

222

A memory of what Alex looked like naked ran through my mind and I felt giddy at the thought. Picturing the deep V cut of the muscles from the bottom of his abs to his hips, sent a wave of heat over me. He was older, so I wondered if he still had it. I knew I didn't look the same naked now as I did when I was nineteen.

To stave off the frustration growing between my legs, I asked him, "Did you ever want children?"

In all that had transpired, I never thought to ask him. No one had asked me either, Auggie just kind of happened to me and there was no question about it. I wanted him from the moment I first realized I was pregnant.

His answer took my breath away.

"I wanted everything with you."

The low toned, deep voiced way he said it didn't help the tension that was eating at me.

"But that was almost thirteen years ago and..."

"And some things haven't changed."

I was speechless. "I don't know what to say."

Near silence passed between us. The rustle of movements on his end came clearly through the phone. Alex was getting dressed. He really was on his way.

"Dr. Allen?"

"Anna?"

I loved it when he just called me Anna. I bit my lip as the exchange continued about as good as what I would imagine phone sex to be like, but without the dirty talk.

"Can I ask you something?"

"Wouldn't you agree we are past the point of you having to ever say that before asking me something? You can ask me anything anytime you like, so just ask."

The way he said it was like he was daring me. I fanned myself, but kept the conversation PG.

"Why me?"

"What do you mean, why you?"

"What made me so special?" I had been curious about that all along.

"You're smart and sweet..." He hesitated and that just drew me in. "And I've never wanted a woman the way I wanted you, the way I still want you even now."

"I'm serious. You could have had any woman in the world." I flipped a hand dismissively, talking with my hands even though no one was there to see my gesture. "And," I added, "'sweet and smart' are the way my mother's friends would describe me. So, why me and why after all these years..."

"I assure you I'm no friend of your mother's." It wasn't what he said, it was how he said it and, again, he taunted me.

I stifled a giggle. "Alex, I'm serious." Hearing myself, I realized I was panting and sounded as if I was begging.

"Remember the night I shot you. I stitched you up and..."

"And I woke up in bed with you hovering over me the next morning. And we fought..."

"Before that. I put you to bed and, yes, I hovered over you. I don't know what possessed me, but I brushed my hand over your forehead, you know, comforting you, over the top of your head. You were completely out of it. I was sure you were asleep, possibly near dead from the shock. It was more to soothe myself and assure me that you were going to be okay. Anyway, I ran my hand over the top of your head and you smiled. A peaceful smile came over your face and you were the most beautiful girl I'd ever seen. You had me right then and it literally scared the Hell out of me."

I sighed, "Auggie's told me that before, that I smile in my sleep."

"He's right, but it's only when you're touched. There were many nights when we lived at the lake house that you did it. It's one of my favorite things about you. It's just this sweet little up turn of the corners of your mouth."

I found myself smiling, not in the way Alex had described, but the big wide, puffy cheeked embarrassed grin, as I listened to him.

"There were nights when I'd lay awake just to touch you and see you smile like that."

I yawned again and stretched before snuggling up to my king-sized pillow, spooning with it and imagining it was Alex.

"If it were only me to consider..." I said dreamily before Alex cut me off.

"We can still be a family." Alex made a case, "We can take back what your father took from us."

"If only it was that easy..."

"It is that easy."

My body and heart ached for him and I wanted to buy into what he was saying, but it wasn't just me now. I had to consider what was best for Auggie.

My heart wrenched as I contradicted him. "No, nothing's instant like that. You only just found out about Auggie..."

"I wouldn't consider what we had a one-night stand so, no, there's nothing instant about this."

As bad as I wanted him and having him back was an answer to all of my prayers from ten, eleven, twelve years ago, I had to think of Auggie. I sat up in bed and cut on the light. Sexual frustration faded away as I explained to Alex, "You understand you are worse than a stranger to Auggie?"

"What do you mean?" I hit a nerve.

"I mean, you're just Alex to me, but to half the world you're Billy Ward and to the other half you're any number of characters you've played over the years. To Auggie, you're Six McMillon, the funny sidekick in that space movie you did. You're not real."

"Fuck, Anna! What do you want from me?"

"Nothing. Never mind that I called." I hung up, thinking if he couldn't figure it out then he had no business being around Auggie anyway.

I tossed the phone on the bed, flopped back on my pillow and ran my hands through my hair and over my face. "Stupid. Stupid. Stupid," I called myself.

I tossed and turned some more. Fifteen minutes must have passed when I heard something hit the side of the house. Figuring it was a tree limb scraping against the siding, I didn't think too much of it until it happened again. That time the noise came from the window. There weren't any branches close enough to hit the window. The third time the noise came from the window again.

I bolted from the bed and threw open the curtains to find a pissed looking Alex throwing pebbles from the driveway at my window.

"Get down here!" He mouthed and motioned toward the yard where he stood.

I shook my head and snatched the curtains back over the window. The stirring feeling was back with one look at him, but I resolved myself. I was not going down there.

Another rock hit the window. I grabbed the phone from the bed and threw the curtain back again. I showed Alex the phone and pointed to the numbers "9-1-1".

"Do it!" he mouthed, raising an eyebrow in challenge. "Or get down here." He pointed to the ground again and then to the pool chairs.

I rolled my eyes, but ultimately, I threw a robe on over the extra-large t-shirt I'd been wearing as a night gown.

From the look on his face staring up at the window, I feared he was going to give me a what for about hanging up on him and how he had every right to see Auggie and all of that. I was wrong. I was barely out of the back door when Alex snatched me into his arms. My chest struck his and I sucked in a shocked breath with my hands going instinctively to his shoulders to steady myself. His eyes blazed in that second of hesitation before he backed me into the wall that joined the porch and the house. Then, Alex threw one Hell of a kiss on me. He gripped one hand

226

around my waist and the other went to my hair, taking a fist full and tilting my head back for him to deepen the kiss.

My knees went weak, my mind went blank and I went all wet and needy for him. I held on tight, my hands, lips and tongue responding to him almost automatically. I didn't even come to my senses when he pulled back.

"I've wanted to do that to you for as long as I can remember," he said, still breathless and not unwinding his hand from my hair.

Being bound like that was a unique and new sensation, like nothing I'd ever felt before. All I could do was blink and blink some more.

"I want you like you can't even begin to imagine."

Alex loosened his grip on my hair just enough that I dropped my head.

"Anna," Alex lifted my chin and tucked a stray tendril behind my ear all the while demanding eye contact from me. "I'm serious. I want my family back and I know nothing's easy or instant or whatever, but I want you to know I'm never..."

"Never say never..." I squeaked out.

Alex gave me a stare down as he started again, "I'm NEVER giving up on you and I'm never leaving Auggie. Make me jump through all of the hoops you want, but I'm never leaving."

"What about your work?"

"I will have to travel for work from time to time, but that's not the same thing as leaving. I think you know that."

"Last time you left and didn't come..."

"Last time I came back and I can't help..."

"Okay, but..."

"Anna, no more buts. I'm never leaving. We've already lost too much time and I'm not about to lose any more." He cupped my cheek in his hand and I leaned into his touch, closing my eyes and giving in to it. "So, name your hoops and let's get on with this."

"Auggie's got a baseball game on Saturday, but I was thinking of taking him to the field for some extra practice tomorrow. Why don't you come by the field?"

Alex pulled me closer and kissed me again. "What - time?" he whispered in a staccato fashion in between small brushes from his lips to mine and I hardly heard him.

"What?" I dug my fingers into the hair on his nape and held him as close to me as he held me. His arousal was firm against my pelvic bone and it appeared he did want me as badly as I wanted him.

"What time do you want me," he paused and there was definitely dramatic effect with that pause, "at the field?"

"1:00 p.m.," I replied, breathy and wanting.

Chapter 23

Alex...

I rolled out of bed with the sunrise that morning. Excitement and anxiety kept me up well past the time it took me to get over the case of blue balls that kiss with Anna had given me in the middle of the night. I was nervous and thrilled about seeing my son. I also wondered what he thought about all of this.

I had the morning to kill as I wasn't due to meet up with Anna and Auggie until after lunch. I tried to fill the time by doing normal things. I thought about Anna and Auggie with every task I attempted. I pulled on a pair of khaki shorts over my boxers, and tugged a polo shirt on over my undershirt. Just down the street, Anna and Auggie were probably doing the same thing. I ordered breakfast, had it delivered and ate alone in my room. Taking a bite of my Belgian waffle, I imagined them doing the same, together with Anna's mother, visiting with her and comforting her the day after the funeral. All I could think was how I should be there with them.

I really didn't know how alone I was until that moment. I forced down the rest of my waffle and strips of bacon and tried to think of other ways to kill time until I was due to meet Anna and Auggie in Wrens. I took comfort knowing I would be with them in a few hours. Each time I thought about the prospect of seeing of them again, my insides knotted.

I kicked back on the bed and contemplated what to do next. Knowing one of Ashley's biggest complaints about motherhood was that she hadn't slept past 7:00 a.m. in four years, I figured she was up. I dialed her number and she answered after three rings.

"Hey. It's me."

Panic stricken she replied, "Is everything alright?"

"Yeah, I think so."

"Then why are you calling so early?"

"Because I knew you'd be up," I teased. Our exchange continued and Ashley explained that I'd never called her before noon, so upon hearing my voice she assumed someone was either dead or on their way to the hospital. Usually she reserved that reaction for folks calling after midnight not before noon, but I was the exception.

For the first time in a long time I didn't hear Addie screaming in the background. And Ashley didn't have to have two conversations at once or hide in her pantry to speak with me. It was a nice change.

After giving Ashley the low down on Auggie she asked, "Have you told Mom and Dad about any of this?"

"No. I fear Dad would be on the first plane up here and Mom, well, I just... I don't know."

"Dad would probably start crying..."

"What?" I didn't get that last statement.

"He does that now. Haven't you noticed? I think his testosterone is low or something. I told him the other day that Addie said her first word and he got all choked up. It was sweet and sad all at the same time."

"I want to see how things go. I don't want to overwhelm Auggie with the whole family just yet. Plus, I've got to fly out to California in a couple of days. The timing isn't right and..."

"Well," Ashley stopped my rambling, "I am dying to meet him. I think you should tell Mom and Dad, regardless of how you think they will react. I mean, they have a grandson and I think Dad would also be thrilled to know there's someone else named after him."

I hadn't thought beyond Auggie having my middle name and being named after me. I hadn't stopped to consider the name August originated with my father, August Madison Allen. Auggie would be the second, or first really, grandchild that carried his name. Ashley's daughter who we called Addie was actually Madison Alex Malone. Ashley's older daughter was Mackenzie Alice Malone, who was named after Ashley's husband's mother and grandmother. I was Alexander August Allen for my mother's father, Alexander, and my father. My sister was named for my mother's maiden name and my father's mother, Ashley Grace Allen. Everyone in our family was named for someone else and it appeared Anna had unknowingly kept with that tradition.

After hanging up with Ashley I decided to kill time by taking her advice. I phoned our mother. She was in the middle of a yoga class and put me off.

"I don't suppose you can call back after lunch?" she asked with a strain.

I didn't let her off so easily. "Mom, it's important. I have to tell you something."

Perhaps I sounded too dramatic as she clearly stopped what she was doing. "Is it your father? Has something happened to him?"

Mother had been furious with us when we didn't let her know when Dad had a heart attack about six years ago. We were perplexed as to her concern and what she thought she could do about it. Ashley and I agreed later that not telling her had been for the best.

I recalled Ashley commenting, "That's all we need is Mother making a spectacle of herself showing up at the hospital with Leslie there."

Although my mother kept a revolving door of male friends, she would have taken my father back at any moment had he only said the word. He was never far from her mind and just for a moment, I found myself identifying with her. She'd always wondered what she did wrong that things didn't work out with them and it appeared after all these years that I'd lived a life wondering the same thing. Unlike my mother, I felt I was genuinely being presented with a chance to put my life back together. I'd never put myself in her shoes before and this time I didn't roll my eyes or snap at her over Dad.

"No, ma'am. It's not about Dad. He's fine," I spoke respectfully and didn't give the air of exasperation that I usually did when she put me on the spot about him.

Sounding relieved, she panted, "Oh, thank goodness!"

"Mom, the thing is," I found myself struggling a little to put into words what I wanted to say. Telling her wasn't as easy as telling Ashley. "Remember a long time ago, I told you about a girl from Georgia and things ended badly?"

"Alex, what's this about?"

I jumped to the point. "I recently discovered that things ended much worse than I thought they did all those years ago."

Apparently recalling my broken heart, the whole family had been worried about me for quite some time following the breakup. "How could it have ended worse than it did? I don't understand?"

"Well, the thing is, she didn't end it."

"I'm not following you."

Words stumbled around in my head and came out my mouth just as jumbled up when I tried to make sense of things for my mother. "As it turns out, she, her name is Anna. I mean, she was pregnant. She found out while I was away. I was in Canada on the set for a movie. She had an accident, a fall, and was placed on bedrest at her parents' house."

"Right, I remember you being furious and hurt that she had her father tell you she didn't want to see you anymore."

"That's just it. She never told him to tell me that. He did that on his own and sent me away..."

"Wait, did you say she was pregnant?" my mother switched gears.

"Yes, she was pregnant and inside his house while he was outside the house getting rid of me and she had no idea. She thought I left her."

Mother was catching on. "What about the child?"

"He's twelve now and I met him the other night."

I'm not sure what happened to her yoga class because my mother proceeded to have an hour-long conversation with me about all that had happened, how Anna's father tricked us both, how Auggie found me and I even told her about the kiss last night. There was nothing normal about my current circumstances, but this was the most normal and honest conversation I'd had with my mother in more years than I could recall.

My mother's parting words were those of wisdom, which is something neither my sister nor myself had ever relied upon from our mother. She said, "Don't expect to pick up where you left off and don't expect to immediately be the boy's father. Most folks say you can't be your child's friend, but Alex, I think you are in the rare situation where you need to cultivate friendship with him first."

"Mom," I said in conclusion, "thank you."

"For what?"

"For the advice. I think you're right about making friends with Auggie first."

"You're welcome, Alex, and I can't wait to meet my grandson. Now, go get 'em," she closed encouragingly.

It was getting on toward 10:00 a.m., and I decided to put off calling my father. He was likely on the golf course with his old Navy buddies anyway. I knew from Anna's directions, it wouldn't take me three hours to get to Wrens, a small town about thirty miles south of where I was, I decided to kill more time and turn in the Corvette to the local rental agency. It wouldn't do for keeping a low profile while cruising the streets in a red Corvette. I needed something more discrete.

By 11:30 a.m., I left the Hertz store with keys to a modern version of the truck I'd purchased the last time I was in town chasing Anna. That truck was the only vehicle I'd ever owned and I gave it to my dad for Christmas. I handed him the keys when I arrived in Florida blurry eyed and devastated the day after Anna's father had delivered his lie. My father still had that truck and it wasn't until taking a seat in this rental that I could stand the thought of that old truck.

233

Settling into the driver's seat and running a hand over the black, leather steering wheel, my mind drifted back to a particular memory of my black Ford. Anna and I had been to dinner in Macon, a place called the Downtown Grill. It was a Saturday night and it was packed, but we had a candle lit table for two in the corner and we were alone. I remember burning for her all through dinner.

Leaning back in the seat, I let my mind continue to wander. Even though it was broad daylight with the sun beating down, it was a dark night with only headlights in front of me, not the pavement of the Hertz parking lot.

I kept one hand on the wheel and guided her, gripping her by the ass as she climbed over the console between our seats. Her hands roamed under my shirt and up my chest and I could feel her hot breath on my neck before the first kiss. It tickled and left me breathless with anticipation.

As her tongue traveled from my neck to my earlobe, she lightly teased with her teeth while her hand traveled south. This was the first time Anna had placed her hand on my dick of her own initiative. She rubbed me over my jeans and as we pulled in the driveway to the lake house, she unbuttoned my fly.

Not realizing our proximity to home, Anna breathed in my ear, "Touch me."

Excited beyond words, I slammed the brakes and the truck slid to a stop in front of the house.

Anna took a tumble within the cab and let out a scream of surprise. I caught her short of hitting the dash. Within seconds I'd scrambled out of my seatbelt and flipped Anna into the passenger's seat.

Reaching across her I aimed to catch the handle to open the door for her while grabbing a few kisses for the walk inside.

Anna pulled me closer, deepened the kiss and when she let me up, she told me with a needy breath between each command, "Take me now. Here. I can't wait."

Fumbling in the dark, I unbuttoned her shirt and slid down her shorts. She let me undress her completely yet we barely pulled my pants down enough to free my cock.

We tested the shocks on the truck that night, making love in the front passenger seat and, after a brief cool down, we made our way to the backseat, too. It was cramped, but Anna managed to lay across me with her head on my chest. I stroked her hair, relaxing with the rise and fall of our bodies in unison as we breathed.

"I've never done this in a car before," I said to her.

Anna lifted her head and the streetlight in the yard lit her face. "I've never done it anywhere...until you." She batted her lashes and grinned all shamefaced-like. "And now I want to do it everywhere with you."

I thought about how sexy she was, with me still mostly clothed and her bare as the day she was born. Anna was no freak, but she trusted me to let go of inhibitions and just be with me.

Growing uncomfortable in reality and getting hard over the memory, I cut the A/C on in the rental and fanned myself. A question then occurred to me. Was it that night in the truck when Auggie was conceived? I wondered if Anna even knew when he was conceived. We made love so often it might have been impossible for her to pinpoint the moment.

Following Anna's directions through Augusta toward Wrens, I continued to reminisce about that night in the truck. With what Anna and I had done, one would think embarrassment would have taken over my face when I presented my father with the keys, but it didn't. My face was near stone and all I could muster was a straight line across my mouth. I had no smile for anyone that day and for so many days, weeks and months after. It was safe to say, I'd nearly forgotten how to smile or feel anything at all.

I found my way down US Highway One. It was lined with pine trees, soybean fields and some pasture land. It was a far cry from the A1A that I was used to in Florida. It was the same highway, but very different. My heart pounded harder with every mile. My palms were clammy and, despite the 65 degrees that I'd set the air conditioning on, I was breaking into a full-blown sweat. I was only moments away from meeting my son, really meeting him, and I was in fear of my deodorant failing and making a fool of myself.

Turning at the red light in what appeared to be the center of town, I glanced down again at Anna's hastily scribbled directions. I was less than a mile away from Chalker Field, the baseball field where she'd instructed me to meet them. I was also early.

The field wasn't grand, but it wasn't a sand lot either. The outfield fence was lined with advertisements for local businesses: M.B. Jones Oil Company, Peggy's Restaurant, Jay's Hardware and several others. One in particular caught my eye. The whole board read, "From colds to cuts, bruises to breaks, come see Dr. Anna Catherine Calloway for all of your boo-boos." It was cute, clever and perfect for an advertisement at a kids' baseball park. It also hit home again, my Anna really had become a doctor. A warmth crept up from my stomach and replaced my nervous feeling with something else entirely. I felt nothing short of proud of her.

There was no official, paved parking lot, just bare spots of dirt indicating where people usually parked. I turned in behind the first base dugout. I'd been parked long enough to take in the sight of the place before a VW Bug pulled in behind me. Anna still drove the same car she had in college. I had memories of that car, too. Those memories were almost as titillating as the ones in my truck, but rated more PG than the triple X.

Not that I wanted to get rid of anything that stirred memories of her at this point, I still vowed to buy her a new car. After all these years and all that she had accomplished, if anyone deserved a new car, it was Anna. Knowing she would be too proud to accept it, I was just going to tell her to consider it a late graduation present.

Chapter 24

Anna-Cat...

"Is that who I think it is?" Auggie asked, spotting driver of the truck parked in front of us.

"Yes," I answered, cutting the car off.

I hadn't told Auggie that Alex was coming. Auggie had been the mix of excitement over finally knowing who his father was and that it was Alex and guilt over being excited about anything fresh on the heels of his grandfather's death. Sometimes guilt won out and he didn't want to think about Alex. Other times, excitement won out and then he felt guilty all over again. It was a vicious cycle for him.

"Auggie, Granddaddy wouldn't want you to be sad about this. He knew how badly you felt about not having a dad." I tried to comfort Auggie, but that hadn't helped.

That statement had only led Auggie to have more questions. "If he knew how badly I wanted a dad, then why didn't he ever fix what he'd done?"

I confessed, "I don't have an answer for that."

True to form, Auggie's first instinct was to jump out of the car and run to see Alex, but as fast as he'd thrown the car door open, he reigned in his enthusiasm. He nearly crept out of the car and poked around about gathering his baseball equipment from the backseat.

I stood in the open door of the car, propped my arms across the top and tried to remain calm myself. "Auggie," I said.

He peeped up from the backseat, looking of the hood at me with the unspoken, "What?"

"Be cool."

"Did you just say, 'Be cool?'"

I nodded with a demure smile.

Auggie let out a long, rolling breath and gave me a deadpan stare.

238

"You don't have to impress him and you don't have to worry if he'll like you." I tried to encourage him.

Auggie shook his head. "I still can't believe he's my dad."

There had been some explanation over the last few days and a great deal of rehashing the story my father had given Auggie, which happened to be the same story Alex had given my mother. Although Auggie understood, he didn't fully understand. How could any of us expect him to understand? After all this time, I still couldn't understand either. Me, basically a simpleton from Augusta, Georgia, and world famous, globetrotting actor, Alex Allen. It was a bit for anyone to wrap their mind around, let alone a twelve-year-old boy who'd been sheltered his entire life.

Auggie gathered up his bag of gear and started away from the car. I lingered behind, trapped in my own thoughts for a moment.

Auggie wasn't the only one that was nervous about seeing Alex again. Whereas Auggie rolled out of bed, brushed his teeth, ran a hand through his hair and was his version of ready to greet the day, I took considerably more time and effort with my appearance. I didn't typically roll my hair for the ballfield or consider what my butt looked like in every pair of shorts I owned, but this morning I did. I also didn't tend to wear makeup to the field either unless it was game day or unless I was coming straight from work. By the time I was done, my hair looked nearly pageant worthy. I tamed it with a twisted bun stuffed through the back of a ball cap.

As always, Alex looked like Alex. He was standing next to his truck, making sexy look effortless. From Alex, I looked toward Auggie who was sauntering over toward him and thought about Auggie's grooming ritual again. "Like father like son," I said to myself.

I lingered a little more, allowing them to introduce themselves again. I watched as they shook hands. I wondered what they were saying but trusted one of them would tell me later.

The word trust shot to the forefront of my mind. I'd trusted Alex once with the most precious thing I had at the time, my heart. Now I was trusting him again with the most precious thing I had, Auggie. Regardless of what my father had done, there was a lingering twitch in my head. It was my father's voice still saying, "If he loved you, he would come for you." Suddenly a burning urge to protect Auggie surged through me and I picked up the pace walking over to them.

Inside of earshot, I heard Auggie asking Alex what he should call him.

Alex said the strangest thing. He said, "Hold on a moment." At that point he reached back into his truck and pulled out a pen.

"Let me see your hand," Alex told Auggie.

Looking skeptical, Auggie dropped his gear and slowly held out his hand.

"That's not your throwing hand is it?" Alex asked.

Auggie shook his head and kept his hand out.

"Okay." Alex proceeded to write what appeared to be a phone number on Auggie's palm. "I don't care what you call me," he looked up at Auggie as he finished writing, "as long as you call me."

Alex smiled at him as Auggie beamed looking up from the number on his hand. For the time being, my trust issues were put to rest.

"So," Alex looked at Auggie's bag, "batting practice or fielding?"

"Can you pitch?" Auggie asked.

"It's been a while, but I'll try." Alex glanced toward me. "And your mom can play outfield?"

I agreed. "Let me get my glove."

After getting the bucket of balls from the car for us, Alex threw some warm up pitches and Auggie caught. I thought watching Auggie play ball was my favorite thing but seeing him play catch with his father was a long, overdue dream come true. It was all I could do to keep the dam on the tears of joy from cracking and flooding the whole ballfield.

Twenty pitches later and Alex was ready. Auggie marked off the batter's box with the handle end of his bat and then stepped up to the plate.

Alex was still athletic and the mechanism of his throwing was just fine. He looked like a natural, except that each pitch he served up like a fat watermelon. Auggie hit a hard bouncer through short stop and I chased it in left center field. He hit another one over the center field fence and Alex was visibly impressed.

Alex went through his wind up to serve another one and I screamed from far in the outfield, "Throw the heat!" and laughed.

Alex let go of the ball and turned to see what I had said. He turned at exactly the same time that Auggie let fly of the bat and cracked the watermelon straight up the middle.

I gasped and let out a scream. It was hard and fast and there was nothing more I could do. Hearing the impact, a solid thud, like something hitting wood, I threw my hands over my mouth and went running.

Alex's knees wobbled, but he didn't fall. Even if he had been paying full attention, I wasn't sure he could have gotten the glove Auggie had loaned him up fast enough or gotten out of the way. Instead he took a line drive to the hip.

Alex hopped on the opposite leg from the impact and rubbed at his hip.

Auggie yelled, "I'm so sorry!" and started toward Alex, continuing to apologize.

Closing in at a full sprint, which wasn't really that fast for me, I heard Alex reassuring Auggie as he started to try to walk it off. "It's okay. It's okay. It's not your fault. I shouldn't have looked away."

"Try walking over here," I said to Alex and gestured toward the first base dugout. "Auggie, go get my glove." I'd left my glove somewhere in the vicinity of left centerfield.

Alex was visibly limping and I tucked my head under his arm to help him walk.

We made it to the dugout and I said to him, "Let me take a look at it."

Alex stood there, perplexed that I'd just asked him to take down his pants, and from the area of impact, knowing he'd likely have to drop his boxers as well.

"Just pull your pants down and let me have a look." I looked him up and down, waiting.

Alex looked shocked.

"Like I haven't seen it before."

"Point taken." He motioned toward the road and the houses of the neighborhood that bordered Chalker Field. "But they haven't."

There was only a chain link fence that made the walls of the dugout so there was nothing keeping anyone passing down the road or stepping out on their front porch and seeing Alex, but I insisted.

"Shit, Dr. Calloway, really?"

I grinned. "Yes."

Alex gritted through the pain and straightened up, standing to his full height and unbuttoned his jeans. Looking me directly in the eye, he slowly dropped his pants. He left his boxers, which looked remarkably like Auggie's sliding shorts, and only stretched them and dipped them down his left hip. He showed just enough skin that I could see, that at thirty-six years old, he still had that deep V.

I leaned down and took a closer look at the mark left by the baseball. It was red and swelling. I pressed a little, feeling for any chip in the bone. I knew I was touching him more as a professional courtesy, but still I wanted to kiss the spot. I resisted the urge and stood up, flushed from the sight of his hip, that dang V and the rising in his boxers which I could not help but notice.

"It's going to leave a mark," I stammered, getting up off of my knees.

"All your years of schooling and that's what you've got?" Alex laughed, offering a hand to help me up.

"You don't have a chipped hip bone or anything if that's what you are wondering."

Alex looked around, checking for Auggie's whereabouts. Auggie was moseying back from the outfield. Having noticed Alex was halfway to an erection, I thought surely, he was going to make a suggestive comment, but no. With pants still around his ankles, Alex said, "He's amazing. You've done a great job with him."

"You think so?" My blushing continued.

Alex leaned down to grab his pants but kept his eyes on mine. "He's great. Well-mannered and..." Alex struggled for words. He fastened the button of his jeans and, when finished he took my hand. "I still can't believe he's mine."

Alex didn't say it in an accusatory way toward Auggie's parentage, but in astonishment.

I beamed as I just listened to Alex go on.

Alex took my hands and held them tight. "Is it odd for me to know that I love him? I do. I can't stop thinking about the both of you." Again, Alex apologized for not being there for us.

Auggie walked up. "Are you okay?"

Alex answered, doing his best to appear completely recovered. "Yeah. I'm made of sterner stuff than one baseball can take down."

Auggie smiled. "Do you want to pitch some more?"

"Or, we could go get some lunch," Alex suggested.

"I could go for a burger," Auggie was quick to admit.

"Auggie, you just ate," I reminded him.

Auggie cocked his head at me and gave a slight eye roll. "I ate breakfast and that was three hours ago."

I shook my head. "You're a bottomless pit."

Alex interrupted our exchange. "So, is there a burger place around here?"

In a snap, Auggie suggested Peggy's, a restaurant in the center of Wrens.

"The place at the red light?" Alex inquired.

243

I nodded and Auggie concurred. "Yep, that's it."

Alex followed us to the restaurant. During lunch we received stares from no less than all ten of the other patrons in the restaurant. Our waitress, who looked as if she doubled as a Dolly Parton impersonator in her spare time, lacked the caution the others shared. Two bites into our burgers and she could not withstand the urge to asked the famous question, "Are you Alex Allen?"

Her timing wasn't the best as Alex's mouth was full and he was chewing. He nodded and tried to hurry along the contents of his mouth, knowing the affirmative had just opened up a door for further questions.

"Well, bless my soul! We have a real live celebrity in here!" she announced to the rest of the room.

I covered my face briefly, embarrassed.

Shifting what was left to the inside of his cheek, Alex titled his head to me and said, "You might as well get used to this."

Auggie laughed at the entire situation.

"What brings you to town? Are you filming in the area? Is there going to be a movie shot here in Wrens?" Before Alex could answer even the first question, the waitress shifted gears. The same thing about Auggie caught her attention that had initially caught Alex's. She took a long look at the two of them and then darted her eyes to me and back to them. We'd been coming in there ever since Auggie was a baby and there was hardly a soul in town that didn't wonder who his father was and now it was as if our server was seeing him for the first time.

A penciled in eyebrow rose to the full height of her forehead and she asked Alex more seriously and waited for an answer, "What *does* bring you to town?"

I really wanted to tell her to mind her business, but I couldn't afford for her to bad mouth me around town. I already struggled to get patients, constantly being told how they missed their old doctor. I could see why they missed him since he recently went to jail for the illegal sale of prescription drugs. One woman got fighting mad with me because I wouldn't prescribe her OxyContin for her ingrown toenail and instead, I recommended a surgical procedure that would have solved her problem once and for all. She voiced all over town that I didn't know what I was doing and, in that one week alone I had six cancellations. They insisted on waiting until the more senior doctor in the office could see them.

As it turned out I didn't have to say a word, Alex fielded the question apologetically, "No movie filming as far as I know. I'm just in town visiting family."

It was priceless. She didn't know what to say. Alex just kept smiling and asked, "May I get a little more sweet-tea?"

She stammered, "Yes, yes, of course," and fumbled for his tea glass.

"Thank you."

Still a bit puzzled by the whole situation, she looked at me for some sort of confirmation, but I didn't give one. I stayed silent, picking over my French Fries.

"The burgers were great as always. Thank you so much!" I said, grinning politely.

My friend Millie, one of the few lawyers in town and the only female lawyer, said the local women didn't warm up to us because we were smart. Both Millie and I had arrived in town about the same time, but she started her practice before I finished medical school. She'd been trying to build her client base longer than I had. She'd been lucky to have been taken in by a senior lawyer in town the same as I'd been taken on by the remaining senior doctor. Millie said we threatened the local ladies and I really threatened them because I was, in her words, "Super successful and an unwed mother. The Bible Belt, what do you expect?"

Lunch wound down and there was a moment of 'now what?' between all of us. Auggie was the first to speak up, but only beat out Alex by a breath.

They spoke over each other with Auggie asking, "Can Alex come over?" and Alex asking, "Do you two want to go for a little road trip?"

My head whipped toward Alex, "What, road trip?"

"No, never mind. We'll do that another time."

"So, Mom," Auggie questioned again, "can Alex come over?"

Even though Auggie was steadily backing me into a corner and, normally I didn't allow that from him, this time I happily consented. "Okay, if he wants to, sure."

Having finished eating and Alex having paid the bill, Auggie and I thanked him for treating us to lunch and stood from the table.

"May I ride with Alex?" Auggie asked.

My face must have shown concern, but before I could turn him down and insist that he ride with me, Auggie leaned into me. "I've never had the option of riding home with my dad like the other kids before..."

I didn't make him elaborate further or beg. I tried to keep the tears out of my eyes as I heard Auggie remind me of what he's missed out on and how he noticed. "If it's okay with Alex."

"Come on Auggie. You can give me directions," Alex told him.

"Okay," Auggie beamed and bounded toward the door leading to the parking lot where both Alex and I had parked.

As old as Auggie was and as mature as he normally appeared, every now and then, he reminded me he was still just a child. This was one of those moments when he gave me the reminder.

Chapter 25

Alex...

The most profound conversation of my life took place in the three blocks between Peggy's restaurant and Anna and Auggie's house.

Among the "turn here and turn there," which he had given even though we were following Anna, Auggie stared out the passenger's side window. "This is the first time I ever got to choose to ride with my dad."

There was a catch in his voice that wasn't the pre-puberty cracking that I'd noticed in it earlier.

"Auggie, are you alright?" I asked him.

Auggie kept his face to the window and shook his head in the affirmative, but immediately changed his mind. He shook his head from side to side.

"Wait! Wait! Pull over. Pull over here!" Auggie demanded.

Scared he was about to jump out of the truck with it still moving, I jerked the truck into a space in front of the Wrens City Hall building and threw on the brakes. To my surprise, Auggie didn't jump out and make a run for it. He stayed seated.

Auggie tugged to stretch the sleeve of his t-shirt up to wipe his eyes. "I don't want Mom to see me like this."

"Okay, Buddy, what's going on?" I prodded him, speaking softly.

My son turned to me and, seeing the tears in his eyes, my heart shattered. "I've always wanted to be normal."

Concern and confusion melded together to form my response. "Who says you're not normal? And what is normal these days?" I asked him.

"You know what I mean. I always wanted to be like the other kids, have a mom and a dad." He sniffled and then

247

added, "Even the kids whose parents are divorced have dads."

"Ah... I see."

Auggie continued, "I know Mom did her best, but..."

"But it wasn't the same."

"Right."

Tears streamed down his face, washing over the freckles that dotted his cheeks and looked so much like mine.

"Auggie, you know none of this is your fault."

He dipped his head, giving the slightest indication of acknowledgement.

"And," I went on, "there's no one to blame but me. Your mother did the best she could, but please understand there is no such thing as normal anymore. There's no family out there like Beaver Cleaver's. They don't exist. I promise you, all of those kids that you think are 'normal,' their families have problems too and I'd be willing to bet that a ton of them would love to be you. You never know what goes on behind closed doors."

Auggie nodded again.

I explained to Auggie about my childhood. "I don't know if you know, but my parents divorced with I was a bit younger than you. To me and my sister, our dad left us with our crazy mother and got a new life, a new life without us. It was really hard for a while. It seemed like he was gone forever, but in all actuality, it wasn't that long before he came back. He came back for us, but not my mother. On the outside we probably seemed like everyone else, normal, but with divorced parents. Let me tell you, just because we had a mom and a dad, didn't make us anywhere near what you think of when you think of normal. I'm not telling you this to make you feel sorry for us, but when I was nine and your Aunt Ashley was six, your grandmother forgot and left us at the grocery store. We sat on a bench out front and waited for her to come back. We missed dinner while sitting there smelling the fried chicken the store was cooking. It got dark and finally the store closed. We didn't know what we were gonna do and we'd never been so scared in all of our lives. Luckily, one of the cashiers lived in our neighborhood and she noticed us and gave us a ride home."

I finished by saying, "You see what I'm saying? You never know what's going on with the other kids and I bet your mother never forgot and left you anywhere."

"No, she's never forgot me." Auggie wiped his face dry.

"I didn't tell you all of that to make you feel sorry for me and, please understand, I can never fully communicate to you how awful I feel that I haven't been here for you, but I'm here now."

"Yes, sir," Auggie shook his head.

"And, I'm always going to come back, but please don't think we will ever be normal, because, Auggie, it really is *abnormal* that makes the world interesting." I smiled at him.

With his face clear of tears, Auggie urged me to get back on the road. "We better go. Mom's going to wonder what happened to us."

"Yes, and, I for one, never want to worry your mother again."

Auggie laughed.

I pulled into the driveway of a small, white Victorian house, the one Auggie had pointed to and said, "That's ours."

Anna was standing on the front porch with her hands on her hips, waiting for us when we drove up.

I cut off the engine but keeping one hand on the steering wheel I reached over with the other and caught one of Auggie's. Before letting him out, I gave him one more statement on normal.

"If one of your measurements for normal is having parents that loved one another when they had you, then Auggie, you have that in spades." I glanced to Anna, still standing on the porch watching us. "I loved her and I still love her, more than all of the stars in the sky."

249

I refrained from saying it, but I wanted to tell him that if she'd have me, I'd marry her and fulfill his idea of normal in a heartbeat. I'd do it for me, but mostly I'd do it for him. To my core, I knew I'd do anything for that boy.

Auggie ran ahead into the house expecting me to follow so he could give me the tour, but Anna stopped me.

Anna crossed her arms and asked me, "What was that about and why's Auggie been crying?"

She came off as if she was about to go mama bear on me, but I shrugged her off and down played our conversation. "It was nothing."

Anna firmed her stance. "Alex, you need to understand, we don't have secrets."

"There's no secret, but if Auggie wants to tell you, he will. I won't start my relationship with him by…" I waved a hand between us, "doing whatever this is."

Anna huffed, "You'll tell me…"

"I won't and you shouldn't press him either. You need to just trust…"

The veins flared in Anna's forehead and her neck went all red, a sure-fire sign she was pissed. "Just leave!"

I leaned in close to her, "What is wrong with you?"

She shook her head, vigorously. "Go!"

I didn't go. I sat right down on the top step of her porch. "Auggie's waiting to give me the tour." I held fast to my non-disclosure but figured since they had no secrets, she surely had some idea about Auggie's desire to be normal and I emphasized that when I added, "When he comes back out to see what's keeping me, we're going to act *normal*."

Apparently, Anna and Auggie had had the similar conversations in the past. She flopped down on the step next to me. "Jesus Christ," she let out in an exasperated sigh. "I get it."

Anna dropped her head into her hands and I put an arm around her. I was paying the tab when Auggie nearly begged her to let him have the chance to choose to ride home with his father like the other kids got to do. I had not heard that at the time and everything made sense to the both of us now.

"I think he's a bit overwhelmed by all of this," I said, pulling her closer to me, "but in a good way."

Anna leaned her head on my shoulder and apologized again. "I'm sorry I was..."

"A mama bear?" I pressed my cheek to the hair on the top of her head. "I wouldn't want you to be any other way when it comes to our son and you being concerned for him."

The situation was diffused. Anna took hold of my hand, "I like the sound of that."

The sound of a floorboard creaking behind us got my attention and I looked over my shoulder to see Auggie. He was standing just inside the screen door, smiling from ear to ear.

"We have an audience," I whispered.

I didn't have to see the expression on her face to know what it was. I could hear it in her voice. Anna whispered back, giving a playful challenge, "Ready to act normal?"

"It's not an act." I said to Anna something similar to what I'd said to Auggie, "Going forward, we are creating *our* normal."

Upon hearing that statement, Anna pulled back from me, looked me in the eye and took my face in her hands. There was a slight pause as she studied me, but it didn't last long. Anna eased up on one knee so she could reach my lips with hers. She kissed me. It was light and not entirely just for Auggie's benefit. It wasn't deep with tongue, but it was sensual and I had to think of babies and all sorts of oddities to keep from getting hard in that brief moment. Pregnancy and babies were usually my go-to thought for stopping an erection, but that didn't work this time. I guess my body knew I didn't mind having a child with her.

Anna finished with a little nose nuzzle. "Thank you," she breathed over my mouth.

"For what?"

"For coming back."

"I told you I would. I'm just so sorry it took me so long."

The hinges on the screen door squeaked as Auggie came out. Both Anna and I held out a hand to him. He might have been twelve, but we pulled him in between us and hugged him into our group as if he was a toddler and he let us. Anna peppered his face with kisses and I just held the both of them.

I was a fixture at Anna and Auggie's house for the next two weeks. I kept my room at the Partridge Inn but went back and forth to Wrens for every waking moment. I even hung out with Auggie and took him to baseball practice the second day while Anna went to work.

"So," I said to them over dinner one night. "I mentioned to you both before, but I have to go to L.A. tomorrow. I've arranged a flight out of Augusta."

Auggie's face fell as if this was the first he'd heard of this. Anna didn't look much better. She was likely having flashbacks of the last time I left on business.

"When will you be back?" Auggie asked.

"I'll only be gone two days."

I had not expected what came next.

"Can I come with you?"

Anna immediately stopped Auggie. "No!" She put her foot down.

"But Mom?"

I backed her up. "Of course, I wish you could come with me, but..."

"But I can," he put up an argument, "It's summer and I'm not doing anything."

"I'm not about to take you away from your mother. It would be inconsiderate of me and presumptuous..."

Auggie cut me off. "You're my father and..."

"August, enough!" I jumped in, speaking sternly to him.

252

Anna's eyes had flicked between Auggie and myself as I had shut him down. At the end, she gave me the most-demure nod of approval.

"It's not that I don't want you with me," I assured a visibly disappointed Auggie. "Never think that, but there's nothing for you in California. I'll be there for work. There won't be anyone to watch you or take you sight-seeing or anything that you would be interested in."

I reached across the table for Anna's hand. "I promise I'll be right back."

We continued to pick over our plates as a shadow had been cast over dinner. Unable to take the silence any longer, I offered a consolation.

"I'll be back by this weekend and I'd like to take you both somewhere." I took a sip of my sweet tea.

"Where?" Anna was the first to ask.

"And, if it's okay, I'd like to invite my family up to meet Auggie. If you don't think it's too soon?" I glanced between the both of them for their answer.

"Too soon? I'm twelve. It's past time for me to meet my grandparents." Auggie's sense of humor about the situation was priceless, causing both Anna and me to laugh.

Mingled with laughter, I clarified, "It'll be more than just your grandparents."

"So, the whole family?" Anna inquired.

"If they can make it. I haven't invited them yet. I wanted to make sure you were up for it first." I went on to tell Anna how the family had grown since she met them all those years ago. "Ashley got married and has two daughters."

I directed my next comment to Auggie. "You have two little cousins."

That seemed to excite him. "I have cousins?" he sought to confirm.

I took out my wallet and pulled out the photo I kept in there of Ashley's girls. I handed them one after another to Auggie. "This is Addie. She's seven months old now.

That was taken in the hospital right after she was born. And, this is Mackenzie. She's three."

Auggie studied the photos. "I've never had cousins before."

Anna leaned in to look at them as well while I thought to myself about his expanding family likely put Auggie closer to his idea of normal. I couldn't help but smile.

I stayed past the summer bedtime that Anna set for Auggie at 10:00 p.m. before driving back to Augusta. Each night before he went to bed, Auggie hugged me and told me goodnight. Tonight was the first time he hugged me and told me he loved me, just the same as he'd done to Anna each night before he left the living room and headed to his room.

As she had the nights before, Anna excused herself to make sure Auggie did in fact go to bed and wasn't just lying in his room watching television or procrastinating in some other way. When she returned, she saw me standing on the front porch.

"Hey," she said, unnecessarily announcing her return. The screen door gave its usual squealing and gave her away.

I didn't turn around. "He told me he loved me." I stiffened and wiped my eyes. I didn't want her to see me crying.

Anna wrapped her arms around me, crossing them over my abs, and laid her head against my back. "It's the most wonderful feeling in the world isn't it?"

I clutched her arms tighter to me and shook my head, unable to speak for fear my voice would hitch.

"I think I cried the first time he said it to me, too."

I'm not sure how she knew, but she knew.

"He was a little over a year old and it came out like 'Lub you Ma-ma.' It was the sweetest, most amazing thing I'd ever heard."

"I would give anything to have been there."

"You're here now."

254

"And I have to leave."

"But you'll be back."

Barely allowing space between us, I turned in her arms. "Come with me."

"Huh?"

"Bring Auggie and come with me to California."

Anna backed up, but I caught her hands. "You said yourself you'll be busy working the entire time..."

"Yeah, but I'll cut things off and come back at night..."

Anna frowned. "No, its... I have to work and Auggie has baseball. We..."

"You're right, but just come with me."

Anna held her ground. "I'm going to trust you to come back. You're coming back and I'm not going anywhere this time."

"I can't lose you again."

It was hot and sticky and what Anna referred to as the "bug man" was making another pass up the street, spraying for mosquitos. He'd just turned the corner at the far end of the street, headed our way, when I decided to say my goodbyes.

"I should be going," I said, breathing in the scent of Anna's hair. Lilacs.

"I'll pick you up tomorrow morning and Auggie and I will take you to the airport."

"Stay right here. I've got something in the truck for you." I sprinted to the truck and back, knowing I still had to get going before the bug man arrived or the fog of the repellant would run us inside.

"Here," I said, handing her the large manila envelope.

Anna took it with skepticism. "What's this?"

"My will."

"What?! No." She tried to give it back. "When did..."

I stepped back, refusing to take it. "I had it drawn up this afternoon. You have to keep it in case anything

255

happens to me. It will supersede the one my sister has giving everything to her girls. Since we aren't married and, I'm guessing, I'm not on Auggie's birth certificate, you'll need this. I mean, just in case."

"This is preposterous! Nothing is going to happen to you."

"I'm flying tomorrow and shit happens. Just take it. I want to know you and Auggie are provided for…"

"Provided for," she laughed, but it wasn't a genuine laugh.

"Anna, I'm serious. I want everything I've worked for to be yours and Auggie's. You don't have to read it or anything." I held up my hands, palms out, again refusing to accept the envelop from her. "I'm just asking you to put it somewhere and hang on to it."

"Fine. Now come here." Dropping the envelope to the floor, Anna took hold of two fistfuls near the collar of my shirt and pull me to her.

I'd kept my libido in check since the night on her mother's back porch, but I wanted her. God, how I wanted her. These past weeks, I'd waited for her to come to me. The most I'd done was reach for her hand and give her a highly restrained goodnight kiss.

I closed my eyes at the last possible moment, watching her face relax into the anticipated touch of our lips. I wanted to remember how perfect she was right that instant. She was always perfect. She always had been, but still, when I thought of her in the days that I would be away from them I wanted to be able to relive this moment. I wanted to revel in the fact that she might want me again, too.

I was wrong. It wasn't the look that I was going to hold in my head. It was the kiss. It started as a sweet caress and ended in my near madness. I was love-struck and lust crazed, half out of my mind with the torment of keeping hold of all decency and not taking her on her front porch. Kicking away the Welcome rug in front of the door and laying her down right there. It was a forcible urge, but I resisted.

I jerked back from Anna, both of us panting. "I've got to go."

I couldn't take my eyes off of her lips. They were full and swollen as she pulled her bottom one ever so slightly. She turned it loose to say, "I know." She was still coming down off of the high the kiss brought. The sound of the buzzing from the mosquito truck growing louder as it came closer barely hurrying us.

Anna closed the gap between us and gave me one more peck. Drawing back, she let her forehead brush against my cheek. "Go and we'll see you in the morning."

I was halfway to the truck when I turned back to her. Anna was still on the top step, watching me when I told her, "I don't want you to take me to the airport."

"Why?" She asked with protest.

"Because I might not be able to leave."

Chapter 26

Anna-Cat...

"Could you pass the salt?" Auggie asked Mama.

My mother had called me earlier in the day and invited herself over for dinner. She was still having trouble adapting to life without Daddy. I readily agreed not only to help her avoid being home alone another night, but to divert mine and Auggie's minds from missing Alex.

Mama picked up the silver shaker, looked at it, looked at what was left of her plate of fried pork chops, stewed tomatoes and okra and then salted her food before passing it to Auggie.

"Thank you." Auggie proceeded to give his potatoes a once over with the salt while I pushed my food around my plate.

My mother tried to make small talk with us, but both Auggie and I were a bit absent minded.

"Okay," she announced, forcefully putting her fork and knife on each side of her plate. "What is going on with you two? Out with it."

I looked at Auggie, seated across the table from me, and he looked back at me. Each of us waited for the other to answer. Auggie sat up straight and gave me a good stare down.

"Fine," I said to him before explaining to my mother. "Alex has been hanging out with us, but he had to go to California for work."

"Here we go again." She pursed her lips and looked disgusted.

"Mother!" I gave her the one-word warning.

"What?" Her facial expression hardly changed. "Do you want me to patronize you?"

"Honestly!" I picked up my plate and carried it to the sink. I dropped it in hard with little regard for whether it might break. I placed my hands on the sides of the sink and braced myself. "You don't know him."

"And neither do y'all."

I reigned in my anger and asked Auggie politely, "Auggie, please go to your room."

Auggie didn't budge more than to turn on his grandmother. "I don't think you are being very fair about my father."

My mother looked aghast.

Auggie continued. "We're all expected to give Granddaddy a free pass on what he did, but you don't seem to want to give my dad a pass and none of this was his fault. You can think what you want, but I know he's coming back for me... and my mother. If you have a different opinion from that..." He paused, working up his courage. "Then you can go home, to your house, by yourself."

Auggie had never been rude or really contrary to my mother before and she was shocked, utterly shocked. I was a little shocked too. I didn't think he had it in him, but he did and I was proud.

Just when my mother started to speak, Auggie added, "And, you should be ashamed of yourself to say one thing against my dad after what was done to him and to us."

Mother started to cry. She took in a deep breath, tried to gather her dignity and placed her napkin in her plate. She didn't say a word as she got up from the table, but it was clear she intended to leave.

"Mother, seriously," I rounded the kitchen island to stop her. "No one wants you to leave." I caught her and took her gently by the hand. "We just want you to respect our feelings about Alex and give him the benefit of the doubt like you would anyone else."

Auggie sat silent, folding his arms across his chest and sticking to what he'd said. It was like we were good cop and bad cop to some degree.

"Do y'all think this is easy on me?" She fretted. "It's not. I don't know what to do or say or even think anymore. We didn't like him for so long. How can you expect me to just change so fast?"

Auggie piped up, "Because it's the right thing to do and you know it." He was on a roll tonight.

I cut my eyes at him, alerting him to the fact that he'd said enough.

Mother slinked back from me and picked up her plate from the table and carried it to the sink and Auggie followed with his dishes.

"What do you say you and I take care of these?" Mother cut on the hot water and started filling the sink.

Auggie didn't argue. He let the subject of Alex drop and grabbed a dish towel. "I'll dry and put away while you wash and rinse."

They got to work cleaning the kitchen while I went to the living room and checked the dial tone on the phone. There was no reason for our phone to be without service, but I was antsy. Alex said he would call as soon as he could. It was after seven here so it was mid-afternoon there. I thought he would have called when he landed, but he hadn't.

The night carried on with us migrating to the living room. Auggie cut on the TV and played along with Wheel of Fortune while Mother explained to me how she'd filled her time writing thank you notes for all of the flowers she received for Daddy's funeral. It wasn't that she was boring, I just couldn't keep myself from glancing at the phone every now and then. And apparently I wasn't as discrete as I thought I was.

"Are you seriously worried that he's not going to call?" She asked right in the middle of a statement about one of Daddy's former Navy buddies stopping by to check on her and asking her out on a date.

"No," I popped back, affronted that she would ask.

"Then stop looking at the phone. You know a watched pot won't boil."

"Look! Look!" Auggie bounced around pointing at the television.

It was a commercial for the episode of Entertainment Tonight that was coming on next. "Alex Allen joins us at his star on the Hollywood Walk of Fame to talk about...Wait for it. Wait for it... Fatherhood," the correspondent said into the microphone while standing in front of a very tall looking and grinning from ear to ear, Alex.

I jumped to my feet and screamed as loudly as the gaggle of teen girls standing in a roped off area behind them.

"He's not really going to tell them..."

I shushed my mother by cutting her off. "I have no idea."

Whether or not Alex told the world he just had a kid or just found out he had a kid... Every aspect of our lives was about to change and all of that was lost on Auggie. "That's so cool!" He exclaimed.

"Cool?" I gasped, still barely able to breathe, but pacing between the couch and coffee table.

"To see Dad on TV," Auggie clarified.

It wasn't even the first time we'd seen Alex on Entertainment Tonight. It wasn't the first time I'd anticipated hanging on his every word, but it was the first time for Auggie. Most of the time that show had only been background noise for Auggie. He was no star watcher, until now.

Auggie waited with baited breath as Pat Sajak signed off for the night on Wheel of Fortune.

I managed to take a seat on the couch, perched on the edge. My mother sat next to me, hip to hip and gripping my hand as tight as I was gripping hers.

"If you were certain he was coming back, what exactly are you worried about now? You had to know all of this about you and Auggie would get out," she whispered, keeping our conversation from Auggie's ears.

"We're in Wrens, Georgia for Christ's sake," I replied in whispered scream.

Auggie whipped his head around, definitely having heard me.

I went on. This time I lowered my voice so only Mother would hear me. "We're basically in a bubble and it's not like the..."

"Here he comes!" Auggie shook the remote in the direction of the television and gave it a few smacks in the palm of his hand before the volume started to go up.

I scooted farther toward the edge of the couch and Mom moved with me. As loud as Auggie had the sound, we still leaned in.

"This is so cool," Auggie clapped his hands. "He's at an early screening for The Dark Knight. I love Batman!"

"We know. Shhhh!"

As it turned out, it was the reporter from the show who had just had his first child. The theme of the show, beyond interviewing all of the celebrities turning out for a prescreening of the latest Batman movie, was to give the reporter advice about being a new father.

"I'll be the first to admit I know nothing about being a father," Alex's eyes all but twinkled as he turned on the charm. "I'm sure I'll rise to the occasion, but I think my biggest fear is that I'll screw up my kid."

"I think we all have that fear," the reporter agreed before he got down to business. "I hear you have a new project coming up."

Alex nodded, leaning down just a bit toward the microphone. "Yeah, I'm pretty excited about it."

"I saw some stills from the shoots." The reporter chatted while movie stills popped up on the TV. "I hear you play a Civil War general."

The photos continued to flip by. Some were of Alex in period dress, a bust shot, one of him mounted on a horse charging to battle, and another of him with a young actress in a hoop skirt and ringlet curls on the steps of what looked like my parents' house.

"Look at his beard," Auggie ogled.

The view on the screen went back to modern day Alex. Never once did he mention me and Auggie directly. My fears were unfounded and we were still in the bubble. It was a relief.

Before the segment with Alex was done, a plug was put in for his appearance later on the Tonight Show.

"Can I stay up and watch it?" Auggie begged.

"No."

In the middle of Auggie pleading, "But Mom," the phone finally rang. I snatched up the cordless and answered.

"Hey. How's it going?" It was Alex and I immediately felt relieved.

"Oh, fine. Auggie and I are just hanging out with my mother, watching some Entertainment Tonight."

Alex laughed. "Really?"

"Yep and Auggie's begging to stay up to watch you on The Tonight Show."

"Are you going to let him?"

"God no! That's way too late for him."

Auggie had been listening with eyes glued on me and ears perked up. "Mom," he whined.

"But I'm going to tape it for him," I added.

My mother listened with little interest, but the same could not be said for Auggie.

"Would you like to talk to Auggie?"

"Not to hurt your feelings, but that's who I was calling for. I was just about to ask..."

My insides leapt on behalf of Auggie. "My feelings are not hurt at all."

"Good." The word slipped off of his tongue almost seductively. "I'll call you back later, okay?"

"Of course. In fact, I'm going to give Auggie the phone before he spontaneously combusts."

I handed the phone to Auggie and watched him as he immediately started out of the room with it.

"I just saw you on Entertainment Tonight. How cool was that?!" Auggie said as he went.

263

I don't know that my heart could have swelled any more without killing me over Alex having called specifically for Auggie. I really wanted to say something akin to "See there!" to my mother but held my tongue.

I hadn't been the only one witnessing Auggie's reaction to seeing Alex on the television or witnessing his excitement over the call. Mother had taken full notice as well.

"Must be nice." I glanced her way. She was gathering up her purse as she aired her observation. "I can't remember ever seeing Auggie that excited."

The phrase "Must be nice," when said by my father didn't mean he was pleased or happy for the person. It meant he was either jealous, was giving them a slap down or code for asking "Who do they think they are?"

"He finally has a father. Of course, he's over the moon. It's all he's ever wanted." It seemed like a no brainer.

Mother caught on to the fact that I thought she was being snarky again.

"Oh, Anna-Cat, no!" She dropped her purse and reached for me, taking me by the shoulders and sincerely looking me in the eyes. "No, I really meant, it must be nice for Auggie. I didn't mean it like..."

I mimicked Dad's voice, "*Must be nice*. Like that?"

We both started to laugh and, through her laughter, Mom said, "No, not like that at all."

"Good because do you know how happy I am for Auggie?"

I wiped my forehead and the sides of my face with both of my hands and mother's touch dropped away. I continued to confide in my mother and she looked transfixed.

"Auggie has a thing about wanting to be normal. I've tried and tried to tell him there's no such thing, but he has in his head."

"Anna-Cat, he really just wants a family." Her head tilted and she gave an understanding smile.

264

"But he's had a family all along," I insisted.

"I know you've done your best for him. We've all done our best, but we've all known it's not the same." Her eyes dripped with sympathy and mine started to pool with tears. "Well, all of us but your father."

The thought I was having about this being the best conversation I'd ever had with my mother was cemented when she said, "I'm sorry about earlier."

I'd never known my mother to be one for being willy-nilly with apologies, but she wasn't nearly as stingy with them as my father had been. They might have been rare, but when she gave them, she did them right.

"I'm not changing my stance about us having hated him for so long." Cupping my face, she further explained, "I'd hate anyone who ever hurt you."

An image of my father flashed through my mind over that statement. I knew she was not telling the full truth, but I understood.

"And, Anna-Cat, when he left or didn't come back or whatever, I didn't even know who he was and I hated him for doing that to you. I may not have been the best mother, Lord knows I've had my faults, but I love you and Auggie more than anything."

I don't know when it happened, but at some point during the conversation, we'd sat down facing one another on the edge of the couch.

I leaned over to her and hugged her. "I know, Mama, and I love you. He might not always show it, but Auggie love you too."

The embrace lasted a moment and then she slinked back, straightened herself and said, "It's getting late and I really should get on the road before it gets too dark."

It wasn't unsettling the way she'd ended our tender moment. I think she was just trying to save face from getting all weepy in front of me. I played along.

"You could stay here if you like, but I understand if you want to go. I don't know about you, but I always prefer my own bed." I shifted the subject a little as she gathered her purse again. "Make sure you watch for deer. Between here and Augusta, those beasts seem to have a death wish."

Mother stuck her head in Auggie's room and told him goodbye before she left. It wasn't long after that before Auggie emerged, giddy as a lark after having spoken with Alex.

"He said the interview we saw was taped earlier and he'd already done The Tonight Show as well. I always thought those things were live." Auggie was in complete awe of Alex and the information.

"So, what's he up to now?"

"He was driving, or being driven," Auggie clarified, "home after the movie. He said the movie was great and that Heath Ledger is really scary as The Joker. He said he was blown away by the performance. He said he would take me to see it when it comes out."

More normal, a dad taking his son to see a comic book movie, I thought, but said, "Sounds like fun," out loud.

"He said he would call you once he got back to his condo," Auggie told me.

Now Auggie wasn't the only one excited. I tried not to show it, but I couldn't wait to talk to Alex. I wasn't a weak woman, but when it came to Alex, I was. I had no will power at all. I knew it was ridiculous to think we could pick up where we'd left off. We seemed to be taking it slow but doing a fine job of being the us that I remembered.

It was nearly midnight and Auggie had long since been asleep. I was in bed, reading the latest copy of <u>American Family Physicians</u>, my favorite medical journal. I was doing all I could to wait up on Alex's call. Despite the recent medical breakthroughs and the light from the bedside lamp, I was minutes from falling asleep when the phone rang.

Chapter 27

Alex...

The day wasn't nearly over by the standards of most in this part of the country, but it was for me. I was so spent I barely had the energy to turn the key in the lock to my condo, a loft space in an area of L.A. that my realtor said was on the cusp of revitalization. That was four years ago and it was as sketchy now as it ever was. The bright side was that no press or fans thought to stalk me here. It was about as far from the bright lights and glow of the Hollywood sign as I could get.

When the key turned and the door eased open, the place was as foreign to me as the hotel rooms I'd been staying in for the better part of the last year. I'd put up a minimal amount of artwork and a handful of family photos adorned a table next to the couch, but still, this place looked generic. It looked like any bachelor could live here. It was stark and cold compared to the homey feel of Anna and Auggie's little farmhouse, which I missed beyond measure.

I'd spoken to Auggie earlier in the afternoon, trying to be considerate of Auggie's bedtime and not call him too late. Anna kept him to a strict schedule even in the summer.

When I spoke to Auggie, I told Anna I would call her later. The thought of talking to them is what had gotten me through today. It was the carrot at the end of the race that had been my day.

Before calling Anna, I took a moment to call Ashley. Like Anna, Ashley was on east coast time.

I skipped past the introduction. My sister was well acquainted with my voice. "Hey, what are you all doing this weekend?"

"Nothing."

For once my sister responded and I could hear her in full. Evidently, I'd called late enough for the girls to be in bed. I looked at the bedside clock for confirmation. It was after 11:00 p.m. their time.

"Good."

"No, not good! My plan is to do *nothing*. No soccer. No ballet. No whatever you want. Nothing." Ashley huffed.

"Wouldn't you like a minivacation at a lake house?" I tempted her, leaving out the part that I wanted the whole family to come.

"Of course, but..."

"Great! Pack your bags. I'll send a car to take all of you to the airport on Saturday morning. I'll be in touch with further details. Love you. Kiss the girls for me. Bye." I hung up before she could protest.

I then called my mother followed by my father. I gave the both of them more details than I gave Ashley. I invited them up to meet their grandson. They were both on board and probably started packing as soon as I hung up the phone.

Another call I'd made last week was to the real estate company in Milledgeville that managed my lake house. I spoke with Jessie Branen the owner of East Sinclair Realty, who assured me his company could accommodate my needs. I needed my house on Lake Sinclair vacated. To do this I offered to purchase a comparable house near the lake and pay for my tenants to move to the new house. Basically, for the right price, anything could be accomplished and this fell into the category of anything. Mr. Branen also assured me he had a crew and connections to paint, remodel and furnish the house if needed. I agreed to the works.

"Please just use your better judgement," I told him. "Spare no expense. Just make it happen for me if you can." I also gave him my number so he could send me where to wire funds.

I took a shower and fell into bed. That bed was the first thing I'd purchased for the condo. I still couldn't believe I'd spent twenty thousand dollars on a mattress, but it was a king size and, when I laid down in it, it was like being hugged by a gentle, fluffy bear. It was the only extravagant thing I'd ever purchased aside of the lake house that I bought on a whim to hold the ghost of mine and Anna's relationship. I relaxed into the bed with the phone in my hand, thanking God I'd bought this bed and the lake house. As I dialed Anna, I made a mental note to order another set of mattresses tomorrow morning for the lake house.

The phone rang twice and a groggy Anna answered with a combined, "Hello," and yawn.

"Hey. I'm sorry for calling so late." I said, sinking back into my bed. It was a little after nine, but it was after midnight in Georgia. I should have been doing more interviews, but I cancelled them to come home and call her. I ached to hear her voice. I ached even more to be back with her and Auggie.

"No," she yawned again. "It's okay. I was still up. I'm in bed, but just doing some reading."

If she was, she hadn't been long for it. She sounded as if I'd just woken her up from hibernation.

"I'm serious. I can call back in the morning if you like," I offered.

"If you hang up on me, I'll fly out there and kill you," she groaned.

"I'll hang up now and take my chances just to get you to fly out here."

"You're not funny."

"I'm not trying to be. I'd do anything to have you here."

Anna and I made small talk for a while. We mainly talked about Auggie and how her mother was doing since her father's death. Finally, things took a turn.

"Can I ask you something?" Anna prefaced.

"I've told you before you don't have to ask if you can ask me something."

"Okay," she agreed. "What's your plan?" I could hear her rustle around in her bed.

"Can I ask you something?" I volleyed back at her.

"Of course." I was sure from the way she said the words, she rolled her eyes at the same time.

"What do you mean?"

"What?"

"What do you mean, 'What's my plan?'"

"Look," she said before laying it out for me, "when the promo for Entertainment Tonight said you were going to be talking about fatherhood, I felt the color drain out of me. I thought you were about to tell the world about Auggie."

"Oh..."

"I don't know what's going on here, but Auggie and I live in a bubble and we do okay."

"Ah." I gathered what he was saying, but wasn't really ready for that serious of a conversation. "Have you ever thought of moving to California?"

"No." Anna was abrupt.

I had only been teasing her about moving to California, but she was not playing.

I pressed on out of curiosity. "Haven't you ever wanted to be famous?"

"I'm one of two doctors in the area. I'm famous in a small town and that's more than enough for me."

"Fair enough," came out with a chuckle, but what she'd first said came back to me. "You do okay, but are you doing great?" I asked as bluntly as she'd asked for my plan.

"What?"

I was more direct, "Okay is not the same as good and good is not the same as great. Do you want to be great?"

"Huh?" She was wide awake now, but obviously confused.

I guess we were having the conversation after all.

"It's been years, but when you were nineteen and I was twenty-four we were great. I know you remember." I took a breath. "My plan is to be great again. I want to be great again with you and with Auggie."

I didn't know what I expected her to say, but when she said nothing it made me nervous. It made me start to ramble on.

"I have some obligations I have to finish up. It will probably take me until the end of the year, but I'll leave all of this movie stuff behind. I'll move to Georgia. I'll move anywhere..."

Anna interrupted, "I'm not asking you to move anywhere..."

"I know you're not asking, but we've already established that you all aren't moving to California..."

Anna cut me off. "You don't even really live there."

"The point is, I want to live where you are." Becoming adamant about what I was saying, I sat up in bed. "I want to be where my family is and you are my family, you and Auggie."

"So, you'd move here?" she asked as if she didn't believe me. "I know this sounds," she searched for a word and came up with, "cheezy, but what about your fans? Are you going to be followed here by..." Anna struggled again.

"Anna, we'll figure it out," I tried to assure her.

"I can't just figure things out," she snapped. "I have Auggie to think about. We can't just wing it. The first time we met, you shot me and you didn't call the ambulance because you didn't want the paparazzi to know. You can't tell me you don't care about that anymore. Plus, I've seen the lengths the press goes to for photos of celebrity kids."

"First of all, *we*." I emphasized, "We have Auggie to think about. It's not all on you anymore. Or, are you telling me you want to give up?" I asked that question before really thinking about it. As soon as I'd said the words, I wanted to take them back. I wasn't sure I wanted to know the answer.

There was a long pause before Anna replied and it caused my insides to swirl. I hadn't been sick over a woman since the last time I lost her. Now, I felt damn near nauseous. "Say something."

"No, I don't want to give up. I just want to know your plan. I fear I might die if I lost you again and that scares the shit out of me, but Auggie losing you scares me more and what absolutely terrifies me is losing Auggie."

"We're not going to lose Auggie."

Anna then gave me a run down on unrealistic parental fears which culminated with the synopsis of the story of the Lindbergh baby. "You are new to this whole parenting thing. You don't get it."

"Oh, I get it alright. Could you not tell by the way I forced that copy of my will on you that I'm petrified something will happen to me and what if something happened to you? How would he be taken care of? As you said, I might be new to this, but let me tell you instinct or something is kicking in. I've never been scared of flying before, but I couldn't focus on anything else other than the thought of the plane going down and never seeing you and Auggie again. What if he didn't know how much I loved him? And, what if you didn't know that I loved you so much I could hardly look at you without feeling an overwhelming since of failure and regret for not being there for you when Auggie was born? And all these years I've already missed with him... When I tell you I'd give up everything for you two, I mean it. I'd leave it all behind and not because you had to ask, but because I want to be with you two. There is nothing in this world I want more than to be with you and Auggie for the rest of my life."

"I wish you were here," Anna sighed.

Knowing the answer, I asked anyway. "Where are you right now?"

"In bed."

"And you want me there?" I wanted to hear her say it.

A breathy response was forthcoming, "Yes."

"Then this is just cruel, huh?"

Anna giggled.

"After all these years you finally want me in your bed again and I'm almost two thousand miles away."

"To be clear, I never stopped wanting you..."

"What are you wearing? No, don't tell me..."

"Black tank top and matching boy shorts."

"Oh, jeez, I said don't tell me. You're so mean."

"Ever had phone sex?" Anna asked shyly.

"No," I stammered, a little shocked that she'd asked.

"Me neither," she confessed.

With skepticism and curiousness, I wondered aloud, "Do you want to?"

"Maybe tomorrow."

"Maybe I'll come home tomorrow and we'll forget about the phone."

A hint of embarrassment hid in the giggle that she gave.

Anna and I carried on talking about nothing and everything and all that was in between. My bedroom was dim and quiet, barely lit by the street light filtering through the blinds. All of the noise of the city faded away and there was a vast nothingness. All I could focus on at that moment was the sound of her breathing.

"I miss everything about you," I confessed quietly.

Her silence spoke volumes. Compliments and declarations embarrassed her more than sexual innuendos.

"I thought I would have to go on missing you forever."

She still didn't say anything, but I knew she was listening.

"I thought about finding you. I thought about it all the time."

"Why didn't you?" she voiced.

"I was scared you would be married, have children, been all the things that I had dreamed we would be." I paused, recalling the times I'd talked myself out of hiring

273

an investigator to find her for me. "I wanted you to be happy. I really did, but I wasn't selfless enough to know that I could handle finding out that you had moved on and forgotten me. It had been years and it wasn't realistic to think you were pining away for me."

"But I was." She let the words hang in the air a moment before explaining. "I was happy with Auggie, but that's a different kind of happy. I was never really happy without you. I tried to move on, but pieces of you were everywhere. I couldn't go to an Italian restaurant without ordering your favorite meal just to feel like you were with us. In fact, I've ordered shrimp scampi so many times that Auggie thinks it's my favorite. I almost bought a black Ford truck once so my memories of riding with you would be more vivid. I was ridiculous."

"Thank God Auggie found me."

"Yeah and I'm so glad you came to find us."

Anna's voice was becoming softer and raspier the longer we spoke. Her smooth velvety southern sound faded as she grew sleepier. It was after 2:00 a.m. her time when I closed our conversation.

"I'll call you tomorrow night, okay? Now go get some sleep so you can function at work in the morning," I told her. "I'll call you tomorrow night."

"I love you, Alex, and I can hardly wait for you to come back to us."

"I love you too and, about Auggie, thank you."

"For what?" Anna yawned.

"For giving me a son."

Chapter 28

Anna-Cat...

A hateful sideways glare, that's what I gave the alarm clock through fuzzy eyes as I tried to come alive. I felt half-dead, but there was no time to give into the strong desire to roll over and go back to sleep.

My twenty-two-year-old self could have popped back to life easily after staying up half the night, but my thirty-two-year-old self needed coffee and Advil to even attempt to get dressed. I knew better than to stay up like that, especially without having a nap earlier in the afternoon the way I did on the days I was scheduled to work in the emergency room at the county hospital, but I would do it again. In fact, I looked forward to staying up half the night on the phone with Alex tonight and that thought would be what got me through the day.

I put one foot on the rug at the edge of my bed and then the other. That maneuver alone was done with calculation and not ease. Today was going to be rough. I knew that going in, but I didn't know just how rough.

Brushing my teeth and, again thinking of my younger self, the image of Sally Ann Watson, Sally McNeil as she was now known, materialized in the mirror before me. For as long as I could remember she had been my best friend. We might not talk for weeks or see each other for months, but we had that sort of friendship that just picked right back up as if no time had passed at all.

"I need to call her," I said to myself after rinsing the toothpaste out of my mouth.

Sally Ann was the only person who knew about me and Alex. She had been the only person in the world, besides my parents who knew who Auggie's father was and she'd known since day one. We never talked about it, but she knew.

Sally Ann married one of the McNeil's from Thomson after college, one of the few McNeil's who actually moved out of McDuffie county. Much like Sally Ann's family, they were old money, just not from the Hill Section like we were.

Randy McNeil was oldest of two boys whose family made their old money from a moonshine still during the prohibition days and parlayed that into a fortune in real estate. He was a feminine man who I would have bet good money was gay. I felt that about him from the first time Sally Ann brought him home. He was portly, unathletic and balding even when we were in college, but Sally Ann saw something in him that others of us didn't. I always thought it was dollar signs, but as it turned out, they fooled me. Randy, as he was aptly named, and Sally Ann went on to have four boys and one daughter.

If anyone asked them, they just said they lived in Charleston, but Randy and Sally Ann lived in Goose Creek, South Carolina. He worked for Boeing as an aircraft engineer of some sort and she was a hair stylist at a prominent salon in downtown Charleston, that is before got pregnant with their first child. Their children were like doorsteps, having been born one right after another with their daughter coming last.

"I just have to have a girl," I remembered Sally Ann telling me.

Sally Ann lived by her word and kept having babies until she got her girl. Little Catherine Anne McNeil was partially named after me and partially after her mother. She was barely six months old and it was on my to-do list every weekend to drive to Goose Creek and meet my namesake, but one thing always led to another.

As thoughts of Sally Ann and her family continued to raid my thoughts, I still could not believe she was my age and had five children under the age of ten. The thought of having more than Auggie boggled my mind, let alone having five and three of them still in diapers.

After struggling to stay awake during my morning appointments, a case of tonsillitis, another of foot fungus, a broken toe, and lastly having to explain to Mrs. Pearl Carter who was all of ninety-three years old that an annual OB-GYN visit just wasn't necessary at her age, I finally started to get my bearings. For lunch, I ate a sandwich that one of the nurses brought in left over from the weekend at her family's restaurant, Cross Roads Bar-Bee-Que, just over the county line. It might have been left over, but it was heavenly and I devoured it as I dialed Sally Ann.

Sally Ann recognized my voice immediately so I jumped right in, skipping the pleasantries. "You will not believe who turned up right after Daddy died!"

Although the birth of Catherine had been sometime past, she was colicky and Sally Ann was not able to attend Daddy's funeral. She sent a beautiful spray and a lovely card to Mother. Everything had been such a whirlwind since Daddy died that this was the first chance I'd had to call and talk to her.

"Who?" she gasped, realizing from my tone that it was someone big, but didn't bother to make a guess.

"Alex, Alex Allen."

The line was silent. She didn't even utter one word of shock and Sally Ann was never one to be speechless.

"Did you hear me? Auggie's father showed up here."

Still nothing more than a very flat, "I heard you," from her end of the line.

I elaborated and told her how Auggie had sought him out in Atlanta and I went on with every detail.

Finally, Sally Ann interrupted, "Did he tell you anything about me?"

I stopped in my verbal tracks, "No." Slight pause. "Why would he?"

It was then that Sally Ann confessed to her part in my father's scheme and filled in some blanks that I hadn't even considered. I'd been bedridden and so single-minded, willing Auggie to stay in the proverbial oven and devastated over Alex, that I hadn't wondered what happened to my things at the lake house. They just magically appeared at my parents'. Seemed stupid now not to wonder about such things, but I had bigger problems at the time.

"What do you mean, 'You're sorry?' What did you do?" I asked, slowly trying to piece together what she was saying.

"Your father paid me a thousand dollars to get your things from Alex's and leave a note on the counter," she started to confess.

"He paid you a thousand dollars? Why so much? You would have done anything for us for free." Before she could answer I mustered up another question. "Did you read the note?"

"The note was from you to Alex saying you never wanted to see him again and not to look for you," she said.

"What? I never…"

"I know…"

"But you left the note?"

"I needed the money."

There were no words to describe the level of shock that befell me. "Did you just say you needed the money?"

"No one knew it, but I got a DUI on the way back to school one night between Sandersville and Milledgeville. I didn't want my parents to know…"

"Sally Ann, what the fuck?" I rarely said the word "fuck" and, even now when I felt the urge to scream the question that ended in that word, I kept it low and I only did that because there were other people in the office.

"I'm so sorry. Please forg…"

I didn't let her finish her request. At that point, I did scream. I screamed, "Never!" and slammed the phone down as hard as I could. I meant for her to feel it like the folks in Charleston felt the 1898 earthquake, the one that rang church bells in Boston.

I left my office, delivering parting words to the receptionist, "Please cancel my appointments for the afternoon," and kept walking.

278

At a brisk pace, I marched across the street and a few blocks down to the office of another of my friends. The one who'd just been promoted to best friend status. I barged in Millie's office like one of her criminal clients needing a fast fix for a pending warrant. I had an urgent need for an attorney and for a friend to listen to me. I needed my will changed and every trace of Sally Ann McNeil being Auggie's guardian in the event of my untimely demise wiped away at once.

Hearing the ruckus of me entering like Cramer entering Jerry's apartment on Seinfeld, Millie came out and escorted me into her back office. She had three. Two in the building there on Broad Street so she could juggle clients and a third out at the Inn she helped run with her husband.

One of the offices in town held her desk and she generally met with individual clients in there. The other office there held a small conference table and she met with groups or did real estate transactions in that one. I knew all of this not just because I regularly ate lunch with her and her secretary at the small conference table, but also because this was the room in which my grandmother signed over all of her property to me before she died. The office at the inn was her work from home type space. She didn't meet clients out there.

Seeing the veins bulging in my head and gathering that this wasn't a social call. Millie put me in the office with her desk while she finished a home sale in the other.

"Have a seat. I'll be right back," she told me.

Millie would have had as much luck telling me to grow wings and fly as she did in telling me to sit down. I paced, back and forth in front of her desk, wearing a path in the deep green shag carpet that was left from when old Attorney Bell had the office. He died recently and, although paint samples and carpet swatches were laying on a side table, Millie obviously hadn't made up her mind yet on the colors.

I was mid-lap of my path in front of her desk when Millie returned about ten minutes later.

"What on earth is going on with you?" Millie asked quietly, shutting the door behind her.

"You won't believe me when I tell you!" I tried to stop walking, but all I managed was ringing my hands and slowing my stride a little.

Millie made her way over to me while calmly giving me the go ahead. "I think you better let me be the judge of that."

I started at the beginning; the storm, the gunshot wound and showed her the little scar on my arm, meeting Alex when he rented my parents' house, living with him, and having the time of my life. I paced and talked.

I stopped to take a breath and noticed Millie seated behind her desk, her chin propped on her fists and elbows on her desktop. Her mouth was dropped open and she had the look I knew she would, disbelief.

I continued, "Alex was in Canada filming a movie when I found out I was pregnant..."

"You're shitting me, right?" Millie's words were the result of utter astonishment.

I stopped walking long enough to look her in the eye and reply directly. "No. Alex Allen is Auggie's father. My parents knew and, you've met Sally Ann, the three of them were the only ones who knew."

I picked back up with the story of how Auggie found Alex in Atlanta just before my father died. "That's when everything started to turn upside down for me."

"So, Alex didn't know about Auggie."

"No," I replied and went on to fill her in about how I thought Alex had dumped me and how he thought I had dumped him. I also told her the part my father played and what I'd just found out from Sally Ann.

"Wow." The word fell out of Millie's mouth as I stopped pacing again and just stood there fuming.

"I am so pissed right now I could physically hurt someone! As if I didn't screw up my life enough by getting pregnant at nineteen, my family and my best friend really hit it out of the park when it came to fucking up my life."

280

Millie's brows went up. She'd never heard me use such language.

I scoffed, "My father did it thinking he was protecting me, but Sally Ann played her part for the thousand dollars my father paid her. She kept my child from having a father for one thousand dollars and to get out of a DUI without her family knowing."

My anger was still brimming, but I know a confused look came over my face. "She sold our friendship so she could skirt trouble that she got herself into. Do you know how much Auggie has missed having a father?"

Now it was my turn to be the one with her mouth dropped open to the floor. I was so furious and baffled and knew nothing could be done to make anyone pay for what they did to Auggie, let alone what they'd done to me. Frustration overcame me and forced the tears. I covered my face with my hands and rubbed at my eyes with my fingers.

I snatched my hands away with a fury. "I need you to rewrite my will. I don't want Sally Ann McNeil to ever have a chance to make any decisions regarding my child should anything happen to me."

"Nothing's going to happen to you."

"Really? My heart is racing right now and I could very well have a heart attack or a stroke, I'm so pissed." I was also hurt.

"I realize you're a doctor and would know better about such things than me, but don't you think you are being a little dramatic about..."

"NO! Please, just change the will."

Millie cocked her head and sighed. "Okay. I'll change the will, but who do you want in place of her?"

"Alex as the primary and you and Gabe as secondaries."

"Isn't Alex a stranger to Auggie? Would he even want..."

"Just trust me. Alex and then you and Gabe."

281

"Okay," Millie agreed. "I'll have the changes made before I go home today."

"Thank you."

There was a lull in the conversation as I started to calm down. I sank down into one of the arm chairs in front of Millie's desk as she called out to her secretary and asked her to print a copy of my will from the computer.

Mrs. Jeannine came in with the document. "Hey, Doc," she greeted me, having been in the back at the copier and missed me when I first came in.

Mrs. Jeannine was a woman of at least sixty and had worked for Attorney Bell from the time he moved to town until he dropped dead of a heart attack in the spot where Millie was now sitting. Watching Mrs. Jeannine walk away, I knew I was watching the equivalent of a bank vault when it came to the secrets. She knew every detail of every divorce, adoption, criminal act, and anything else for which anyone in town would disclose to an attorney.

The biggest secret Mrs. Jeannine kept was that she'd carried on a thirty-year affair with Mr. Bell. That only came to light because she had some explaining to do when she and Millie called me in a panic the day of Mr. Bell's heart attack. At their ripe ages, Mr. Bell and Mrs. Jeannine liked to spice things up. They were doing a bit of Monica and Bill role play with her under the desk and Mr. Bell's pants nowhere in sight. He was a large man, and though Mrs. Jeannine managed to push him enough to get out from under the desk, she and one hundred and ten-pound Millie couldn't move him to get his pants on and neither of them were keen on touching a dead body. That's when they called me and as far as anyone knew when they called the ambulance, he died working at his desk and fully clothed.

I knew Mrs. Jeannine's secret, but neither Millie nor I saw the point in tempting her with mine just yet.

"I'll make the changes myself and we won't let anyone else know about this."

"Thanks. I know it's going to come out sooner or later, but I'd rather put it off for now."

282

"I understand."

After I calmed down and Millie started to ask questions about Alex coming back starting with, "What's he really like?"

"Are you a fan?" I gave a sly grin.

"Who isn't?"

The both of us had a big belly laugh and Millie's tiny frame shook as she cackled, "I have wondered all these years which married man around town you were protecting..."

"Oh my God!" I started to protest. "You thought I'd had an affair with some married dude? You think so little of me!" I placed my hand over my chest and gave a good impression of 'Well I never.'

"Seriously, I'm real proud of you! You landed Alex Allen." Millie continued laughing.

I answered sincerely, having put away the giddiness. "He's wonderful. He always has been."

"You still love him?"

I nodded. "I've loved him ever since I first met him. I would have never left him and I'm fairly sure he wouldn't have left me either." Feeling the anger starting to boil again, I tried to soothe it by airing it. "I'm so pissed that we were cheated out of the last twelve years, but I'm more pissed for Auggie! Seriously, I could murder someone over this."

"You don't have to convince me," Millie was quick to heap on an assurance. "You know about Gabby's real mother. If I ever see that bitch again..." Millie trailed off without giving the full description, but I understood her quite clearly.

Millie and her husband, Gabe, had two daughters that were basically the same age. One was their biological child, George-Anne. Their other daughter, Gabby, was adopted. It was a sordid story, but Gabby was the biological daughter of one of Gabe's former girlfriends and a married man. His ex-girlfriend had tried to pass Gabby off as Gabe's and then basically abandoned her to Gabe when she was just days old.

The girls were beautiful, but only an idiot would have mistaken them for twins. George-Anne was the perfect mixture of her parents, both with blonde hair, and she was fine boned and tiny like Millie. Gabby had jet black curls and green eyes. She was tall and thin and the only person anyone could say she looked like was Vivian Leigh as Scarlett O'Hara. Millie and Gabe raised both girls as their own and, although it wasn't a secret that Gabby was adopted, the circumstances of her adoption weren't widely known.

As far as Gabby knew, her mother gave her up because she couldn't take care of her. The real truth, as far as Millie saw it, was that Gabby's mother threw her away and Millie hated the woman for it. She hated "that bitch," as she almost always referred to her, who didn't have any regard for Gabby at all and I think that's what I was having trouble with, too. It was as if my father and Sally Ann never once thought of Auggie as a person with rights and feelings when they did what they did.

Chapter 29

Alex...

"Hey, I didn't wake you, did I?" West Coast time, it was only a little after 8:00 p.m., but East Coast was another matter.

"No. I took a nap earlier so I could stay up late."

Anna was all yawns last night, but tonight she sounded damn near spry.

Anna began to direct the conversation. "Do you know what I like about you?"

"What?" With baited breath, I waited for her answer.

"I like that you specifically call for Auggie. You can't imagine how much that means to him." I could hear the smile in her voice.

"Although I appreciate you saying so, I didn't do it so you would like me better."

I did it because my father had set a good example for me. When I was little and he was still married to my mother, if he was away for business, he made a point of making a call for each of us. He made each of us feel special and he never cut things short and asked us to pass the phone to the next. After they divorced, he kept up that practice. Ashley got a call around 7:00 p.m. and I got a call at 8:00 p.m. We could almost set our watches to it. He also called on different nights so it didn't seem like he was making the calls out of obligation.

"Well, I like it." Her voice was serious, almost seductive sounding and I liked that.

We went on to talk about Auggie's day and exchange details about our own days. It went on like that for about thirty minutes and then Anna went serious again.

"What would you do if something happened to me?" she asked.

Why couldn't she ask me something like, "What are you wearing?" or "Are you in bed?" That's what I was going to ask her next. I was wearing a pair of boxers and I was already in bed. No parties at Chateau Marmont for me and being photographed out and about at night was not a part of my obligations for this trip. Morning voiceover work at the studio and afternoon interviews for the movie I'd just finished was all that was on tap for it.

"What do you mean?" I'd just found her again. I didn't want to think about losing her.

"About Auggie, what would you do?"

Shit. I hadn't thought about that.

"And don't start by saying, 'I guess I would...'"

"I've never played Twenty Questions before and if this is it, I don't really like it." I tried to lighten the mood.

"No, I'm being serious. Would you take him or..."

"Of course, I would take him!"

"You just met him..."

"Stop it. I would take him." I was adamant.

"And where exactly would you take him?"

"Anna, nothing is going to happen to you." I found myself sitting up in bed as I tried to stop this line of conversation. I loathed the thought of not having her in my life.

It was then that Anna finished telling me about her day. She told me about, calling her former friend and her involvement in deceiving us and keeping us apart. That former friend had been who Anna had appointed to take care of Auggie in the event that something happened to her. Needless to say, her day culminated with the changing of her will. I found this slightly amusing since I had just done the same for Auggie's sake and Anna refused to take a copy of my new will until I forced it on her. She'd found the whole idea of anything happening to me and my being prepared, just ridiculous at the time. It wasn't so ridiculous when she was worried about Auggie being cared for in the event something happened to her.

"I know it sounds like a bunch of girl drama, but I wouldn't trust her to comb his hair at this point!"

"It doesn't sound like girl drama. It sounds like you're long overdue for cutting her off, you just didn't know it until now." With no thought of how this woman's actions had derailed my own life, I was furious on behalf of Auggie and Anna. What I went through losing her was excruciating, but my misery paled in comparison to what Anna and Auggie had gone through.

"I won't leave him to my mother because..."

"No need to explain..."

"I have another set of friends, a married couple with two girls about his age, that have agreed to take him if..."

"Anna, seriously, please stop. I said I would take him. He is my son."

Anna continued the exchange, "But he lives here."

"I know that, and nothing is going to happen to you, but if it did, I would likely already be there so if you think I wouldn't live there to make his life more comfortable, you're wrong. Plus, we already discussed my living situation last night."

Anna let out a sigh of relief and stopped arguing. "Okay," she said simply.

"Now," I started, determined to change the subject, "about tomorrow. Were you able to get the afternoon off?"

"Crap! I had forgotten about that." I could picture her face, all screwed up and frustrated with herself. "I had to reschedule this afternoon's appointments and I think my staff may have just moved them until tomorrow. I'm so sorry."

"No problem, but you'll be done by 5:00 p.m., right?" I asked gingerly.

"Yeah, I should be done by then."

"It's okay for Auggie to miss practice this weekend, right? And, you both will be packed?"

"I can't believe I am saying this since you haven't told me where we are going, but yes." The spry sound in her voice had returned.

"Good and it's a surprise so just go with it."

"Fine. I'll just go with it." Anna teased me.

"Perfect. So, my plane gets in at noon and I'll come straight to Wrens. Will Auggie be home?" I settled back onto my pillow and relaxed now that all of the business appeared to be out of the way.

"He has practice in the morning so he'd better be home when you get there." Anna gave a laugh, but not one of real amusement. What she said, had the ring of something my step-mother would have said about me when I was his age.

"Okay. I'll just have some father/son time with him. You don't mind, do you?"

"What's to mind? I think it's a great idea and Auggie will love that. Make him take you out to Seven Springs." Anna went on to tell me about the friends that she said would take Auggie and how they owned an inn called Seven Springs and it had a creek that ran around it. "Auggie loves to go out there and wade in the creek. You can have lunch out there too, if you like."

The flight the next day from L.A. to Atlanta was damn near enough to make me swear off flying. The heightened sense I had over my own mortality combined with the turbulence that jolted us more than the handful of earthquakes I'd felt during my time in California, did not make for a fun ride. It was terrifying and when I changed planes for the flight to Augusta, I contemplated renting a car and driving. The only reason I didn't rent the car was because I had plans with Auggie that I didn't dare break.

The flight to Augusta was, thankfully, uneventful. The plane landed and I went on with my day just the way I'd planned. I picked up Auggie, we ate lunch at a cool restaurant at the inn and I got to meet Gabe, one of the owners of Seven Springs and apparently the guy who would be raising my son if anything had happened to Anna if I hadn't agreed to step up. He seemed like a great guy, but the days of anyone raising my son but me were over.

After lunch, Auggie and I played in the creek. It wasn't more than shin deep, but the water ran so cold that our lips turned blue.

"Sixty-eight degrees year-round," Auggie had touted his knowledge about the creek. "That," he pointed to the old hotel, "was built around the turn of the century and was a major tourist stop on the railroad between Louisville and Atlanta. That's what folks around here say."

"Interesting," I acknowledged before splashing him again.

We must have looked ridiculous, but even if there had been anyone around to see, neither of us would have cared. Auggie and I played like giant children, kicking water at one another and seeing who could last the longest standing in the water before succumbing to the cold and jumping back onto the bank.

"They also say this creek starts from the side of a hill," Auggie added.

"Do you think we could walk up stream until we find the beginning?"

Auggie grinned, seeing this as a challenge. "We can try."

With those words, he started walking up the creek and I followed. We continued to talk and splash one another as we went.

Far upstream and way back in the woods, Auggie brought up a subject that I'd purposefully avoided, his mother and the guy to whom she'd been engaged.

After the intro to the subject, Auggie described how they met. "She saved him in a wreck when they were in college."

I flashed back to a night when I was living at the lake house, a night just before she officially came to live with me. She was working at a restaurant in town part-time and that night after she got off work, she witnessed a horrible accident on the way out to the lake. She stopped and pulled one of the drivers involved from his vehicle and waited with him until the ambulance took him away. The next morning, in an attempt to soothe her mind about whether he lived or not and while she slept, I went to the hospital to check on him. I found that he was busted up really good, but he was going to live. In that moment, I recalled exactly what that bloody, scraped, bandaged and casted boy said to me. He said he was going to marry that angel who saved him the night before.

I snickered and under my breath, I said, "I guess you tried."

"What?" Auggie glanced back at me as he ducked under a vine hanging across the creek.

"Nothing."

"I didn't think he was right for her," Auggie continued, lifting the vine as high as he could for me to pass under.

"Why's that?" I asked, not so much out of curiosity, but to keep up my end of the conversation.

Auggie stopped, turned to face me and stood to his full height. "Because he didn't like me."

The way he looked at me, I couldn't tell whether he was searching my face like a test to see how I felt about him or what? The look was definitely more than just assessing my abilities to navigate the stream. Either way, I stopped and stood up as well, shaking off the water on my hands from where I'd used them to crawl under a low hanging branch.

"What makes you think he didn't like you?"

"Because..."

"That's not an answer."

Auggie started up stream again.

"Auggie, come on. He didn't do anything to you did he?"

Auggie barely looked back, shrugging off what he was about to say. "He referred to me as 'the Little Bastard' when he thought I wasn't listening."

Auggie's delivery was so matter of fact. It was clear that he cared or he wouldn't have brought it up, but he did his best to give off an air of apathy.

"You heard him? Who did he say that to? Not your mother?" I was anything but apathetic.

"No, not her." Auggie was quick to defend Anna. "He was on the phone both times I heard him say it. He always sent me to play outside when he would come over or, if they went on a date, I was never invited. I had to go to my grandparents' house."

"Oh." I continued to follow Auggie and listened closely to hear him above the sound of the babbling water.

"He didn't want me. They probably would have gotten married if it weren't for me." Auggie held another branch for me.

Despite knowing this wasn't about me, my gut took a punch then. I focused on the branch and Auggie's consideration in holding for me.

"Thanks," I said, taking it from him and dipping my head to go under.

"I was seven and it was scary."

Stopping in my tracks, I reached for Auggie, turning him back. "What was scary?"

"He gave her a ring and, well she doesn't know I knew, but a week later he told her it would be best for everyone if," tears rose in his eyes and he stuttered to get it out. Apathy was gone. "If I went to live with my grandparents. He told her he wanted her to move to Charleston where he was from and it wouldn't be fair to take me away from..."

My temper flared. "Fair?" I was about to give an answer to my rhetorical question, but checked myself. Obviously, Auggie knew full well what wasn't fair and me expounding upon it wouldn't do him any good. All I needed to do was let him know that I was on his side and would never try to get rid of him.

I pulled Auggie into a hug. I wrapped my arms around my son and guaranteed him, "I will never, ever send you away or even try. You, August Allen Calloway, are my child. Mine. And, I will never try to take your mother away or make her choose between us. I choose you, Auggie." I paused and then repeated, "I choose you."

I loved Anna more than just about anything, but there was something inherent in me which I knew for certain. I knew if there was ever any circumstance that would force me into a choice, I would choose Auggie. I felt to my core that good parents would choose their child above all others.

The boy, nearly as big as I was, sobbed in my arms and called me, "Dad," and said, "I'm so glad you came back."

Auggie didn't have to say it, but I knew without a doubt Anna had chosen Auggie too and sent that sack of shit packing. That sack of shit whom I now wished had died in the streets of Milledgeville all those years ago. I wished that on him because he'd hurt my son.

Once he'd calmed down, Auggie wiped his eyes and started further upstream. He was still determined to find the origin of the spring. He also carried on with details of Anna's dating history or lack thereof. He told me that Anna had given up dating after she dumped the asshole.

"Really, he's the only one I remember. She didn't have time for it between school and work and me. That's what my Granny said."

"And Granny is?" I wondered aloud.

"Granny, was Mama's grandmother. We live in her house."

After walking and walking in the freezing water, Auggie and I found the start of the creek. Upon the discovery, Auggie acted much like Rocky having topped the stairs, jumping around and fist pumping. I high fived him, but didn't see it as the Olympic triumph that he did. What I did see as a bit of a triumph is knowing that Anna had not dated hardly at all in the years when we were apart. Of course, I wasn't so full of myself that I attributed it to how she couldn't get over me, rather I believed Auggie's account of her having a full schedule.

We made our way back downstream and hit Gabe up for ice cream at the inn. We ate the ice cream in the truck on the way back to Wrens. I'd managed to get the same truck I'd had earlier in the week.

Pulling into their driveway, Auggie and I found Anna's car.

"Looks like your mom's home already." I nodded toward the car.

"Oh, no, that doesn't mean anything. She walks to work."

I cocked my head at him and the look of disappointment must have shown on my face.

"Don't worry. She'll be home soon." Auggie shook his head.

"Am I that obvious?" I smirked.

Auggie smiled and nodded, "You have it bad, don't you?"

"What do you know about having it bad?"

"I know all about having it bad." He sounded so confident.

I couldn't help but laugh. "Because you've had it bad so many times?" I asked, referring to his vast experience.

"God, no!" Auggie was offended. "Because Granny used to make me watch her soap operas with her."

I just rolled my eyes and laughed. He was fine with me knowing he watched soap operas, but not thinking that he was some sort of a little Casanova.

Chapter 30

Anna-Cat...

A sight for sore eyes was waiting for me on the steps of my front porch when I got home from work. I could see him sitting there when I turned the corner onto my street. I noticed him long before he saw me. I wanted to run to him, but I willed my legs to keep their pace to a walk and that was a struggle.

It wasn't like I didn't know he was there, that he was back. Auggie had called me at work and left a message telling me that Alex was taking him out to lunch. I knew he had come back, but seeing him really hammered it home. He said he would come back and he did. I managed to keep my body from racing to him, but I couldn't stop my heart.

Alex stood up to watch me coming when I was still two houses away. He waved and I waved back. I wondered if he could see me smiling stupidly from there.

The closer I got, the better I could see him. To me, I always thought he had the ideal male figure and the way he wore a pair of jeans was almost sinful. As I walked along, I could hardly take my eyes off of him, speculating that he didn't wear Wrangler's or Levi's like the guys around here. I'd never taken the time to notice the brand before, but it must have been really expensive or maybe he had them made specifically to fit him. The way they hung from his hips and flowed straight down his legs, barely pooling at the top of his sneakers, they weren't too big for him, but they weren't tight either. I wouldn't describe them as fitting, but hanging. His jeans hung and his t-shirt clung. Eye-candy, that's what he was. He always had been.

Coming closer, I made out the writing on his t-shirt and suddenly I recognized it. The words pulled tight across his chest, "Georgia College."

"Oh my God! I can't believe you still have that t-shirt," I said to him, turning into my driveway.

"Yep," he called back. "It's my favorite."

"I love it!" I said, amazed that he still had it.

It was a t-shirt I bought for him at the college book store back in 1996. It was one of a few that I gave him with a couple of the college baseball caps to wear around town so he would blend in. I didn't really believe it would work, but the ball caps, shirts, a perpetual five o'clock shadow and sunglasses kept him incognito while he lived there.

Alex met me at the bottom of the steps with open arms and eyes that looked me over hungrily.

I wanted that welcome home kiss and Alex appeared to want as bad as I did, but I warned him off. "You may not want to get too close."

"Says you!" Alex disregarded me.

Still smiling and very tempted, I turned my shoulder, slinking back. "No, I need to shower first."

"Shower before kissing? No way, Babe, I've been dreaming of this moment every minute for two long days."

"This," I pointed up and down, from my head to my thighs, "is not sexy. I've got the vomit of a six-year-old on me from here to there." I motioned from my knees to my neck, adding, "and all in my hair. We ain't even shaking hands right now."

I cut past him playfully and I thought Alex was going to give chase.

"Alex Allen, don't you touch me!" I squealed as I darted up the steps toward the front door.

"No worries about that now!" Alex laughed.

Having heard the commotion, Auggie threw open the front door to see what was going on just as I reached for the door handle.

"Ewe! You stink!" Auggie announced, holding the door.

I ducked past him into the house. "Thanks, son!"

Once in the shower I went through the whole beauty routine, washed my hair, scrubbed and shaved here, there and everywhere. It wasn't a quick process so naturally an impatient knock came on the door.

295

"You've got ten minutes and then I'm coming in!" Alex yelled through the door.

"You wouldn't!" I gave a teasing yell back.

"Try me!"

Luckily, I was about done, but I wanted to dry my hair before he came in. I didn't want him kissing me while I looked like a wet cat any more than I'd wanted him kissing me while I smelled like a stomach virus.

"Just be patient," I hollered one more time.

His seductive sound came through the door. "Oh, I've been patient. I've been real patient."

I was as giddy over him as I'd ever been, hiding in the shower, stifling giggles, and half hoping he would come in while praying he wouldn't.

Twenty minutes later, my hair was mostly dry, a light layer of makeup had been applied and I was dressed in a baby blue wrap dress with matching strappy cork heeled sandals. I felt sexy and worthy of kissing him now.

Alex tapped three times again. "The anticipation is killing me!"

Alex was leaning against the door and almost fell in when I opened it.

"Wow!" he said, seeing me and catching himself. "Oh, my brown-haired girl. You are breathtaking."

I wasn't used to anyone ogling over me the way he did and, again, my embarrassment set in. I dipped my head, to hide my red face and the return of the stupid smile. One nice word from him and it was like I had no control over my face.

"So where are we going on this road trip of yours?" I asked, still looking at the hardwood floor around my feet.

With a quick, deliberate move, Alex had me in his arms. "Shut-up and kiss me."

His arms crossed over my back and he held me to his chest, arched me back and kissed me so hard it took my breath away. My lips swelled, my breasts heaved and my knees went weak. Regardless of how I felt about him and the electricity that ran between us, Alex was one Hell of a kisser. He so knew what he was doing and it drove me half out of my head. It was like he knew better than to just release me, he wound it down and weaned me off like an addict.

Loosening his hold on me, Alex panted, "The only reason we're stopping is because I want to get where we're going before dark."

"Where are we going?" I asked again, and again Alex responded coyly, "That's for me to know and you to find out soon enough."

I thought I was done traveling the road between Wrens and Sandersville. I thought I was finished getting stuck behind chalk trucks between Sandersville and Milledgeville. I thought they might one day finish the Fall Line Freeway, the name of the four-lane highway they were building between Wrens and Milledgeville. I was wrong on all accounts.

Well before Sandersville, Georgia, I had an idea where we were going. It wasn't just any old road trip, but it was our first road trip as a family and I was certain Alex was taking us to Milledgeville.

Auggie was asleep in the backseat by the end of the street we lived on. I was in the passenger seat and my hand was in Alex's before we left my driveway. Now, my head was leaned back on the headrest relaxing as Alex dodged the caution barrels separating the lane from the latest road construction.

"You are so beautiful," Alex said in a soft voice that could have melted cement.

I'd been looking out of the passenger's side window and thinking about nothing when he spoke. I let my head roll toward him and my eyes slowly fell his way. Feeling the heat rise in my cheeks, I bit my bottom lip and dropped my eyes to hide the flustered smile that came over my face every time he complimented me.

"Thank you." I blinked, letting my eyes rise to his face again.

Alex drew my hand to his mouth and kissed the back of it. His eyes were heated as he took them from the road for a moment and lent them my way.

"Don't..." I began.

"Don't what?" He gave me the same once over.

"Look at me like that."

"Why? What's wrong with looking at you?"

I whispered, "Like you know what I look like without..."

"I do know what..."

I argued back, "Not now, you don't and be quiet. Auggie will hear you."

Alex brought my hand back to his mouth. He drew a circle with little licks and in between each one he kept up the exchange. "I doubt much has change." Again, he let his eyes float over me. "And we can correct any misconception I might have at any time."

I giggled, embarrassed at his blatant suggestion.

Our banter and innuendos continued to the heart of downtown Milledgeville and only stopped when Alex parked the truck in front of The Brick. Brewers was gone. Now The Brick, a pizza place that was a staple to my diet while I attended college there, had moved down the street and taken the store front where Brewers had been.

"No more Brewers, huh?" Alex observed.

"Guess not," I said sadly. I would have given anything to have had dinner there for old time's sake.

A groggy Auggie, who'd napped the whole way, yawned through his question. "Where are we?"

"We're in Milledgeville," I replied. "Get your shoes on."

Auggie yawned again. "Okay."

"Y'all up for pizza and wings?" Alex shut the truck off.

Auggie perked up. "Always." He also rustled around in the seat, quickly digging around in the floorboard for his Nikes.

Over the basket of wings, I told Auggie and Alex, "This place still has the best Buffalo wings I've ever had."

During dinner Alex explained to Auggie about Brewers and that I was working there the night he came to find me.

"Your mother was the absolute most gorgeous girl I'd ever seen. I wanted to impress her so badly, but I came off more like a stalker when I showed up here while she was working."

Auggie looked at me, slightly blushing over how Alex had described me, but still listening to him attentively.

Alex didn't stop. Between bites of his slice of pepperoni pizza, he filled Auggie in on how we met, but glazed over the gunshot portion. He told Auggie how his family told him to go find me after Master's week and how he did. Alex focused on how we dated when he first came to Milledgeville to find me and Auggie listened intently.

It pulled at my heart strings for Alex to give Auggie his story of us and I appreciated the fact that Alex kept it PG. I also loved the idea of what we must have looked like to others in the restaurant. No one recognized Alex, thanks to ball cap and vintage Georgia College t-shirt which he'd brought back with him from his home in California. We looked like everyone else, like a normal family, mom, dad and son having a conversation over dinner.

Back in the truck after dinner and waiting for the light to change at the corner of Hancock and Wilkinson streets, Alex adjusted the rearview mirror so he could glance back at Auggie. "Have you ever seen where your mother lived when she was in college?"

"I see it every day?" Auggie replied.

Alex furrowed his brow and shot Auggie a puzzled look.

"He meant my dorm at college. Alex, we lived with my grandmother ever since Auggie was born. I drove back and forth to school while I finished my undergrad degree at Augusta State so Auggie didn't mean to answer like a smarty pants. Did you, Auggie?"

I had been less than pleased with the tone of Auggie's response.

"No, ma'am," Auggie replied, sounding more respectful.

"I don't know why I assumed you graduated from here." The light changed and Alex gave it the gas. He also pointed to the first of the white columned brick buildings to our right that made up the front campus of Georgia College. "Well, that's Bell Hall, where your mother lived when she was going to school here."

Gazing out my window and reminiscing about a kiss Alex and I shared on the steps of Bell, I reached over and placed a hand on Alex's thigh. "I had some fun times there," I told them.

"Why didn't you keep going here after you had me?" Auggie leaned up between us in an effort to feel more a part of the conversation.

Before answering him, I asked him if he was wearing his seatbelt and he immediately sat back and I heard the clicking. The response that came to my mind first was that there were too many memories for me to return there, but the main reason was, "I had to have help with you and I couldn't afford to hire anyone and rent an apartment." I didn't fully spell it out for him that my parents had cut me off.

Alex made the zigzag around the main campus and eventually we turned onto North Columbia Street and headed in a familiar direction.

"Are we really going where I think we are going?" I drew back and looked at him, waiting for confirmation.

Each time either Auggie or I had asked where we were going, Alex simply replied, "It's a surprise." This time he just looked at me and grinned widely.

"I thought you said it was rented." My smile grew bigger.

"It *was*," he said with emphasis on the word "was."

My mouth fell open and my insides did flips. All I could say was, "Oh my God," and in a giddy way.

Auggie leaned in again, but not as far this time due to the restraint of his seatbelt. "What are y'all talking about? Where are we going?"

Alex took his eyes off the road for a split second, giving a quick turn to Auggie. "We're going home to my house."

"What? I thought you lived in California."

Alex cut his eyes at me. "He doesn't miss a thing, does he?"

I gave a little laugh.

Alex simplified his explanation, "I own a house on Lake Sinclair. I haven't lived there in a very long time, but I've always considered it my home."

"Oh," Auggie slumped back in his seat, not really understanding what Alex meant.

"Actually," Alex started to correct himself, "now home is wherever you and your mother are."

I looked back at Auggie. The sun was setting and the street lights hadn't fully kicked on, but I could still see him and he was beaming. The wattage in his smile was nothing short of a thousand and it was priceless.

A turn here, a turn there, and finally we were on the last leg of our trip. We were on the road to the lake house. A few more houses had popped up over the years, but little else had changed.

Even though there wasn't another soul on the road, Alex put on the blinker for the driveway. Seeing the headlights hit the mailbox and scan across the front yard, my stomach knotted and my color drained. The anticipation of seeing the house was almost too much.

A light was on at the front porch and the glow of a lamp shown through the big window in the living room. The headlights came to rest on the front door. The front door was still painted red, exactly the same color as the knockout roses that grew in flower beds along the front of the house. The white paint on the exterior of the house and the black shutters really made the red pop and it was as pretty as it had ever been. Everything was exactly as I remembered it and it looked like it was waiting for us to come home.

Taking it all in, I covered my mouth with both hands. It was all I could do to hold back tears. In my heartbroken state after Alex didn't come for me, I could never bring myself to drive out here. It seemed so ridiculous now.

Feeling the dam of tears budging, I said to myself, "I'm not going to cry." I couldn't help but think that if only I had come out here, I might have found Alex. We might have avoided all of... I shook off the notion.

There were so many memories, wonderful memories, tied to this house. Snippets of those memories flashed before my eyes as we pulled down the driveway. I glanced down at my ring, catching and twinkling in setting sun that shown through the cab of the truck, and remembered the day the UPS man delivered it. He'd come right up to the door, presented me with the package and, as I signed for it, he remarked on how it came from Canada. I opened the big envelope and, to my surprise and delight, I found the most extravagant gift I had ever been given. Looking at it now, it looked exactly the same, a circle of flawless diamonds encased in platinum. I also remembered how I nearly fainted at the sight.

The memory of the ring was the least of the memories that house held for me. I also made love to Alex for the first time and almost every time there. Auggie was conceived in that house and he should have grown up in that house, but I shoved that last thought aside.

"Take these and go have a look around. Pick out your room." Alex handed Auggie the keys from the ignition after we came to a stop.

Auggie, remarking with enthusiasm about how we had a lake house, was eager to follow Alex's instruction and sprang from the truck.

Alex also got out and rounded the truck. Opening my door and offering his hand to help me out, he grinned. "Come on. Let's go home."

My insides jumped for joy. All thoughts of what ifs melted away like the setting sun. Seeing the delight in Alex's eyes with Auggie running through the front yard full of excitement to see his new home, all I could think about was how this was a dream come true. My dream for as long as I could remember, was finally coming true.

Chapter 31

Alex...

Anna and I were barely through the front door when Auggie ran past, screaming, "I found my room!"

"Auggie, don't run in the house!" Anna chastised him and he slowed to a canter still struggling to contain his excitement.

Remembering himself, Auggie paused long enough to ask if he could go see what was out back.

"Sure, but don't go out on the dock without one of us..." Anna instructed and followed with an explanation to me, "He can swim fine, but parental paranoia and all, you know."

"There's a dock?!" The night was having more of an effect on Auggie than if we had turned him loose in a candy store.

"What kind of lake house would it be without a dock?" I asked jokingly like his question was absurd.

Auggie went running out the backdoor as Anna stood wide-eyed, taking in every detail of the room. I'd hardly been able to take my eyes off of her all night and now was no different. I waited and watched her, hoping the new décor met with her approval.

It was the first time I'd seen the house in years, too. I probably should have inspected the handiwork. I'd paid the real estate company a hefty sum to take care of the house in preparation of our return. I continued to watch Anna to see if she was pleased. If she was pleased and if she was happy, then it was all worth it.

The bangle bracelets on her arm clanked together as Anna ran a hand along the arm of the couch, feeling the fabric. It was an overstuffed, beige couch that looked to be the length and width of a twin bed. Anna glanced back at me, "This is different."

304

"Do you like it?"

The house wasn't exactly the same, but I still felt nostalgic over it. I told myself that even if we had never left, it could very well look like this now. We would have bought new furniture, repainted the walls and changed out the pictures and artwork on the walls over the years.

Anna tilted her head toward the floor. I couldn't see her face, but I knew the look. She did like it, but she was cautious about revealing just how much.

Anna took in everything from the deep brown leather accent chair, a wide, hobnailed and tufted seat with a matching ottoman, to the photos on the walls. The chair was a masculine piece and I loved how the room was built around it and the photos of us. I'd sent copies of the only photos I had of us together from when we lived here. I asked to have them blown up in black and white and hung on the walls. I wanted it to look like it was our home and, in my opinion, the decorator had succeeded.

Someone had taken the liberty of editing the photos and made an entire gallery series on the wall by zooming and cropping them. They managed to turn three photos that I'd held onto from when we were young and a copy of the few Anna had shared of Auggie into an arrangement of family photos on the living room wall. The photo in the center was a 20 by 30 inch that was all Anna. In the original version I was standing behind her, holding her around her waist and looking over her shoulder. In this version, I was the blur that made up the background.

I never really noticed until that moment just how she was looking back at me. The dimples in her cheeks were on full display and I could see every freckle that dotted the bridge of her nose. Her lashes were as long as my pinky finger and her eyes were cutting up and back. On her lips, in her eyes, her full cheeks; her smile was infectious and it was a true picture of happiness.

The other photos, a close up of her hands crossing over mine as I held her, and other tidbits cut from the originals, those paled in comparison to the big center photo and the ones of Auggie. Even Anna studied the arrangement for a moment, focusing more on the center photo and commenting, "That's a bit much, don't you think?" before moving on to the kitchen.

"That picture has always been my favorite of you," I replied. Even before the magnification, it was my favorite photo of us. I remembered every detail of the exact moment surrounding when Sally Ann snapped it.

In the kitchen, Anna commented, running her hand over the kitchen countertop the same as she had done to the couch,

"It's exactly as I remember it."

I leaned against the door jamb inside the space the size of double doors that joined the kitchen and the living room. I just watched in silence.

Anna focused in on one spot on the countertop. "I'm pretty sure Auggie was conceived right here."

"Say what?" She completely caught me off guard.

"Yep. I'd be willing to bet good money that this is it."

Mouth agape, I managed to formulate the question, "How do you know?"

Anna blushed. "We... well... you know," she patted the spot next to the sink, "right here one night." Anna paused, trying to push through with the details. Her face turned a bright red and she could hardly look at me as she explained deep thrust.

"You really gave it your all one night," she described, slightly coding her meaning. "And, it hurt a little. I would have died before I said anything, but I held out on you for a couple days after that." Anna chuckled, still rosy in the cheeks over her disclosure. "I'm pretty sure it happened then. The delivery and the timing and what not seemed to line 1up."

"Oh." I tensed, finding myself slightly embarrassed as well. I don't think I'd ever had a girl use the phrase "deep thrust" to me before.

"To think of it," Anna said, again keeping the conversation light-hearted, "there really wasn't a surface in this house that had not been exposed to my bare ass." She laughed through her words and fanned herself. "I really don't know what's come over me."

"You're happy."

"Yeah," she bobbed her head. "Let's go find Auggie."

I left the threshold of the door and made my way to her. "Wait a minute."

Fingering the tendrils of loose hair, I tucked them behind her ears before cupping her face in my hands. I would have been content to be lost in her eyes, those doe looking eyes with lashes batting so slowing, their own Morse code that blinked out a signal telling me to come closer, look deeper, and never stop.

Her full lips moved and a whisper came forth, "I love you."

The words I'd have sold my soul to hear, echoed again and again in my ears.

"I love you," came forth again, firmer and more confident.

"I'd let you have me time and again on any surface around here." Anna fisted my shirt in her hands and pulled me down to her, locking eyes with me more fiercely, "I regret nothing."

My Lord, I relished the words, "I love you," and that was enough in itself, but the way she said "I regret nothing," the pitch and tone and emphasis, was like verbal garters and stockings. My dick went from zero to full erection in the span of a breath and had the squeaking of the back door not gotten my attention, I may have embarrassed us all by tearing off Anna's clothes with my teeth and taking her on the kitchen counter right then.

"You know what this place needs?" Auggie announced, bursting through the door.

307

Returning to her normal voice and guarding the view of my bulging pants, Anna stepped casually around me. "I think it's perfect just the way it is."

Anna squeezed my hand, prompting my question. "What does it need, Auggie?"

"A dog!"

Anna looked back at me, pursing her lips. "He's been wanting a dog forever."

I sided with Auggie. "I've always thought this place needed a dog, too. Something like a Golden Retriever that would fetch sticks and tennis balls from the lake?"

Auggie's eyes went as wide as saucers and he popped back with a vibrant, "Yes! Exactly! Can we get one?"

Anna and I spoke over each other.

I indulged him. "I think we should!"

Anna was the voice of reason, "We're only going to be here two days..."

"Mom..." Auggie's hopes sounded dashed.

Talk of puppies put the kibosh on my hard-on, so stepping to Auggie's side was viable at that time. "She has a point, but maybe there's a pet store in Macon and we can call there tomorrow morning. If they have a Golden Retriever, then we'll drive over and get it."

"Really?!!!" Auggie perked back up.

"And then what?" Anna asked. "You live in a hotel."

"About that," I started to correct her. "I'll be living here, for now."

Auggie stood looking on as Anna and I continued to discuss my living arrangements.

"That reminds me, what happened to the renters?" she asked.

"They live two houses over now."

"Huh?" she scrunched her nose.

"It's really cute you when do that, just so you know." I referred to the face she made.

"Stop it! What..."

308

She had more questions, so I jumped right to the explanation. "I wanted this house back so…"

"You just made them move?" Anna seemed offended on behalf of my renters.

"Not exactly." I held up my palms, trying to calm her. "I bought the house that was for sale on the other side of the one next to this one and I had them moved over there."

Auggie rejoined the conversation, "Now you have two lake houses?"

"Yes and no," I replied to him.

Anna still looked put out with me. "I thought you said they lived here for years and years."

"To be clear," I went on the defensive, "they got the better end of the deal. It's a bigger house over there. You should see it."

"That's not the point."

"Isn't it? Aren't you accusing me of being unfair by making them move? Well, I'll walk you over there tomorrow and you can have a look and see who got the better end of this deal. Their rent stayed the same and I paid the movers, too."

"Auggie, would you excuse us?" I said politely.

"I'm going to watch TV in the living room." Auggie went one way as I took Anna by the hand and led her out onto the back deck.

The door had barely closed behind us when Anna started in. "You can't just wave your checkbook and…"

Not in a confrontational way, I went nose to nose with her. In the same way she'd delivered her statement about regrets, I said, "I can, I did and I will."

Anna pressed her palms to my pecks, trying to keep the space between us, but I didn't stop.

"What's done is done and I'd do it again just to see the look on your face when we turned in here. The look when you walked inside and the knowledge of when Auggie was conceived, yeah, to see that and have that, you bet your ass I'd do it again."

I leaned closer and wrapped my arms around her, planting my hands firmly on her ass. I could see her chest heave over the shock of the ass grab. I whispered with an unwavering stare, "And, I'll get him a dog, too."

"You..."

I didn't let her finish. I skimmed my lips over hers, before giving her behind even more of a squeeze. She didn't resist, but moved her lips with mine, parting and opening, allowing me to devour her. Our hips met with the tightening of the grip one of my hands still on her ass. Her arms were around my neck pulling me in as I crossed my other arm around her back. We pulled at one another with a fever that could have melded us together. All the while, ravaging her mouth, I prayed Auggie found something on TV to watch and that he didn't come out.

I eased back just enough to bury my face in the hair that hung near her temple. "What are the odds of getting him to go to bed early?"

With her face in my neck, still giving little laps and nibbles, Anna replied. "Not favorable."

"Shit," I chuckled, with the shaking of my laugh rolling from me through her.

Just as quietly, she asked, "Are you sure you really want a dog?"

I wound her hair in my hand and pulled it back, lifting her face. "Are we going there again?" I kissed her, lightly.

"It's not ten yet and, if there is a pet store in Macon, it's probably still open. I'm just sayin..."

"You're not suggesting we go now?"

Anna's face grew more concerned than playful. "I'm not real keen on dogs."

"Why not?" No sooner had I asked the question did I remember the story of Anna's brother and the family dog. With the flash of the memory of how they'd both died, I immediately apologized. "I'm sorry. I wasn't thinking."

"No, you were doing a good thing for Auggie and..." She had to work up the courage to put the words out there.

310

"I've been putting him off for years about getting a dog, but he...well..."

"Anna, it's okay. We don't have to..."

"No, we should... for him."

"Dr. Calloway, I just love that you are so smart!"

Anna inched away. "One thing, though."

"What's that?"

"When's your family getting here? Aren't they supposed to arrive in the morning?"

"Right. The plane comes in at 11:00 a.m."

"So, you'll have to be at the store when it opens."

Anna and I continued to make plans about tomorrow. I told her not to worry about anything because I had a local chef coming to prepare the meals and so forth.

"I can cook," she protested. "And they should stay here."

"No. I love your cooking, but I want you to enjoy yourself and not work. Secondly, they can't stay here. This is a three-bedroom house and there are seven of them and one of them cries all the time. So, no, they're staying at a bed and breakfast on Liberty Street. Trust me, this is best for everyone."

"So, where am I staying?" Anna nuzzled into my neck again and wrapped her arms around me.

"With me?" I dared to hope.

"I think that could be arranged."

A few minutes later, Anna and I drug ourselves apart and back in the house. I found the phone and took it to the master bedroom to track down a number for any Petland that might be in Macon while Anna corralled Auggie to the shower and then to the bedroom that he'd claimed. He was too old to be tucked in or read to, but they had a night time ritual. They prayed together and I watched from the doorway.

After the completion of their ritual, I entered the room. "Sleep well." I tussled his hair, not sure if it was appropriate for dads to kiss their twelve-year-old sons goodnight. Perhaps he was too old for that.

I fumbled over the words, "Goodnight," wanting to add, "I love you," but Auggie took over.

"Night, Dad. I love you." He sat up in bed and reached to hug me.

I leaned down, wondering why I didn't think of the hug and initiate it.

Back in the hallway, Anna aired her observation with amusement. "That looked awkward."

"I have no idea what I'm doing." I shrugged and then reached to take her hand.

"You're over thinking it." Anna said, leading me toward the master bedroom.

"And trying too hard?" I followed.

Anna didn't say anything. She didn't have to.

"They didn't have a Golden Retriever or a Yellow Lab."

Anna smiled, knowingly, "You know that's for the best, right?"

"Oh, I'm getting him a dog!" In addition to my original intention of pleasing Auggie, I saw it as a challenge now.

"Yes, but you realize giving him a puppy on the very day he's to meet your whole side of his family for the first time wouldn't help him make a good impression? And, he's never had dog before so he'd spend his time ignoring them and doting on the dog. You can see how that's not..."

I slapped my forehead. "Dammit! I didn't even think of it like that," I let out a huff. "I'm sorry."

"Hey, you didn't tell him you were getting him a dog tomorrow so there's no harm, no foul. Just settle down a bit."

"Have you always been a natural at it?"

"At what?"

"Him and knowing just what to do?"

"God no! I had my grandmother and now you have me."

312

Anna said a few more things, but I'm sure my eyes glazed over and my hearing kind of stopped for my mind to dwell on her comment, "You have me."

Finding myself in the master bedroom with Anna wrapping her arms around me, my mind returned to the present.

"The best piece of advice my grandmother gave me was 'Say what you mean and mean what you say.'" Anna looked up at me and reached to caress my cheek. "Fatherhood looks damn sexy on you."

I'd been called sexy by millions of women since I was teenager, but it never meant anything to me. I even made People Magazine's list of sexiest men alive one year, but I didn't even get a look at that issue, let alone buy a copy. It was just a word, another objectification that fell on deaf ears until that moment. I never took it as a compliment until it came from her.

"Thank you," I replied sincerely, meaning it for the first time in my life when it came to someone referring to my looks.

Chapter 32

Anna-Cat...

I hadn't slept naked in years, not since the last time I slept in this house, and I never slept with my door locked. Last night I did both of those things. In that cat nap phase between asleep and awake, I relived exactly what I did, what we did the night before.

Many nights I'd dreamed of the things Alex used to do to me, how he'd made my toes curl and first showed me what an orgasm was. Many mornings I woke up wet from the experience my mind had played out while I'd slept. None of those dreams really compared to the real thing. Nothing compared to what I'd been missing. This morning the catnaps brought back fresh memories as flashes of images on the backs of my eyelids replayed acts and emotions.

A hand on the small of my back with slight pressure from his fingertips, just inside the bedroom door, Alex's touch commanded me to turn to him. His hand stayed right where it was as I obeyed. For a moment, he stood looking at me. His face was a melding of disbelief and burning flames. Suddenly, I was shy under his gaze.

Two fingers under my chin, he lifted my face just in time for me to feel the deep breath he took before meeting my lips. Blindly kissing, backing me up to the bed and scooping me up, he gently laid me crossways on the king-sized bed, but never broke our connection.

From the slide of his hand going from my ankle to my thigh after he unhooked my sandal to the way he parted my legs with a knee, Alex took his time. Slow and deliberate, he undressed me one garment at a time all the while tempting and teasing me with kisses.

Alex sat me up, buried his face in my cleavage, and for a moment, I was nineteen again. Chills sprang up and down my arms and legs as the whiskers of his five o'clock shadow tickled my breasts and his fingers fumbled to unhook my bra. The bra, having a mind of its own, took a little more effort and, when it finally gave, it did so with a pop causing me to give a not so quiet yelp of surprise immediately followed by giggling.

"Shhh." With a low rasp of heat, Alex cautioned. "You don't want Auggie to hear."

Making love to Alex hadn't been far from my mind from the time I'd first laid eyes on him again and I knew tonight was the night. I'd been nervous all day, knowing what was on the horizon. My body wasn't what it once was. I wasn't overweight, but I wasn't rail thin anymore either. I had a few curves now and a few stretch marks from having had Auggie, too. I'd feared Alex seeing me, all of me, and how he would think I measured up to my former self. Now, as I bared myself to him, all of those fears fell away.

My bra slipped from my shoulders and I was down to my panties. I'd purposefully worn one of the few matching sets that I owned, but I wasn't sure if Alex had even noticed. And, if he'd notice anything different about my body, he didn't stop to raise any objection. He kept at his task and before I knew it, he was kissing on the thin layer of material that was the only thing keeping me from being completely naked. Oh, the sensations that radiated through my body as he kissed and licked there! I'd never felt anything like it and I never wanted it to stop. In no time at all, my panties joined the bra and my dress in a crumpled heap on the bedroom floor, but all I could think about was the sensation building up in me and never wanting it to end.

I'd been so distracted with what he was doing to me that I hadn't bothered to help undress him. It apparently didn't matter. Hovering over me, one hand balancing on the bed, Alex used the other, with a little help from me, and pulled the Georgia College t-shirt over his head. With the flick of his wrist, he flung it in the direction of the far side of the bed. I didn't watch to see where it landed since I couldn't take my eyes off of him. I was, as always, completely mesmerized and I had to have him. I had to feel him, completely.

Alex's fair, sandy hair flopped over his forehead and hung tussled above me. Running my hands through it, I tugged. Slowly, Alex came down, studying my face as the anticipation built.

No words were spoken. No instructions were needed. Alex knew exactly what I liked as he was the one who'd taught me what I know. Oh, how I'd missed his scent, his touch, his kiss. Yet, he was with me. Right here, right now. And he continued kissing me deeply. His hands roaming, caressing, making my body quake with anticipation on what would happen next.

Circles made by his tongue around my nipples and the touch of his teeth, ever so slightly grazing across the sensitive flesh, caused my toes to curl and my hips to nearly turn themselves inside out. The gentle hand he slowly ran from my thigh to my ankle commanded my leg to draw up. He didn't just get to me. He made me lose my mind. With nothing more than a touch, he sent my body into a frenzy and I wanted to beg for him to take me. I wanted to scream his name, scream that I wanted him, needed him, was going to die if he didn't stop with this glorious torture.

Leaving a trail of kisses and licks, from my right earlobe, between my breasts to my naval, Alex went lower, gliding over me, raking his stubbled little beard over my hyper aroused skin, tickling and teasing me. He kept going, interchanging kisses, drags of his tongue and a gentle suction every so often all the way from my head to my toes. When he came to my instep and the edge of the bed, he gave me a bite, which was something he'd never done in the past. It was something that I never knew could blow my mind, but it did. Alex watched, unzipping his jeans and letting them down, as my reaction could not be concealed. I arched my back, writhing with need for him.

For a moment Alex stood at the edge of the bed in all of his glory. Naked and on display, he lingered. He wanted me to look and, unable to help myself, I couldn't tear my eyes away. As they floated over him, I admired him for the specimen that he was. Men of his age didn't normally have chiseled abs, cut arms or thighs of a high school running back, but Alex did. He looked every bit the picture of a stallion as he ever did. He was beautiful, absolutely beautiful.

When my gaze came to rest on his face, his eyes were hooded and full of purpose. The exchange of looks had clearly been a turn on for him, and I knew that without glancing south again.

In a flash Alex was back on the bed, hovering over me. I was putty in his hands. Alex could have flipped me over and taken me in any number of scandalous ways. I would have let him. He didn't.

Missionary style, it wasn't boring. It was intimate, the most intimate thing I'd ever experienced. To give it that term was so understated for what it was.

Alex settled in between my legs and the length of him rested at my opening. On the third dip of his hips he slid in, filling me gently, slowly and completely. I wanted to cry out, but not from pain. Not pain at all. I wanted to cry to God, thanking him that this man was mine again.

I rose to meet him at every thrust, but it wasn't because my mind was actively participating. My head was swirling and giddy with the joy of being with him. The world was slipping away and my body was on autopilot, moving on instinct and reactionary to Alex's every touch.

Only a thin layer of sweat was all that separated his chest and mine. He bucked his hips and ground into me time and again and every single time his pelvis met mine, I wanted to open wider. Each time wider, taking him into me more, I just couldn't get enough of him.

My hands were pinned above my head with my fingers clasped in his. From my shoulders to my hips, I was clear of the bed, arching to keep my skin against his. The pleasure was unreal, like nothing I'd experienced since the last time he'd made love to me.

The quaking, the quivering, the rising of my pulse, the heat my face, the water filling my eyes, I was going to cum soon. I'd never cried when I came before, but tears were going to fall. It wasn't voluntary, but my eyes bulged. I was almost there.

"Bite down on my shoulder, if you need to," Alex offered. He felt what was happening, too.

Times in the past I'd cried out his name loudly, followed by that of our Lord. I'd rarely failed to heap on praise and gratitude for a thorough job with those three names and Alex remembered.

I twitched under him and came undone.

"Sweet mother of God, I have missed you," I panted breathlessly against his neck as he flopped down over me, his orgasm having come as the last wave of mine washed over me.

Still twisted together and clinging to one another, Alex whispered, "I have something for you."

"Something better than that?" I asked, maneuvering to lay my head on his chest.

Alex's chest shook beneath my head as he laughed. "Nothing's better than that. Well, just laying here like this is pretty great, but nah. I don't think anything beats that."

For a moment, we just laid there, coming down off of the euphoria.

"So," I finally spoke up, "what is it?"

"You'll find out tomorrow."

My head popped up. I grabbed for the bed sheet to cover myself and acted as if I'd been slighted. "Oh, that's just mean to tease me like that."

Alex grabbed me and flipped me on my back. "I'm not nearly done teasing you tonight."

The ease with which he tossed me left no question to his upper body strength. I never thought I'd be one to find being man handled a turn on, but God help me, my engine was revving again.

By 2:00 a.m., I'd had three orgasms and were it not for his family coming tomorrow and having to get up to see about Auggie, we probably wouldn't have stopped then.

Drifting off to sleep, Alex moaned, "I've always loved you."

I reflected on those words as I floated in and out of sleep that morning, coming to in Alex's arms.

I rolled over, blinking rapidly to focus my eyes and found Alex watching me sleep.

"Good morning, my love." He smiled, smoothing back the tendrils of hair from my face.

"Morning," I yawned and kept my stretching to a minimal, not doing the full star over the bed that I tended to do when I woke up alone. Finished stretching, I settled on my side facing toward him.

"Sleep well?" He didn't sound sleepy at all.

I nodded, the urge to stretch coming over me again. "What time is it?"

"Almost 9:00."

I scrambled, but in little more than two moves I went from flat of my back in the bed to flat footed on the floor. "Oh crap, Auggie!"

"Hey, don't worry about him." Alex reached out and caught my wrist. "I got up with him about an hour ago and fixed him breakfast."

"You did?" I stood frozen.

"Yeah. I took care of him." Alex patted the bed for me to sit back down. "He's playing video games in the living room. He's fine."

A rush of relief went over me immediately followed by a wave of self-awareness. I remembered I was naked, really, stark naked. Noticing this, I decided to take it in stride. I tried to straighten my back and draw up to my full height, but instead I bent with a fit of laughter. I didn't know what came over me other than the knowledge that I was really standing there naked in front of Alex and last night really had happened.

Alex sat up, watching me as I laughed until I cried. I cried tears of joy.

I should have been fretting over his parents' arrival, but it didn't even enter my head. Sheer joy filled me. I was utterly happy, too happy to contain myself. I covered my face as I continued to laugh, trying to pull myself together.

Alex made his way across the bed. He reached for me and caught me by the wrists.

"Don't you dare hide your face," he said in a low voice in which I'd only ever heard him use on me. Standing on his knees, we were face to face as he pulled my hands down and my eyes fell into his. "I love seeing you laugh."

The giggles left me and I succumbed to the notion of just being near him again. I nuzzled my nose into his neck, drawing closer to him, pressing my chest to his. My nostrils filled with a combination of pure Alex and the scent of fabric softener that lingered on his skin from the fresh sheets. I was smelling Heaven, my version of it anyway.

The stubble on his chin prickled over right my temple as our heads tilted towards one another and chill bumps ran down my arms. His chest rose and fell against mine bringing my nipples to full perkiness. Barely six hours ago, he'd given me my third orgasm of the night and now all of my senses were heightened and my body was on the very verge of begging for him again. With each touch, the sensation came over me that I'd never wanted him more.

Barely beyond my climax, a breathless whisper slipped from my lips, "Alex Allen, you are bad."

"In a good way though, right, Dr. Calloway?" Alex rolled off of me and laid proudly on his back next to me, breathing rapidly, coming down the same as me.

"Like you have to ask." I teased before adding more seriously, "I've missed this." My fingers clasped in his, I brought his hand to my mouth and kissed the back of it.

Alex rolled to his side, facing me. "All you have to do is say the word Dr. Calloway and I'm yours whenever you want."

I didn't know whether I liked it better when he just called me Anna or when he called me Dr. Calloway. Whereas the rest of the world called me Anna-Cat, it had always been a treat to my ears the way he alone called me Anna. Now, the way he said Dr. Calloway damn near set my panties on fire. I really needed to stop him from calling me that or I'd never be able to look at anyone without blushing when they addressed me in what should be a professional manner.

"So," I hearing the rasp in my own voice, "Dr. Calloway is off duty so it's just Anna here."

"I like calling you Dr. Calloway." He said it again in that husky, eyes blazing, fire starting way.

"So do I and that's why you've got to stop."

Alex's face shifted to a slight shade of bewilderment and he sat up.

"Let's just leave it at I won't be able to look at my patients straight faced if you keep it up."

Getting my meaning, Alex let out a roar of laughter.

By 10:30 I was dressed and ready with thirty minutes to spare before Alex's family was to arrive. I was excited for them to meet Auggie, but nervous as to how they would feel about me. Alex said he'd told them that I hadn't broken his heart on purpose all those years ago. He didn't use the words "broken heart", but that was the jest of it and he told them what really happened. Essentially, he tried to rewrite history so they wouldn't hate me.

"They don't hate you." Alex tried to convince me as I milled around the kitchen, straightening all of the items on the countertops.

"If someone did Auggie the way you thought I did you and I found out about it, you better believe I would hate them." I didn't go so far as to telling him that I better not ever seen that bitch again, but that's what I meant.

"I promise, they don't hate you."

"If I were your mother, I would hate me." I stopped rearranging the small appliances.

"You never met my mother. I don't think she has it in her to hate anyone. She's actually weird that way." Alex stood calmly on the other side of the kitchen. "Actually, there's one person I think she might hate and I'm not sure I can really commit to the word hate either. I think resent is more accurate."

"And, who is it she *resents*?" I laid on the word thickly and played along.

"My step-mother." Alex clarified, "Don't get me wrong. My mother fully believes my step-mother stole my father, but she resents and envies her more than anything."

Alex was right. The Thanksgiving that we'd hosted his family at the lake house, only his dad, step-mother and his sister came. They hadn't invited their mother. That brought me to a new level of nervousness. This would be the first time I'd met his mother. After his disclosure about her, I envisioned some peace-loving hippie, but the thought of her still unnerved me.

Picking up on the ques when it came to anxiety, like how I started wiping down the spotless counters, Alex came over and took the dishcloth. "Remember, it's not about you today. They're coming to meet Auggie."

"You're right. I know. I know." I dropped my head, feeling a tad ashamed.

Also, the nearness of him sent a flush of heat through me and snippets of memories from last night flicked through my head. Just standing next to him at the kitchen sink wasn't close enough. My arms acted without thought and went around him. I wanted to kiss him again and I couldn't seem to squelch that urge.

"And, Anna," he said, wrapping his arms around me. "You've done such a good job with him," lifting my chin, he forced me to look him in the eye, "all the other nonsense will melt away."

My knees went weak as Alex's lips slid over mine and any thoughts but those brought on by the sheer ecstasy of his touch left my head.

Chapter 33

Alex...

I never used drugs, not one sniff of anything, not one drag. The strongest thing I'd ever had was whiskey and I'd had my fair share of that. I knew what being drunk was and now I knew what getting high was like. I knew there was more than alcohol and drugs that folks used as a means for getting high. I knew it from all of the ads, afterschool specials and a couple of movies I'd seen and one or two that I'd been in during my teenage years. I also knew this because I'd been chasing my own high for almost thirteen years. My high came from being with Anna and last night I hit that high and again this morning.

Studies and experts say an addict can never attain their first high again and they will spend their lives chasing it. I spent a long time chasing my high, burning through women like a crack-head on a pipe. Of course, I could never recreate the feeling I had when I was with Anna and it didn't take me long to figure out that it wasn't the sex that caused what I craved. It was her. She was my euphoria. That notion was hammered home last night, I knew now more than ever, she was my drug. There was no amount of distance that could be put between us and no kind of rehab that could make me want to stop. I would live and die chasing her and my version of high.

Slightly past 11:00 a.m., the two black Suburbans turned into the driveway. My dad and step-mother were in the front vehicle and my mother was in the second with Ashley and her family. Ashley's husband was driving.

I went out to greet them while Anna and Auggie waited inside. Crossing the front yard, I looked back at the house. Through the picture window I saw Anna making over Auggie's hair and tucking the tag in the collar of the shirt he was wearing. Anna's earlier chastising went through my mind.

"If you had told me who was coming and what your intentions were, I would have packed better clothes for him." As it was Anna had only packed t-shirts and shorts, comfort clothes for Auggie. "A t-shirt advertising the latest video game is not my idea of a good first impression."

"Stop worrying. He could be wearing a Budweiser shirt, Speedos and a pair of cowboy boots and I assure you they wouldn't care," I told her.

She was having none of it. "He is a reflection of me and I care."

I had never thought about Auggie like that before. I just knew I loved him and I didn't see past that fact. Now, seeing her still fretting over him, I realized that I had done them a disservice. I'd made her worry about whether Auggie would be liked and question what she could have done to prevent him being disliked.

I stopped in my tracks, turned around and went back inside.

Hearing the whine of the unoiled front door hinges, Anna and Auggie looked my way.

"Come with me," I said, holding out a hand to each of them. "We're going out together, like the family we are."

It wouldn't make a difference to my parents or my sister how Auggie was presented, but a squeeze from her hand and the change that came over her face let me know it mattered to her. He was our son and we would introduce him together and I'd do anything to keep her looking at me like that forever. It was a warm look of adoration that beamed from her eyes straight to my soul. Anna had me in the palm of her hand.

As the two vehicles pulled to a stop, one behind the other in the driveway, I wondered which of my parents would be the first to meet Auggie or would Ashley out run the both of them.

We made a united front with Anna and Auggie standing on each side of me. I couldn't tell whose smile was bigger, my mother's or my father's. I struggled to smile through the pain.

I leaned to Anna. "If you grip my hand any tighter, you're going to spend your afternoon setting the broken bones."

She immediately released the vice. "I'm sorry. I'm just so..."

"Nervous, I know." Still within hers, I gave my hand a little shake to get the blood going again. "It's going to be okay."

The car doors started opening and my attention was shifted to Auggie.

"That's your grandpa." I nodded to my father. "You and I both have his name. Well, his middle name. It's August."

Auggie's face lit up even more.

"And, you know what they say about step-mothers?"

Auggie gave me a cocked eye.

"None of its true when it comes to my step-mother. She's the best and she's going to spoil you rotten." I slipped my hand from Anna's and used it to scruff Auggie's hair.

He twisted away. "Stop. You're messing up my hair."

"That red-headed lady, that's your grandmother." I really didn't know how to elaborate on her and spit out the first thing that came to mind. "She makes really good grilled cheese sandwiches."

Ashley gathered her girls from the backseat of the vehicle and trailed behind, but her husband lingered by the car, not bothering to follow. I was shocked to see that he'd made the trip in the first place.

"That's your Aunt Ashley and your cousins. The little one's Addie and the big one's Mackenzie."

My descriptions were cut short by the spectacle my mother made running to us. I didn't realize she could still run so that in itself was shocking.

"Mom!" I threw out my arms, but she went past me, ignoring me completely.

"You must be Auggie!" She said in a pitch that made me wonder what she'd had to drink on the flight there. She'd certainly never been that excited to see me before. I wasn't jealous, just observant.

My father lingered back, rolling his eyes, but Leslie approached Anna.

Leslie reached for Anna, taking her hands. "It's so good to see you again, Anna-Cat."

"Thank you," Anna said shyly, shrugging her shoulders and looking up through her lashes. "It's good to see you again, too."

"Oh my God," Ashley gushed, pushing Mom to the side and passing the always whaling Addie into her arms.

"You are so much bigger than I expected." Ashley threw her arms around Auggie before he knew what had him.

Ashley's five-foot ten-inch frame towered over Auggie as she came into his personal space. Auggie stiffened, not knowing what to make of my sister's overly familiar actions.

Ashley squeezed and spun around with Auggie. "I am so glad to meet you."

"Mommy?" Mackenzie tugged at Ashley's skirt as she came full circle with Auggie. "Mommy?"

Ashley let go of Auggie and leaned down to Mackenzie. Mackenzie was four and confused by the fuss her mother was making over what must have appeared to her as a strange little man. "This," she said, picking Mackenzie up, "is your cousin, Auggie. Doesn't he look just like Uncle Alex?"

The whole family stopped and marveled over Auggie. There was one thing that was not a carbon copy of me, his eyes. They were the color of Anna's and they grew wide as everyone looked him over and made comparisons. He was the proverbial deer in the headlights.

"I don't know if Alex was as tall at this age," my mother observed.

"Oh, he was tall," Ashley contradicted, "and just as skinny."

Leslie chimed in, "They even have the same cowlick."

My mother shifted Addie, still sniffling, to one hip, and made a gentle caress with her other hand, tracing her thumb over Auggie's cowlicked eyebrow. "It's uncanny."

Auggie smiled under the scrutiny.

Anna chimed in, "They have the same mole on their cheek, too."

Anna gave an indication toward my right cheek as I noticed my father, fingering the mole on his cheek while taking a long hard look at Auggie as best he could from the outside of the circle of women.

"Y'all give the boy some space." My dad stepped forward, guiding Anna and Leslie apart to make room for him to get closer to Auggie.

"I hear you're named after me." My father's voice caught in his throat and I saw what Ashley was talking about just before he pulled his shades over his eyes. There were tears building in his eyes.

Auggie smiled that sheepish, self-conscious smile. He might have had my looks, but he had his mother's mannerisms.

Auggie extended his hand to my father. "I'm August Chandler Calloway. They call me Auggie."

As my father took Auggie's hand and they shook, he corrected Auggie. "No, your name is August Chandler Allen." My father pointed to the mole on his cheek. "I'm an Allen." He nodded my way, "He's an Allen."

Dad didn't point out the mole on Auggie's cheek, the one that grew a little smaller with each generation. He released Auggie's hand and placed his own on Auggie's shoulders. Auggie was transfixed on him, hanging on his every word.

"And, you're an Allen, too," my father said before pulling Auggie into his arms.

Unlike with my sister, Auggie didn't stiffen. He wrapped his arms around my father and my father pressed that same DNA riddled cheek to the top of Auggie's head. Auggie held on until my father was ready to let go.

My father wasn't a rich man. His education wasn't nearly as extensive as Anna's father's had been. He'd served two years in the army, two years that he talked about as if they'd been forty. Those were the years that taught him the things his father didn't teach him, honor and what it meant to be a man. He'd made mistakes and there were a few that I remembered clearly. They'd affected me directly and deeply, but all of that was washed away when I saw the way he was with Auggie. Before me was a man who loved his family, who loved my son, his only grandson, at first sight. I don't think he could have loved Auggie more had he been a newborn baby. Despite the Ray-Ban's, I could see the depth of his love written all over his face. In that moment, I wanted Auggie to be the kind of man my father was. One that had the capacity to love like that.

I'd been afraid that the bond Auggie used to have with Anna's father, and some sense of loyalty to him, would force Auggie to keep my father at arm's length. But my fear was unfounded. From that moment on Mom, Leslie and Ashley were afterthoughts.

Leslie trailed along behind Dad and Auggie wherever they went, contributing little more than any wallflower would. Auggie led them out back to look at the lake. I overheard him explaining that the place needed a dog and a boat.

"Preferably a pontoon because that would be big enough to hold all of us," Auggie specified.

I chuckled to myself thinking how Auggie's list of needs for the place had increased since last night.

Anna and Ashley migrated to the back deck with the girls. They insisted on setting the patio table for lunch in anticipation of the first delivery from the chef I'd hired. I showed Mom the house since she was the only one who'd never seen it.

Ashley's husband was nowhere to be found. He'd never been much of a joiner during my past visits so I didn't pay him much attention. I always figured he was shy or didn't like the fuss that was made over me when I came home.

I ended my mother's tour of the house in the kitchen. Looking over the kitchen island, past my mother and through the window on the back wall of the kitchen, I watched Anna as she got reacquainted with my sister.

Anna was showing Mackenzie how to wipe down the table as she was preparing it for lunch. Ashley stood on the other side of the table from Anna, her back to the window, swaying with Addie cuddled to her chest and Addie's head on her shoulder. Addie's face was red, but it appeared she'd settled from full blown screaming to sniffling. I looked past them to Anna.

Anna's hair was blowing in the breeze that floated across the backyard, swirling it around her face. She lifted her hand and wiped the tendrils from her face, but they were back before she reached the crown of her head. It was as much a losing fight as was me tearing my eyes from her.

I was hardly paying attention to my mother speaking to me until she mentioned, "I've been seeing a life coach," my mother said, "and I realize now that your father and I were never a good match."

I'd heard of life coaches before, but never put much stock in them. Now I figured they might be some sort of miracle workers if this one managed to help her come to this realization which was twenty-five years overdue.

My father, who'd become instantly enamored with Auggie, was on the dock with my step-mother and Auggie. I could see them beyond Anna and Ashley. For a moment, I watched Auggie and my father skipping rocks off of the dock. I remembered what he'd told me before agreeing to come to the lake house, after learning my mother was coming, too.

"I've told you before that I am not apologizing to your mother for leaving again. Don't ask me," my father

329

warned, but he added a concession, "I'll treat her as I would any old friend that I haven't seen in a while. Just don't let her read anything into it."

Catching my mother in this state led me to tell her a truth that I hoped she was open to hearing. My mother always thought that Leslie stole my father from her and, were it not for Leslie, they would still be married. The truth was that my mother failed to realize that as far as my father was concerned, their marriage was dead long before he met Leslie. Meeting Leslie only gave him the motivation to leave. The truth was, Leslie never gave him the time of day and told him she never would because he was a married man.

I told my mother Leslie's side of the story, the story Leslie told me after I was well into my twenties.

"I didn't tell him to leave your mother," Leslie had said to me. "I didn't think he would. In fact, I thought he was a dirty pervert, hitting on me when he was married and I told him so."

I told my mother how I was dumbfounded at Leslie's description of my father as a "dirty pervert" and how I'd exploded with laughter at her description, nearly snorting the Sprite I was drinking through my nose.

Leslie hadn't noticed my reaction and carried on with her story. "The next time I saw him was six months later when he told me he was recently divorced, showed me the papers and set about chasing me until I agreed to go out with him. I only caved so he would go away and leave me alone. I kind of thought he would get over his midlife crisis and go back home to your mother."

The truth I wouldn't tell my mother, no matter what terms she'd come to, was that looking back over the memories I had of my father with Leslie and those I had of him with my mother, he never looked at my mother the way he looked at Leslie. He never watched my mother the way he watches Leslie when she's not looking. He's fascinated with her the same way I'm fascinated with Anna, the same way my mother was with him.

For the first time in a long time, I felt sorry for my mother. Thanks to the way I felt about Anna, I understood the depths to which my mother's heart had been broken, but I wanted her to be able to move on and I felt terrible that she'd never been truly loved. I also felt horrible that her unrequited love had poisoned the best love she could have ever known, the unconditional love of her children.

I leaned into my mother as she processed what I'd told her about my father. I couldn't remember the last time I'd put my arm around my mother, but I put my arm around her. "It's not too late you know."

She looked up at me curiously.

"Forget about Dad," I offered the best advice I could. "Focus on your grandchildren and I bet you will find more love than you could ever imagine."

I knew it wasn't the same as romantic love, but I knew from personal experience, that would come when you least expected it.

The doorbell rang before my mother had a chance to express her thoughts on what I'd told her, which I felt was for the best.

Lunch arrived and although my mother offered to help set everything out, Anna insisted. She sent my mother outside to help Ashley with the girls and call everyone to the table.

Anna went into the pantry, a tight spot, but big enough to walk in. "Could you help me reach something?" She asked while my mother was making her way out the back door.

"Sure," I replied, wondering what she could need from the pantry considering the delivery bags contained everything right down to plasticware, plates and even little packets of salt and pepper.

The backdoor gave that little click, the one that doors do when the mechanism within the knob catches in the door jam and the two pieces meet. It was louder than the actual closing of the door. My mother had always been a stickler for not slamming doors to the point that it was a strain to ever hear her close one.

I squeezed into the pantry with Anna, looking over her shoulder to the shelving.

Anna requested something, but it wasn't for a stack of paper plates or anything located out of her reach. "I like your family and all, but I would give anything to just stay in here with you."

Her hands went under my shirt and splayed fingers slid up my chest and my dick went instantly hard. She was thinking the same thing I was.

I pulled the handle on the door and slid it shut, cramping the space even more and forcing Anna's hands around me. Her clipped nails dug into my back as she clung to me. I locked my lips over hers in demanding fashion.

With little room to do so, after a moment of abandon, Anna pulled her face away from mine, "We've got to get back out there before someone comes looking for us."

"Can't we just stay in here?" I pleaded.

My pleading was cut short when the backdoor flew open and the sound of Leslie's screams accompanied quick footsteps into the kitchen. My head snapped. She was screaming in a rush of panic, demanding help. My first thought was of my father. He'd had another heart attack. That's what I thought as I nearly broke down the accordion door that concealed us in the pantry.

"Dad!" I shouted as I sprinted past Leslie with Anna running after me.

Chapter 34

Anna-Cat...

I left the flip flops I'd been wearing in the pantry and ran barefooted after Alex. My greatest fear about the lake house was in the forefront of my mind. I feared one of the children had fallen in the lake. My heart was pounding, but I was fully prepared to sprint to the end of the dock and dive in.

Alex ran straight for his father who was rushing back toward the house with Auggie in tow. Spotting Auggie, I felt a flash of relief, but it was quickly over shadowed by the scene on the dock.

Alex's mother was standing, her hands pressed tight over her mouth. Her body was jerking, convulsing and tears were streaming down her face.

Alex's sister was on her knees clutching her baby. Her husband was on his knees as well performing an act I knew all too well. Arms straight, palms flat, he pressed, withdrew, pressed, up and down, counting. He stopped, pinched the nose of the sopping wet child laid out on the dock and sealed his mouth over hers. A frantic father was doing his best to breathe life back into his child. To no avail, he stopped and started the compressions again. He performed CPR on little Mackenzie, but nothing gave.

Alex hardly paused as he passed his father. He was six inches taller than me and had strides measured at least a yard per step, but I passed him. I don't know how or where the adrenaline came from, but I did. I outran Alex to get to the child.

I yelled to anyone behind me who was listening, "Call 911!"

With no regard for manners or consideration, I shoved the child's father out of my way and took over with the compressions. He let me, but he stayed close, hovering, looking for any sign of life. He was fully clothed and dripping with water from having jumped in to save his child.

"How long was she in the water?" I panted as I kept up my work, noticing that Mackenzie's face was turning blue.

No one answered.

"Come on!" I shouted, giving it all I had, pumping her chest.

"Not long," Alex's mother answered. "She leaned over to see her reflection and fell in."

The man beside me broke and his response came in sobs. "She got stuck under the dock and I couldn't find her at first."

I stopped, pinched her little nose and closed my mouth over hers. I huffed in air through my nose and pushed it from me to her with all I had.

"Mackenzie, wake up for Mommy," Ashley begged through her tears and the whales of her baby.

I leaned up and started the process over again.

"Breath, Baby!" I demanded.

I didn't allow the worry to enter my mind. I only knew that even if only through will alone, I would save this child. Five minutes passed and then six. No ambulance. I hadn't given up, but I'd never performed CPR this long. I wasn't going to give up, but it wasn't looking good. I forced away the thoughts that were trying to come from the back of my mind to the front.

By eight minutes I was getting winded. By twelve minutes I was struggling. CPR was like sprinting. Short distances were fine, but it wasn't something you wanted to do in a marathon.

"Where is that fucking ambulance?!!" I let loose in a venomous bite.

The lake house was the definition of off the beaten path, but even someone from a volunteer fire department should have arrived by now, not that they could have done more than a licensed M.D. like myself.

334

Around minute fourteen, I could hear the ambulance in the distance. Sirens were blaring. Maybe it was Alex that called or maybe it was Leslie. I had no way of knowing. I was single mindedly focused on saving Mackenzie.

Pushing through exhaustion from the physicality of performing compressions this long, I fought past the statistics that were chirping in my ear. Most people gave up CPR after fifteen to twenty minutes.

Minute seventeen, yes, I was glancing at my watch, I grabbed a mouthful of air and leaned over to pinch her nose again. That's when the most beautiful sound, short of Auggie and Alex telling me they loved me, came forth. A little cough and then another and before I could lean back Mackenzie let off one Hell of a blood curdling scream right in my face. My ears rang as if I'd been slapped. Pure terror came from her, but to the rest of us, it was the most glorious sound in the world.

Ashley's husband grabbed up the child as Ashley passed the baby to her mother. Mother and father piled onto the little girl, praising the Lord for letting her live and showering her with hugs and kisses.

I crawled out of the way. I would have kept sitting on the dock, but Alex offered his hand to help me up. I wouldn't consider myself out of shape, but my arms and legs were Jell-O. I hardly had the energy left to stand, but he was there to pull me up and steady me.

"Thank you for saving her." Alex pulled me to his chest. "You're amazing."

I'd lost patients before. I'd lost children before. I'd lost ones that I'd worked harder to save. I didn't cry when I lost lives and I certainly didn't cry when I saved them. It was my job. It's what I did. I wasn't amazing. I wasn't gifted. I was well trained and lucky, but that was all.

Today, I got really lucky. Mackenzie had been oxygen deprived for, as far as I could tell, going on twenty minutes. After four minutes there was a very real possibility that she could have had severe and irreversible

335

brain damage, but from the looks of her reactions to her parents, she was fine. After fifteen minutes, it would have been within medical acceptability for me to stop CPR and have the hard conversation with her parents, but I didn't stop.

Today, I wasn't so full of myself that I took all of the credit, but my decision to become a doctor was reaffirmed. I did the thing I'd intended to do from the day I witnessed my brother die. I helped save someone I loved from the grief I saw in my father when my brother died in his arms.

The urgent sounds of the ambulance drew into the yard. There was discussion in on the dock to send them away.

I interjected, "She needs to be seen at the hospital." As all eyes turned to me, I elaborated with caution as not to scare them again. "They need to make sure there's no..." I paused to allow for the delicacy of the word, "damage."

Ashley clutched Mackenzie, understandably, unwilling to let go. Her husband was the voice of reason.

"We'll ride in the ambulance with her." He looked to me as Alex and I stood on the outer circle of the family. "Anna-Cat will ride with us. She'll make sure Mackenzie has the best care."

I wanted to bow out. I didn't know how to do it, but I wanted to be excused from the hospital trip. Even though I'd always wanted to be a doctor so I could save people like my brother, but the elation I'd felt after saving her fell away. A fear gripped me, raising the question, what if I'd lost her? There was no answer to that question.

From that moment on, I found myself reluctant to be involved in the treatment of anyone remotely related or not exactly related to me. I never wanted that pressure again, but as Ashley held out her hand to me, begging that I come along, I nodded and agreed. I'd go wherever they needed me and do whatever I could.

I straightened my back and put on a smile. "Sure. I'll be glad to come, but I don't have privileges at the hospital here so..."

I didn't have to explain further. Ashley grabbed my hand. "You're coming. That's final."

It was good that she could not tell that I was trembling inside. It was good she didn't know how very close we came to losing her daughter. She knew it was close, but no one knew how close but me.

Mrs. Allen, the second Mrs. Allen, kept the Addie, after she was passed by her mother to the first Mrs. Allen who abruptly passed her on. Leslie gladly accepted the child and held on to her even as she waved to us when the ambulance pulled away. Alex stayed behind with Auggie and all three of his parents. They waved from the driveway with everyone else.

Ashley and I rode in the back of the ambulance with Mackenzie and her husband followed in the Suburban in which they arrived. Mackenzie was laying quietly on the gurney, taking comfort in cuddling with her favorite stuffed animal. She was tired and wanted to go to sleep, but I kept prodding her each time she looked as if she was going to drift off.

Ashley gave my hand a squeeze. "I'm glad you're back in Alex's life." She added clarification, "I'm glad you're back in all of our lives."

"Thanks." Had we not all just been through a trauma, I would have grinned from ear to ear. That would have been music to my ears, but as it stood, I forced a smile. The image of Mackenzie's limp little body was still too fresh in my eyes to be happy about much.

Tears filled Ashley's eyes again and for the first time I noticed that looking her in the eye was as if I was looking in Auggie's. Ashley, Alex and Auggie all had the same long, thick lashes, same color, same arch of their brows and the same nose, too.

She did her best to stop the pooling in her eyes, but it was to no avail. "Thanks for saving her. I don't know what I would have done if..."

"Hey," I stopped her. "She's going to be fine."

As it turned out, Mackenzie was going to be fine.

"She probably won't like swimming much anymore, but other than that..." the doctor explained light heartedly.

The doctor at Oconee Regional Medical Center was a white-haired pediatrician who'd clearly perfected his bedside manner with both children and their parents. He was so calm. He was who I wanted to be, not a pediatrician, but calm and reassuring. I was a general practitioner and I was usually those things.

The doctor insisted on keeping her overnight, but just as a precaution. I was as relieved as if she'd been my own child.

Despite the argument he put up on staying with Mackenzie, as her mother, Ashley won the debate. She was staying at the hospital with her daughter.

With hands tightly locked in his wife's, Mark offered, "I'll go and get your suitcase."

"Don't worry about it. It's only one night. We'll be fine." Ashley glanced toward Mackenzie, "We have Mackie. That's all we really need to get by."

Mackie must have been the name of Mackenzie's stuffed animal. She was clutching it around its neck with the arm that connected to the thumb she was sucking even as she slept. After all of the tests were finished, the little thing fell fast asleep. The color was back in her cheeks, blonde ringlets falling over the pillow, and such a serene look on her face, she was a doll. She reminded me of Auggie when he was her age.

As her parents said their goodbyes for the evening, I watched her sleep and thanked God he allowed me to save her.

Ashley walked with us and waited with me at the front door of the hospital while Mark brought the car around. We stood there awkwardly for a moment, the sound of an ambulance approaching made my feet itch to run to it, to go into emergency assistance mode and make myself useful. It was interesting that the thought of treating a stranger left no room for worry, but treating someone the equivalent of family made me a nervous wreck.

My head snapped back to Ashley when she broke our little silence.

"I don't know what, but I know Alex had something special planned for you this weekend and I'm sorry we ruined it," Ashley said apologetically.

"He just wanted you all to meet Auggie and you did so nothing's been ruined. Plus, your daughter is going to be fine. That's all that really matters," I assured her.

"Auggie's great, you know." Ashley smiled warmly as she heaped on compliments about Auggie. "You've done a great job with him, despite everything."

"Thank you. You saying that means a lot to me," I told her.

"Anyone can tell, you're a great mother."

I put my arm around her. "So are you. And," I added, my doctor voice coming through, "Please don't ever think what happened this afternoon was your fault or that you could've prevented it. Accidents happen despite our best efforts."

At that point, Ashley grabbed me and threw herself around me. She sobbed uncontrollably. The dam of emotions, pressure and relief broke free once again.

I held her and caressed the back of her head, smoothing down tendrils of her blond locks. "She's going to be fine," I soothed.

After a minute or two, Ashley eased back. She wiped her fingers under her eyes, trying to clear any running mascara to no avail. "I'm not usually an emotional wreck like this."

"It's okay. I'd be worried if you weren't a wreck right now."

She gave a helpless roll of her eyes. "I can't let her see me like this."

"Once when I was little, my mother lost me in the K-mart in Augusta. Seriously, I was missing for about an hour. This was a few months after my brother died so needless to say, she was scared out of her wits. When they finally located me hiding in the middle of one of those circular racks, I'd scared her so badly that she beat me within an inch of my life. Before that, my mother had never even swatted my hand."

Ashley looked at me, near horrified.

"It's okay to let our children see that we're human and that we love them so much they can scare us out of our minds." I gave Ashley my best, most reassuring smile, "Just don't beat her within an inch of her life, okay?"

A vehicle rolled up to the curb next to us. From the corner of my eye, I could see it was my ride.

"Addie will be fine with us. Not they your mother or Leslie will probably let me, but I'll take special care of her until you get back."

Ashley dried her eyes again and nodded.

Mark came around the Suburban. I kind of thought he was coming to open the car door for me and I was going to tell him that wasn't necessary. I didn't have a chance to as he walked right past me and embraced his wife. He kissed her and assured her the same as I had.

"Baby Girl's going to be okay. Anna-Cat said so." Still holding her, Mark told Ashley, "Call me if you need me. I'll come running."

They parted with the mutual exchange of "I love you."

Chapter 35

Alex...

Mom and Leslie were trying to entertain Addie, playing any number of baby games; peak-a-boo, making funny faces, and even pretending to injure themselves which brought on hysterical giggles from the baby. Dad and Auggie were throwing the baseball in the backyard while I was pacing in front of the living room window. Everyone had their way of keeping their mind off of what had gone on earlier with Mackenzie, but it was a struggle for each of us.

Ashley had called with an update and word that Mark and Anna were on their way back. I was anxious for them to return, anxious to see Anna. Seeing her was the only thing that would ease the memory of Mackenzie's lifeless body lying on the dock. I paced and paced, wanting more than anything just to lay eyes on her, to know that everything was going to be okay. Ashley had said Mackenzie was going to be fine, but I wanted the assurance that only came from seeing Anna's face.

At half past seven, they pulled into the driveway. The chef I'd hired had come and gone, but no one had stopped to eat except Addie, who insisted on being fed.

"I'm starving," Mark said as he came around the vehicle, but I barely heard him.

"How is she?" I asked, opening my arms to Anna.

Walking into my embrace, Anna answered. "She's going to be just fine. The pediatrician that saw her said she'll probably have a healthy fear of water from now on, but other than that's she's perfect."

Auggie and Dad heard the car pull in and came around from the backyard. Anna held out an arm to invite Auggie into our hug and he readily joined us.

"She's really going to be okay, Mom?" Auggie asked, looking at Anna.

"She's right as rain, baby." Anna let go of me to focus solely on Auggie and making sure he was alright.

A heavy sigh came from behind me. It was my dad and it was definitely a sigh of relief. I brought him to our group the same way Anna had brought Auggie in. Until recently, Mackenzie had been my father's first grandchild. Although she was no longer the first in the birth order, my father would forever be wrapped around her little finger.

I'd never seen my father cry before, but Ashley warned me that as he was getting older, he was becoming less able to hide his emotions. Now, I saw it firsthand. My father wept openly over the relief of the news that Mackenzie was going to be alright.

"Dad, she's going to be okay." My words of comfort were nothing compared to what came next.

Auggie gave my father a side arm hug and added, "Yeah, Grandpa, Mama said she's okay and Mama never lies." He cut his eyes up at my dad's, "I mean, not ever."

All eyes turned to Anna and she blushed.

"She was great," Mark added and then gave me a bit of a ribbing. "I don't know how you managed it, Alex. I mean, she's way smarter than you are and she'd definitely a keeper."

Mark passed by me and took Addie from Leslie who'd brought her out to greet him. She and my mother had also come out to hear firsthand the news about Mackenzie.

"Come to Daddy," Mark smiled and nuzzled his nose to Addie's neck, making her squeal. "Sissie's gonna be just fine. Don't you worry."

"You all must be starving," my mother announced, joining the small circle of us in the yard. "Diner's ready and it looks great."

After the day she'd had, no one would have blamed Anna if she'd lingered in the living room and waited to be called to the table, but she didn't. She joined Mom and Leslie in the kitchen, helping set the table, put ice in the glasses and all of the last-minute things the chef I'd hired hadn't been able to do since we weren't ready to eat while he was there.

I stuck my head in the kitchen and asked, "Anna, do you need any help reaching anything in the pantry?"

"We know that's code for something," Leslie piped up before Anna could answer.

Anna stopped in her tracks, between laying down a knife between a plate and a fork. Her face turned redder than I'd ever seen it turn before.

"I think it's code for Seven Minutes in Heaven," my mother snickered.

"Mother!" I gasped, faking shock. "What do you know about Seven Minutes in Heaven?"

Leslie hooted with laughter and Anna's eyes grew big.

"And what do you know about it?" I directed my quip to my step-mother who promptly blushed.

"More than you think we do." Mom gave Leslie a wink as she moved through the kitchen, carrying tea glasses to the table.

Arriving at the table, Mom sidled up to Anna, before she could say anything Anna let out a giggle. "Y'all are nuts!"

"We might be, but if we don't laugh right now, we just might cry. Now say 'y'all' again. No wonder he wants Seven Minutes in Heaven with you. You're so dang cute and smart." Mama gave Anna a long pat down the length of her hair.

Leslie carried the last remaining glasses to the table. It was a picture I never thought I would see, my mother on one side and Leslie on the other with Anna in the middle.

"All teasing aside," Leslie said as she wrapped an arm around Anna's waist, "We are so glad you are here and not just because of Mackenzie."

My dad joined me in the doorway, watching as I did.

"She's the one, huh?" he asked quietly.

343

I tilted my head. "Yes, sir, she's the one."

"Then what are you waiting for?"

The truth was that I had been waiting on sunset and I was going to propose out on the dock with everyone watching, but that plan was shot. I saw no need to disclose that then.

"For Ashley to be here," I replied, also realizing that I would like for Anna's mother to be there when I proposed as well.

"Stop waiting for the perfect moment and ask her."

"You don't think it's too soon?"

While my father imparted his wisdom, from the corner of my eye, I saw the conversation between the ladies had morphed into a group hug with Anna at the center. I tried not to think about it, but I could not help wondering if Anna weren't in the equation, would my mother still be making nice with Leslie.

My full attention was called back to my father when he pointed out the outlandishness of my statement. "Too soon? It's been over a decade in the making. How much time do you need?"

"I mean, I just found out about Auggie and we've only been, well, back at this for about a month."

"Lord, Son!" He shook his head in disbelief. "Just get on with it!"

I laughed. "That's your fatherly advice? Get on with it?"

My father cut his eyes at me sharply. "You know what I mean."

Anna fell asleep as soon as her head hit the pillow that night. I was not so fortunate. Thoughts of Anna hovered over Mackenzie giving CPR lingered in the forefront of my mind as I watched Anna sleep. The fact that she had single handedly saved my niece was nothing sort of spectacular. I could never do anything so amazing.

Laying there watching her I remembered something that she'd said to me right after I came back. "I never had time to let myself dwell on having a broken heart.

344

I was pregnant and, when I wasn't pregnant, I had an infant and college to worry about. Then when I didn't have an infant and college, I had a toddler and medical school and then a kid in elementary school, a grandmother with cancer and so on. There just wasn't much time to focus on my feelings."

Anna's life had been full even without me. She never needed me. I had movies, millions of dollars, thousands of fans and I dwelled on the fact that I was alone. In the early days after losing her, I drank to cover the heartbreak. In the years following, I worked and went to school, but she was always missing. I never stopped needing her.

I had never been more in awe of her than I was on this day. She was the one people should clap for and chase to be near, not me. She was the smartest, most capable person I'd ever met and my measly Doctorate of History didn't hold a candle to her.

The next morning, Ashley saw to it that Mackenzie was released bright an early. Anna had insisted that Mark and Addie stay our guest room. One thing led to another and, despite the fact that I'd booked hotel rooms for the lot of them, they all stayed over. Mark and Addie took the guest room, Dad and Leslie took Auggie's room, my mother took the pullout couch and Auggie slept on a pallet on the floor next to the couch. I let Mark sleep in and I went to pick Ashley and Mackenzie up at the hospital.

"I slept, if that's what you want to call it, in a chair." That was Ashley's greeting as she handed me Mackenzie.

While I put Mackenzie in the booster seat in the back, Ashley climbed in the front and flopped her head back on the headrest with a moan. "I'm too old for this."

"Mommy, I'm hungry!" Mackenzie announced.

Ashley said nothing.

"Would coffee help?" I asked Ashley when I reached the driver's seat.

"Only if it is being served by the gallon."

"I'm hungry!" Mackenzie repeated with more force.

"Grandma's making pancakes just for you." I glanced at her in the rearview mirror.

Mackenzie stiffened her upper lip and gave me a stare down. "Mama says Gramma can't cook."

I tried not to laugh as Ashley came to life. "Mackenzie, no!"

"You said it," my niece continued to argue.

"Not one more word little girl!" Ashley put the kibosh on further words from her daughter.

What Ashley saw as a core, correcting her daughter and making Mackenzie a good person, I saw as an opportunity I missed with Auggie. Not that Anna needed any help making Auggie a good person, it was just another reminder that I hadn't been there to make him who he was. I voiced as much to Ashley.

"He's a fine boy and..."

"And I had nothing to do with that..."

Ashley's head snapped around. "You don't know that. There's a whole world of studies out there about nurture versus nature. Your DNA is just as much a part of him as hers is and it counts for a lot. Plus, it's not too late for you to start helping with the nurture part. You invited us up here for something so get on with it."

"What? I invited the whole family up to meet Auggie," I swore.

"Really? You don't have the ring in your pocket right now?"

My sister really did know me too well. I had the ring in my pocket, but I'd had it in my pocket for years. It was the solitaire that went with the eternity band that I'd given Anna for her birthday that first year. I'd bought them as a pair, I remembered thinking it was stupid at the time, but had convinced myself it was fate or I was just having faith. Of course, I thought about asking her to marry me. I thought about it all the time.

"Did you talk to Dad last night?" I asked Ashley.

"No, why?" She yawned.

"Because he basically told me the same thing."

"Well, you might want to listen. Especially since I heavily implied to Anna-Cat yesterday that you were going to ask."

"You what? You told her?"

"No, not exactly. I just told her that I thought you were planning something big and I implied."

"You implied?"

Ashley and I went back and forth as Mackenzie pointed out every American Flag along our way.

"Yep, I implied. I don't know what you're waiting for anyway?" Ashley yawned again and stretched.

"That's exactly what Dad asked last night! And, I did not plan anything big other than for you all to meet Auggie. Isn't that big enough?"

"Is it?" She looked at me directly and almost clear eyed. "I mean, it's big enough for me, but is it enough for you?"

"There's no rush," I countered as I made the turn onto the last leg of the trip back to the lake house.

"But there's no reason to keep waiting either. You've loved her since you first met her and, now, you have Auggie and I can see how much you adore him." Those were Ashley's final words on the subject and I didn't bother to argue any more either.

The rest of the weekend went off without any more near drownings, any trips to the emergency room and without a proposal. A lesser man would have caved, but not me. I wanted to ask Anna to marry me, but it just didn't seem like the right time.

Ashley may have hinted to Anna that I was going to propose, but Anna never let on. Things between us carried on as they had been before the trip to the lake. Anna went back to work, Auggie went back to baseball and I rented one of the cabins at Seven Springs, the Inn Anna's friends owned. I spent my days reading scripts that my agent insisted on sending me, but nothing caught my eye. No script and no amount of money appealed to me enough to leave Anna and Auggie.

I kept a low profile around town and most folks kept their distance. Most looked at me, had a dawn of recognition, but wouldn't let themselves believe that such a celebrity was cruising the aisles of their IGA. They gave a nod in passing and went along their way. It was good to be anonymous. The ball cap, shades and a five o'clock shadow served me well when attending Auggie's baseball games with Anna. For the most part, things just rocked along, until one day they didn't.

Chapter 36

Anna...

Blood, pus and the contents of a stomach covered me and it was just another day at the office. I smelled like antiseptic and used tacos. It was the cologne of doctors and nurses everywhere. That's how I left the office that day and most days.

"By 11:00 a.m., I had diagnosed my third case of Mono of the morning. This time it was for the head cheerleader from the high school," I carried on to Alex about my day.

"The kissing disease?" I mimicked the girl's mother, gasping and throwing my hand over my chest for dramatic effect as I gave Alex a play by play of my day.

Ever since we got back from the lake house, Alex had been a fixture at my house. Every afternoon I arrived home to find him sitting on the front porch steps waiting on me. As soon as I turned the corner onto Stone Street, I started looking for him. I loved finding him there and it made me look forward to coming home more than I already did.

Realizing how I smelled, I broke character and turned back into just Anna as he watched attentively. "Now, if you don't mind, I'm going to go take a shower."

"Make it fast. We're due at your mother's house by seven for dinner."

I barely had my hand on the handle of the screen door. "What?" I whipped around.

"Yep. Get a move on!"

"No," I whined.

It was then that I took in the picture that was Alex. A collared shirt with the sleeves rolled up, his best jeans, and loafers, not the flip flops he'd been wearing for days, he was dressed to impress.

"I don't feel like going out and since when did you and my mother start making dinner plans?"

"Since now so go get dressed."

I grumbled a little more, but Alex wasn't budging. "Go!"

Alex followed with a shout into the house for Auggie. "Hey, buddy, come out here I've got to ask you about something."

I never entered through the front door at my parents' house, but with Alex holding my hand and leading me from the car, he headed toward the porch. I fretted over Auggie's hair, specifically the Alfalfa sprouts that were sticking up in the middles of his crown, while Alex rang the bell.

My mother arrived at the door wearing an apron and oven mitts. "Don't stand on ceremony here. Come on in!" She held the door open wide with one of the mitts.

I was barely inside when Mother jumped with the ding of the oven timer.

"Make yourselves at home," she said with a backward flip of her hand as she ran down the hall back toward the kitchen.

Not having to be told twice, Auggie brushed past me headed for the living room, specifically the television remote.

Alex was pointing to a spot on the floor at the base of the stairs. "Is that..."

"My blood?" I finished the question and answered, "Yes."

Alex caught me by the waist and pulled me close. "I guess we've come full circle, huh?"

I would have been happy to just stand there and smell him all night. Alex smelled like mint and leather and a little bit like a bakery, which was a new addition to his cologne regimen.

Alex nuzzled my ear and whispered, "You are every bit as beautiful as the first moment I saw you."

"I was unconscious the first moment you saw me," I teased him.

With no one around to see, Alex cupped my face and kissed me sweetly.

Dinner at my mother's was a drawn-out affair. I suppose with my father gone she had nothing else to do with her time, but cook. One would have thought she was recreating the last meal of the Titanic with the volume of food she had prepared, all seven courses. First was wine and cheese around the kitchen island, followed by appetizers of stuffed mushrooms in the living room. Finally, the mingling was over and she allowed us into the dining room. Salad was served, followed by soup, a lobster bisque which she swore she made herself.

"I'm so full I can't see," I said after finishing my soup.

"But we haven't even had the main course yet," mother said, placing her spoon down and reaching to start clearing the table of our bowls.

Auggie was a bottomless pit so he was eager for whatever else his grandmother was about to trot out.

"I'm going to have to pace myself," Alex commented.

"Because we are at an eating marathon?" I snickered, lowly as Mother left the room.

"Be nice. She's gone to a lot of trouble," Alex chastised me.

"But, why?" I was quick to question.

"Because she loves you."

Mother returned with plates already filled for each of us. Prime rib with au jus, mashed potatoes and broccoli. I had no idea she could cook like this.

After dinner, we didn't dare decline dessert, but we did ask that it be delayed while all of the other food we'd eaten settled.

My mother insisted Auggie help her clean up the kitchen.

I wasn't the only one who was a little whiney that night.

"Why do I have to help?" Auggie asked begrudgingly.

"Because you liked eating here," my mother replied sharply.

While Auggie washed and rinsed, my mother dried and put away, and Alex led me to our chairs by the pool. We sat in silence, our two hands linked between the chairs. It was nice just to sit there and breathe the night air. For a change it wasn't sweltering in Augusta in September.

"I miss this," I sighed, hardly breaking the silence and letting my head fall to the side to look at Alex.

There was very little light out. No street lights shown in the backyard. There was nothing more than the light from the back porch and that from the sky and Alex looked so peaceful in it. I loved looking at him, but turned my head quickly when he looked my way. I didn't want him to catch me staring. Although I ogled over him, I didn't want to be one of the throngs of women who did that so I never let him catch me.

I heard him stir and from my peripheral vision, I saw Alex slide from his chair. Curious, I turned my face in his direction just in time to see him take a knee. With a hint of an idea of what was about to happen my smile broadened and my cheeks bulged. I whipped my legs around the side of the chair and sat up. I bit my lip to hide the excitement that was rapidly taking hold of me.

"I wish I had something poetic to say, but the truth is..." Alex stammered, nervously. "The time for poetry for you and me has passed. The time for me to ask you this has long passed. Wasted time, missed opportunities, misunderstandings. I don't want any more of that. I thought it was enough just to..." He stuttered again and repeated himself.

"Just to be with you. With you and Auggie," he clarified. "It's not enough."

I waited with bated breath. I knew what he was getting at, but I wasn't about to help him. *Say the words.* I pleaded with him in my head. *Say them. Ask!*

Alex reached in his pocket and produced a small box. Extending it to me, the drawing out of the situation came to an end. All batting lashes, nervous and never sexier and, for once, vulnerable, Alex asked, "Will you please marry me?"

Ignoring the ring, I threw myself into him. "Yes! Yes! Of course!"

Alex, barely having enough time to open his arms and catch me, lost his balance and we toppled over. We crashed into the chair in which Alex had been seated, sending it flying up. Tangled in kisses and limbs and laughter, we hardly felt it when the chair landed on us.

"Yes? Are you sure?" Alex gasped in a staccato fashion, a word between each kiss.

"Yes! This very night if you like!" I could hear the joy in my own voice.

We didn't get married that very night. Eventually we went back inside to find dessert waiting on us along with my mother, Auggie, Alex's parents, his sister and her family, Millie, Gabe and their girls, our friend Jay, Dr. Farrell from my office and his wife, and a few of my mother's dearest friends. It was evident this had all been a set up.

My mother passed Champagne, but before the toast, I turned to Alex, whispering and joking, "What if I wouldn't have said yes?"

Millie over heard me and replied, "You would have died before you wouldn't have said yes."

Millie was right. I never wanted anything more than to marry Alex Allen. I'd wanted it since the moment I'd met him. At first, I wanted it for me, but I didn't just want it for me anymore. I wanted Auggie to have everything he ever wanted and that included what would be our new normal.

Dear Reader,

Thank you for giving your time to my latest creation. I hope you enjoyed <u>The New Normal</u> and will take a moment to leave a review for it on Amazon.com. I also welcome you to email me with your thoughts and comments at <u>TSDawson1996@yahoo.com</u>. I appreciate your comments, concerns, critiques and suggestions for improvement to my work.

I apologize for it taking me so long to produce <u>The New Normal.</u> You may rest assured that I am already working on my next project and will keep you apprised of its developments via my author page on TS Dawson on Facebook. You are also welcome to contact me via the comments or messages through that page.

Thank you again and I look forward to hearing from you.

Sincerely,

-Terri
AKA TS Dawson

61214541R00212

Made in the USA
Columbia, SC
21 June 2019